"Mr. Free—or rather, the person we call by that name—has concealed a talisman. The acaryas do so at times, putting by their unearthly crowns and orbs to walk among mortals. Now he lacks strength to take it up again. But if we could find it . . ."

"You mean this," Barnes said. "You're serious."

"I was never more so. Do not think to cheat me of the prize, Ozzie. You could no more wield such a talisman than you could summon the green-haired wantons of the sea. But if you help me, you shall be my vizier in an empire encompassing the world." The witch's hands toyed with his own, stroking their backs, tickling their palms.

Icy though the room was, his face was damp with sweat. "I wish I knew if you're crazy."

GENE WOLFE

A TOM DOHERTY ASSOCIATES BOOK

FREE LIVE FREE

Copyright © 1984, 1985 by Gene Wolfe

First printing: November 1985
First mass market printing: November 1986

A TOR Book

Published by Tom Doherty Associates, Inc.
49 West 24 Street
New York, N.Y. 10010

Cover design by Carol Russo

ISBN: 0-812-55813-8
CAN. ED.: 0-812-55814-6

Library of Congress Catalog Card Number: 85-51761

Printed in the United States of America

0 9 8 7 6 5 4 3 2 1

"The country needs and, unless I mistake its temper, the country demands bold, persistent experimentation."

—Franklin Delano Roosevelt

FREE LIVE FREE

Chapter 1

FOUR ROOMERS OF WAR

It was not yet night, though the streets were already dark. A few stores and restaurants had switched on their lights. A neon sign thrusting like an erection from a bar on the corner winked redly at thirsty patrons who were not present. There was rain in the wind, and the feeling that the rain would soon turn to snow.

Stubb swore, rounding the corner. He took off his glasses and wiped their bottle-bottom lenses on the sleeve of his trenchcoat, then swore again as they were spattered with fresh rain. A Checker passed, throwing fine spray at the sidewalk. Stubb entered an alley and walked it with ferocious energy from end to end and back, looking in doorways, occasionally stopping to examine a garbage can, at last emerging where he had come in. Half a block down the street, a fat, blond girl in a white plastic raincoat waved to him, and he nodded almost imperceptibly.

She was waiting for him in the musty little hall, rain trickling from her coat and white plastic boots onto the worn linoleum. "How'd you do?" she asked. She loomed over him, a head taller than he.

"How'd *you* do?" Stubb said.

"I haven't yet. I just went out for gum and stuff."

"You shouldn't smoke," he told her. "Screws up your lungs."

"Yeah," the fat girl said. "That's right." She opened her purse and took out a pack of Viceroys. Two were gone. She pulled out two more. Stubb reached up to light hers, and she smiled.

"Going to be a lousy night," he told her. "You ought to stay in."

"I think maybe I will. Till eleven or twelve anyway. You going to watch TV? It's *Hellcats of the Navy*."

Stubb shook his head, drawing on his cigarette.

"You like the oldies almost as much as he does."

"I saw a piece of it."

"I wish they'd run *The Wizard of Oz* again," the fat girl said. "That's the one I like. But I could watch this."

"I've got things to do."

"Okay."

She waited for him to go up the stair, then toiled after him. The parlor door was half open, but if the three people in the parlor had heard them, they gave no indication of it.

They sat before a television set as they might have sat around a fire. On the small screen, images hardened to harsh lines of black, then spread the shadows of humanity again. The voices of the film murmured like little waves, and like little waves seemed to die.

The most impressive of the three was an old man. He sat in the largest chair and gripped its arms as though for him it were a seat in a plummeting plane. He was bald. He had once been a powerful and perhaps even a fearsome man; now his chest had fallen in, and his blue eyes seemed awash in milk.

The man on his right aimed at a prosperity his check suit did not confirm. The leather of his wingtip shoes was polished and cracked, and his carefully knotted rep tie revealed at the knot an area worn threadbare by the heavy stubble of his chin. His broad mustache and thick hair shone black and oily as fresh paint. A tarnished chain stretched across his vest, ending in an empty pocket; there was a rubber daisy in his lapel.

A young woman in a black toque sat on the old man's left. Her long-sleeved lace dress suggested Italy or Spain, but there was something of the East in her thin, strong face and dark eyes. Suspended from a silver cord about her neck was a circlet of silver from which three points radiated; it was no bigger than a small coin.

The man with the black mustache asked, "Would you like something, Mr. Free? A glass of sherry, maybe. Or I could make you some coffee."

The old man seemed not to hear him.

"You may go to the kitchen and take whatever you can find," the woman said. "He will not object."

The other man glanced at her, and then (perhaps because he feared his regard had somehow offended her) looked around the room as if taking inventory of its dusty furniture. His eyes, slightly divergent and dryly black, might have been buttons of jet.

"Go on, Mr. Barnes. You are so hungry."

"Can I bring you something?" the man called Barnes asked.

"For eight days I have fasted," the woman said.

"Maybe then—"

"Nothing."

Barnes rose. "I'll fix tea, if there is any."

Neither of the others answered, and he went into the kitchen. There he washed a teapot and put a pan of water on the stove. There was a tablespoon of black tea loose in a cannister, and, to his surprise, a little sugar in the sugar bowl. In the refrigerator he discovered a small cube of cheddar, which he ate. When he carried his tray into the parlor again, neither the old man nor the dark woman appeared to have moved.

"You like some, Mr. Free?" Barnes asked. "I brought you a cup."

The woman said, "How was the cheese?"

For a moment Barnes stared at her. The color drained from his florid face. Then he laughed. "You smelled it," he said. "Smelled it on my breath. That's terrific! Listen, Madame Serpentina, I can take a joke as well as anybody. Better, in fact."

"I cannot," the woman said.

"Hey, you ought to. There's nothing in the world better for you, for your health and your whole outlook on life, than a good laugh."

"I laugh often, but not at jokes."

Barnes grinned. He had large, square, slightly yellowish teeth, like a horse's. "That's because you haven't seen mine. But if you'll excuse kind of a personal comment, I've been watching you since we got here, and I've never seen you laugh."

"I am laughing now," the woman said. "My spirit laughs, because I did not come here with you."

"We both came Monday," Barnes said. "Answered the same ad. That's all I meant."

The woman did not reply, and after several minutes had passed in silence except for the muttering from the old television and the rattle of the rain, Barnes said, "Nice weather."

For the first time, she turned her head to look at him. "You like this?"

"Sure I do." Barnes grinned again. "Made three sales today, and selling weather is as good a weather as Ozzie Barnes ever asks for."

"You have sold nothing, or you would go into the street and buy bread. You are very hungry."

"I didn't say I got any money. I got orders. Tomorrow I'll send them in, and when the merchants pay, I'll get my commission. I do like this weather, though. You probably don't believe that."

"Belief insults the mind. A thing is so or it is not."

"Say, that's good. I'll have to remember it. But I like this weather—not many customers coming in, which is always good for a salesman, and then, too, some merchants feel a little sorry for me. That makes them readier to listen. The whole secret of selling, let me tell you, is just getting your customer to listen to what you're saying. Nine times out of ten, a man will stand there and stare at you like he's hearing every word, but what he's really listening to is something he told himself a long time ago, or maybe just his wife telling him not to lay in any more stock. He no more hears you than Mr. Free here does."

The woman said, "He hears."

"Okay, but he doesn't pay attention."

"That is so. We are to him what that," the woman's eyes moved briefly toward the television set, "is to us. We are that to me also."

"Is he following the story, you think?" Barnes's voice dropped to a whisper. "I wouldn't want to bother him."

"Less than you. Less even than I."

There was a knock at the door. The old man rose at once and went into the narrow hall, where pools of water from the fat girl's raincoat still lingered sullenly. Behind him, the voices of Barnes and the dark woman mingled with the roaring of piston-engined aircraft.

The newcomer was a uniformed policeman, his shoulders white with snow. The old man bobbed his head and led him into the parlor.

"I'm Sergeant Proudy," the policeman said. "Thirteenth precinct. I'm looking for Bernard Free."

The old man nodded. "Sam'l Benjamin Free, son. That's me. Call me Ben."

Rising, Barnes said, "There's no Bernard anything here Sergeant. This is Mr. Free."

The policeman nodded and took an envelope from the inner pocket of his overcoat. "Who are you?"

"My name's Osgood M. Barnes. I'm in sales."

Proudy nodded. "And you, Ma'am?"

"I am Serpentina."

"I bet you are. You a snake charmer?"

"I am a witch."

"It's against the law to tell fortunes in this city," the policeman said.

"I do not tell fortunes."

Proudy shrugged. "I don't give a damn what you do outside this precinct, but—"

The fat girl's voice floated down the stairwell:

"The bosun's pipe, it felt like tripe,
The Chaplain's it was good . . ."

"That's Candy!" Proudy said. "Candy Garth. You know her?"

"I have sat at table while she ate," the witch said. "That was not today."

Barnes put in, "Madame Serpentina's fasting."

"Candy ought to take lessons—she'd do more business. She lives here?"

Barnes nodded. "This is a rooming house. It belongs to Mr. Free."

Proudy turned back to Free. "You let whores stay here, sir?"

"No Horace here. You from the Building Commission, son? You can't tear my house down—we got five people living here right now."

Barnes said, "He doesn't know, officer. Take it easy on him, huh?"

Proudy fingered the envelope he held, and for a moment looked tired. "Yeah," he said. "I bet he forgets to collect his rent sometimes too."

Free said, "They live free. I don't charge."

"And maybe you might lend your boarders a little something. If they told you a real good story. Old folks are like that." He was not looking at Free, but at Barnes.

Barnes looked away. The witch said, "I do not believe he has anything to lend."

"You ought to know."

"You asked of Candy Garth, does she live here. She is upstairs on the left."

"Thanks." Proudy handed his envelope to Free. "Nobody's going to live here a hell of a lot longer. Yeah, it's the Building Commission, old man. You got to be out tomorrow, understand? That's all the time you got."

"Used to have a lot more," Free said slowly. "All of it. I'm not going. Going to die right here."

Barnes said, "And we'll help you."

"I'll bet you will," Proudy said.

A moment later they heard his feet on the stairs, then a hard rap and the word *Police* at the fat girl's door. Barnes sat down again and looked at the flickering television, where rotary-engined fighters warmed up on the deck of a black-and-white aircraft carrier. "All the time there is. I know what you mean, Mr. Free. When I was younger I used to feel the same way. I guess for you this is practically a new show, isn't it?"

Free shook his head. He had pushed Proudy's envelope into his shirt pocket unopened. "Ages ago, Mr. Barnes. Whole ages."

The fat girl's voice came faintly from upstairs, followed by the sound of a blow. A moment later, Proudy tramped down the steps and went out into the snow, slamming the door.

"I'm hungry," Free said suddenly. "Anything left in the kitchen?"

Barnes shook his head. "You could have some tea."

The old man fumbled in his pockets. "Not a continental dollar. Got to sell some skins tomorrow. But if somebody's got money today, I'll get us something."

"I'll have some for you Tuesday, Mr. Free. Believe me, I will. Twenty dollars, I swear."

The witch said, "You are overgenerous with your oaths, my friend."

Free did not seem to hear her. "No rent," he told Barnes. "Live here free, like I said. You just help hold 'em off. I'm a mite hungry, though."

The stair boards creaked. They heard the fat girl's sniveling, her wheezing breath.

"She must have something," Barnes said. "I'll talk to her."

"No." The witch touched his arm. "She has nothing. She gave him what she had, and it was not enough. Here."

As if she were alone, she pulled up her skirt and took a rolled bill from the top of her black stocking.

"Take this," she said. "But you must go, not Mr. Free. Get fruit and bread, and if there is money remaining, whatever you like. I expect a receipt and my change."

Chapter 2

THE MEN

Stubb's room was the smallest and least desirable in the house, the left side back. Paper peeled from its walls, and its only window faced the abandoned house next door across an areaway filled with debris. There was barely space enough to hold a dresser and a narrow bed. His trenchcoat hung on a corner of the door of the stale-smelling little closet; his damp hat slumped on the shelf inside. His shoes stood on the radiator, and his sodden socks lay flaccid beside them.

Stubb himself lay on the bed in his shorts. He was neither reading nor sleeping. Without their glasses, his eyes seemed inadequate for his face, though it was, overall, not a large one. Several hours before, he had discovered Free, Barnes, and the witch as they finished their meal. There had been little left, but he had eaten what little there was—an odd slice of bread and as much potato salad as had lodged in the corners of the carton.

Perhaps with some vague notion of pleasing the witch, Barnes had bought a can of tamales. Unobserved, Stubb had swallowed the liquid that remained and stuffed the greasy paper "corn husks" into his pocket so he might lick them clean in privacy.

Now he muttered, "Cliff, you're a herpid mother-fucker," and put his legs over the side of the old bed. They did not quite touch the floor. He looked at his wrist, then looked away again and ran his fingers through his thinning hair.

"He could," he said. "For old times' sake. What the hell." He dressed again, augmenting his still-wet socks with newspaper shaped like the footprints of dance diagrams. One held Free's ad, and Stubb paused to read it again.

FREE LIVE FREE Live w me, pay no rt.
Hlp sv hs. B Free, 808 S 38th.

Outside, snow no longer fell; an inch was turning to slush on the sidewalk. Stubb walked up the street to a diner where a plump young man sat reading a magazine behind the counter. Stubb glanced at the clock in back of him and boosted himself onto a stool. "Coffee," he said. "Heavy cream and sugar, Murray. I like a lot of sugar."

"I know you do, Jim," Murray said as he put the cup on the counter. "You'll get fat."

"Not me."

"You little guys eat the most. You never get fat. I don't see how you do it. I don't eat anything, and I'm as fat as a pig."

Stubb lifted his coffee, holding it with both hands. The cream had cooled it, and it was syrupy with sugar.

"How the hell do you do that? Just pour it down your throat like that?"

"I guess I was thirsty," Stubb said.

"I guess you were. How's the op business?"

"Up and down, like any other business."

"Coffee's thirty-five cents."

"Jesus, no wonder you're fat."

Murray looked from Stubb to a sign that read PLEASE PAY WHEN SERVED, then back to Stubb; but Stubb appeared not to see him. After a moment Murray went down the counter to refill a napkin holder, and Stubb, rising rapidly on his stool and bracing his feet on its rungs, leaned across the counter and reached beneath it for a telephone.

"Listen, you've got a customer who hangs around, tall man, about six one, one-seventy maybe one-eighty, Caucasian, clean shave, reddish hair going gray. . . . Yeah, that's him, I want to talk to him. . . . Mike, this's Jim. How's it going? . . . Yeah, sure. Right. . . . Yeah, I figured you'd be in there, a night like this. No use freezing your butt off. . . .

Listen, Mike, how'd it be if I came over and took it for an hour? Give you a chance to have a crap and maybe a look at the paper. What you getting an hour? Seven-fifty? . . . Mike, I didn't say that's what I'd want, I'd do it for five, and you'd be two fifty to the good. You know Cliff had me on it when they had six guys on him. . . . Mike, I'll split it down the middle. Three seventy-five, and that's my last offer."

There was a click like the closing of the napkin holder. Stubb hung up and got down from his stool.

"You owe for the coffee," Murray said. "And that's not a public phone."

"I'll make it up to you," Stubb told him.

It had started to snow again, flakes drifting down around the street lights. He pulled his trenchcoat tight at the neck. When he was some distance from the diner, he turned and glanced back at its window, still shining among the darkened stores: SANDWICH SHOP. He shrugged.

Free's house was dark. Stubb rummaged through the kitchen, found nothing, and at last returned to his room. From a dresser drawer he took a ring of keys. With them in his pocket, he made his way to the door of the room in front of his own.

The bolt squeaked back. He stepped inside and closed the door carefully behind him before switching on the light.

It was a much bigger room than his, with two windows facing the street. There was a smell of perfume and stale ashtrays. Soiled lingerie, peach, pink, and black, lay in a corner. Jars of cream and bottles of cologne littered the dresser; in the center, precisely parallel to the dresser top, lay a Baby Ruth of the dollar size. Stubb reached for it, then drew back.

Swiftly he searched the drawers, leaving them no more jumbled than he found them. He looked under the pillow and the mattress, and even under the tattered throw rug. Then he switched off the lights, stepped into the hall, and relocked the door.

He had taken several steps from it before he saw the witch standing on the other side of the stairwell watching him. He grinned at her, though he could not see her expression in the dim light. "I've got a key, Madame S. She gave me one. I was going to wait for her, only it's getting too late."

The witch said nothing. He could just make out the whites of her eyes and the darker dark that was her hair.

"It'd be better if you didn't mention it. Nicer—you know what I mean?"

Slowly she vanished. There was no shimmer, and her disappearance was not sudden like the bursting of a soap bubble, nor did she disperse like smoke or melt like the ferns of frost on a windowpane. She was and was not, with between the two a moment, the knife edge of time, when she was and was not.

Stubb was alone in the hall. He went around the stairwell until he stood where she had, fished out the paper matches with which he had lit Candy's cigarette, struck a match, and held it up until it scorched his fingers, peering at the floor. Shaking his head, he rapped his temple and returned to his room.

Once more stripped to his shorts, he lay in the dark with his hands beneath his head. When he had rested so for perhaps half an hour, he muttered, "She doesn't think more of that Baby Ruth than I do of my prick."

Barnes's room was across from Stubb's. It was larger than Stubb's, smaller than the fat girl's, cleaner than either. Its walls were decorated with ads for various jokes and novelties. These were:

a bottomless drinking glass;
a swizzle stick that smoked when put in a drink;
a cigarette lighter shaped like a dog, operated by lifting the dog's hind leg;
a cigarette lighter shaped like a toilet, operated by lifting the seat;
a rubber fly;
a real fly entombed in plastic ice;

a deck of cards in which the spades and clubs were red
    and the diamonds and hearts black;
a deck whose backs could be read with tinted glasses;
a deck in which the jacks simpered, the queens winked
    and beckoned, and the kings leered;
semen, vomit, and excrement reproduced in soft plastic;
a watch decorated with a nude woman whose arms were
    its hands, depicted at a relatively modest 6:30;
and a watch numbered counterclockwise.

Besides all these, there was one picture that was more or
less conventional. Suspended from a stick-on hook like an
erectile penis, it showed a voluptuous blonde whose gown,
brassiere, and panties would vanish if the room became
humid.

It was not humid, however, and the blonde appeared fully
dressed. Barnes was dressed too, in tattered nylon pajamas
and a robe. His room boasted a small table in addition to the
bed and dresser, and he sat before it composing a letter on the
florid, gold-crested stationery of the nearby Hotel Consort.
He wrote slowly and laboriously, the tip of his tongue
occasionally protruding from one corner of his mouth. From
time to time he kissed the point of his souvenir pen.

Dear Lois,
    Wonderful to hear from you. I know now you don't hold
a grudge. Me neither. It's over but it might have been
different. I think about that alot and I bet you do to.
    Can't understand what happened to the child support. I
would have my bank stop the check but then what would
happen if it's just stuck in the mail and later got delivered
to you alright. Let me know when you write next—if not
I'll have them stop and send you a new one, no joke.
    Doing alot of business but the weather is so bad I wish I
was south like you. Rain and snow. I know you said I could
visit Little Ozzie and of course Lois so did the judge.
    But, I'm not sure you mean it. Tell you what. If you
mean it get me a plane ticket and send it. (Address c/o Mr.

B. Free who is District Manager here.) Then I'll know you mean it and I'll pay you back when I get there.

    Kiss Little Ozzie for me.

    See You soon.

Big Ozzie

When he had completed this letter, Barnes drew an S-shaped flourish under his signature. After carefully retracting the point of the souvenir pen, he picked up the letter and read it with evident satisfaction.

    Taking up his pen again, he addressed an envelope, crossing out the location of the hotel and substituting that of Free's house. When the letter had been folded and sealed inside, he took a quarter-sheet of stamps from the table's shallow drawer, tore off one, moistened its back with the tip of his hard-working tongue, and (with the greatest attention to its position) gummed it on upside-down.

    After satisfying himself that it had adhered, he added the letter to a modest stack of similar ones on the left side of the table, stood up, and stretched. In his stocking feet, he padded across the room to the light switch. Drawing the blind down the single window left the room in a darkness that was nearly total.

    The whisper of his feet on the floorboards came again, followed by a nearly imperceptible scraping as he shifted the picture of the voluptuous woman with the disappearing gown to one side.

    The hole in the wall behind it showed no light. His finger explored it, and at last he thrust the souvenir pen into it. When he had satisfied himself that it had not been blocked, he replaced the picture and switched on the light again. Taking up a soiled supermarket tabloid from the bed, he began to read the classifieds.

Chapter 3

THE WOMEN

Stubb had fallen asleep, but the noise woke him. He flipped the wall switch and opened the door to illuminate the dark hall. Candy lay halfway up the stair, trying to rise.

He found her purse, hung it over his wrist, and bracing his feet on the worn wood, got his hands beneath her arms. "Hold the rail," he told her.

She nearly fell backward, taking him with her.

"Jesus!"

"'S all right," she said. "I'm swell." Her tongue was thickened almost to unintelligibility.

After a moment, he realized she no longer knew whether she was going up or down. "You want to go to the john?" he asked. "Up here."

She shook her head. "Go bed."

"Swell. Your room's up here too. Jesus, what have you been drinking?"

"Had li'l party."

"I bet." He put a hand under her knee and lifted until her foot was on the step where he stood. "Come on, you can make it. Hold on to the rail." He tugged at her, and she lurched upward.

Once he got her to the top, it was easier. Half steering, half carrying, he brought her to her door. Her key, chained to a rabbit's foot, was near the top of her purse.

He pulled her coat from her shoulders and maneuvered her to the bed, then closed the door and locked it. Candy staggered up at once, nearly falling, fumbling at the side of her skirt.

"That's fine," he told her. "Go to sleep. I haven't got the bread anyway."

The fat girl's hands fell helplessly. "Undress."

"Hell, it won't hurt you to sleep with your clothes on."

She began to fumble with the closure of her skirt again.

"All right, I don't want you stumbling around getting hurt. What happened to your shoes, anyhow? God damn it, this thing's tighter than you are."

The zipper at the side of her skirt was open already, or perhaps had never been closed. When Stubb released the straining catch, a gap as wide as his hand appeared between the ends of the waistband.

"Thanks."

"Sure."

Her blouse buttoned up the front. He ran nimble fingers down the buttons, pulled the blouse away, and threw it over the headboard. Her belly, white, soft as gelatin, and balloon-like in its distension, overhung the elastic of her panties and propped the swollen breasts in her sagging brassiere. Swaying, she embraced it, lifting and fondling it as if to compensate it for the discomfort it had endured.

"Candy, if you'd just charge 'em by the pound, you'd make a fortune."

She belched. "Pizza. Lots of pizza. Went up to his place. Marty."

"I thought they were all named John."

She belched again. "Pizza and boilermakers."

Stubb shook his head. "He give you anything, or did you just take it out in food and booze?"

Quite suddenly the fat girl took two tottering steps backward and fell across the bed. Stubb lifted her feet onto the mattress and rolled her on her side. A tin wastebasket half full of crumpled Kleenex stood beside the dresser; he put it on the floor near her head.

Her eyes fluttered open, closed again.

"If you get sick, use that," he told her. "Stay off your back. You could choke."

He bunched the pillow behind her shoulders and pulled

blankets over her. "Well, you won't freeze tonight when they turn off the gas. You might be the only one who won't."

At the sound of his voice, her lips twitched in a smile, then she began to snore. He squatted on the floor and dumped her purse onto the rug. The pack of Viceroys still held four cigarettes; he took one, lit it, and inhaled deeply. If she had ever had a billfold, it was gone, but there were loose bills among the soiled tissues, chewing-gum wrappers, and exhausted lipsticks. Twelve dollars in singles, two twenties, and several dollars in change. He took five singles and one of the twenties, making a roll he tucked into the crotch of his shorts.

"I earned it tonight, Candy," he told the sleeping girl softly. "For a minute there, I thought we were both going down those steps."

The rest he swept back into her purse.

On the roof, old Ben Free was speaking to the witch. "It's coming closer," he said. "I feel like I can hear it."

"I cannot hear it," she told him. "But you are correct. It draws so near. Soon it will be in Virgo."

The snow had stopped again, but not before it had covered the rooftop with a fluffy layer. The old man's booted feet left shambling tracks that might have been a bear's; the witch's footprints were so tiny and sharp they might have been a doe's, and in places they did not appear at all. The sky had cleared. In the moonlight, the shadows were deep blue.

"I'm talking about the wreckin' ball," the old man grumbled.

"I speak of Saturn. It is the same."

"Horseshit."

"You say that, who can hear it swung already?"

He seemed not to hear her. "Anyway, they'll find me like I always knew they would. It was a long chase I give them."

"The years, you mean."

"You know better, Ma'am, or you wouldn't be up here on the roof with me."

"Whom do you mean, then?"

"It ain't your affair."

"I tried to give you a gentlemanly escape, but you would have none of it. Do you prefer rudeness, Mr. Free? I do not." The witch put one foot on the parapet, and holding up her black skirt in the parody of a curtsy, stepped onto the coping and began to walk along it.

"You'll fall," the old man said. "You'll bust your fool neck."

"I do not much care, Mr. Free, and because I do not, I will not fall. Anyway, we are said to fall more slowly than others. We float when ducked, and given the least crust of ice, we can run over the snow like wolves."

"You tell lies, too."

"Not I." The witch laughed; her laughter was clear and yet unpleasant. "I used to as a child, I confess. But I soon found the truth more disconcerting."

"Next thing you'll tell me you knew I was here, and that was why you come."

"Not at all. I am as destitute as the rest, or nearly. Like them, I attempt to live by my wits; and though I wish to think I have more, I live as badly as they."

Free looked at her and shook his head. "You're proud of it, though, girl. Proud you're whatever you are."

"Whatever I am is the best thing to be. I am the only person I have ever met who is not a fool."

"Present company excepted, I s'pose."

"You tell me you are awaiting destruction and your death. If I were you, I would welcome them; but you do not, and neither do you flee."

"Where I just come from, men don't die easy. Women neither."

"I am properly rebuked. Why don't you run? Even if you have no money, there are places that will accept a homeless old man."

"I can't. I won't. You think you can see thirty foot into the hill, don't you, girl? You can't see a thing."

"What can I not see, Mr. Free?"

"You think this here me that's talking to you is all there is.

Don't you know there ain't a man to either side of the Muddy that's all held in his skin?"

"There is something in what you say."

"You think these walls are mine. I'm telling you these walls are me. Here's where I started out from. Here's where I've come to lick my wounds for—well, a sight of years. More than my whole life. Here's where I'll live as long as they stand, and here's where I'll die when they come down. See my chimney there? That's as much me as what you're talking to."

"We live inside you then, we four. I find that amusing. Like worms in a corpse. Very well, Mr. Free, will you speak to me out of your chimney? Or is your flue hoarse from smoking?"

One of the tiles of the coping slipped under the witch's feet. She nearly fell before it shattered on the pavement two floors below.

As the night wore on, the old house became cold. Barnes stripped the blankets from his bed, wrapping one about his shoulders, the other around his legs.

Dear Box 188B,
    I do not know what else to call you so I will call you that. I think it is a nice name. The 1 means you are alone and I am 2. That is a pun I guess but I really am. The 88 makes me think of a piano which has 88 keys. I used to play and I bet you do too. To tell the truth I was never very good but I admire people who are. Now since I am a salesman and live in hotels I can never practice. B is for beautiful. It is a womanly letter to me and always has been. A & C is male and so is I. (More puns.) Since I said I was a salesman I bet your thinking I am one of those guys who goes on the road and cheats on a wife. I am single (divorced) I really am. Your ad says you are a JW. I am a GM. I am not prejudiced and do not see why you should. I am 35, 5 ft. 9 in. with black hair and mustache. But, I am not Black. I am White of course.

If you would like to have my picture send me yours and I will send mine right away.

Could be Yours

Oscood Barnes

When he had inspected this letter and sealed it in its envelope, Barnes threw off the blankets, stood up, and stretched. For a moment he looked thoughtfully at the picture of the voluptuous blonde, now as thoroughly clothed as was possible for her. Then, shrugging, he flipped off the wall switch.

This time he was rewarded. Light gleamed from the hole, and he put his eye to it.

It penetrated the wall only a few inches above the top of the witch's dresser, where some bulky object (he had never learned what it was) cast a shadow on it. From it he could see most of her bed, much of the rest of the room, and a part of the door.

The witch was seated on that bed, fully dressed, nervously smoking a long cigarette that boasted lavender paper and a scarlet tip. For an instant she seemed to look directly at him. She exhaled a stream of smoke and rose; he recoiled instinctively, half expecting to see the burning end of her cigarette come through the hole.

When he looked again, she was seated once more and holding a hairbrush. She drew long pins from her hair, which tumbled in a cascade of night. Under his breath, Barnes began to count the strokes with her. One, two, three . . . Then he realized she was not counting but brushing to the rhythm of verses she murmured in a foreign language.

He stopped counting, but he was sure she had gone far beyond a hundred when she threw down her cigarette and lowered her brush. A moment later he heard it clack on the dresser top. She came into sight again, head bent as she removed contact lenses.

He expected her to undress, and she did not disappoint him, first removing her boots. They were small and spike-heeled, apparently of black kid, now wet and much worn. She looked critically at the sole of each before putting it down.

Her dress she pulled over her head with one easy motion, then padded away to her closet, presumably to hang it up. Under it she wore a black corset with garters, and Barnes was in ecstasy.

At that point, however, she seemed to lose interest in the process. She paced her room, looking for all the world like a panther transformed by some incomplete magic. Barnes took the picture from its hook, straightened for a moment to ease his back, then looked again.

Her hand flashed past the peephole. An instant later he could actually smell the perfumed smoke. She had lit another cigarette, and with it she continued her pacing. Carefully, he grasped the back of the chair before his table and pulled it over, then found he could not sit on it and continue to look. He thought of his sample cases and was about to carry one over to put on the chair when the witch went to her closet again. He saw a flash of scarlet as she opened her door, then heard her knock at his own.

Chapter 4

THE OLD MAN

"Hello, Mr. Stubb," Free said. "I hadn't figured to see you in my kitchen this hour of the night, though you're mighty welcome. Might I to ask what brings you here?"

"Hunger, sir," Stubb told him. "Hunger and curiosity."

The old man massaged his forehead with one big gnarled

hand. "You're seeking to shame me because we didn't save you some of what Mr. Barnes brought this evening. You're right to do it, and you've done it, Mr. Stubb. I'm most heartily sorry about that."

Stubb waved the apology away. "From what I hear, it was the Serpentina woman's money. Besides, you probably figured I ate somewhere else."

"I didn't figure, Mr. Stubb. That's what it was. My mind was otherwhere, thinking about old times."

"We all do that, sir," Stubb said. "And I wasn't trying to put you down when I said I was hungry. See, I got a little money tonight—I was able to help somebody out. The diner where I usually eat was closed, so I went to the all-night grocery and got a frozen TV dinner. It's in your electric oven now. Fried chicken, mashed potatoes, and green beans. If you'd like to split it with me, you're invited to."

"No, no. I've had my dinner, thanks to Madame Serpentina and Mr. Barnes. Heat feels good, howsomever, and I wish you full enjoyment, Mr. Stubb. You're welcome to my tea, if there's any remaining."

The old man began to back out of the room, but Stubb halted him with a gesture. "There was one other thing, sir. Curiosity, I said. Remember?"

"And what's that, Mr. Stubb?"

"When I was getting dressed to go out, I heard some peculiar noises."

"Old houses like this make such creakings," Free said vaguely. "Stands to reason."

"On windy nights they do, yes, sir. And just about any house will creak and groan when it cools down. But they hadn't shut off the gas then, and I've been out twice tonight and haven't noticed much wind either time, though it was windy earlier this afternoon. No, Mr. Free, I listened to those noises for a while and eventually I decided it was somebody walking on the roof above my head."

The old man nodded, and crossing to the kitchen table where Stubb sat, pulled out a chair and sat down.

"It wasn't Candy Garth, because I'd just left her. It wasn't

Barnes either. His room's right across from mine, and all I had to do was stick my head out to hear his chair squeak and his pen scratch; he'd been in there writing something almost ever since you people ate. It could have been the Serpentina woman—her room was dark—but I didn't think she was heavy enough. That left you, so I took a peek in your bedroom downstairs before I went out. You ought to learn to lock the door when you're not in there."

"I'm gone sometimes," the old man explained softly. "Every blamed thing in there worth stealing has been taken long ago."

"I've heard people talk like that before, but it was always before they got ripped off. Not afterward. Anyway, just as I was about to go out, a tile almost beaned me. I know it was a tile because I picked up a piece and had a look at it when I got to the grocery. I don't think anybody was laying for me, because I hadn't stepped through the doorway when it hit. Just the same, I was damn near killed, and I'd like to know what was going on."

"You were correct about me," the old man said. "I have no doubt it was my steps you heard. But you were wrong concerning Madame Serpentina. She was with me."

"Ah," Stubb said. He took off his glasses, breathed on them, and put them on again as if waiting to hear more.

"I'm sorry about that tile, I really am. Had no notion anybody might be down there that time of the night."

"You dropped it then, sir?"

"I'm responsible," the old man said. "You've got it. I was trying to show that girl something."

"Show her what?"

"I don't mean to get you riled, Mr. Stubb, but I don't believe that's your affair. Besides, that dinner of yours is about cooked. You're lucky they haven't shut off the electric yet. Better take her out now."

Stubb glanced at his bare wrist. "I suppose you're right, sir. I left my watch upstairs."

"Hope you locked your room. Anyway, she's done. I wind her."

Stubb turned off the oven and carried the foil-covered tray to the table. "Sure you won't have any?"

The old man shook his head.

"Mr. Free, what you were doing up there isn't my business, I admit. But I'll make it my business—if you want me to."

"They're going to tear this place down. I told you about that."

"Uh-huh." Stubb selected a drumstick and bit into it.

"They shut off my gas an hour ago. Tomorrow the electric will go off too, and the wreckers'll come. I want you to help me hold out. I told you about that."

"I know you did," Stubb said. "I will."

"If we can keep the walls standing, that's all the help I need. If we can't, nothing's going to do me good." Free paused. "Reckon to die, but old Ben Free don't die without a fight."

"You love this place."

"Suppose I do. Should it shame me, Mr. Stubb?"

"Everyone's got to love something."

The old man nodded. "That's so, I believe. I love this country, I suppose, or I used to. Loved a wife and daughter once. What do you love, Mr. Stubb?"

Stubb chewed and swallowed. "I don't know. My work, maybe, when I can get it. I haven't got a woman or a house."

"You're a detective, I think you said?"

"I'm an operative, sir. To be a private detective, I'd have to be licensed. As it is, licensed private investigators hire me to do the work they'll bill their clients for. If you think of a doctor and the clerk who sells you the aspirin he tells you to take, you'll about have the right idea."

"I believe I'd be clearer thinking about a farmer and his hired man. The farmer, he owns the land. He says, 'Time to plow for winter wheat,' and the hand, he plows and sows. He takes his wages and the farmer takes the crop."

"You've got it, sir."

"Thought I had." The old man pushed back his chair. "I'll make you some tea to go with your dinner."

"I'd be finished before you could get the water hot, Mr. Free. I'm all right."

"I'll get you a glass of water anyhow. I was a hand once myself." Free chuckled. "A hand for a bunch of letters."

Stubb nodded politely.

"Up in the High Country, that was." The old man waved at the ceiling. "That's where I come from to start with."

"Uh huh. How'd you get here, Mr. Free?"

"Oh, by my own doing. Come here and many another place too. Nobody made me. I'll let it run for a minute, so it'll be cold."

"Fine."

"You'll say I was a fool. Well, you'd be right, too."

Stubb swallowed again. "I've done some pretty dumb things myself."

"Adventure, that's what I wanted. Save the world. I come up here looking for a new world, but in all them years I never caught the sight of it, and now I guess I wouldn't hardly care to. Danger? Plenty of that, here and there. Love? I got some, but not enough to pay, if you catch my meaning. Pain, lonesomeness. Plenty of each. I'd like to go back, but it's too late. I'm old."

"A bus ticket doesn't cost much, Mr. Free."

"I have my ticket, Mr. Stubb. There won't no bus take you there, but I have my ticket. I saved it and I'll save it still, though it can't do me any good. It's still where I left it, there in the wall."

"In a wall?"

Free nodded. "I was fearful I'd lose it, you see, and I hid it there. Listen to me, Mr. Stubb, and I'll tell you what don't many know. Most of them that went lost theirs. Some used them and went back. I'm the only one I ever got the smell of that didn't do either. 'Cept you could say I lost mine too, 'cause I can't use it now."

"I haven't got the slightest idea what the hell this ticket is, sir," Stubb said. "But if you want me to, I'll try and help you find it."

The old man sighed and put a glass of water on the table.

"Maybe you could. If they don't tear the place down, we'll see." He leaned on the back of his chair, supporting his weight on his arms.

"And if the Serpentina woman's giving you some kind of trouble, I'll do what I can to help you with that. All you have to do is ask."

"She's more like you than you think, Mr. Stubb. I believe she'd help too, in her way."

"Serpentina's a good name for her, if you ask me, sir. If she bit a rabbit, it would die. I know the type." Stubb took a swallow of water and began to scrape up what remained of his mashed potatoes with his fork.

"Where I come from there was rabbits all over," the old man said softly. "Bears too, and deer. Here, I've never seen a one. Or any other wild creature, 'cept maybe a pigeon or a rat. You people don't know how poor you are." He straightened up, squaring shoulders that were still wide. "The creatures are all gone now, Mr. Stubb, as I soon shall be. Murdered."

Stubb leaped up. By the time he reached the door, the parlor beyond it was empty. So was Free's bedroom.

Returning to the kitchen, he removed his glasses and produced an almost clean handkerchief. When he had wiped the lenses thoroughly, he took a notebook and an automatic pencil from his shirt pocket and, twisting his face in a laborious grimace, wrote something in an almost microscopic hand. That done, he scanned the earlier pages, tearing out some and wadding them into balls he dropped into the empty tray.

The task complete, he carried the tray and its load of paper and chicken bones to the garbage container. A mouse ran from behind it as he dropped the tray in. Stubb froze; the mouse stopped to contemplate him, sitting up like a little kangaroo. Slowly, Stubb fished out a penknife and opened a blade at each end. The second clicked as it sprang into place, and the mouse resumed its dash for safety. Stubb threw, but missed by a foot.

Outside, new snow sparkled under the stars. He kicked it

to find the shards of tile, then turned up his collar and walked, occasionally halting to peer upward.

The woman behind the register looked up and smiled when he came in. "My best customer."

"Right. Am I the only one tonight?"

"The only soul. Leastways, there hasn't been nobody in since you was here last. Need somethin' else?"

"Forgot to get a paper," Stubb said.

"These's yesterday's now. You want to wait twenty minutes, the new ones'll come."

"Maybe." Stubb picked up a paper.

"How 'bout some coffee? On the house."

"Sure, it's cold outside."

"The company gives it to us so we can give it to the prowl-car mens. Havin' them come in for it keeps the place from bein' stuck up so much. We get to drink it ourselves and give it out, only we're not supposed to make the first pot till after midnight. What you lookin' for?"

"Story on the new freeway," Stubb told her.

Chapter 5

THE VISIT

"A moment," Barnes called. "Just a moment." In the dark he had mislaid the picture. He scrabbled for it—not finding it dove for the light switch, located the picture, hung it over his peephole, and threw open the door.

"I am so sorry," the witch said. "You were sleeping. I should have been more thoughtful."

"I wasn't asleep. Wide awake, that's me. Honest." He stumbled backward. "Won't you come in?"

She nodded and stepped inside. Without her high-heeled

boots, her head came only to his shoulder. The scarlet robe was oriental, embroidered with writhing black dragons; she clutched it at her chin, and with her long, dark hair she might almost have been Chinese.

"You are so very kind, Mr. Barnes. You have every reason to be annoyed with me."

"Never!" The chair was still facing the picture of the gowned blonde. He seized it in an agony of haste and held it for her, seating himself on the bed only after she had consented to sit down.

"You have taped up pictures, I see. I would guess that you are the only one among us who has labored to decorate his chamber."

"These are what I sell," Barnes explained. He cleared his throat. "Having them here reminds me of them, and I think about what I can say about them."

"System," the witch said admiringly. "You are correct, Mr. Barnes. System is everything." Her eyes, which until now had been more impressive than inviting, were melting.

"I try," Barnes told her.

"Often with great success, I am sure." The witch released the collar of her robe and folded her hands demurely in her lap, permitting Barnes to see her decolletage and a triangle of the black corset. For the first time, she seemed to notice the hook on which the picture of the blonde hung. "You are religious too. How refreshing to find that in a man! Mr. Barnes, I have come to you for help."

He swallowed. "If you mean, financial, I'm afraid—"

"It was I who gave you the money for our food tonight. Have you forgotten?"

"No, Ma'am, not at all, and I promise you when I get my commissions—"

"There is no need. I meant only to show you that I do not require money from you. Doubtless other women you have known have in this way or that always demanded it."

"No, no," Barnes told her. "Not at all."

"Really? You are an exception then. At any rate, I am

asking for your help, Mr. Barnes. I wish to enlist you under my banner, as it were."

"Anything I can do, Ma'am, why I'd be delighted—"

"Perhaps you should hear first. Do you credit the supernatural?"

"Why, ah . . ." For a moment Barnes looked embarrassed. "I can't really say I believe or I don't. I suppose you could say I've always thought there was more to everything than anybody could really know, but frankly I haven't thought about it much. I've never felt it concerned me. Maybe when we die we'll find out."

"There is little reason to think so, Mr. Barnes. People are inclined to believe that in this world the higher world is obscure, and in the next it will be made plain. But is it not equally probable that while we are here the higher world is revealed, and if we perish in ignorance of it, we shall remain in that ignorance in the next?"

"I don't know," Barnes admitted.

"As a man, you would no doubt be more impressed by science than by the symbolism of the mystics. To you I would say that to speak of a higher world is to speak of a higher state of energy. That is nearly always, you will note, what we mean when we speak of height—the stone upon the mountaintop, for example, possesses greater potential energy than the stone at the bottom of the tarn. If one end of a poker is red, we say that end is of a higher temperature, or that its thermal energy is higher. When we die, by the Law of Entropy, which all scientists acknowledge, we pass from a higher state to a lower. Since we will then be further from the higher world, how are we to see it more clearly?"

Barnes said, "I'm afraid I don't know much more about science than I do about the supernatural. In fact, they often seem about the same to me."

The witch nodded and smiled, perfect teeth flashing in her dark face. "They are indeed closer than most scientists—or most mystics—are willing to admit, Mr. Barnes. If I have provided your first lesson in science, let me give you your first in mysticism also. It is that we live surrounded by signs—signs we are often too blind to read. I am such a sign and you are such a sign and that bed on which you sit is a sign. If we knew what all the signs mean, we should be creatures of a higher order. If we knew only what many of them mean, we should have power and great riches. Do you understand?"

"I think so," Barnes said.

"The air and light of the living are signs then, and the dirt and dust of death. If we who can see the stars cannot see what is higher, how shall those who dwell beneath the roots of the trees in a land of worm and stone and water see it? I say to you, Mr. Barnes, that knowledge comes to those who seek to learn, sight to those whose eyes are opened, understanding to those who ponder the mysteries."

"That's wonderfully put," Barnes said. "I can see why you believe it, ah . . ."

"My name is Madame Serpentina. You may call me that."

"I know. Only I thought maybe . . . well, for instance, it might be more friendly if you were to call me Ozzie."

"Very well, I will call you Ozzie, and you will call me Madame Serpentina."

"Of course, Madame Serpentina, if that's the way you want it. I was going to say that now that I've heard you put it so well—that is, if I could sell my merchandise the way you do your ideas, why I'd be rich. I believe it, too. Only I don't know what it is you want from me."

The witch smiled again. "You are a wonderful man, my Ozzie. You are practical, you are persuasive, you have to an unusual degree the masculine force of character. What would any woman want of you?"

Barnes's eyes strayed to the stack of letters on the table. "Well, as you said yourself, Madame Serpentina, what most of them are after is money."

"Your protection, your courage, your strength, and your cunning at her side. But, Ozzie," she leaned forward and caught his hands in her own, which seemed to him as cold as ice. "You must first understand that I am what I say I am. I have been called a witch, and indeed I have called myself that—it is the closest word English has for what I am. Do you know what it means? Wit meant knowledge once. To wicken was to enchant, only a thousand years ago. To wikken was to prophesy. Wih meant holy."

She said all these words rapidly, so that *wikken* sounded much like *wicken*, *wit* like *wih*. Barnes could only gasp, "You certainly are enchanting."

"I am indeed, my Ozzie; you speak more truly than you know. I have often noticed that when others speak to me—doubtless it is my aura. But what you must understand is that I am one who has lifted the veil. I am enlightened. We spoke, you and I, of seeing a higher world. I have on occasion glimpsed it, or its reflection. I have made the study of it my life."

Barnes nodded solemnly.

"You are here now, and I am here, Ozzie, in a house on the brink of destruction. Why are we here?"

"Well," Barnes said slowly, "I can't really speak for you, Madame Serpentina. But me, I always read the classifieds, especially the personals. And a couple of days ago, I saw this ad in the Sunday paper that said free rooms. I cut it out, and I believe I've got it here someplace."

"You need not search for it."

"Anyway, it said there would be free rooms at this address until the building came down. To tell the truth, I'd been having some trouble where I was staying then. I owed rent, and once they padlocked my door, only I was able to show the woman that unless I could get my sample cases and present a respectable appearance, I couldn't ever make the rent, and she let me back in. So when I saw this, I went after it. Old Mr. Free was turning away undesirables, and my impression was that we would all be respectable people here, which I should say we all are, except one."

The witch waved the cavil aside. "Let me tell you now how I came." She paused, and for a moment appeared to see something over Barnes's left shoulder that he would not himself have seen. "I had observed certain portents, in the stars and elsewhere. Because of them I was excited. You may think me, my Ozzie, a woman of the indurated kind, but it is not so—I am capable of feelings that would burst the hearts of many. Like you, I had experienced certain difficulties; at times I am wakeful for long periods and at odd hours. I enjoy music that is—shall we say—an acquired taste, and my visitors are sometimes unconventional."

Barnes nodded solemnly, having observed something of all these himself.

"Although I paid an excessive rent for an inadequate apartment, I was no longer welcome. I saw the advertisement you saw, and despite its appearing too small a stroke of good fortune for the promises extended to me, yet it was a favorable day, and I came."

"Let's say the good fortune was ours, Madame Serpentina."

The witch ignored this compliment. "All the rest of the day I waited the blessing promised. It did not appear. I returned to my old building hoping some message had come; there was nothing. That night I watched the stars again. I had not been mistaken. You may believe I wondered long over that."

Barnes nodded again. "I can see how you would."

"After you left us tonight, I talked with our host. He told me something of his sorrows, his fears. Much more, I think, than he thought himself to tell, because he believed me unenlightened. He is old, and his mind is full of death and no longer so clear as he thinks. In the end, he could not resist a small demonstration of his power."

"Are you saying Mr. Free is, well, somebody like you?"

The witch's smile flashed. "You are a man of intelligence indeed, my Ozzie. Like me and yet unlike, for I could not have done what he did. I believe him one of the lesser acaryas. Unless a student is contacted by them, as sometimes happens, she is fortunate to meet and recognize one such in a lifetime. Tonight he let slip something of the greatest importance. My Ozzie, have you never wished to be rich? Powerful? I do not mean what is called wealthy. Nor do I mean power in the sense that a mayor or governor is said to be powerful. I speak of endless riches, of real gold, emeralds, sapphires, and diamonds, and of the power of life and death over hundreds of millions."

"More than anything else in the world!" Barnes looked surprised at his own vehemence.

"Mr. Free—or rather, the person we are told to call by that name—has concealed a talisman. The acaryas do so at times, putting by their crowns and orbs, regalia more than earthly, to encounter us at a level. Now he lacks strength to take it up again. But if we could find it . . ."

"You mean this," Barnes said. "You're serious."

"I was never more so. Do not think to cheat me of the prize, Ozzie. You could no more wield such a talisman than you could summon the green-haired wantons of the sea. Less. But if you will help me, you shall be my vizier in an empire encompassing all the world." The witch's hands toyed with his own, stroking their backs, tickling their palms.

Icy though the room was, his face was damp with sweat. He drew one hand away and wiped it with the faded sleeve of his robe. "I wish I knew if you're crazy."

For an instant the witch glared, then she laughed. "In comparison to me, you are all of you lunatics. No, idiots— save Free. You said you longed for wealth and power, and you are destitute. What have you to lose, my Ozzie?"

"I don't think you're crazy," Barnes told her. "What do you want me to do?"

Chapter 6

BREAKFAST

The fat girl tottered into the kitchen. A golden trumpet of sunshine striking the scuffed linoleum made her squint and press her temples with plump, pink hands.

Her robe was pink as well, pink with the violent, almost ferocious, fluorescent pinkness found only in discount stores. Like her disordered yellow hair, it made her seem an immense doll, still bright, yet abandoned and bedraggled.

The old man rose and pulled the shade.

"You got any coffee, Mr. Free?"

Free shook his head. "Sorry. There ain't one thing."

"I couldn't eat," Candy said. "I just want some coffee."

"I ain't had nothing either."

"No breakfast?"

"That feller Barnes went out last night and got some stuff, but it's all gone now."

Candy yawned, pulled out the top of her pink robe, and glanced down at herself. "Wait till I get dressed."

"Got nothin' else to do," the old man said. When she was gone, he opened a closet, got out a broom, and began to sweep. The kitchen had not been swept for a long time. Strange crumbs and crusts mingled with the gritty dust; there were bent beer-bottle caps and little splinters of broken glass. He opened the back door and pushed them all into a backyard filled with rubbish and gay with morning glories.

"Here I am," the fat girl said. Under the plastic coat she wore a pink sweater (near relative to the pink robe) and a black wool skirt. Her shoes were open-toed sandals with thick wooden soles. "Get your coat, Mr. Free. I'll treat you to some eggs."

"That'll be good." The old man sighed. "I ain't had no eggs in quite a time." He stood the broom in a corner.

Outside, sunlight danced on the snow. "Your feet's goin' to freeze," he told her as they went down the front steps.

"Lost my boots," the fat girl said. "I must have left them up at Marty's."

"And come home barefoot?"

"He drove me," the fat girl said. "Anyway, somebody did. Maybe I'll have to buy some more." She was combing her hair with her fingers. Its short, springy curls came closer and closer to their normal appearance each time her fingers passed through them. "If I seem kind of crabby, don't pay attention. I've got the most terrible headache."

"You seem real fine to me."

"Thanks. I feel like I'm going to chuck."

"I ain't never had words with an egg in my whole life."

Candy giggled. "Me neither."

The Sandwich Shop was open again; they took a booth near the front. "I love these damn things," she said. "I'm never comfortable in a chair."

The old man nodded solemnly.

"They ought to take into account that some people are bigger. Like, look at those stools at the counter. They'll kill you. Sitting on a bed is okay, but you can't rest your back."

A middle-aged waitress brought them menus.

"I just want coffee," the fat girl said. "You've got the bottomless cup, right? All the refills I want?"

The waitress said, "Fifty cents."

"Uh huh."

"I can't read this," Free announced. "But I know what I want. I want two basted eggs. Can I have some ham?"

"Ham," the waitress said.

"Uh huh, go ahead," the fat girl told him.

"Then I want some. Tea, if it ain't too much trouble."

"Tea." The waitress nodded and went behind the counter. "Blind 'em. Country on the side."

"Coffee will fix me up," the fat girl said. "But it's better with a little liquor in it."

"That'll go for most things."

Candy giggled again. "I bet you were a swinger. A big, good-looking guy."

The waitress returned with ice water, cups, and tin teapot. "You want cream and sugar?"

"Lots of sugar," the fat girl told her. She dumped three packets into her cup, stirred it negligently, and drained it, then sat for a moment with her hands pressed to her temples. "More!" she called after the waitress. Free was moving the tea bag up and down in his pot; the fat girl leaned toward him, lowering her voice. "Can you still get it up, Mr. Free?"

He chuckled. "How'd I know that?"

"If you want to try, just ask me. When I'm not so wasted, okay? If you can't, don't worry about it. I've seen it happen with a lot of younger guys."

"You're a kind-hearted woman, Miz Garth."

The waitress refilled the fat girl's cup and dropped a fresh handful of sugar packets on the table. They bore the likenesses of poets: Byron, Shelley, Keats.

"I'm a sick one," Candy said. "My head hurts me like you wouldn't believe." Her plump fingers trepanned the poets.

"Wish I knew something to help you."

"I know already. I took four aspirins before I came downstairs the first time, and I drank about a quart of water. Now just give me six or eight cups of coffee and I'll be fine."

"Used to know a man that breathed steam. Him and me had a pot we'd make stew in and suchlike, and he'd fill her with water and set her on the fire till she boiled. Then he'd take her off and put his head down and pull a blanket over him."

"That was a different kind of headache," the fat girl told Free. "Or maybe not." She had drunk half her coffee while he spoke. "See, what I'm doing is maybe the same thing, only on the inside. Your buddy put his water in his pot and I put mine in mine." She patted her belly. "Now I'm boiling it. When we get back to your house, I'll pull the blanket up for three or four hours."

"You might not get your sleep out," the old man said. "They're comin' today."

"Who's coming?"

"Them that'll wreck my house."

"They tell you that?" the fat girl asked.

Free did not reply.

"Just a hunch, huh? Mr. Free, you know I'll do anything I can. But hunches don't always work out."

"Mine do, Miz Garth."

The waitress brought Free's eggs and ham, and more coffee for the fat girl.

"Listen, I used to have a boyfriend who was a hunch

player. Like, he'd look over his form and see a horse called Try Me, and it would hit him. That was his horse. 'Guilty,' I'd tell him, but he'd go nuts unless he had something down on Try Me. Or he'd see a robin fighting a glass door, and then there'd be this horse Gallant Portal. Sometimes they paid, but he never had any cash, and he took mine."

The old man looked up, interested. "Gallant Portal win?"

The fat girl shook her head, then looked as if she was sorry she had. "Finished three or four places out of the money. Andy—his name was Andy—was always after me to lose some weight. I was always after him to quit the horses. It got to where we made each other feel awful all the time."

She stirred in sugar. "One time I was in this hotel, and I met this really nice, kind of elderly dentist. Some girls will meet a john like that and say a hundred bucks and if he says no they'll say seventy-five and so on depending on how low they're willing to go, and sometimes I do that too, only it depends on the john, what I think he's like. This time what I said was listen, I'm starving, you take me to dinner and we'll go up to your room and it'll be great. So we went down the street and I had a lobster and maybe a dozen oysters, plus the baked potato and that junk.

"About an hour after that I was going uptown and I went past a pizza joint. The dentist had slipped me fifty and I was feeling flush. With a certain type, mostly your older johns, you can let them feed you and then give them a good time and act like you like them, and they're liable to give you damn near anything. Anyway, I went into the pizza joint and got a large with everything, and I was sitting there in the booth with a bottle of Diet Pepsi and it came to me that Andy was like me and I was like Andy. I could have walked right past that pizza joint, but if I had there would have been another one down the street, and I would have gone in because I passed up the first one. And if I couldn't, I'd just as soon die."

"Ain't you never wished you didn't want to eat so much?" the old man asked.

The fat girl was waving at the waitress. "More coffee, and a pecan waffle with sausage on the side."

"Not that it's my business," the old man said.

"I never have," the fat girl told him. "Only I wish sometimes I wasn't so—you know—obese. Once I roomed with a girl that would go out and eat a big meal and come back to our place and stick her finger down her throat. Puking so she'd look good to the johns. She cut her wrist once in the tub. It didn't kill her, but various things went on after that, and I don't think I ever saw her again."

"Miz Garth, don't you do that."

"Not to worry. What were we talking about? I forgot."

The waitress called to the cook, "Step on the nuts. Pigs."

"Headaches," the old man said.

"Yeah, only I wish you hadn't reminded me. I got a winner." The fat girl ripped a paper napkin from the dispenser at the back of the table, dipped it into her water glass, and pressed it to her forehead. "My brain hurts. Why don't they ever have contests for stuff I can do? If they gave cups for headaches like they do for bowling, I could take a bath in mine. We got any hot water?"

The old man lifted the lid of the tin pot.

"I mean back at your house. I could use a nice bath—just lie in the tub and soak. That might make me feel better than anything."

"The heater went when they cut off our gas, but I got a little bottle-gas job set inside the furnace to keep the pipes from freezing. I'll have to keep a eye on that anyway so's it don't blow up the place 'fore the wreckers come. Maybe I could pipe some bottle gas over to the water heater for you."

"Thanks," the fat girl said. "I mean that. You really think they're coming today, huh?" Without removing the napkin from her forehead, she emptied her cup and put it down.

"About them prizes," the old man said. "They don't amount to a spot on a hog. You take bowlin', you mentioned that yourself. What matters is that a certain feller can get down all the pins about any time his turn comes up. The cup just tells that. It ain't the shingle makes a doctor."

"Liquor makes you sleep too hard," the fat girl murmured. She had shut her eyes, and was leaning her head against the padded backrest. "Last night you couldn't have got me up with a gun."

"You got things you could win prizes for, if they gave them. Maybe they don't, but you've got them things, and that's what counts."

"With you," the fat girl said.

"With me, yes. What counts, period."

"You're a gentleman, Mr. Free. They're damn near all dead."

"There'll be gents when Ben Free is gone and forgot, Miz Garth."

The fat girl opened her eyes; they were large, bloodshot, and startlingly blue. "I think it's going away. I feel a little better."

"I figured you did when you asked for that waffle."

"That was just a habit," the fat girl told him. "If you're like me, you eat when you feel good because you feel good, and you eat when you don't because you don't." She dropped the damp napkin on the floor and rummaged in her purse for a cigarette. "You smoke, don't you, Mr. Free?"

"Sometimes."

"Here, have one of mine." She braced her wrists on the edge of the table to strike the match, and when the waitress brought their food she asked for a pack of Viceroys.

"This here is a good cigarette," Free told her. "Usually when I smoke, it's a pipe, or maybe the doc will give me a cigar."

"I thought blind people didn't," the fat girl said. With her own cigarette between her lips, she was cutting up her waffle.

"I ain't blind! I can see *smoke*, for Pete's sake."

"I didn't mean to make you mad."

"I ain't mad!"

"Okay. Like some of my waffle?"

"I got plenty," the old man said. "Thanks to you."

"You won't forget about fixing the hot water for me?"

Shifting her cigarette to her left hand, the fat girl forked waffle into her mouth.

"Course not. You think I'm mad. I ain't mad, I just ain't blind. Never will be, neither. Won't live that long."

"Really." The word was nearly drowned in maple syrup.

"I s'pose you'll be feelin' better when you've had that bath?"

The fat girl nodded and swallowed. "Maybe I ought to tell you when I'm out? I mean, so you can turn off the heater and all that stuff."

"Your room's right over mine," the old man said. "I'll hear the boards creakin'."

Chapter 7

IN A WALL

"Ah, there you are, Mr. Free," Barnes said. "I've been looking for you."

"Not in the right spots, I reckon. Me and Miz Garth was out to breakfast."

The fat girl smiled at Free. "I'm going to go upstairs now and get ready for that soak. I'll be seeing you." On the second step she turned and blew him a kiss.

"Got to fix up the hot water," Free said. "Promised I would, and it'll take a bit for it to get hot."

"Of course." Barnes drew his threadbare topcoat around himself more tightly. "I'll come along and help, if I can."

"Don't need no help, but you can come. You want to see me?"

Barnes nodded. "It's rather . . . I can't say personal. Private, right? Perhaps we should go—"

Free interrupted him. "You come with me, then. I got to go pipe up that heater, and down there's about as private as

anyplace." He shouldered his way past Barnes and without
looking back to see if he were following strode off toward the
rear of the house.

"I think I should explain that I'm not really here on my
own behalf," Barnes began, hurrying after him. "Madame
Serpentina asked that I talk with you."

"If she's cold, I can't help it—they shut off my gas. You
tell her if she's got any more complaints to make them
herself. I'll listen, and I don't bite much. I got nothing to
work with here, but I'm doin' the best I can."

"I'm sure you are, Mr. Free. And believe me, all of us
appreciate it more than you know."

The old man pulled a rusty key from his pocket and
opened a door. Warm, stale air, musty with time and decay,
poured out. He started down creaking wooden steps into the
dark.

"Aren't you going to turn on the lights?" Barnes called
after him.

"Ain't none." Free's voice seemed to float like a ghost in
the blackness. "Never has been. Come on down, Mr.
Barnes. Just keep a hold of that railin'."

Hesitantly, Barnes came.

"Some steps's broken. Got to be careful." There was a
rasping noise and the flare of a match. "She's a deep one, I
guess you can see. Just keep on comin'."

The stair had been repaired often and badly. Or perhaps it
had never been repaired at all, only built of such odd scraps
as had come into the builder's hands. Some treads were no
more than two or three unplaned sticks laid side by side;
some showed paint at their edges, fragments of letters and
pictures.

The match flickered and went out.

"Naught to worry about, Mr. Barnes. I never strung none
because I didn't want no one coming down here, but I been
up and down them steps a hundred times. Good thing,
too—they'll be shuttin' off the electric any minute. S'pose
they caught us down here? You say that witch asked you to
talk for her?"

A second match flared. For a moment, Free's big, hunched body was interposed between Barnes and the light, then the golden radiance of a candle appeared.

Barnes managed to say, "She was up on the roof with you."

"I know that. She got up on that little wall that goes around it. It was a damn fool thing to do."

"She said you—ah—confided certain important facts." Barnes's foot touched the grimy surface of the floor, and he heaved a sigh of relief.

"She did, eh? I hadn't reckoned she'd pass that on."

"Madame Serpentina and I are friends." Barnes cleared his throat. "You might say we've a relationship, if you know what I mean. I'm sure she didn't tell me anything you asked her to hold confidential."

"I know, but I ain't sure you do. There wasn't anything like that."

In the flickering light, the ancient furnace seemed a monster, lifting tentacles as thick as a man's body to the overhanging dark. The monster was dead, its rotting flesh weeping asbestos, corroding the old-fashioned cabinet that spun wiring in its shadow.

"I didn't mean anything improper—"

"Neither'd I. Just thought you thought maybe I said somethin' I didn't want spread around. I didn't. I'll be on my way to meet with my daughter 'fore sundown, I reckon, so what do I care? You like women, don't you, Mr. Barnes?"

"Like them?" Taken off guard, Barnes considered for a moment. "Not really. I want them, and since I can't have them, usually, I don't like them. But I want them, I suppose you could say that. I admire Madame Serpentina."

"Do you now?" Free said. A length of hose ran from a small propane tank into the mouth of the monster. Stiffly, he bent and reached inside.

"She has pride, intelligence, and vivacity. Her profile is wonderful, and I don't think I've ever seen a woman with finer eyes."

Free looked over his shoulder. "Interestin' you should say

that. Because, Mr. Barnes, I been just now wonderin' about yours. The black part in a man's eye usually gets big in the dark, just like a cat's. When I lit this here candle, I noticed only one of yours acted so. Your one there looks about the way it always did, I believe."

"It's glass," Barnes admitted. "You don't think it looks too unnatural, Mr. Free?"

"Never noticed it till now."

"I'm glad of that. Sometimes I think I see people looking at it when I'm making a call. Appearance is very important in sales, and someday, when money's easier, I'll buy a better one. The best are made in Germany, but they cost a bundle."

"It looks fine," the old man told him. "It's the most natural thing about you."

"It would be better if the others, especially Madame Serpentina—"

"You don't have to worry about me. I'll be gone anyway, just like I told you. When I got you people in here, I kind of hoped they'd leave the old place stand because folks was still livin' here. It ain't goin' to work, though, and I know it. I look at my walls, and I can see that big, black ball comin' through 'em."

"I'll do what I can, Mr. Free," Barnes said. "I know the others will too."

"I believe that, Mr. Barnes."

"I know that none of you—except for Madame Serpentina—think a hell of a lot of me. Just a bunch of talk, a hand-pumper and a back-slapper. But I don't walk away from my friends, Mr. Free. Not unless I'm forced to."

Free nodded. "You're a bigger man on the inside than on the outside, Mr. Barnes. I knew it when I seen you hadn't got nothing for yourself last night 'fore you brought our grub to us. There's a few like you."

Barnes smiled and squatted beside the old man. "I'm glad you feel that way, Mr. Free, because it's going to make it quite a bit easier to talk to you. When you were up there with Madame Serpentina, you told her—this is what she says—

about something valuable you hid away and more or less lost some years ago."

Free nodded. "Quite a few years. I'm surprised, though, she told you. I guess I said that." He had picked up a screwdriver, and his hands were busy. He did not look at Barnes.

"Believe me, I would never betray Madame Serpentina's confidence, and she knows it. She's asked me to help her."

"Well, now."

"Just as you've asked me to help you, Mr. Free. And I'm going to try to do my best for both of you."

"Good for you," Free muttered. "Now you have a look at that bottle gas. See the valve? Shut her off."

Barnes did as he was told. "Madame Serpentina's a very intelligent woman, but she has a certain view of life. A view of the world. She sees things in, um, spiritual terms."

Free straightened up, the hose end, a hose clamp, and the screwdriver all in one big hand, like a bouquet of soiled flowers. "That's got her loose. Smells funny, don't it?"

"Speaking man-to-man," Barnes continued dauntlessly, "what she told me was nonsense. What I mean to say is, it was nonsense to me, right? I don't look at things the way she does, but I suppose if you look at them that way, she might be right. Anyway, what she indicated to me was that you told her you once had a—ah—crown, or something of that sort, and you had hidden it. Last night, she said, you told her where, more or less, and that it would be all right with you if she got it. When you—ah—have met your daughter and have no further use for it."

Free chuckled. "A crown? That's what she said?"

"Something like that. She used a lot of words I don't know, but that's what it seemed to boil down to. Regalia? I always thought that meant a yacht race, but I believe it was one thing she spoke of."

"And she said I told her where 'twas? Mr. Barnes, don't you think if I had a crown, and knew where it was, I'd go get it?"

"Not where it was, exactly." Barnes was stubborn. "Only that you had hidden it away a long time ago."

The old man chuckled again. "I gave her more than that, Mr. Barnes. I doubt she told you everything."

Barnes smiled. "Then there is a crown. That's wonderful, Mr. Free."

"Not a crown." Free's voice grew grave. "I never said it was a crown."

"I didn't think so. It doesn't seem probable, after all."

"Trouble is, I want to tell you what it was, Mr. Barnes. Only I can't."

"I would respect your confidence, Mr. Free. Trust me."

"'Taint that." The old man shuffled awkwardly, like a boy. "It's a treasure. That's all I can say. A treasure. Something I brought from the High Place, and there's no words I could use to tell you what it was and make you believe it now." He held up his hands as if depicting a fish or a putt. "It ain't too big. Not much wider than that."

"But it would be worth a great deal," Barnes persisted, "if we found it?"

"Oh, you could sell it for a sight of money, I s'pose. 'Cept you never would. Once you had it, you couldn't part with it. Not for money. Maybe not for anything. I never meant to, you see, Mr. Barnes. I'd used it, and I'd learned a whole lot. I only wanted to put it to one side for a while and stay where I was at. Then one thing and t'other happened. I thought about it sometimes, but the time never seemed right to go. There was always corn to plant, or this or that. Anyway, I got older—which we all do, Mr. Barnes, treasure or none. And I knew it would be harder. I kept thinkin' one day I'd feel better, and some days I did, only it never lasted. Then it was too late for me. I started askin' myself what I'd do with it now, and I'll tell you the truth, there wasn't much of a answer."

"I see."

"No you don't, Mr. Barnes. You don't see a thing." The old man shambled off in the direction of water heater.

"I only meant that I can sympathize. My grandfather had a

farm and lost it. I still remember how depressed he was. I understand how you feel."

The candle went out.

"You're wrong, Barnes." The voice was Free's and yet not Free's, as though a new and different Free had come suddenly with the dark.

Barnes gasped, "Where are you, Mr. Free?" and patted his pockets helplessly. "I've been trying to quit smoking, and now the candle's—"

"I know that, Barnes. Don't be any bigger fool than you can help. A moment ago you said people don't respect you. I said I did, and I do. But you're involved in something you don't understand. That's the simple truth."

"Don't you have—"

"You're trying to ask me where I put my gizmo, and what it is. A way to make me tell you what I hardly know myself about something you don't understand. Well, I put it where I told you. In a wall. I could have put it someplace else, but it was a wall I chose."

Barnes took a step. He hoped it was toward the stair, though he felt a chasm had opened before him.

"And I put a sign on it. I'm not sure you'll ever see that sign, Barnes, but if you do I think you'll know."

Chapter 8

THE DEFENDERS

Sergeant Proudy mounted the steps of 808 South Thirty-eighth and knocked at the door. It was a fine old door, high, wide, and solid. The Proudys lived in an apartment with a fireplace; Sergeant Proudy wished briefly that he might have that door. It would burn for weeks.

There was no sound from inside. Proudy pushed up the tail of his overcoat, took a blackjack from his hip pocket, and used it to knock again.

After several more knocks, Barnes opened the door. He was half a head shorter than the policeman, who wedged one of his large, black shoes between the door and the jamb.

"You still here, bud?" Sergeant Proudy grunted. "Where's the old man?"

Barnes hesitated. "I'm afraid Mr. Free's presently engaged, officer."

Proudy pushed open the door. "I have to see him. I've got a paper here for B. Free. Where is he?"

Barnes backed away. "I think he's—ah—upstairs. It would probably be better if I went up and asked him to come down and see you."

"I'll go up with you," Proudy said firmly. He followed Barnes up the steep, narrow stair. "You're still living here?"

"Yes, I am," Barnes told him. The house was icy cold, but a radio banged and grumbled upstairs.

"You're going to have to get out. You and the old man and everybody else, if there's anybody else left."

Barnes halted, his hands clutching at the banister. "Not now, officer. There are five of us."

"As of noon of this date."

Barnes shook his head. "That's impossible. I've only made a couple of calls today—a few neighborhood places. I wanted to see Mr. Free myself, so I couldn't go very far. I'd make a call or two over in the next street, you follow me? And then I'd come back and check. The first time he was still asleep, and then he was out having breakfast. Probably I waited too long because I got a good order at the second place, and I had to write it up and promise the guy it would be here in ten days or less. You know how it is?"

"You get on upstairs, and while you're doing it, I'll make this completely clear. What I got here's a court order." Sergeant Proudy had a large nose. He rubbed it. "It says you got to be out at noon because they got to wreck this house. Come noon, we carry you out, and we carry your stuff out, and we dump everything in the street. If you don't want that, move before then.''

"I really don't think that's reasonable, officer," Barnes said. "Or right, either." The sergeant was crowding him, jabbing him just above the belt with the end of the blackjack to force him up the stairs. "People, old people like Mr. Free particularly, should have some rights."

"The law says he's got the right to take what the state says his house is worth. Ain't that right? Now go get him."

"In here, I think." Barnes trotted past Stubb's door and knocked at Candy's.

Bedsprings creaked. The door swung back, the ugly sounds of the radio grew louder, and the fat girl appeared in the doorway. She was heavily powdered and rouged, but she wore the pink robe.

Barnes could see a little of the unmade bed beyond her; it was empty, but something flat and furry and larger than any cat lay there. "I don't like to bother you," he said stiffly. "But do you know where Mr. Free is?"

"Not any more. I was taking a nap." The fat girl yawned as though to prove it, then glanced at Sergeant Proudy. "I'm broke, remember? You were here yesterday."

Barnes cleared his throat. "He says they're going to make everyone leave at noon."

"Not me. I won't be up then." The slam of the fat girl's door was followed by the snick of a night bolt.

"Ozzie, the wrecking. It will be today?"

Across the stairwell, Sergeant Proudy saw a slender, dark-haired woman in a black dress.

"At noon," Barnes said. "We have to be out by noon." There was an unspoken appeal in his voice.

"I will try," the dark woman said. "It will depend, perhaps. Where is Stubb?"

Sergeant Proudy broke in. "The hell with that. I got to serve this paper. Where's Free?"

"Stubb couldn't do anything."

"One never knows, my Ozzie. He might help you."

"Help me do what?"

"You are intelligent and resourceful. What you will think of to do." The dark woman opened the door behind her and slipped through it.

Stubb was in the Sandwich Shop, with the telephone, an ashtray, and a half-empty coffee cup before him. He sat listening intently to the telephone while drawing on a Camel, his head cocked. "Yeah," he said. "Yeah, sure. Who would know?"

A heavy, middle-aged woman stood behind the counter staring at him.

He covered the mouthpiece with one hand. "What's eating you?"

The woman looked down the counter at the young man who had waited on Stubb the night before. "Murray, you gave him more credit?"

"He paid up, Mom."

"Okay, switch me," Stubb said. "Let me talk to him."

"So help me God as I live and breathe, Mom, he paid up. He paid for that coffee there, too."

"Hello, Charlie, this is Jim Stubb. You remember me? I'm a friend of Tinker's. . . . Charlie, I need a little favor, just a two-bit thing. Tinker'd do it for me in a minute, but he's down in Florida reeling 'em in, and I don't want to bother him. . . . Yeah, I do too, haven't done any fishing in a year. Too busy, you know how it is. . . . Charlie, what it is, is this place over on the south side where they're putting the new freeway through. It's scheduled for demo, but the old guy that owns it is a friend of mine. He hasn't had time yet to get his stuff out. I was wondering if you couldn't—Hell, Charlie, there's got to be something else they could do for a couple of months anyway. They've been *planning* the God-damned freeway for eight years. . . . Sure, I understand. What's the number? I'll try him."

"You want more coffee?"

"Thanks, Murray."

"Do me a favor, huh?"

Stubb had hung up the telephone. He picked up the

handset again and began to dial. "What're you whispering for, Murray?"

"So I'm whispering. Order a doughnut."

"Commissioner Carson's office, please."

"You're asking them for a favor, I'm asking you for one. Order a doughnut. I bet you didn't eat breakfast. What can it hurt?"

"My name's Jim Stubb, and I'm active on the south side. I'm a very good friend of Tinker Bell's. Will you tell Commissioner Carson I'd like to talk to him? What the hell, Murray, you gone crazy?"

"A little favor I'm asking. You ask me for favors all the time."

"Hello, Commissioner? . . . I believe we did meet last summer at the picnic. . . . No, no, I was just in the audience, you probably wouldn't remember me, but I heard your speech. We shook hands afterward. . . . Yeah, you gave 'em hell, everybody loved it. That's why I'm calling, Commissioner. You know how it is, you have the party's interests at heart, maybe you stick your nose in sometimes where it doesn't belong. But you say to yourself, the party's been good to me, maybe I should stick my neck out and pay back. The thing is, Commissioner, they're going to knock down this old house here on the south side. It's full of people who've got nowhere else to live and the whole neighborhood's pretty steamed. . . . Sure, the snow and all. . . . It's going to hurt us with these people, and the way I figure it, just a little cooling down period, just a few weeks maybe, could make all the difference. . . . No, white. Not Polish or anything. . . . Okay, Commissioner, I'm not going to argue, there isn't a white vote. But whites vote. . . . Okay, I'll call him. Maybe you could call him too?"

Stubb hung up and stared into space for a moment. Into nothingness. Then he took a torn dollar bill from his pocket and laid it on the counter. "Hey, Murray, give me some more coffee and a couple doughnuts, huh? Not them, the big greasy kind."

Murray took two from a plastic canister on the counter and

stacked them on a saucer for Stubb, then took the dollar and
rang up ninety cents on the cash register. As he brought his
dime to Stubb, he whispered, "So she could see you paying.
It'll get me off the hook later."

"Sure."

"One would have been okay. The twenty-cent kind would
have been okay."

"You do me a favor, I do you a favor. Nobody can say Jim
Stubb cheated him unless he cheated Jim Stubb or his friends
first."

"Well, thanks anyway. Who'd this commissioner want
you to call?"

"Charlie, the guy I talked to first." Stubb picked up a
doughnut and broke it in two. "I thought I asked for more
coffee. Holy Jesus, Murray, aren't I ever going to get some
more coffee?"

In the room belonging to the witch, a foot or two to one
side of the area visible through Barnes's peephole, stood a
machine consisting of a keyboard that was like a typewriter's,
except that it lacked provision for the lower-case letters, and
a screen like a television's. The witch pressed a switch on the
keyboard, and the screen glowed palely green. She pressed
keys. A succession of letters appeared at the bottom of the
screen:

AZXDFGHBRTGHJM

This line was lifted by another appearing below it:

OIJNUHBYGVTFCR

The witch glanced at them, then pressed an additional
sequence. The next line read:

WAZXS CGHTVE NFAERTI

She nodded to herself and began to undress, tossing her
clothes onto the bed. Naked, she removed her contact lenses.
Taking a black glass bottle from a dresser drawer, she poured
a small quantity of unguent into the palm of her left hand and
smeared herself with it, beginning at her feet and giving
special attention to her vulva, rectum, and breasts. It smelled
as weeds do crushed beneath the tires of a truck in spring.

The anointing completed, she turned off the light. Dull winter sun leaked around the blind, yet left the room nearly dark. The screen pulsed yellow-green:

SACG HRCMLO LOBZYTGKK
BSCNLP EANAL YNSSFINNO

The witch herself now possessed a slight luminescence. She replaced the bottle and took a yellow pastel from the same drawer. This pastel, if it glowed at all, did so only feebly, but when she scribed a circle on the floor, the line seemed almost a trench of flame.

Leaning to reach the drawer without leaving her circle, she took out a small drum. Its body was of blackened metal; its head carried a blurred picture of a rose, executed in blue and red. The witch placed this instrument in the center of the circle, then with the pastel inscribed the words *ADAM TE DAERAM* around the interior of the circle, and outside it: *AMRTET, ALGAR ALGASTNA*. That done, she tossed the pastel back into the open drawer.

Cradling the drum between her crossed legs, she tapped it with her fingers. The sound was like the beating of a heart.

After an hour or more had passed, she sang in a clear contralto: *"Palas aron ozimonas, Baske bano tudan donas, Geheamel cla orlay, Berec he pantaras tay."* This little song ended, she was silent for a time, staring at the pulsing screen as she drummed.

At length, she began a new song: *"Bagabi laca bachabe, Lamac cahi achababe, Karrelyos. Lamac lamec Bachalyas, Cabahagy sabalyos, Barylos. Lagoz atha cayolas, Samahac et famyolas, Harrahya!"* Before she had finished it, the screen flamed:

AMRTET ALGAR ALGASTNA
ADAM ALCAR DAGERAM

The old house trembled slightly, as though some subway train, blocks from the tunnel through which the trains ran, had gone beneath it. As though some old motorman, asleep and dreaming, had sent his train hurtling through the earth.

The witch smiled.

Chapter 9

THE ATTACKERS

The machine came down the street on the back of a flatbed truck. Not that it could not move by itself; it could, on two stubby, treadless tracks. Its neck, which lay stretched upon the flatbed, was not stubby but longer than the neck of any giraffe. Like a giraffe, the machine was bright yellow but smudged.

The flatbed truck parked five doors down from the Free house, and the operator and the driver got out. Heaping one splintery timber on another, they built a ramp at the back of the truck. The operator climbed onto it and into the machine; its engine roared; oily black smoke belched from a pipe shaped like Lincoln's hat.

A second truck brought the ball. The ball too was black; it might have been the bowling ball of a giant.

The machine lifted its head slowly but smoothly and looked about at the snow-powdered neighborhood. It crawled down from the flatbed and picked up its ball.

Through the windshield of his squad car across the street, Sergeant Proudy watched the machine with somber satisfaction. It was the policy of the Department to overawe resistance with a show of force, and he had brought two patrolmen with him; their names were Evans and Williams.

"Here we go," Proudy said. "Let's make sure everybody's out." They left the squad car, and the two preceded him up the steps. Both were younger and taller than he.

Williams rattled the knob. "Locked, Sarge." He rapped a panel with his knuckles. "There's a fire station a couple blocks down. I could borrow an ax."

A large and very neatly turned out man in a blue overcoat was watching them from the sidewalk. "You three busy now?"

None of the three answered.

"Don't worry about me. I can wait until you've got a minute."

"Hit it again," Proudy told Williams.

Williams drew his revolver and used the butt to pound the door. "I could shoot the lock off," he said hopefully.

"The three of us will take it with one shove," Proudy told him.

Evans asked, "We got a warrant, Sarge?"

"We don't need one. This building's condemned—it's city property. Altogether on three now. One . . . two . . . THREE!"

Three shoulders crashed into the door, which did not budge.

The man in the blue overcoat mounted the steps. "I'll give you a hand," he said. "I used to be pretty good at it."

Evans said, "We got too many now. We're gettin' in each other's way." He had a round, ruddy, freckled face. In ten years, he would look angry all the time.

Williams, who was black but otherwise much like Evans, asked, "You plain clothes?"

"Used to be," the man in the blue overcoat said. "Had seven years of it. Eighteen on the force. I'm Mick Malloy." He extended his hand to Proudy, who took it.

"I make you," Proudy said. "Eleventh precinct, ain't that right?"

"Right."

"Williams, you see if you can get that ax. Leave the car here. We'll have another shot at the door while you're gone."

Williams nodded and went down the steps. The sidewalk was white with snow; his footsteps compacted it without melting it. Evans said, "Maybe those guys could swing their wrecking ball and hit this door, Sarge."

"And maybe there's somebody standing in back of it."

"I never thought of that," Evans admitted.

Malloy said, "A cop can't think of everything, and one slip-up's all it takes. Maybe somebody else gets it, or maybe he does." He rattled the knob. "We used to have a guy at the Eleventh we called Whitey Nelson. One night they found his cruiser parked in front of an empty store. Whitey was inside the store with one in the pump. Nobody ever found out why he went in there or what he walked into."

"Probably he saw a light or somethin'," Evans said.

"Maybe. He left a wife and six little kids. You want to have a go at this?"

Proudy said, "You and Mick do it, Evans. I'll count. I wouldn't want to get in your way. Get set now, boys, and give it all you got. One—two—THREE!"

The two big men slammed their bodies against the door; it shivered but remained solid.

There was a rattle and a bang as a window on the second floor opened. The two policemen and the former policeman looked up.

A woman with a wide face and curly blond hair leaned out. "Fuck off, you bastards!" she yelled. "We're not leaving!"

Sergeant Proudy started to say something, but she withdrew. A moment later she was back, holding a tin wastebasket. "Fuck off!" She upended the wastebasket. The three men jumped to avoid the water, and the window slammed shut.

"Assaulting an officer in the performance of his duty," Proudy said. "We'll get her."

Evans nodded. "Damn right, Sarge."

Malloy shrugged and smiled. "Hell, it was just water. Suppose it had been acid or something? We could all be dead, or maybe crippled for life."

Evans said, "I bet they got a crowbar in one of them trucks."

"Good idea," Sergeant Proudy told him. "You take a look, Fred. You're getting in my way up here anyhow."

As Evans turned to go, Malloy said, "You married, Sarge?"

"I look like a fairy?"

"Hell, I've known single guys that were as straight as you or me. Sometimes the wife dies first, you know? You'd be surprised how often that happens. Got any kids?"

"No way."

"That's a shame. I got three, myself. Back when I was on the Force, I used to think if anything happened to me, they'd look after the old lady."

Sergeant Proudy nodded as if acknowledging some deep-drawn confidence. "A guy can't stay on the Force forever. You do something, maybe, for one guy. Then bingo, it's another guy that's in, and you're out on your ass. Or you don't do it, and you're out even faster. Everybody slips up sometimes."

"Hell, it was nothing like that. It's my heart. I got angina."

"Maybe you shouldn't have hit that door."

"Don't worry, Sarge, I know what I can do. I got it under control. Besides—"

A small crowd, mostly children, had gathered to look at the machine. Now a short, red-faced man with an attache case was elbowing his way through. Catching the police-man's eye, he called, "Are you Sergeant Proudy, sir?" He gave a somewhat theatrical start as he appeared to see Malloy for the first time. "Hello, Mick."

"Hi, Steve."

"Mick, if you're making your pitch, I'll wait. You know me, I'm one of the boys."

"Sure," Malloy said. He sounded tired.

"A lot of guys would horn right in. Not me. I don't consider that ethical." The red-faced Steve turned his attention to Sergeant Proudy. "I'm S. B. Marshal." He extended a business card. "I just want to caution you at this time to wait and hear us both. I'm not asking you to do that out of fairness to me, but out of fairness to yourself and your family. As an intelligent and dedicated public servant, you can surely see it's to your advantage to shop around and get the best."

Malloy said, "I wasn't making any pitch, Steve. The Sarge

and me were just talking about old times. Never having been a cop, you wouldn't understand."

"In that case, Sergeant, there's a little diner up the street. Maybe we could get out of this cold and have some coffee? On me, naturally."

From the sidewalk, Evans reported, "They haven't got no crowbar, Sarge. They said how about the back? Maybe the back door ain't strong."

Proudy rubbed the side of his nose. "That's the first sensible thing I heard today. Mick, you going to be around for a while?"

"Sure. I got something I want to talk to you about."

"I thought you did. Okay, you stay here till we open it from inside. If Williams comes with the ax, tell him we're around back. Mr. Marshal can stay to keep you company, if he wants to. When we got this wound up, you and me will talk."

On one side of the house, a narrow areaway choked with debris led toward the rear. Sergeant Proudy entered it and Evans followed; it was too narrow for the two to walk abreast. Abandoned trash cans waited there with engine blocks and fenders, lightless table lamps, and broken stoves bereft of heat. It was dark as midnight, and everything lay under a film of snow.

The policemen took their flashlights from their belts and used them to light their way until Sergeant Proudy slipped on the tilted side of an old Frigidaire and fell, smashing the lens and bulb of his. Evans helped him up. One hand was skinned. Proudy sucked it and wrapped it in his handkerchief.

"Let me go first now," Evans said.

"How are you going to get past? You want me to lie down so you can walk over my back?"

"Take my flash then, Sarge."

"With my luck, I'd break that too. Shine it around my feet. Kind of through my legs so I can see where I'm going."

"Sarge—"

"Yeah, what?"

"You hear somethin'?"

For a second the two stood listening. "Just the traffic over on the freeway."

"This ain't like that."

Sergeant Proudy wiped his nose with the handkerchief on his hand. "So what's it like?"

"I don't know. Like a engine turnin' over real slow. Thub-ub, thub-ub, thub-ub, like your heart."

"You're hearing your own heart, that's all. The pulse starts pounding in your ear and you hear it. Happens all the time."

"This ain't my heart," Evans said.

"Oh, yeah? Turn it off and see if that noise don't stop. Now shine that light at my legs like I told you." Sergeant Proudy attempted to grip the wall with his good hand as he clambered across the junk. "Got to be careful here," he said. "Bedsprings."

"Maybe there's a alley. We could go down to the end of the block and see."

"What's the matter with you, Fred? We're halfway there."

"It still goes back a long ways," Evans said.

"These houses aren't that big."

"What's the big black thing at the end?"

"What the hell are you talking about?"

"Down at the end, Sarge."

"There isn't a damn thing."

"It's gone now," Evans said.

Sergeant Proudy, seeking a toehold on a pile of frozen garbage, snorted. "Probably a car or a truck in the alley."

There was a narrow alley, but no car. The yard into which Ben Free had swept his fragments of glass, his bent bottle caps, stood side by side with a dozen others much the same. Or perhaps instead of standing, it slept beneath its snow. Perhaps they all slept.

And it was snowing much harder now, and a cold wind had sprung up to swirl the falling snow. There is a legend that horizontal snow will drive you mad; it is believed by those who believe in aspirin in cola and the piety of politicians. If they are correct, there was much madness behind the windows of the shabby houses. Their bricks were brothers to the bricks of Belmont Hospital; their blind, staring, half-opened eyes, their quarter-open and slit eyes, luminously yellow, peered from the skulls of lunatics.

"Here it is," Evans said, then he too slipped. His flashlight fell clattering into the corpse of a jukebox, and the red and green glowed again with the ghost of its old plastic gaiety.

Sergeant Proudy swore and shouldered him out of the way to grope for it himself.

"We're even," Evans said. "Anyway, mine didn't go out."

"Yeah, but you dropped it."

"That's what I said, Sarge."

"So I'm going to borrow it for a while, okay? I'm surprised mine busted. Those things are usually built pretty good."

"I cracked the glass in mine once. I socked this gambler with it. You got it?"

"Yeah. . . . No, damn it, this's something else."

Snow swirled about the two men.

Chapter 10

THE ASSAULT

Glasser wore blue-tinted spectacles and a large and rather hairy tweed coat. The coat was burdened now with snow; the spectacles made Glasser appear blind, though he was not. He hurried forward, hand extended, as a real blind man might who had been informed of the proximity of the Messiah. "I'm Nate Glasser," he announced. "Pleased to meet you, Sergeant."

"Not no sergeant," the policeman with the ax told him.

"I'm sorry," Glasser said. "I thought you were a certain Sergeant Proudy."

"Huh uh."

"You see, as I walked past the police car, that one back there, I couldn't help but overhear the radio. They were asking for Sergeant Proudy."

"That's our unit," the big policeman said, quickening his step. "I believe I better see about it."

He swung open the squad car's door and jerked out the microphone. "This Unit Twenty-three, Dispatcher. Citizen say you calling us."

"You still at that demolition site, Twenty-three?"

"Parked across the street."

"We got a call, a seventeen fifty."

"What address?"

"Caller didn't say. Just that it was the Baker house, and there was a cruiser out front, but she didn't see any officers. Then she yelled and hung up. We thought it might be you."

"I'll have a look," the policeman said and tossed the microphone onto the seat.

Glasser touched his arm. "What's a seventeen fifty, officer?"

"Home invasion. You know a Baker house 'round here?"

"I'm afraid I'm a stranger. I'm with Pee, Em, Gee, and Dee."

"Hey!" The policeman raised the red ax he carried and trotted toward a group standing chatting on the sidewalk.

Loping beside him, Glasser told him, "They're no good. They're agents too. I know the whole bunch. Except the little guy."

The little guy had turned at the policeman's shout. Unlike the rest, he was shabby. His thick glasses scarcely reached the second button of the policeman's coat.

"Sir, you know the Baker house?"

"Sure," the little guy said. He pointed to the house next to the one before which he had been standing. "Not condemned. If they really build the ramp, it'll be right next to the supports."

The policeman was not listening. Ax in hand, he mounted the stoop, taking two steps at a time.

The door opened and a second policeman looked out. He had a round, freckled face. "I thought that was you, Bill. You got it, huh?"

Williams relaxed and lowered his ax. "Yeah. What you doing in here?"

"Playin' with a kitty."

"What you say?"

"You asked me. Come on in."

Williams did. Like a shadow, the little guy slipped in with him, ducking under his arm as he closed the door. Inside, an old woman sat in a rocking chair, smiling indulgently. Sergeant Proudy crouched on the worn oriental carpet before her. He held a length of string from which was suspended a crumpled ball of pink paper. A kitten with intelligent yellow eyes watched the paper with fascination, occasionally extending a tentative paw.

"This place sure don't smell good," Williams said under his breath.

"It's just the cat box, Bill."

Sergeant Proudy glanced up. "You got the ax."

"Yeah," Williams said slowly. "Right."

"Chop the door yet?"

"What you mean? I just got back. Dispatcher say somebody try to bust in here, and here I am."

"That was me that called," the old woman in the rocker said. "I hung up when I saw it was the police. No use crying wolf when the fire's out."

Williams asked Sergeant Proudy, "What happened, anyhow?"

"Fred dropped his light and we got the wrong house. I knew something was the matter as soon as that door went flying open. The Free place has doors like a fort."

Evans added, "We were pretty cold, so when Mrs. Baker here asked us in it sounded good. Then the Sarge got to playin' with her cat."

"Puff," Mrs. Baker explained.

Sergeant Proudy said, "I happen to like cats. Some people do, ain't that right? It's no crime."

Williams shook his head. "'Course not. Me, I'd rather have a dog, but it's just what a man's taste run to. I believe, though, they're 'bout ready with that big machine outside."

The little guy who had slipped in behind Williams said, "They've had some kind of breakdown—I think they said something about a cylinder head." He had taken off his trenchcoat and battered felt hat. Perhaps everyone there except Mrs. Baker herself thought he belonged in the house.

"We ought to get them out anyways," Williams said. "Get it done."

"Yeah."

Puff had changed tactics. She was clapping both gray paws now.

"If you ain't going to go, I believe I'll just go out and set in me and Evans's cruiser. Something might come over the radio."

Sergeant Proudy stood up. "You trying to smart off, Bill?"

"Not me. I just meant what I said. Not a thing else."

The little guy glanced at Mrs. Baker. "Maybe you'd like some coffee before you go out. I know I would."

"I don't have any," Mrs. Baker told him. "Just tea for two and cooco. How about some cooco? It always goes so nice on a cold day."

"Yes'm, I'd like some," Williams said. "I got mighty cold walking all the way down to that fire station."

"We were out in it as much as you were, ain't that right?"

"I never said you wasn't, Sarge. I never said you went and set in the cruiser or anything like that. I know you must have got cold too. Probably that's why Fred dropped his flash. A man's fingers gets cold and he start dropping things. Why I just 'bout dropped this ax a couple times on my way back."

Sergeant Proudy looked at Williams dangerously.

Mrs. Baker murmured, "I'll Polly put the kettle on," and bustled off. The little guy offered helpfully, "If you're really worried about that radio, I'll go listen a while. I'm not cold. I'll come in and tell you if anything comes over it."

"There's a man out there with blue glasses on that's probably listening now," Williams said.

The doorbell rang, and the little guy opened the door to see who it was. The snow had slackened again, but enough had fallen to form a minute glacier at the bottom of the door. The man on Mrs. Baker's stoop wore sunglasses, a coconut-fiber hat, a colorful sports shirt, and shorts. His face looked sunburned. "Could you let me inside?" he asked the little guy.

"I might. You another insurance salesman?"

"No." The man in the sports shirt raised one hand solemnly. It was shaking. "I swear to you on my mother's grave, on my honor and everything I hold dear, that I am not selling insurance."

"I'd let an insurance salesman in," the little guy said. "I just wondered if you were one. There's quite a few out there." He stood aside and let the man in the sports shirt across the threshold.

"Thank God. I'm freezing."

"You look it."

"I always have a couple gin slings before I go out on calls—we've got them free in the office—but by God, I don't think they help a bit."

"I may come up to your office sometime."

"We'd love to have you. I mean that." The man in the sports shirt reached into its pocket and took out a card. "Any time. Let me know." The card read:

Sim Sheppard
"SUNSHINE ESTATES"

The little guy said, "I think you're looking for Sergeant Proudy, am I right? I'm not him, I'm Jim Stubb. Proudy's the one with the kitten. Come on, I'll introduce you."

Barnes tapped Stubb on the shoulder. "What is it?" he asked. Like Stubb, he stood in the snow, his coat collar turned up against the wind.

"You don't know, huh?"

Barnes pursed his lips. "Salesmen?"

"Yeah. There must be a hundred of the bastards. Insurance. Stocks and bonds. Florida real estate."

"I called them. I said I was Proudy and told them to meet me here."

"I thought it was something like that. You're a clever devil, Ozzie."

"Madame Serpentina wanted me to do something, and I had to think and think before I came up with this. I don't believe it will stop them. Not really."

"It's sure as hell slowing them down."

The three policemen were fighting their way through the mob. It might have been a riot.

"I think we should go up and stand in front of the door," Barnes said. "It may be the last thing we can do."

"Watch your step. Candy threw some water out of her window a while back, and it froze."

"I should have thought of that," Barnes said. There was no rail on the stoop, and the two roomers clung to each other to keep from falling.

"Anyway, she did," Stubb told him. "Candy's a straightforward girl. Hey, look at that!"

Down the street, a van with an elaborate antenna on its roof loomed through the falling snow.

"Channel Two News," Stubb said. He took off his glasses and wiped them on his sleeve.

Barnes glanced at him admiringly. "You call them?"

"If I called them, they wouldn't come. But I called a hell of a lot of politicians, and I figured somebody would tip them. There's always somebody in politics who wants to make a little time with the media."

Williams flourished the fire ax over his head. Beside it, Evans's nightstick rose and fell. One of the salesmen yelled. A siren howled in the distance.

"More police," Barnes said.

Stubb nodded. "I was afraid of that."

"Think we ought to lock arms?"

"We're not young enough, but sure. *No nukes! Save the whales! Free's an endangered species!*"

They locked arms. Stubb used his free hand to take off his glasses and slip them into a pocket in his trenchcoat.

Evans was thrusting with his nightstick now, using its blunt end to punch the bellies of the salesmen. Williams and Proudy broke free and mounted the stoop, Williams still brandishing the ax. "Get out the way!" he ordered the two roomers.

The yellow machine's operator revved its engine.

"Not us," Stubb told Williams. A rusty, bulbless porch light thrust forward from the bricks. Stubb was just able to grasp its bracket to steady himself.

The salesmen surged after Sergeant Proudy. Beyond them, a little class of varicolored children and a gaggle of old people watched with interest, wiping their noses on their sleeves. The camera crew had taken in everything at a glance and was already shooting as a reporter advanced with a microphone. Down the street, a black-and-white police car skidded around the corner.

"It's you," Sergeant Proudy said to Barnes. "Where's Free?"

"Yes, it's me," Barnes told him.

Williams asked, "Why you want to do this anyway? What this old house mean to you?"

"I've been thinking about that," Stubb said. "To tell you the truth, I'm damned if I know."

"Well, move. I'm just going to have to carry you off."

Stubb shook his head.

Sergeant Proudy threw his arms around Barnes, pinning Barnes's own to his sides. From nowhere, as it seemed, there was an explosion of white dust. Sergeant Proudy began to sneeze violently, and on the third sneeze, he released Barnes.

Williams yelled, "Get out the way!" and shouldered Stubb aside. Swiftly the red ax flashed up, then slammed forward. There was a scream of wood as Williams wrenched at the blade.

Behind him, Mick Malloy lost his balance on the icy steps

and fell heavily against Nate Glasser and Ozzie Barnes. Both of them fell against Williams. The long, sharp wrecking spur of the fire ax flew wildly back just as Sergeant Proudy straightened up from yet another sneeze.

Vaguely through the falling snow and the fog of myopia, Stubb saw the white of bone and the gush of blood.

Chapter 11

THE CASUALTY

When Captain Davidson stepped out of his car, the street was calm again. The television crew had departed for a more visual disaster, and of the varicolored kids and old folks, only a corporal's guard remained. Four policemen, in attitudes diversely self-important, oversaw the conversation of the salesmen. A fifth drooped some distance away. "Now then," Captain Davidson demanded. "What's going on here?"

A big, red-faced policeman stepped forward. "They got him in there, sir."

"The hell they have."

"Yes, sir."

"You were here when it happened?"

"Yes, sir. I been here the whole time. I come with him. I'm Evans, sir."

"And you let them take him inside?"

"I couldn't help it, sir. The doctor did it. The sergeant was down on the sidewalk floppin' around, with these salesmen steppin' all over him—"

"Did you say salesmen?"

"Yes, sir. Them over there, sir. Then this old doctor come runnin' up from someplace. I think he lives around here, sir. He was yammerin' about stoppin' the bleedin'. Then the door opened. This big fat gal in a pink robe that threw the water at us opened it, and the doc yelled help him up. So I did, and the first thing I knew, the doc had his shoulder on one side and the guy with the mustache was on the other side, and the two of them carried him in the house and locked the door, sir."

"And you didn't go with him."

Evans shook his head. "I tried to, sir, but all the salesmen was tryin' to get in too, and the fat gal was pushin' them away. She's a good pusher."

"This whole God-damned operation has a curse on it," Captain Davidson said bitterly. "It's already taken ten times as long as it should have and used up ten times too many men. Now this."

"Yes, sir."

"You looked like you were going to say something, Evans. Spit it out."

"No, sir. I wasn't goin' to say anythin'."

The captain jerked his head toward the construction vehicles parked along the curb. "Where are the operators?"

"Down the street, sir, gettin' some coffee."

"I don't blame them."

"No, sir."

Captain Davidson walked to the stoop and leaned forward to peer at the door.

"Watch it, sir. It's icy."

"So I see."

"Think we'll get much more snow, sir?"

Captain Davidson turned around to look at Evans. "Not before we have them out of there, no. Not before I have the whole God-damned bunch of you screw-offs back on the job. Who's got the ax?"

None of the policemen spoke.

"You heard me. Somebody hit this door with an ax. Williams, you beaned Proudy with it. Where is it now?"

Williams muttered.

"Speak up! If you're afraid to swing it again, I'll do it myself. Where is it?"

"Somebody got it."

A slightly disheveled man in blue spectacles separated himself from the knot of salesmen. "A little guy with thick glasses got it, Captain."

"What?"

"This officer was somewhat dazed—I think we all were—and this little guy came up to the officer and said, 'I'll take that,' and took the ax from his hand. That was the last I saw of it."

"Who are you?"

It was said briskly and even abruptly, but the man in the blue spectacles stepped forward smiling. "Nathaniel Glasser, Captain." Like a stage magician producing a miraculous bouquet, he extended his card. "I'm an investment counselor. Possibly you've heard of us—Papke, Mittleman, Glasser & Dornberg. We got our clients into women's pre-perfumed bras right at the beginning. They made millions, and we steered them into tax shelters. Our own percentage is very small, of course." The card was in Captain Davidson's hand. Glasser stepped back, still smiling.

"The sunlight troubles your eyes, Mr. Glasser?"

"Hm? Oh, you mean these?" Glasser removed his blue spectacles. "Yes, it does. When the sun's out, I mean. Reflects off the snow. I'm not wanted, if that's what you're thinking, Captain."

"No, I suppose not. The sun's not out now, Mr. Glasser."

"They have my correction," Glasser said, and replaced the blue spectacles.

Captain Davidson turned away. "Evans, you're pretty big. I want you and Williams here up on that stoop. You two—" he gestured toward a pair of policemen who had been watching the salesmen. "You go around back. You, Peters," he pointed to his driver. "You come—"

At that moment, the door of the Free house opened; Mick Malloy stepped out, closing it behind him.

"What are you waiting for, you dumb bastards! Evans! Get that door!"

Evans lunged for it, slipped on the ice, and caught himself

by grabbing the knob. After a moment he got his knees under him and tried to turn it. "Locked again, Captain."

"Yeah, I bet." Captain Davidson stalked across to Malloy. "Who're you?"

"Eighteen years on the force," Malloy said. "Seven in plain clothes. I'm Mick Malloy. Used to be Eleventh Precinct, Captain."

"You live in there?"

"'Fraid not, Captain. I was just in there talking to Sergeant Proudy; I'm his insurance advisor." Malloy's hand dipped into an inner pocket and came out with an official-looking document. His eyes sought out a red-faced man in the crowd. "I just signed Sergeant Proudy up for twenty-five thousand whole life."

The red-faced man stepped forward, swinging his attache case. "You signed him while he was lying there bleeding? You dirty cocksucker!"

"He was anxious to sign," Malloy said happily. "He *wanted* to sign, Steve. You should have heard him thank me afterwards. I could have made it fifty. I'm kind of sorry I didn't."

"Suppose he dies?" Marshal asked angrily. (Captain Davidson watched the two of them in silence.)

"He won't."

"The hell you say! You're no doctor."

"The doctor's a doctor. He's got him in there taking stitches in his head. He's not yelling about oxygen and transfussions, is he?"

"How the hell would I know?"

Captain Davidson said, "You said you didn't live there, Malloy."

"I don't, Captain."

"Then you wouldn't mind if we had a look at your keys, would you? Just friendly. You say you're an ex-cop. You ought to know how it is."

"I'd like the keys back, Captain. I hope you'll keep the card. You know how it is."

"I don't. I never sold insurance."

A shivering man in shorts and a short-sleeved shirt appeared at Malloy's elbow. "Did you say twenty-five thousand whole life?"

Captain Davidson tossed the keys to Evans on the stoop. "Double indemnity. Beneficiary's his wife."

"That's what I thought I heard," the shivering man said. He was nursing a styrofoam coffee container. "One of the guys was talking about it when I came up. I had him—" He paused to wipe his nose.

Glasser pushed him aside. "Look, you're leaving, right? Malloy, right?" He thrust out a hand, and Malloy took it. "Nat Glasser. You got nothing to lose, so tell me. What kind of a presentation did he go for? Man-of-the-world? Serious? We've got something opening up that—"

"How do you know I don't have a concussion?" Sergeant Proudy asked argumentatively.

"Do I look like God?" the old doctor said. "I don't know." As a matter of fact, he did look like God. He was a small, elderly man who sported a little white beard and an even whiter mustache; the collar of a tattersall shirt—an almost infallible sign of the presence of deity—peeped above the collar of his overcoat.

"Suppose I do have a concussion?"

"You're blacking out? Seeing spots?"

"No."

"Dizzy?"

"Not much."

"Your fingers are numb. You drop things."

"Not since I dropped that flashlight, and that was before I got hit."

"Then supposing you have a concussion, I'm ordering you to go home and go to bed. In the morning, see your regular doctor and tell him what happened."

"That's what you said before."

"I noticed it myself." The doctor glanced at his curved needle and put it away. "Concussion is a bruising of the brain. It can be so slight there's practically no symptoms at all. The main thing is to leave it alone until it gets better. Don't play football. If you see somebody trying to hit you with a ball bat, duck. (Nurse, let me have some tape.) If you want to find out for certain if you have a concussion, we'll perform an autopsy. If you think you might have a fractured skull, go to the emergency room of the nearest hospital and tell them that. They'll zap your head with a few X-rays, and it's a poor X-ray man that can't find a little crack someplace if he looks hard enough. He'll tell you to give up football until the bone knits. Okay, all done, put on your hat and you can go home."

"You're through bandaging?" Sergeant Proudy's fingers groped at the gauze.

"Why do you think I was pulling you around while I was talking to you? I warn you, if you press it, it's going to hurt."

Candy Garth said, "Here," and extended a pink plastic hand mirror. Proudy accepted it and inspected his bandage.

"I made it look worse than it is. If a dressing doesn't look bad, nobody ever believes the patient is hurt."

"I'd hate to be hurt as bad as that bandage looks."

"You'd be dead."

Candy asked, "Is it going to leave a scar?"

"I'm afraid so. He's losing hair up there. Of course a plastic surgeon could erase most of it."

"I'll keep it." Sergeant Proudy rubbed his hands together. "When some rookie asks me what happened, I'll just tell him I got it in the head with a fire ax. You got any aspirin?"

"I never carry it. My theory is that any patient too dumb to buy his own is too dumb to live anyway."

"I'll get some," Candy said. She bustled out, and they heard the stair groan beneath her weight.

Barnes said, "That girl enjoys nursing. You ought to hire her, Dr. Makee." He stood with his back to the fireplace, where the wreck of a table burned.

The physician shook his head and snapped his bag shut. "There was a time when I would have taken you up on that. Now I've had to learn restraint."

Sergeant Proudy stood, swayed, and gripped the back of a

chair to steady himself. "How much do I owe you, Doc?"

Dr. Makee winked at Stubb. "I can always tell when they're getting better. They call me Doc."

"How much? If it isn't more than I got on me, I'll pay you now."

"Ten dollars. Quite a few years ago, I swore I'd never charge more than ten dollars for a house call."

Stubb said, "Nobody else even *makes* house calls." The bloody fire ax lay across his knees.

"I don't either. I'm retired, or that's what I keep telling people."

"Here's the aspirin," Candy announced. "I'll get you a drink, if the pipes aren't frozen yet." To Barnes she added, "Madame Serpentina's packing. I listened outside her door."

Stubb glanced at the dark and silent television. He whispered, "Where's Free?" but Barnes only shrugged.

Sergeant Proudy gulped down two aspirin tablets and wandered across the room to look out the window.

"There he is!" Sim Sheppard shouted.

Everything stopped. Everyone turned to look. For perhaps twenty seconds, the prominent nose and small eyes of Sergeant Proudy appeared at the parlor window, still recognizable beneath a rakish cap of white surgical gauze.

Sim's coffee was trampled in the snow. Steve Marshal's attaché case came unattached. No physicist could say how hard the front-runners struck the door. They were weighty men, most of them, police and sales alike; they had been sprinting, and they were unable to brake on the ice. Behind them were a dozen more even weightier and equally unable—or unwilling—to stop.

The weakened door made a sound much like that of a large model plane jumped upon by a small boy.

Chapter 12

THE RETREAT

"You too, huh?" Barnes asked.

Stubb looked around at him. "Yeah, me too."

It was night, and snow clouds hung over the city; there was no light anywhere that was not mankind's. It might have been a city of clouds, with a few stars peeping through. They might have been in some vast, dark, rolling country, a land of hills and black pines.

"I thought they'd have more down."

"It was almost quitting time when they got Candy out." Stubb chuckled.

"What was that gunk under her robe?"

"Baby oil, I think."

"I'm the one who's supposed to know about novelties. If I had greased the floor in the hall . . ."

"They probably would have dropped her and broken her neck."

"Or she would have gone through to the basement. How much does she weigh?"

"How the hell should I know? Two hundred, maybe."

"Two hundred and fifty, at least. Maybe three hundred."

"Maybe three hundred," Stubb conceded. "Who gives a damn?" He tossed his cigarette into the snow. "It's God-damned cold out here, Ozzie. You got a new place to stay?"

"Yes, I do."

"Not me. They let me put my bag behind the counter in the Sandwich Shop up the street, and I'm still looking around."

"Yes," Barnes said again.

"We kind of worked together this afternoon, right? And it didn't go too bad. Hell, with Candy it almost went good enough."

Barnes nodded.

"Ozzie, I was wondering whether I could bunk with you. Just for tonight. I'll get a place of my own in the morning."

There was an instant's silence, then the soft voice of the witch said, "Ozzie has no place to stay, Mr. Stubb."

Both men whirled. "Where'd you come from?" Stubb asked.

"I fear he lied to you. He is here, staring at this ruined house, for the same reason you are. He wonders if he might not occupy his room one night more. Do not do it, gentlemen. It is very cold tonight. You would freeze."

Stubb asked, "What about you, Madame S.?"

"I am here because I was forced to leave behind certain belongings. I have returned to fetch them."

Stubb said, "We'll help you carry 'em. Where are you going?"

"What is the nearest hotel of good quality?"

"The Consort. It's only about four blocks."

"From such a neighborhood as this? I am amazed. Then I go to the Consort. And yes, you may carry my things for me. You will save me the price of a taxi. Ozzie, you are a man and know about such matters. How may I pass through this fence?"

The barrier the wrecking crew had erected was not actually a fence, but a pack-train of yellow sawhorses carrying indolent orange lights, harnessed with an orange cord. Stubb cut the cord with his penknife, and Barnes moved one aside.

Not even the front wall of the house that had been Free's was entirely gone as yet. Its outline remained, bricks hanging from their mortar to make a crazy arch that framed the dollhouse interiors of the front rooms. Under drifted snow, the hall was still recognizably the hall, with its stair vanishing upward into blackness. On its right, the parlor was changed mostly by the dying of the fire and the absence of the stuffed bird, its glass bell, and the table they had burned. To the left,

Free's bedroom seemed to bare all its poor secrets; his rumpled sheets cowered on the bed under a thin blanket of snow. Above, Candy's room and the witch's were only half exposed.

"Look!" Barnes pointed. "I saw something."

"Where?" Stubb craned his neck and lifted his small body on tiptoe.

"Up there. Something moved."

"Probably just the light."

"Or Free. It could have been Free. I never saw him after this morning. Did you? Did anybody?"

The witch glanced back, her face half buried in the fur of her coat collar. "Free is dead."

Stubb grunted. "You see the body?"

"I walk into it now."

"Without a flashlight. Ozzie, you got a light?"

Barnes took out what appeared to be a small chrome-plated pistol and pulled the trigger. A blue flame an inch long burned at the muzzle. "Butane," he said. "You like it?"

"I'm crazy about it." In the dim, blue light, Stubb examined the trampled snow. "Kids been in here. See that little sole with the hole in it? Neighborhood kid. Madame S., I hope you hid whatever you got, or it won't be there now."

"My things are here still. I feel them."

Barnes hurried to catch up with her. "Hold onto the rail, please, Madame Serpentina, or you'll fall."

"Not on this. Not even without your light, Ozzie. I do not require it, nor would I if this place were entirely dark."

Something creaked.

No one spoke; but there was in the air the almost palpable agreement not to speak, to ignore whatever it had been. The old house seemed to sigh. Perhaps there was no wind—the snow never stirred. Perhaps there was no sound.

"We'd better hurry, Madame Serpentina. The butane won't last long."

"I have told you I do not need light."

Stubb muttered, "Well, we do."

The door of the witch's room was locked. She took her key

from her purse and opened it to reveal one wall half dissolved in space and streetlights.

"I'm surprised the kids didn't break in," Barnes said.

"They were in fear, my Ozzie. They did not venture to the top of the stair, I think."

"Tracks?"

"I do not need to look at tracks."

Stubb said, "Somebody came up here. Big feet. Probably the wrecking crew."

"No one has entered my room. That is all I care about. Ozzie, my bags are beneath that bed. Will you get them for me?"

One was an old suitcase, the other a bag in actual fact, a sack of hairy goatskin as big as a laundry bag. Its knotted thongs were sealed with a lump of wax that looked black in the faint light.

" 'Now I am done.' So speaks the poet. If you will carry these for me, gentlemen? Mr. Stubb, it would perhaps be better if you were to take the suitcase. Ozzie, you may have the honor of the other. That is somewhat heavier, I think."

Stubb was already maneuvering the suitcase through the narrow doorway. After a final, lingering glance around the room, the witch followed him, leaving Barnes to bring up the rear.

"What a day has this been, and what a time in my life! You say, Mr. Stubb, that it is not far to this hotel?"

A voice out of the darkness asked, "Did somebody say *hotel*?" There was a flicker of light on the opposite side of the stairwell.

"Candy, is that you?"

"Jim?" The fat girl's face appeared as the moon appears with the passing of a cloud. She struck a match and held it up.

"Candy, what the hell are you doing here?"

"Getting some stuff. Celebrating." She smiled, and despite its unfocused quality, the smile made her pretty. "This is where it was, right? I thought," (she belched softly) "that maybe before they tore down the stadium I'd go stand on the mound again."

"Yeah," Stubb said. "You had them going."

The witch added, "And we should be going."

"To a hotel, you said." The fat girl still wore her white plastic raincoat, but her lost white plastic boots had been replaced by enormous black ones. She carried a flight bag and brought the malty odor of beer with her. "I met this guy I know, and he said sorry I'd like to but I don't have the bread, right? And I said tonight he didn't need it—just let me sleep over. So we went up to his place, and then he said come on, I know where there's a party tonight."

The witch pushed past Stubb as he stood listening; Barnes followed her.

"So we got in his beater and drove way the hell out. Shadylawn. Sounds like a graveyard, doesn't it?"

"Yeah," Stubb said.

"And then he said give me a cigarette, and I said I didn't have any. I'd been smoking his on the way out. So we went by a drugstore, and he stopped and dug out a buck and said here go in and get us a pack." A tear splashed on Stubb's hand.

"And he split while you were inside."

"Buh huh."

"Jesus Christ. No wonder you feel down. How'd you get back?"

"Hitched."

"Jesus Christ," Stubb said again.

"It wasn't so bad, except I was afraid I was going to get picked up by the smokies." The fat girl swallowed and snuffled. "Jim, we'd better go. We'll lose them."

"Sure we will. I got her suitcase here. Can you make it down the steps okay?"

"I made it up. You don't have a drink on you?"

"I got two cigarettes, and that's it."

"Up at Harry's, I knocked down six or eight beers, and now I can feel them dying in me. You know what I mean?"

"Sure."

She was going down the stairs beside him. There was just

enough room for the two of them with the suitcase between them. At the bottom, she asked, "Let me have one of those cigarettes?"

"Sure," Stubb said. Barnes and the witch were already some distance down the street. Stubb put down the suitcase, took out his last two Camels, and crumpled the pack and tossed it into the gutter. He lit their cigarettes from a paper match, as he had before.

"This lady picked me up. She was about forty, I guess. Her husband was out of town and she was going downtown to have dinner with another lady she'd gone to college with. Hey, let me carry part of that—see, I can just hook a couple fingers in the handle."

"All right."

"Now we kind of walk in step. I told her I was on a date and he wanted me to come across, and when I wouldn't, he shoved me out of the car."

"Happens a lot, I guess."

"Not to me. Anyway, she bought it. At first, you know, I thought she was just pretending to make it easier for both of us, but she really did buy it. I was kind of messed up."

"Like now," Stubb said.

"I guess. I didn't give her any big act. Just what I told you. I asked her about this college she and the other lady went to. It sounded great. When I got out, she said how far, and I said oh, 'bout eight blocks, but you wouldn't want to go down there, and she gave me a couple of bucks for a cab."

"You can't hardly open the door of a cab for two bucks."

"I don't think she gets downtown much."

"Tell me about coming back to Free's."

The fat girl belched again, letting out the air with a puff of smoke. "Jim, am I walking all right?"

"Good enough."

"She knew I was a little—you know. Tippy."

"Tipsy."

"I didn't laugh or do anything crazy, but she must have smelled it on me. I think I cried a little."

"She'd expect you to."

"Uh huh. Do we want to catch up with them?"

"No. Let's just keep them in sight."

"Then we ought to slow down a little. This thing's heavy anyhow."

"Sure."

"I was all messed up, see? I'd spent the whole damn evening, and all I had was three bucks to show for it. I didn't have anywhere to stay."

"Yeah."

"And I remembered—you know? Once in my life I had come over everybody. You remember when they came in and I was sitting there all slicked down with Johnson & Johnson's? They just about went bananas. You remember, Jim?"

"Sure I remember."

"One time eight of them tried to pick me up and they couldn't do it. Then that captain, that smart fucker, said to put me in the rug. And the rug tore."

The fat girl began to giggle, and for a time it seemed she might never stop. Her chins jiggled as if each knew some joke of its own, and her belly, to which she pressed the flight bag and a hand like a plump, pink starfish, jerked up and down uncontrollably.

"They finally got me out—did you see it? They handcuffed my hands and feet so they could stick their arms through without them slipping out. It hurt like hell. How many were there?

"Carrying you? Six."

"And that captain threw the rug over me. It was a good thing he did. The benches in those paddywagons are metal, and I put the rug down and sat on it."

"They must have brought your clothes," Stubb said.

"Uh huh. Except my boots, because I lost them last night."

"You didn't have them when you got back to Free's."

"I don't remember seeing you, Jim. I don't even remember going home." Her merriment faded.

"I heard you on the steps. I went out to see if you had cigarettes."

"Did I?"

"Yeah, you gave me one."

"How was I?"

"Okay. Pretty tight, sure, but okay except for not having shoes." Stubb tried to shrug. "Hey, how about changing sides with this thing? My arm's giving out."

They set down the witch's suitcase, walked solemnly around it, and picked it up again. Barnes turned to look back at them, waved, and hurried on.

"This morning I wore those open-toed pink straw things I had. They got soaked. I put them in the closet."

"You should have got them a minute ago."

"To hell with them. They were coming apart."

"This isn't too heavy for you, is it?" They said it together, then looked at each other and laughed.

Chapter *13*

THE CONSORT

It had been the function of the Hotel Consort to end poverty, and it did it very well. A cynic might have said that was the only thing it did well. An old Italian neighborhood had been demolished. The shops that had sold salami and crucifixes were gone. The cleaners who had offered invisible reweaving had disappeared. An ugly Walgreen drugstore had gathered its narrow aisles like skirts, wrapped itself in the perfume of its fine smells, and hastened off to oblivion. The funeral parlor, once almost smothered in carnations to the honor of a numbers baron, had withered in death. The people who had so often been janitors, nurses, and cops were gone too. No one could say where.

Certainly they were not at the Consort. Its guests were

businessmen, almost to the last. Its maids were black when they were not Puerto Rican, its assistant managers college-bred hoteliers who had skimmed Melville and Mark Twain in the course of learning to bully cooks and pad bills, its manager a computer no guest ever saw. Poverty was ended, having vanished from sight.

The many elegant chambers of the Consort are almost too well known for description, since they are found in all major and many minor cities. There is the Gourmand Room, with false European furniture and plastic walnut paneling. The Gourmand Room is open for lunch and dinner. There is Top o' the Consort, featuring live entertainment, potted plants, and a view that changes every hour. The Top o' the Consort is open for dinner. There is the Quaint, on a floor not reached by most elevators; the Quaint is open for breakfast and lunch. There are the Apache, Sideburn, and Vermont rooms, all of which can be divided and provided with folding chairs. They are always open except when locked.

And there are those seldom considered rooms, the halls—long, narrow rooms opening into hundreds and thousands of "private" rooms, some of which open into each other. Perhaps the halls are so seldom considered because they are the best rooms of all, and do not command attention. Bad food is not eaten in them, and those who tell bad jokes there are not paid for it. They have the simplicity and dignity conferred by their carpets, which are already beginning to wear. For the most part, they are mercifully silent.

They held something of that silence despite the witch and her bellmen. She, striding along in four-inch heels, only emphasized the quiet with the soft froufrou of her nyloned thighs. The bellmen puffed, groaned, and grunted, so that a dozen such would have sounded like a herd of swine driven to market; but there were only three, and their sighs, their groans and grunts were so muted as to be scarcely audible. When they reached seven seventy-seven, the first set down the bags he carried with a thump; but it was a silent thump, a mere trembling of the structure of the Consort.

"This here's a lucky room, Ma'am," he said.

"I do not come to gamble. I endeavored to rent number thirteen-thirteen, but it was unavailable."

The third bellman said, "There's no thirteenth floor, Ma'am."

The first bellman rattled the witch's key in the lock. "Here you are, Ma'am. Get those, will you, 'Cisco?" He swept in, leaving the bags he had carried in the hall.

"Closet here, bath over here, TV there. Here's a remote control for your TV." He switched it on, dialing down the sound. "Nice picture."

The witch said, "I do not require two beds."

"They come with the room, Ma'am."

"Perhaps if I stay here, I could have one taken away. I would prefer a chaise longue, I think."

"I'll tell the assistant manager you'd like to talk to him about it, Ma'am. You can probably get a weekly rate too."

"Thank you. You have been very kind." She fumbled in her purse. The other bellmen were piling her luggage in the closet.

"This your first trip to America, Ma'am?"

The witch smiled. "Do I speak your English so badly?"

The second bellman wiped his forehead with a red bandanna. "Oh, no, Señora. Your English is beautiful." He was Puerto Rican and the *is* was *ees*.

"Where you from, Ma'am?" the first bellman asked.

She drew a crisp bill between her fingers as though it were a handkerchief. "And from where do you think I am?"

"Greece?" guessed the first bellman.

"Argentina," said the second, anxious for the honor of Hispanic nations.

"Belgium," ventured the third, a devoted reader of Dame Agatha Christie.

"Ah, you are all such very, very intelligent men. Perhaps you are all correct. Perhaps you are none of you correct. I should give you something, no? So is it done here." She spread the bill long enough for them to glimpse it, then ran it backward and forward between her fingers again. "In my country it is the other way—one gives something when one leaves."

"You can tip us when you leave if you'd rather, Ma'am," the first bellman said virtuously. "Only you're right. Here, we usually get the tip when we take the guest to his room."

"I have only this one hundred dollar bill," the witch said. "It is too much, I think, even for three."

"That's okay, Ma'am. We'll see you later."

"Also I have some one dollar bills. They are too small, I think. Is it not so?"

The hundred flashed among the witch's fingers. None of the bellmen spoke.

"So I will do this. I will give my one hundred dollar bill to you," she looked into the eyes of the first bellman, "and you will take it somewhere where they will—how do you say? Make small ones."

"Break it. Yes, Ma'am."

"Then you will give yourself ten dollars, and to each of these other men who have helped me ten dollars. The rest you will return to me. Will you do that?"

The bellman smiled and came close to making a little bow. "Of course, Ma'am. Thank you very much." The others chimed in: "Gracias, Señora." "Thank you, Ma'am."

"It will not take you long? Half an hour, perhaps?"

"Less than that, Ma'am."

"Good." Suddenly, impulsively, the witch clasped his hand. "I trust you. You will bring seventy dollars back to me."

The bellman nodded, glanced at the bill, and thrust it into his pocket. "Let us know if you want anything, Ma'am."

"I will. Oh, I will!" The door had swung nearly shut. She pushed past them to open it. "Thank you again."

"Thank *you*, Ma'am."

When they were gone, she threw the night bolt and hung up her coat. "I like you, room," she said softly. "I am going to stay with you at least a month. At least one month I shall stay here. Yes." On the television, a beautifully colored man strangled a beautifully colored woman. She retrieved her purse from the desk and flipped the catch.

Stubb stepped from behind the drapes. "You really give them the hundred?"

She whirled on him, eyes blazing. "What are you doing here?"

"I'll tell you in a minute. You really give them the hundred? Professional interest."

"I will call the desk. They will have you out at once!"

"Sure. But you'll be cutting your own throat. A slick worker like you? I don't think you're going to do that."

"And why not?"

"See? You're not all that sure of yourself. If you were, you'd be on the phone right now. Okay, to start with, I'm on to you. Or anyway, I'll say I am. I may not be working, and I may not have much money, but I'm still a private operative. You get hotel security up here, and I'll tell them you're a bunco artist."

"I can pay for this room, Mr. Stubb."

"Sure, but you don't want to. And whatever it is you're going to try here isn't going to work if I tell them— they'll be watching every move you make. You want to phone?"

The witch shrugged. "You are an old friend. Besides, I am curious."

"Yeah, you and me both."

"How did you get here, Mr. Stubb? You know nothing of magic, but that was like magic."

"No trick at all." Stubb sat on the bed. "When we dumped your luggage outside the hotel—you didn't give us any hundred, but maybe we were lucky at that—you expected us to split. I didn't. I waited and followed you in. You were at the desk, and I got on the other side of the big guy next to you. The clerk said your room number when he shoved the key at the bellhop. I got an elevator while he and his buddies were rounding up your computer and the bags you'd brought here earlier. That was bullshit, when you asked us about the closest hotel; you'd already picked this place and got most of your stuff here, but you didn't want us to know you'd carried it yourself.

"Anyhow, the elevator got me here maybe two minutes before you came. It took me about fifteen seconds to open the spring lock with plastic slip. Your window there is recessed behind the curtain, so that's where I stood, with my ass pushed up to the glass. I'm a little guy, as you've probably noticed, and sometimes that's handy. Now, how about you?"

"What do you mean?"

"Tell me about the hundred."

"I have already told you, and when you hid behind my drapes you must have heard. I gave them a one hundred dollar bill. They were to take ten dollars each and bring seventy to me. It was my emergency reserve."

"And you trusted a bellhop with it and gave thirty bucks in tips? Sure you did. Was it queer?"

"I wish this hotel to believe I have a great deal of money. Thus I can stay a long time."

"Sure." Stubb patted his pocket. "I'm out of smokes. You got any?"

"I do not smoke."

"You smoke; I've seen you. What you mean is, you don't smoke much in public. Give me a cigarette, please."

The witch said nothing, staring at Stubb.

"Okay, forget it—it'd probably be poisoned anyhow. When I jumped out of your curtains, you had your hand in your bag. Want to tell me what it was doing there?"

"Certainly. You are correct. I was reaching for a cigarette." The witch picked up her purse and took out an oddly shaped box covered with Arabic script. "They are Turkish." She extended the package to Stubb.

He selected one and lit it with a paper match. "A little dry," he said, emitting a puff of smoke. "Maybe they were too long on the boat."

"I am most terribly sorry. You may give it back to me if you do not like it."

He chuckled. "That's better. For a minute I was afraid

you were going to go ladylike on me. You're cute, aren't you? You're a cigarette psychologist."

"I fear I do not know what you mean."

"When I asked you for a cigarette, you said you didn't have any, because you figured sooner or later I'd go out after some, and you could lock the door. Then when I started on the handbag, the cigarettes came out to take my mind off it. It won't work, Madame S. If I ever wanted to smoke that bad, I'd quit."

"So I was condemned for not giving you a cigarette, and now for giving you one. Such condemnations come cheaply. Very well, you wished for a cigarette and you have one, though you do not like it. What else do you wish?"

"I've already told you. I want to know your gimmick with the hundred."

"And I have told you. I gave the porter one hundred dollars—a hundred dollar bill, not counterfeit as you seem to think. He is to return seventy to me."

"Okay, I'll guess. Will you let me see that handbag?"

"Certainly not!"

"Any way you want it. It would be better to have some verification, but here's my guess. When I got my mug out of the curtains, you were at the bag. You might have been going for your lipstick, but if you had been you wouldn't be so up-tight about it. So I say you were putting the hundred away for next time. Want to comment?"

"I say only that I am going to have you put out of this room."

"Either you never really gave the bellhop the hundred— just let him see it and switched it at the last minute—or you got it back somehow. If I had to bet, that would be the way I'd go, because you keep insisting you gave it to him. Want to tell me what he did with it? No? When I'm flush, I usually tip bellhops about a dollar, and I've never yet seen one get out his wallet and put my buck in there—they don't want you to see how much they've got. What most of them do is stick it in their front pants pocket. For somebody with magician's fingers, it wouldn't be much of a trick to get it out of there."

The witch spit like a cat. "I do not do tricks!"

"Sure you do. We all do. What you mean is you don't do them on stage or at parties to impress your friends, if you have any friends."

"Not like you. You, I am certain, have many, many friends."

Stubb pointed a finger. "Don't sneer at me. I warn you, it's the only thing I can't take. You sneer at me, and sooner or later I'll get you."

"Yes, so many good friends, little man!"

He raised his fist, then let it drop. "You know, I'm glad you said that. It reminded me of something. Want to pass me that phone?"

"Hardly."

"I think you'd better—"

The telephone rang. Stubb reached for it, but the witch was nearer and quicker. "Yes, this is she. . . . How did you discover . . . No, do not come; you will not be admitted."

Stubb leaned toward the receiver and said loudly, "Come on up. I'll let you in."

"You fool! You damnable fool!"

"Don't you think you should hang up before you call me names?"

The handset slammed down. "You are unendurable!"

"Sure. It's part of my shtick to be unendurable when I want to be. I do bill collecting when I can't get anything else. On the other hand, I can be as nice as pie when I'm on your side. Wasn't I nice when I damn near broke my arm carrying your suitcase? Candy helped too. What'd you carry?"

The witch was calm again, but there was no blood in her dark face. "Are you such a fool as to think I cannot curse? I can, and though in the ordinary course of life I would not waste my efforts on such small prey, for you I will make an exception. Wait and see what I shall do!"

Stubb chuckled. "Going to curdle my milk? Madame S., I'm flat broke. I'm nearsighted, and there's newspaper in these shoes, and I think I'm getting an ulcer. Anything you could do now would just put me in jail or the hospital, and either one would be a hell of a relief. Curse away, and meantime I'll be cursing you, in my own inimitable fashion. Or would you rather have me working for you?"

Chapter 14

IN THE LOBBY

"I lost it," Majewski declared.

Fuentes looked daggers at him as the house telephone rang.

The mystery fan said, "I'm not calling you a liar—there's no evidence of that. Did I call you a liar?"

Majewski shook his head as the house telephone rang again.

"All I'm saying is seventy dollars of that money belongs to the woman in seven seventy-seven. You lost seventy dollars of her money. You're going to have to make that up. Ten belongs to 'Cisco and ten to me. You're going to have to make that up too."

The house telephone rang yet again, rather pettishly.

"Damn right," Fuentes said.

A sub-assistant manager called, "Joe, will you *please* get that phone?"

"Yes, sir!" Majewski answered with unaccustomed smartness, and picked up the handset, happy to escape.

"This the bell captain?"

"Yes, sir," said Majewski, who was not.

"Captain, I want you to do me a favor. Somewhere around there's a young lady in a white raincoat. Garth. Gee, ay, are, tee, aich. Garth. Stout. Blond. Look around. You see her?"

Majewski glanced at the overstuffed vinyl furniture and the guests. "No, sir."

"She's probably in the lobby, but she might be in one of the bars, or even outside on the sidewalk. I'd try the street-level bar first. Could you have one of your boys find her and tell her to come up to room seven seven seven?"

"Yes, sir, I will, sir. If she's not around, I'll give you a ring, sir."

"She's around. You got pay booths. Look in them too. She might be making a call. Young, stout, blond, white raincoat, Garth. Got it?"

"Got it, sir," Majewski said, and hanging up, turned back to his colleagues. "Look, I owe each of you ten, right?"

"Right," the mystery fan announced firmly; Fuentes nodded.

"Okay." Majewski drew out a money clip. "If I pay you, we're square, aren't we? The seventy's between the woman and me."

"Right," the mystery fan said again, this time more hopefully.

"Fine." Majewski handed him two fives and Fuentes a five and five singles, emptying the clip. "Now I want you and 'Cisco to do something for me." He described Candy. "Her name's Ms. Garth. Find her, and when you do, come tell me."

"What for?" the mystery fan asked.

"Because I want to talk to her, that's all. The guy on the phone gave me a message for her, all right? So look around."

Fuentes went into the bar of the Gourmand Room. It was dark, smoky, and packed with the late crowd. Three bartenders in red jackets sweated behind the bar. A pianist in a midnight blue ruffled dinner jacket grinned and played, the brandy snifter on his instrument well stuffed with bills. Under a blue spot, a busty woman in a low-cut blue gown sang:

"Oh, she never told her mother,
For mothers' hearts will break,
She never told her father,

About her big mistake,
She never told her sister,
'Cause sisters always tell,
She never told the Monsignor,
And so she went to . . ."

"*HELL!*" shouted a dozen enthusiastic drunks.

"A finishing school in New Jersey
Where the work was always hard—"

"*Mees* Garth," sang Fuentes. "Call for *Mees* Garth!" The pneumatic blonde gave him a disgusted look.

A man in a check suit left the bar. "What do you want with Miss Garth?"

"Got a message for her."

"Give it to me. I'll see she gets it."

"She's in the powder room?"

The woman near the piano kissed her fingers to her audience.

"Now don't forget her lesson,
For it is true, you know.
Don't do a thing without a ring,
And now I've got to go."

She hitched up the blue gown, which became a coat that hid most of her startling cleavage. When she stepped out of the blue spot, the coat was no longer even blue. Her audience clapped and whistled, and someone called, "Hey! Finish it!"

"I have to see a man about a bed," she shouted back.

Another man stepped away from the bar. "How about having a drink with me first?"

"I'll take a rain check, and I'll see you real soon. Ozzie, what's happening?"

Fuentes said, "You are Mees Garth? Go with me to the captain's desk. We ask there for Joe."

"Right. You better come too, Ozzie."

Barnes whispered, "Aren't you going to tell the piano player he has to split with you? I was watching, and there's plenty in there."

Candy shook her head. "Mostly ones and fives. You don't get big dough in a joint like this, because how the hell are they going to get it on their expense accounts? They've got to pad it on, call it a cab ride or something, and the company back home will only stand for so much."

"You should have had half, anyway. It was more than half for you."

Fuentes said, "One floor down, Señor, Señorita. In lobby." He held the elevator doors for them.

"Ozzie, asking isn't getting. He'd have bitched like hell and ended up giving me twenty bucks, and the next time I wouldn't be welcome. The way it was, I got a couple of free drinks, and I'll get star treatment any time I come back. Golden oldies—did you notice? Nothing real raunchy. They loved 'em. If I hadn't had to leave, I could have taken my pick of four or five johns, and with any luck he would have given me fifty or a hundred."

The doors slid open, and they crossed the lobby to the bell captain's desk.

"Joe's looking for you," Fuentes said. "I get him."

Barnes said, "I wonder what she wants?"

"Who?"

"That chicky at the desk. Tam. Tweed skirt."

"What do you care?"

"When you find out what this Joe's after, whistle." Barnes straightened his tie and pulled down his jacket.

"I know she's here," the young woman in the tweed skirt was saying. "I phoned, and you connected me."

"She doesn't wish to see you," the clerk said. He used the world-weary tone of one who drops a polite pretense. "She called and said we weren't to give out her room number, and she's not taking calls. If you went up there—if you found out the room number—you might make a scene, but you wouldn't be admitted."

"But this is Serpentina! She's got to see somebody!"

Barnes cleared his throat. "You're looking for Madame Serpentina? As it happens, I'm a friend of hers."

The young woman looked around at him. Her face was lively rather than lovely, but it was a very attractive liveliness, reminiscent of blindman's buff played at a fifteenth birthday party. "Can you take me to her? Will you?" The sub-assistant manager seized the opportunity to move away.

"Not so fast," Barnes said. "I don't want to inconvenience her, not unless there's a reason for it. But I might be able to talk her into seeing you. Let's go over there," he gestured toward one of the vinyl couches, "and discuss it. Who are you?"

"I've got a card," the young woman said. She opened a purse nearly as big as Candy's and jerked out a compact, a glasses case, and a package of nonnutritive gum. "Here they are!"

The card read:

ALEXANDRA DUCK
Associate Editor
Hidden Science/Natural Supernaturalism

with the usual address, telephone number, and so on.

"Miss Duck?" Barnes murmured uncertainly, returning the card.

"That's Ms. Duck," the young woman said, "and no quacks. Sandy Duck. If you're really a friend of Madame Serpentina's, call me Sandy."

"Call me Ozzie," Barnes told her. "Madame Serpentina does."

"Swell." Sandy Duck held out a hand in a knit acrylic glove.

Barnes shook it solemnly. "Is that a magazine or a newspaper? *Hidden Science and Natural Whatever It Was?*"

"It's magazines. Or I should say they are. We publish them in alternate months. *Hidden Science* in January, March, May, and so on, and *Natural Supernaturalism* in February, April, June, and like that. It has to do with shelf life. The supermarket kids will leave the January–February issue of *HS* standing right next to the February–March issue of *NS*. Or anyway, we hope they do, and sometimes it works."

"Supermarket kids?"

"The ones that straighten the magazine racks in the supermarkets. That's where we sell, mostly. To women in the supermarkets. What's she like?"

For a moment, Barnes thought wildly that he was being asked about his ex-wife.

"Madame Serpentina," Sandy explained. "She's getting to be quite famous, you know. I've met a dozen people who've met her, but you're the first who claimed to know her well."

"Well, she's very beautiful. . . ."

"I've heard that."

"Black hair, dark complexion, dark eyes, and she has a wonderful figure. You think of her as tall, but she isn't really. Just medium height, maybe two or three inches taller than you are." He paused to reflect. "She doesn't exactly have an accent, but I don't think English is her native language."

"Don't you know?"

Barnes shook his head. "It isn't something you can ask somebody right out, now is it? She doesn't talk about herself—or only once in a while. Sometimes she doesn't talk at all. She's imperious, very queenly."

"Do you—" Sandy broke off to look at the fat girl looming beside her.

"Seventh floor, room seventy-seven, Ozzie. We're off to see the wizard."

"Who was Joe, and what did he want?"

"It's Jim, I thought it was. He's up there. He phoned down, and we're supposed to come up. Say bye-bye to your little friend."

Sandy jumped up. "Is that where she is? Madame Serpentina? Seven seventy-seven?"

"Ozzie, who is this?"

"I'm from *Hidden Science*. One of our readers tipped me that Madame Serpentina was here. I telephoned, and a man's voice said to come over, that he'd get me in to see her."

Candy pursed her mouth. "That must have been Jim."

"Who's Jim?"

"A friend of ours. Maybe you ought to come with us."

Chapter 15

BAKER'S DOZIN'

"Come in," Stubb said, and all three tried to crowd in together, Sandy Duck caught and crushed between Candy and Barnes.

"God, but I'm glad to see you," Candy said. She sat on a bed, kicked off one of the galoshes the police had given her, and began to rub her plump, pink foot.

"What are you doing here?" Stubb asked Barnes.

Candy grunted, obstructed by her belly as she tussled with the other galosh. "I made him come, Jim. I was talking to him while you were up here, and he hasn't anyplace to stay tonight. He just parked his sample cases and stuff in the bus station."

Their hostess snorted like a small, well-bred horse. "Am I to have this mob domiciled with me?"

"Not me, Madame Serpentina," Sandy Duck declared. "I only want to interview you—I told you over the phone."

"And I told you that I do not grant such interviews. I am a witch, not a politician!"

There was a brief flash and the click of a shutter. Sandy lowered her little one-ten and looked at it with satisfaction. "That's great, I think. With your head back like that. It looked like you were exorcising."

"I would gladly ring my bell and light my candle, if they would make you go. Ozzie, I certainly did not invite you to my room, but now that you have come, please get this creature out."

Barnes smiled. "I'll be happy to, Madame Serpentina. But of course it might be better not to have a commotion. I think the best way might be to work out a compromise that would leave good feelings all around, and since you've laid it in my lap—if you'll excuse the expression—here's what I propose. Let Sandy ask three questions. I'll see to it that she doesn't pack them, doesn't ask two questions as if they were one. You answer them fully and fairly, and when you've answered the third, Sandy will go out with no urging. Won't both of you agree that's reasonable?"

Stubb chuckled. "You should have been a diplomat, Ozzie."

"She must also promise not to harass me in the future."

Still clutching her camera, Sandy raised her hand. "I won't harass. I may ask to see you, but if you say no I won't push."

"All right then, it is agreed—with the proviso that my answers need satisfy only my own sense of my own worth. I cannot promise they will be satisfactory to you."

"Okay!" Barnes was beaming. "What's the first one, Sandy?"

"Wait a minute." The associate editor's fingers fluttered as she jammed her camera into her purse. "I have to think. . . ."

"I have not got all night."

Stubb added, "Hell no. There's something I have to talk over with the rest of you when this girl's gone."

"Well, I have to think about it. I came up here with a list of about a hundred questions. Now I'm only going to get to ask three. The least you people can do is give me time to decide which three it's going to be."

"I said, *I have not got all night!*"

"Hey," Stubb put in. "I'm hungry as hell—I don't think I've eaten since breakfast. While she's making up her mind, how about getting on that phone and asking room service to bring up a club sandwich and a cup of coffee?"

Candy laid a pink hand on the telephone. "Wait a minute, if anybody's going to eat around here, I'm in. There's probably a menu in this drawer."

"What is the use!" The witch gave a theatrical gesture of despair. "Perhaps we should ask for stuffed pig, did we not have one already."

"If you mean me, forget it. A pig, maybe. But stuffed? Forget it. I'm so empty I can feel my stomach folding up. Now listen to this." Candy held up the room service menu. "'Pompano Amandine—luscious filets of fresh pompano, flown up daily from Miami, broiled in a mixture of farm butter, fresh-squeezed lemon juice, and grated almonds.' That's for me."

"Right," Stubb said. He had taken a small notebook and a mechanical pencil from inside his coat. "What to drink?"

"Beer. Pie afterwards. Peach, if they've got it. Or apple. They've always got apple."

"Right. What about you?" He looked toward the witch. "It's your room, after all."

"I am delighted you recall it. I had thought it forgotten that I will be paying for all this."

"Sure. By the way, it's about time you phoned the desk to ask about your seventy bucks. But wait till I get this order in. What'll you have?"

"I do not eat flesh or dairy products. Is there anything there for me?"

Candy scanned the menu. "Large fresh fruit salad—includes pineapples and mangoes, other fruits in season."

"That will do. I will have a glass of white wine also."

Stubb glanced at the salesman. "Ozzie?"

"Filet mignon with mushroom caps. Scotch on the rocks."

"Got it. Sandy?"

"Nothing. I don't want anything."

"We can't just eat in front of you. How about a drink?"

"You're going to have coffee, aren't you? I'll have that. A cup of coffee."

"Got it." Stubb took the telephone, rang room service, and began to read out the order.

"I can't decide which questions." Sandy was staring at a scuffed notebook as though the scrawled words there represented some indecipherable code.

"You must," the witch said. "Or give them to me. I will decide." She reached for the notebook.

"A minute. Can't you give me just a minute?"

There was a knock at the door.

Stubb put a hand over the mouthpiece and looked significantly at the witch. "There's a peep-hole in the door. Use it."

"I need not," she said, standing up. "Our visitor means no harm." She opened the door, but stood in the doorway.

A little, gray-haired woman in a shabby coat waited on the other side of the threshold. "I know you," she said as the door opened. "You're Miz Garth." She sighed as a traveler who has come to the end of a long journey. "You're a sight for some eyes, being from Mr. Free's house and all. Can I come in?"

"I have visitors, and though you say you know me, I do not know you. What is it you wish?"

"I know all of you," the little woman said, peering around the witch's shoulder. "Or anyways, most all, almost. A difference without a disinclination, is that what they call it? I just want to ask you about Mr. Free."

"Let her come in," Stubb said. "Come in, Mrs. Baker."

The witch took a half step back, and Mrs. Baker slipped past her. "I know you," she said. "You were in my parlor when that nice policeman was playing with Puff. I've seen you over at Mr. Free's too. You're Mr. Barnes." She turned her vague, sweet smile toward Candy. "And you're Miz Snake, the fortune teller. Oh, I do so love to have my fortune read! There's truth in tea, I always say."

Candy grinned at her. "I'm afraid you've made a Miz Snake, Mrs. Baker."

The old woman did not appear to hear her. "But I don't know . . . Well, where did she get off to? Where's the other girl? I'm sure I saw three when the door opened."

No one answered. Stubb stepped to the drapes and jerked them aside, but there was no one there.

The witch said, "Certainly she did not go out."

Barnes called, "Sandy? Ms. Duck, where are you?"

A muffled voice replied, "In here."

"Oh, hell." Barnes sounded relieved. "She's going to the bathroom. I must be getting jittery."

"I'll come out when I've got my questions!"

Candy sighed. "I was just about to go in there myself. Ozzie, you brought her, tell her to hurry up."

"That'll just fluster her worse," Barnes said. "Leave her alone. She'll be out in a minute."

Mrs. Baker smiled at them. "Haste makes worst, I always say."

"I'll bet you do," the fat girl said.

Stubb interposed. "While Sandy's out of the way, we've got a chance to talk to Mrs. Baker here. Let's make use of it. You said you wanted to find out something about Mr. Free, Mrs. Baker. What was it?"

"Where he's at, of one thing. A bird in the hand's worth two in the brush, they say."

The witch, who had been watching the old woman expectantly, let her shoulders droop a trifle. "Then you know no more than we. I had hoped you did."

"Because some ladies were asking around and about him. They're from the Government, I think. And I'd like to know myself. It's been prying on my mind."

Stubb said, "These ladies from the Government, were they police? Like Sergeant Proudy, who played with your cat?"

"I don't think so. They weren't uniform. Besides, they drank my tea. It was my obsession, when those two nice policemen broke my door, that policemen bought and large won't drink tea, only cooco. Tea and symphony is what they say, and policemen bought and large don't care for music."

"Can you tell us what they told you? Please think carefully. It might be important."

"Only that they had seen Mr. Free broadcased, and they wanted to talk to him—"

"They saw him on television?"

"Yes, and I did too, clear as day sight on the TV pogrom. It was just after they showed that nice sergeant getting hit with the ax. They say fool's names and fool's cases are often aired in public paces, but I thought Mr. Free gave his case about as good as anybody could. He didn't sound like a lawyer—he sounded like he was telling the truth."

Barnes said, "That must have been while the rest of us were inside looking after that cop."

The old woman shook her head. "It was the six P.M. Morning Report."

Stubb grunted. "They had it taped, Mrs. Baker. Maybe even from before we moved in, when a lot of people were protesting the new ramp. What else did these ladies say?"

"Nothing match. Just that they had been looking for poor Mr. Free because he had crash coming, but when they got there he wasn't here. Factually, the whole kitten caboose of you wasn't. A missus as good as a mile, like they say, even if maybe they were married. They didn't take their gloves off, either one."

"They must have given you their names."

Mrs. Baker hesitated, chin tucked in. She was sitting in the vanity chair, her back as straight as its own.

"First names? Last names? Anything?"

"I know they said them, but I was in a fluster. Then the little one saw Puff and asked what's Puff's name, and I told her Puff, and she run over and hid under the divan like she does, and I never thought to ask again. Do you think it's a lot of crash?"

Stubb shook his head.

"Still, it *might* be a lot to him. The widow's might, it's called, I believe. You could call it the widower's might nearly as good. Mr. Free was a widower, I expect."

"But you don't know?"

"He always seemed so widower-weedy, if you know what I mean. Not like a old bachelor—they're always so crispy. The worst old women is the ones that wear pants in the family, they say. But I think old bachelors are worse even, and Mr. Free is so sweet. He casts his spelling over you."

The witch asked quickly, "Just what do you mean by that?"

Mrs. Baker smiled her vague smile. "Why if I could say, it wouldn't be spelling, would it? But Mr. Free used to come over and chew the rug now and then. The late Mr. Baker was a deer bomber in the war, and Mr. Free liked to hear about that and talk about his old company that he used to work for, Louise Clerk I think it was." She sighed. "The closest I can put it is I never felt truffles was important when he was around. He had a beam in his eyes, like the Bible tells, and it lit up within."

Barnes nodded and cleared his throat. "You know, I felt like that too. I felt like it wasn't all that important whether I made the sale. I made some good ones too, just before we had to leave."

"Yesterday I saw you go out my window," the old woman said. "It wasn't nosiness, it's just that looking at the street's more real-like, sometimes, than TV. I knew you were sailing because of those big valances you carried, and I thought someday you'd come to my door to sell me pans or bicyclopedias. You'd have thought I fell for your line hook and ladder, because I would have let you in and looked at everything. If you'd have told me about Mr. Free, I might have bought a new rooster too. I need one."

Stubb was thumbing the telephone book. "No Louise Clerk & Company," he said. "No Clerk, Louise in the residential section either."

"I think they're out of business," Mrs. Baker told him. "They went backripped, I suppose. He said it was years black."

Candy put in, "He would have retired at sixty-five, Jim, and I think he was over seventy."

Stubb nodded. "I'm afraid we don't know where Mr. Free is any more than you do, Mrs. Baker." He slapped the telephone book shut. "But we'd like to find him. I'll write down the hotel number and the number of this room for you. If you find him or hear where he is, I want you to call me. Don't tell those women anything until you hear from me. I doubt that there's any money. That's something all investigators say when they want to find someone."

"I was thinking—" Mrs. Baker took a handkerchief from her purse. "I was thinking if he'd crashed in he might have saved his house. Paid on somebody. I used to think how lucky all of you were to room in board there." She blew her nose, a sound like Puff sneezing. "He told me all your names, but I think I've got them stirred up now and you aren't who I thought. Just the same, I feel I know you from those years ago. The dark lady's Miz Garth, because he said Miz Garth was an adventuress, and she's so pretty. That makes the other lady—"

The bathroom door flew open. "I have my questions!" Sandy Duck waved her notebook triumphantly.

Chapter 16

CATOPTROMANCY

"Who was that woman anyway?" Sandy asked when she had settled into the plastic-cushioned hotel chair Barnes vacated for her.

"And is that the first of your questions?" The witch raised an eyebrow.

"Oh, no! I was just curious."

"But you are not curious about the subjects of your other questions."

"Yes, I am, of course. Very much so." Sandy's round little face was confused and concerned.

"Then this question is of a piece with them, and counts as the first. Her name is Mrs. Baker, and—"

"Wait!" The notebook waved again, now a placard of protest. "You're not in good faith. You're just playing with me."

"And are you in good faith? I spend my entire life, nearly every waking hour, in the pursuit of eternal truth and transcendent authority, and you come here with your three questions for an idiotic article that will be thrown away as soon as it is read. Is that good faith?"

"Yes," Sandy said. "Yes, it is."

The witch stared at her.

"In the first place, I didn't come here with just three questions. I came with scads, and you were the one who said only three. In the second place, sure some copies we sell will be pitched out as soon as they've been read once, but a lot won't be. To start with, we keep two sets in the office. They go clear back to 1927, when *Who Knows?*—that was our original title—was founded. The Mary-Sue Jordan Smith Memorial Library of the Occult in Belhaven, North Carolina has a complete set too—"

"She was a fool," the witch interrupted.

Sandy looked baffled, and Stubb said, "The Smith woman?"

"Yes, I knew her. She had some talent, perhaps, but she had no judgement. She was appallingly ignorant as well."

Sandy looked at Candy Garth as though for support. "I think she died in nineteen forty-seven."

"Pah! Nineteen forty-five. Continue."

"That's all." Sandy held up her hands as though she were balancing two coconuts. "I was just going to say that lots of our readers keep all our issues for years and years. They write and tell us, or say they have everything except a certain one, and ask if we'll sell them that. We do, for five dollars, if we've got it."

"How could I not cooperate with a publication so high-minded? Very well then. My favorite recording artist is a man in Senegal, of whom you have never heard. I sleep in the nude. If I were stranded on a desert island—"

Candy shouted, "Oh, shut up! For God's sake, let her ask

her damn questions and get out of here. I'm tired and I'm not buzzed any more and I'm so damn hungry I may faint. You!" She glared at Sandy. "Ask the first one. She'll answer it or I'll sit on her."

The young woman from *Hidden Science/Natural Supernaturalism* cleared her throat. "Madame Serpentina, you are one of the most profound practitioners of the occult today. In your opinion, what one thing can the average person do that would most improve his or her position vis-à-vis the unseen world?"

"See."

"I beg your pardon?"

"Apprehend, if you wish a longer answer."

"This isn't a question, but I'd appreciate it if you'd enlarge a little on that. You promised to answer 'fully and fairly' after all."

"Most unenlightened people believe they see what they believe they will see," the witch said. "They should not do that. To see the unseen world, it is necessary to look—that is why wisdom has so often been depicted as a third eye."

Sandy hesitated, then nodded. "I see."

"I doubt it."

Stubb interposed. "Time for the second question, I think."

"All right, second question." Sandy took a deep breath. "Madame Serpentina, by what simple test—if such a test exists—can our readers determine whether they themselves or others who in their opinion may possess them, actually have occult powers?"

"Certainly such a test exists." The witch straightened her shoulders and with both hands smoothed the black lace of her skirt. "You must understand that we are speaking of talents, just as one who might seek to isolate a future symphonist from a group of students would be intent upon talents. Occult talents differ from musical, or mathematical, or athletic talents in certain ways, but they are talents still. Those who possess them show signs of the same sort. I mean an easy mastery of the rudiments combined with a 'signa-

ture'—a characteristic their teachers may or may not appreciate that distinguishes their work from that of others."

"But—"

"For example, a woman who believes herself clairvoyant
should, more than once and more than twice, attempt carto-
mancy. If her most surprising predictions are often validated
by subsequent events, she may proceed to more difficult
things. A man who puts himself forward as a medium, let
him call up spirits—then see if they come."

Sandy remained speechless for a moment, then sighed.
"Now I'm just dying to ask you about fakes, but you
wouldn't answer, would you? Unless we counted it as the
third question?"

The witch shook her head.

Stubb said, "I'll answer. I've checked out a few of those
guys for nervous relatives. And what the hell, you're not
interviewing me, so anything I say is free. So what I say is, I
never in my life met a man that had a dog that would come
every time he called it. But I've met a lot of stage people
who'd go into their acts every chance they got, and sometimes for no reason at all. If a guy comes up with some sort of
spook every time he tries, you can bet the rent he's a
performer. The guy whose dog stops coming if somebody
looks hard to see if it's a real dog or a kid in a dog suit's a
performer too."

The witch's lip curled ever so slightly. "Since Mr. Stubb
has seen fit to put himself forward as enlightened, I have no
alternative but to proffer an answer—or at least half an
answer—myself."

Sandy started to speak, but the witch raised her hand to
stop her. "Do not thank me. Whatever gratitude you may
feel should be directed to him, not me. My half answer is
this—that the real problem confronting one who would
judge mediumship is not distinguishing true spirits from
bogus ones, as Mr. Stubb appears to believe. The great
problem that confronts such a person is distinguishing honest and beneficent spirits from dishonest and malicious ones.
One who can do that will have no difficulty unmasking

shams; but one who cannot do it, and do it reliably, had much better have no traffic with spirits at all unless he can procure the assistance of a trustworthy expert. Now let us have your third and last question, please."

"All right." Sandy gulped. "The third and last question, but before I read it I want to tell you I *am* grateful to you, whatever you say.

"Third question. Madame Serpentina, what event of great importance to America do you foresee within the next ten years?"

The witch laughed. Her laugh was charming when she wished it to be, and it was charming now—Barnes felt she had never been so desirable. "I do not cast the nation's horoscope every day. Indeed, I do not much approve of the casting of horoscopes at all, as that art is commonly understood. One baseball team will defeat another, a short politician will be beaten by a tall one, valleys will flood, and the ground will shake; aircraft will plummet from the sky. I can tell you all that, but there is nothing of the unseen world about it—it is all the world that is too much seen, and in fact the world that does not have to be seen at all, since anyone can read of it in a newspaper. I will couch all those things in suitably cryptic verse for you, if you wish."

"But that wasn't my question—none of it was my question. I want to know just one event of great importance, as specifically as you can give it to me. We'll print your prediction, and don't forget that your reputation will depend somewhat on what you say. If you have to cast a horoscope, go ahead and do it."

The witch shook her head. "Casting the horoscope of an entire nation—as I do such things—would require weeks. I will make a prediction because I have promised, if I can. If I cannot, you must leave without one. Are you familiar with catoptromancy?"

"I don't even know what it means."

"Perhaps you will see some. Ozzie, would you please open the drapes?"

Barnes fumbled for a moment before finding the cords at

one side of the window. The stores and offices across the street were in three and four-storied buildings for the most part, so that the window looked out over a dark panorama of ugly roofs.

"Cloudy," the witch said. "Very cloudy. Nevertheless, perhaps we might try. Ozzie, Mr. Stubb, I wish the mirror to be taken from that—that thing there. The dresser, or whatever one calls it. Can you do that for me?"

"I doubt it," Stubb told her. He jerked the article in question away from the wall and glanced at its back. "Big tamper-proof screws. I might get it off in half an hour if I had a tool kit, but I don't."

"Then you will have to move the whole affair until it faces the window. Not right against the glass necessarily, but fairly close. Ozzie, assist him."

Sandy pushed her chair back to let them past.

"Good. That is fine. Now open the window."

"It's cold out there," Barnes protested.

"I am aware of it. Miss Garth, would you prefer that I call you Candy?"

"No," Candy said.

"I do not blame you. Miss Garth, will you please extinguish the lights? You are nearest the switch, I think."

The room was plunged into night. Sandy stirred in her chair and made one of those little moans for which there is no name. Barnes was wrestling with the window catch in the blackness. He won and slid back the glass.

"Now what?" Stubb asked.

"Now you wait until I tell you otherwise."

Candy, rummaging the floor near where she sat, found her white raincoat and draped it about her shoulders. None of the others moved.

The faint noises of traffic rose from the street below. There was no wind, but the room quickly became cold. Somewhere nearby, the door of another room opened and closed.

"If you don't—" Sandy began. The witch, leaning forward from her position on the bed, touched her knee to silence her.

An airplane droned far overhead. At thirty-five hundred feet the dark masses of snow cloud parted. Moonlight reached down toward the spire of the Consort, shone through the open window of Room 777, touched the mirror, and was reflected back and lost in the lightless sky.

"Shut the window," the witch said. "Close the drapes. Now you must all listen to me and do as I tell you. You must not look into that mirror. When Miss Garth turns on the lights, you may talk among yourselves, or walk about, or do anything else you wish, but you must keep your eyes from the mirror. Do not speak to me; I will not be able to answer you . . ." She continued, rapidly yet solemnly, but the words were in a tongue none of them understood.

"Hell, we *can't* look into it," Stubb said.

Barnes told him, "I think she wants us to put it back where it was."

Candy flicked the switch and called to Sandy Duck, "Get up and help them. That thing must weigh a ton." With a woman at each front corner and a man at each rear corner, the vanity was restored to its original position.

"Now what?" Sandy asked. She was the smallest of them all, shorter even (if the heels had been pulled from her shoes) than Stubb, and she was panting a little.

"Now we don't look in it," Barnes said. "You heard her."

There was a knock at the door.

"Oh, Lord," Candy muttered. "What now?"

A voice outside announced room service.

Candy opened the door, and the third bellman wheeled in a laden cart. She looked frantically at Stubb, who waved a reassuring hand.

"Four dinners," the bellman said. "I'll put them on the table for you. Fish. Pie. Club. Steak. Fruit. Two coffees. Beer. Scotch. Glass of wine. That everything?"

"I think so," Stubb said.

"Lady will have to sign for it," the bellman said. "Unless you're paying. Say, is she all right?"

The witch relaxed and nodded. "I am fine. I will sign. May I put a tip for you on the bill when I sign it?"

"Yes, Ma'am. That will be fine, Ma'am. Thank you very much."

She took the check and his pen. "Your friend—do you know whom I mean? He has not returned with my seventy dollars. If you should see him, will you ask him to do so? I am somewhat inconvenienced."

"I certainly will, Ma'am. Joe ought to have got back to you with that quite a while ago. I'll tell him."

Stubb said, "Maybe he's off already."

The bellman shook his head as the witch handed back the check. "He'll be on the rest of the night. We don't get off till seven." He grinned. "That's very generous of you, Ma'am. Thank you."

"Think nothing of it."

"I do think something of it, Ma'am, and I appreciate what you gave when we carried your bags up, too. Ma'am— maybe I shouldn't say it, but I know something, something confidential, that maybe I ought to tell you about."

"Then tell me," the witch said. She had speared a section of mandarin orange, and she punctuated the words by thrusting it into her mouth.

"It's confidential." The third bellman looked around at Stubb, Sandy, Candy, and Barnes. "Maybe you could step into the hall with me for just a moment?"

Barnes said, "You don't have to do that, Madame Serpentina. We'll go outside if you want us to."

Stubb's smile was wide and nearly genuine. "What is this? Aren't we all friends here? Listen, if the lady's in some sort of little embarrassment, I want to know about it so we can help her out."

"I'm not sure it is her," the bellman admitted. "I just thought she ought to be told."

"Enough of mysteries," the witch said. "I wish to eat my fruit and drink my wine in peace—or at least, in as much as I may have. If you are not even certain I am concerned, out with it. Or let it be, and out with you."

"Maybe it's another one of you," the bellman said. "Or all of you. But you've been staked out by the authorities."

Chapter 17

PROPHECY . . . AND A POLL

"What the hell," Stubb said. "What the hell?"

He was the only one who spoke.

"Listen, buddy," he said to the bellman, "do you mean the house dick? You can see for yourself that there's nothing going on here. This lady," he gestured toward Sandy Duck, "came up to interview your guest for her magazine, and the rest of us came to talk business with her over a late snack. What the hell's wrong with that?"

"Not Mr. Kramer," the bellman said. "The real authorities." He did not say that he wished he could say Scotland Yard, but he did. "I told him I wanted to see his credentials, and he showed me his badge. It was the real thing."

Candy looked toward Stubb. "Jim . . . ?"

"Yeah. This sounds like my department. Where is he?"

"Three doors down. Seven seventy-one. It's an empty room."

"He didn't rent it?"

The bellman shook his head. "When he opened the door to talk, I saw he'd taped the latch, so he could go out without the door's locking behind him. If he'd paid at the desk, he'd have a key."

"Right. He stopped you while you were coming with the cart?"

The bellman nodded.

"And what'd he say?"

"He asked where I was taking it, and I told him. Then he

said when I got finished to come back and knock on his door and tell him what I saw in here. He said to keep my eyes open. That's when I told him I wanted to look at his credentials and he showed me his badge."

"You're going to need an excuse for staying in here so long. What do you plan to tell him?"

The bellman thought for a moment. "I could say the lady was foreign, and she asked me a lot of stuff about how to get around the city—where things were."

"Then he'd say what about the other people—he must have seen all the dishes on your cart—why didn't she ask them? And he'll sure as hell want to know where she wanted to go. No, you tell him that we had a bunch of papers spread all over the table. You couldn't see what they were about. We made you wait until we had shuffled them around some before we put them away so you could serve the food. We didn't say anything particular while we were doing it. Just, 'Here, you take this,' and 'Are these in order?' Stuff like that. You got it?"

The bellman nodded. "Is it okay to tell him what you look like?"

"You'll have to, but if he's got the room staked out he's probably made us already. Now listen, he'll take you over everything three or four times if he's a good cop. Keep it simple and remember to forget anything you could possibly forget. He didn't give you his name, did he?"

"No."

"He didn't say, 'I'm detective so-and-so?' Anything like that?"

"No. I would have remembered."

"You said he showed you his badge. What was the number?"

The bellman hesitated, then said, "I guess I didn't notice."

"Okay, when you go back, don't knock like he told you. Go straight past. He'll stop you again. Tell him you're not sure about him, and say you want to see his badge again. Take a good look—make him let you see it in a good light—and remember the number. When you get back downstairs again, phone this room and tell me what it was. What did he look like?"

The bellman thought for a moment. "Not as big as most of them. I'd say maybe just over middle size. Big nose. He had a bandage around his head."

"Forget the badge number," Stubb told him. "I know who he is."

"So do the rest of us," Candy said when the bellman was gone.

"Except her." Stubb nodded toward Sandy Duck.

"You're right," Sandy said. "I certainly don't know. I also don't know why the police should want to watch Madame Serpentina. Of course they always view major psychics with distrust except when they beg them to solve their cases for them without a fee."

The witch smiled. "I believe you yourself wanted a certain prediction. I did not hear any mention of payment, but then perhaps I was inattentive."

"I wish I could," Sandy said frankly. "I can't. Our magazines don't have the money. I'll tell you what we'll do, though. Any time you want, we'll run a one-page ad for free."

The witch laughed.

Stubb said, "Don't knock it. Sandy, I'll send you Madame Serpentina's copy tomorrow. To run as soon as possible, either magazine. How do you want it?"

"If there are pictures, we'll need camera-ready copy. If it's just text, you can tell us what you want to say and we'll lay it out and spec the type."

"But now," the witch said, "I must earn this advertisement with my prediction. First, however, I will answer several more questions, questions you would ask if I permitted them. Yes, I did indeed see something in the mirror. No, you would not have seen what I saw, had you looked—you would merely have ruined the operation. And lastly, what I have done is the verso of necromancy; I summoned the spirits of the unborn to reveal the future.

"You desired to know of a great event—one affecting the entire nation—that will occur within a decade. Is that correct?"

Pencil poised, Sandy nodded.

"Very well. The greatest event of the coming decade will be the quadrumvirate. Four leaders, unknown today, shall unite to take political, financial, artistic, and judicial power. They shall create a revolution of thought. Many who are now rulers shall be imprisoned or exiled. Many who are now powerless shall rise to places of great authority. The rich shall be made poor, and the poor rich. Old crimes, long concealed, shall be made public, and their perpetrators given to the people as to a pride of lions. The four shall be hated and idolized, but their rule will not end within the period specified by my prediction. That is all I was told."

The pencil flew. "You don't know the names of these men?"

"No. That information would be very difficult to obtain. The spirits, as you should know, have great difficulty providing answers in terms of specific words. It is somewhat as though you—who we shall say speak Chinese—were to ask a woman who knew no other tongue the name of an American she met last year. If you were most fortunate, you might hear 'Beloved Disciple of the Iron-Smiter,' if the name was John Smith."

"They will come to power in ten years?"

"Much sooner, I think."

Sandy rose. "I realize I've asked more questions than the three we agreed on, and I don't want to wear out my welcome. Mr. Barnes, Ms. Garth, I want to thank you for bringing me up here. I know as well as you do that I couldn't have gotten into this room if it hadn't been for you. Mr. Stubb, you've come to my rescue more than once, and I appreciate it. Madame Serpentina, I know you never grant interviews, but you've given me one tonight and let me take a picture and everything, and I appreciate it more than I can say."

The witch inclined her head graciously. Candy looked embarrassed, Barnes grinned, and Stubb snorted.

"I'll go now, but I want you to know that nothing I've heard in here—I mean, nothing beyond what I myself was told—will go into my article."

Stubb said, "I'm a good deal more worried about what you're going to tell the cop. Do you want to talk to him?"

Sandy shook her head. "Not if I can help it."

"Swell. According to what the bellhop said, he's between us and the elevators; but this hotel's built in a hollow square, if you know what I mean. Turn right instead of left when you go out the door, and you should be able to walk around the long way and get to them without passing his room. Will you do that?"

"Of course. But if I'm stopped, I won't tell lies—I just won't say anything. The courts may say the police can examine a journalist's notes now, but they won't find anything there I wouldn't put in my story."

"Good girl," Stubb said. He opened the door for her.

Candy sighed as it closed. "Wow. That's over. Ozzie, why'd you have to bring her up here?" She tried to cross her legs, failed, and settled for crossing her ankles.

Barnes shrugged. "She looked like she needed help."

Stubb said, "Our friend Ozzie's a soft touch. How was your fish?"

"Tasty, only there wasn't enough of it, or enough beer. You want the rest of your sandwich? How about that pickle?"

"You can have them." Stubb pushed his plate over. Barnes said, "It's that cop that got hit with the ax, isn't it? Sergeant Proudy, his name was. I let him in this morning— my God, it feels like a year ago."

"We've all had a tough day."

Her mouth full, Candy mumbled, "'S not over yet." She swallowed. "Why's he watching us?"

Stubb nodded. "You're right, that's the first thing we have to talk about. Anybody got any ideas?"

"Maybe they found out about Ozzie calling all those salesmen. I heard you and Ozzie outside the house through the busted wall. Maybe somebody else heard you too."

"So what? It was just creating a nuisance, and if they wanted him they could pick him up. Besides, Proudy's not on duty."

"You've been taking lessons from the Wicked Witch of the West over there, Jim. There's no way you could know that."

"Nuts." Stubb leaned back in his chair, removing his glasses and pinching the bridge of his nose. "I don't know how she does it—or if she really does. But I know how I do it, and anybody willing to think for a minute could do it too. Proudy got it with the spike end of a fire ax. I saw it. He got stitches and bandages and so on. You saw that, in fact you helped. He may not be in a hospital. He may not even be lying down, even if he should be. But there's no way in hell the Department would put him back on duty after that. Not today. Not tomorrow. Not till he's pretty well healed up."

The witch pushed aside her fruit and lit a cigarette. "You are right in what you say. But that is not the question."

Stubb nodded.

Barnes said, "Let me try. What are we going to do about him?"

"That's not it either," Stubb told him. "Anyway, who says we have to do anything?"

"*Why*," the witch said. "That is what we must discover, Ozzie."

Candy was staring at the witch and Stubb. "All of a sudden it seems like you two are pretty close."

"Yeah. I'll tell you about that in a minute. For now, let's get back to Proudy. Anybody got any more suggestions about what he might be up to?"

Barnes said, "Remember those women who came to see Mrs. Baker? Could he be working for them? And anyway, what are they doing?"

"I don't know," Stubb said. "When she told us all that, I

more than half thought she was making it up, or blowing a couple of nosy neighbors into spy stuff. Now I don't know."

Candy asked, "You think he *could* be working for them?"

"No. Not working for them. But he could have got onto them, and he might have talked to the Baker woman for all we know, and be trying to cut himself a piece of cake. He's on his own for sure, and when a cop goes on his own when he could be home in bed, he smells a promotion or money. Any of you a mass murderer?"

"Don't try to be funny, Jim."

"Okay, then it's money. We'll talk about that later too. Should we ring him up and ask what the hell? I'm serious. He's in seven seven one, and all we have to do is pick up the phone and dial his room."

"I'm for it," Barnes said. "After all, we carried him in and got him patched up after one of his own men hit him. If he's after us now, I think we're entitled to some kind of explanation."

"One in favor," Stubb said. "How about you, Candy?"

"You know as well as I do that it'll end up with me getting busted."

"One against." Stubb glanced at the witch.

"It seems to me we should know more."

"One for later. Make that two for later—when I talk to a cop, I like to have something I can pry with. Later it is."

The telephone rang.

Chapter 18

FROM THE HIGH COUNTRY

Stubb reached for the telephone. The witch said, "This is my room. You may hand it to me." He nodded.

Candy nudged Barnes. "You think it's him calling us?"

"Yes," the witch said into the receiver. "This is she." Then, "Of course you are. I knew your voice at once. What is it you want?"

There was a long pause while the witch listened.

"No, I did not. I will not say I never call invisible powers, but I have done nothing to him. . . . Everything affecting human lives involves spirits. That is nothing. There are many other explanations. . . . I would suggest that you go home. It is very late—if this were summer, you would see dawn at the windows." She hung up.

Stubb was leaning back in his chair. The light from the weak hotel bulb above the table showed how waxen his skin was under a dark stubble. "You going to tell us?" he asked casually.

Ignoring the cigarette that smouldered on her plate, the witch got out another and her gold lighter. The flame trembled ever so slightly.

"Later, maybe," Stubb said.

"I will tell you now, if you wish. It was the girl who just left. She was curious about the policeman and went past his room after all. She said he came out and tried to question her, but she would tell him nothing; when she threatened to scream, he released her. She asked if I had laid a curse on him."

"And you said you hadn't. Why'd she ask?"

"I assume because he looked or acted like one who had been cursed. She was prolix, but she really told me very little. I gathered she thought him irrational."

"Did she tell you what he asked her?"

"Only that he wanted to know if we were all here, and that he seemed to expect her to know who he meant by *all*. She described us, and he asked who else was here."

"Swell." Stubb sounded bitter.

Candy asked, "What's the matter, Jim?"

"Well, for one thing, I didn't want her to talk to him. She has, and she's sure as hell told him something. You can't describe four people without telling an investigator who's listening a lot, just to start with, and who knows what else she told him? For another thing, now I've got some idea of what he's looking for."

"And what's that?" Barnes asked. "Or is it a big secret?" He had loosened his tie and unbuttoned his shirt.

"It's no secret and it's just a guess. But I think it's a good guess. Who's not here, Ozzie? Which of us isn't here?"

Barnes's eyes rolled as he looked about the room, the glass eye not quite tracking with his real one. "Why, we're all here," he said. "Everybody's here."

Stubb shook his head.

Candy asked, "You don't mean Mrs. Baker?"

"Close, but no cigar. Who was *she* looking for? Who were the women who came and talked to her looking for? Last night, folks—just last night—there were five of us living together in the same house. Who's missing?"

Barnes nodded. "Free, of course. I guess I didn't think about him because we'd already talked about him when Mrs. Baker was here."

"We're going to talk about him some more. I didn't want to do it then because that Duck girl was in the bathroom and so forth. But that's why we're here." Stubb walked across the room to the television set and switched it on. "I don't like talking against noise any more than the rest of you—maybe less. If anybody can guarantee no one's listening in, I'll turn it off. Anybody want to try?"

No one spoke.

"It stays on, then. The last we heard, Proudy was a couple of rooms away, but he may have got closer by now. There's half a dozen tricks for listening through a hotel wall, and all of them work pretty good."

Candy blurted, "All right, Mr. Free's not here—and I don't give a damn about the God-damned TV. If you knew how much talking I've done against rock tapes and radios and everything else— What I want to know is why are *we* here. If the crystal gazer wants to put me up for the night, fine. I could have found some other place, but this is as good as any. Only if you're going to tell me it's out of the goodness of her heart, forget it. In the first place, I don't think she's got one.

In the second place, if she does there's no goodness in it."

"Thank you," the witch said. "I am delighted by your gracious acceptance of my hospitality."

"Knock it off," Stubb told Candy. "What the hell do you think the rest of us are—a choir? This is a business meeting. You and Ozzie might as well know right now that before you came up Madame S. and I formed a little partnership. We're going to help each other instead of fighting each other, and we're going to split whatever we make right down the middle. She didn't get you up here, I did—the room is just in her name, that's all. And I didn't get you up out of the goodness of my heart either. I did it because we want to invite you in. You get to hear our offer, and if you don't take it you can split."

Barnes was suddenly alert. "All right," he said. "What's the offer?"

"Let me ask you something first. Did Free ever say anything to you that made you think he had something valuable hidden?"

Barnes shut his eyes as he cast his mind back. "Suppose he did. Why?"

"We think he did. I'll give you this just to show we're dealing off the top. One time Free told me he came from what he called 'the High Country.' He said he had a ticket hidden away that would take him back there if he wanted to go, but it was too late to use it. What do you think of that?"

Barnes shrugged. "What do you think of it? That's what seems important to me. You were there and you heard him, and now you say you're going to make me an offer. What do you think?"

"I haven't got anything but guesses," Stubb said, "but I'll let you have them—I've given them to Madame S. here already." He took off his glasses, inspected their lenses and put them on again. "Ever since I talked to him, I've been wondering what the High Country might mean, because if I knew that, I'd have a pretty good idea what kind of a ticket it would take to get you there. Madame S. has her own ideas, but I'll lay off them—she can tell you herself if she wants to.

In the first place, the High Country could really be another country—Switzerland, maybe, or someplace else that's got a lot of high ground; maybe the highlands of Scotland. In that case, the ticket's probably his passport. Anybody buy that?"

He looked at Barnes and Candy, but there was no reply.

"Me neither. Here's another guess. Free could be a hillbilly—he talked like one. Maybe he was from someplace in the Smokies. Anybody like it?"

Candy said, "Jim, I think he talked different depending on who he was with."

"You sure of that?"

"No. I can't really put my finger on it. Maybe it was something I just imagined. Only that's the way it seemed to me. I don't have a hell of a lot of education, Jim. I dropped out of high school. And I don't think you do either. So I think maybe when he was around us he talked a little simple, so we'd relax."

"Fine. That's a good point, and I want to come back to it in a minute. For now, let's hold it and clear the decks a little. Anybody go for the hillbilly idea?"

"No," Barnes said. "Go on."

"Then where are we?" Stubb paused and looked at each of them in turn. A televised war crashed to a close, and an announcer began to speak earnestly about soft drinks. "If he wasn't from someplace that's really high up—here or in some other country—what's left?"

"Craziness," Candy said.

Barnes swiveled to look at her.

She said, "You ever talk to those old bag ladies in the street? I have, when I've had a fifty or hundred-dollar trick and three or four shots afterwards. I'll be floating along, and I'll sit down beside one someplace, or one will sit by me. One I met was a princess. One was the bastard of some President. All of them have some crazy story, and if I ever hear one that makes the bag lady not so important as she looks instead of the other way, I'll give her a five if I've got one. But I don't think I'll ever need to."

"You really think Free was crazy?"

Candy thrust her chins forward as she considered. "I'll have to think it over. But right now, yes, I think maybe he was. He let us into his house, didn't he?"

The witch said, "And described us to his neighbor long before he did so, or so it sounded when she spoke of it. Was it only I who heard her? Whatever else may be true, Free was not mad."

Stubb nodded. "I don't think so either. Of course, Candy, what you think is up to you. For me, as far as I can see, if the guy wasn't really from the mountains someplace, and he wasn't nuts, there's only one thing left. He told me he came from the High Country, and he came for adventure, and other people did the same thing, and he had his ticket—that was what he called it—hidden away, but it was too late for him to use it."

Barnes said, "Then we look for it. It's probably in the house someplace."

"We will. Or rather, I will, tomorrow when it's light; and if it's in the house, I'll probably find it. But suppose I don't? Suppose it isn't in the house at all? He told me one time that everything valuable had been stolen from his bedroom one time when he was away. It would be a lot easier to find the ticket if we could find Free."

Candy put in, "You said there was only one thing left, Jim. Lay it on us."

Stubb smiled and leaned back. "He called it the High Country. Maybe we'd call it high finance, high society, or the high life. I think Free, and that name's a ringer if I ever heard one, came from a wealthy old family, that kind that's been playing ambassador and governor and maybe even President for so long they've forgotten who great granddaddy stole the money from in the first place. I think when he got out of Harvard, or maybe even before he got out, he went to the Good Will store and bought some old clothes and went on the bum. A lot of them do. Just for an adventure, like he said. And I think that whatever the reason was, he stayed a whole lot longer than most of them do. Maybe he got mixed up with some woman. Maybe he was dodging something up there where he came from; maybe he didn't want to spend his life running Amalgamated Copper or whatever it was. Then they decided he was dead, and he was ashamed to go home."

He took off his glasses and polished them on his sleeve; when he looked up for a moment, his eyes seemed grotesquely small. "But before he started his little adventure, I think he left himself an out—something that would bring him back to Harvard and Newport and all that if he ever wanted to go. Something that would make him rich, really rich, no matter what his family did while he was gone. Even if he was declared legally dead, for example.

"I'm not going to ask if anybody buys that idea. Somebody does—me. I've talked it over a little with Madame S. here, and although she doesn't see it my way, she agrees that Free wasn't nuts, and he really did have something very valuable salted away." The thick lenses back in place, Stubb looked toward the witch. "Right?"

Her nod was guarded, but unmistakably a nod.

"So I talked to her. I said, listen here, whatever it was, I'm going after it and you're going after it too. You've got your way of operating and I've got mine, and it's even money we'll just screw each other up so somebody else gets it or nobody gets it at all. I've never doublecrossed a client, and I never will. Let's join and split it down the middle. She's a smart lady; she agreed. Now we're making the same offer to you two. You lived with him just like we did. It's likely one of you—maybe both of you—heard something we didn't, something that might be important. Throw in with us, and you're each in for ten percent of whatever we find. But it's got to be now, and you've got to be willing to work for the partnership as well as talk. Do you want in?"

"We get ten percent," Barnes said.

"Right."

"You said you were giving us the same deal you made with Madame Serpentina, and you said the two of you were going to divide it equally."

"Divide what?" Stubb snorted. "We don't even know if

anything's really there. If it is, ten percent could be a fortune."

Candy yawned. "Jim, if it was just you, I'd be in. You know that. The way it is . . ."

Barnes said, "And I'd be delighted to assist Madame Serpentina; but that would be—uh—a matter of gallantry. This is business, and not very good business, not very profitable business."

"Candy said she thought Free was crazy. Do you think so too, Ozzie?"

Slowly, Barnes shook his head.

"What do you think?"

"I'm going to reserve that," Barnes said. "I'll tell you in the morning. Maybe."

"In the morning?"

Barnes shrugged. "You're going to have to let Candy and me stay here. As Madame Serpentina said a few minutes ago, it's already so late that if it were summer it would be getting light out."

Candy said, "That's right. Dibs on the bathroom."

"If you two stay here, you're going to be sleeping on the floor," Stubb told them. "I should have said we will—all three of us. Let's get that straight right now."

"What the hell!" The fat girl stared at him openmouthed. "There's two double beds."

"Right. And if more than one person uses them, the maid will report it, and the hotel will know there's been more than one person staying in the room. We can't afford that. It's Madame S.'s room, so she gets a bed. The rest of us bunk on the floor or in chairs—or not at all."

Chapter 19

EGO VENDO

Candy was in the bathroom, in the tub. As Barnes lay on his back, almost precisely where the table from which they had eaten had stood, he could hear her singing, and occasionally splashing.

> "Oh, the Captain's it was lofty,
> And Chips, he always would,
> The Cook's was hot and greasy,
> But the Mate, he never could!
>
> They sailed down to Rio,
> They sailed back again,
> But six days out of seven
> Was all she saw of men!"

He would get up, Barnes thought, and have a shower when she was finished. He wished he had clean underwear. Perhaps Madame Serpentina would not object if he washed what he had, and left them—undershirt, Jockey shorts—to dry on a towel bar. On the shower curtain rod. He would sleep in his pants and shirt. Would Stubb object if he pressed his pants under the mattress of the spare bed? No, he couldn't do that. Tomorrow—today—he would have to get his bag, his sample cases, from the lockers in the bus station. They were good for only twenty-four hours. They had taken almost the last of his money. Would Madame Serpentina allow him to store them here? Surely she would, even if he couldn't sleep here again. In the lobby, perhaps, for a time. If only she had gone naked to bed. He would have seen her, no matter how dark the room. He had seen more, much more, through the hole. It didn't matter now—the house was gone anyway—the black ball swinging. He would have to sell something to get more coins for the lockers. His watch, perhaps. No, that was gone, already gone. The ticket was in his wallet. Free's ticket? Could that have been what old Free meant? Was it in pawn, whatever he had possessed, the thing he had so obliquely spoken off? Or was it oblique, the knight hooking left, hooking right, the bishop sliding off to one side? Perhaps it only seemed so now, Free's treasure. Money or bonds, Stubb thought. Madame Serpentina thought it was a crown, though she hadn't said so. A treasure in a wall; a wall with a sign, Free had said. An unmistakable sign. The picture was in one sample case now, but the hole was no longer behind it. Would never, never be again. He slid aside the picture and reached through, drew forth a treasure . . . a what? A chest filled with gold and emeralds. Slithering from some childhood memory, an old cobra, white and blind, twined about them. Surely not that. That was not like Free at all, Free who had owned no turban, whose complexion had been, if anything, lighter than his own. And anyway such treasures are found under floors. This was in a wall. Did the others know? Candy, Madame Serpentina? Free had break-fasted with Candy, she said. Or Stubb, Stubb was much too clever to be safe, but he couldn't sell. He hadn't sold them on it, and he had wanted to so much. Perhaps because he was too clever, too clearly dangerous even for Candy who loved him.

No one, Barnes thought, has ever loved me. Possibly Little Ozzie would have if things had been different. I can sell, he thought, but in the end they find they've been sold a bill of goods, of bads. I'm never as good as they've been led to believe, never earned as much as they thought I would. Still I'll have it on my stone, he thought, if I can. "He Could Sell." If I were rich I'd have a gate so I could have a stone shield over it: *Meus Vendo*. Something like that—the ones who carved the shield would know. They'd have to.

"The Bosun's pipe, it felt like tripe,
    The Chaplain's it was good;
    The Cabin Boy's was just a toy,
    The Mate, he never could."

There was a grunt and a heaving splash—presumably Candy was rising from the tub.

I wonder if she's left me any hot water, Barnes thought, then remembered that he was in a hotel, with hot water enough for a thousand bathers. He wondered if she had left any dry towels. *Meus vendo, ego salum.* Lois had wanted a big house. He would show it to her sometime. "That's the gatekeeper's lodge, of course. We could follow the drive up to the main entrance, Lo, but the poplar walk is really nicer, and we might see some deer. That? Just a peacock, we've got quite a flock. Going to have one for Christmas dinner, just to thin them out."

The bathroom door opened, releasing a gush of steam and blinding light. The towels of the Consort were voluminous indeed, and Candy had contrived, though barely, to wrap herself in one. Wet, her always tousled hair hung in ragamuffin curls. Her immense legs, thick as pillars at the thigh, glowed pink above feet like boiled shrimps. Barnes sat up. "Finished?"

Candy shook her head. "I just want to borrow a pair of tweezers, if I can. I need to do my eyebrows."

The witch spoke from the bed. "I do not have them."

"Sure you do. Come on, give me a break. I'll give them back."

"I do not tolerate the touch of iron unless I must."

"Listen, I didn't want to say this, but I've seen your eyebrows. They look very nice."

"Shall I show you what I use?" the witch asked.

She threw back the bedclothes and stood up, all in one smooth motion. Her nightdress—if it was in fact a nightdress—was of an unrelieved black, not silk or nylon, Barnes decided, something rougher and less lustrous.

"Here. They are clam shells. What you call the razor clam."

"Clam shells?"

"You hold them like this. You see, while he lived, the clam made a perfect seal between the halves of his shell. If the finest hair comes between them, it is caught. Come, I will show you."

The bathroom door closed behind the two women, leaving the room in darkness again. Barnes put his hands under his head. Backed as it was with soft urethane, the carpet felt as soft as a mattress. Candy's voice came faintly through the door: "Ouch!" From the doorway where he lay listening for footsteps in the hall, Stubb said, "Well, you never can tell. Sisters under the skin. Who said that?"

"Kipling."

"He was right. You know, you don't come over as smart, Ozzie, but I think you really are. That stuff with the salesmen was pure genius. The sneezing powder too."

"I'm like Candy," Barnes said. "I want a chance to sleep on it."

"Sure."

The bathroom door opened and the witch came out. Her nightdress, or whatever it was, was slit up the side—Barnes saw a flash of skin against the dark fabric. She slipped back into bed.

"Stubb," Barnes asked, "how do you spell your name?"

"Ess, tee, ewe, bee, bee. Why do you want to know?"

"I just wondered. I never came across it before, and I write down a lot of names, taking orders and so on."

"There used to be an Eee on the end. We lost it someplace."

"Stubbe," Barnes said, pronouncing it *stew-bee*. "I think it means a room. Something like that."

"Stubb," Stubb told him. "Now it means me."

The witch announced, "I am going to sleep. The one who wakes me will be very sorry."

Stubb told her, "That's easy for you to say. You've got a bed."

"I have a knife also. Anyone who enters this bed will learn where it is."

"Sure."

No one else spoke. The imposing gate loomed at the end of a road that wound among mountains. *Ego Vendo*. The red car had right-hand drive and was as long as a bus.

Little Ozzie peeped out his window as the dark woods gave way, past the wall, to lawn and grounds. "Is there broken glass on top?"

His father nodded. "I don't like unexpected company to wake me up."

"Gosh!"

The big car tooled along the drive, rolling over some gleaming substance Barnes could not quite identify. Other drives branched to right and left, and eventually he took one. Lions roared, confined in big, gilded cages like birdcages.

"We let them roam at night," he told Little Ozzie. "Here." He took something from his pocket and hung it around Little Ozzie's neck on a silver chain. "This'll protect you if you go outside after dark. Don't run, though. Let them smell you."

"Gee!"

"When they get used to you, you can even ride on one. Would you like that?"

A million stories down, the doorman's whistle blew faintly. Who would want a cab at this time of night? Barnes lifted his wrist, but no scarlet numbers burned there. The last parties were leaving the bar where Candy had sung, the street-level bar, and all the other bars, all over the city. Glass clinked in the bathroom. Madame Serpentina's toiletries must be in there, he thought, and the fat girl's using them. Wonder if she minds.

"Here's the main bath for your suite. The copper door leads to the hot pool, the marble arch to the cold one. We tried just putting in temperature controls when we built this place, but it took too long to cool the water down or heat it up. Want to see the cold one first? Seals, polar bears, stuff like that? All tame."

"Gee, it sounds neat."

"It is neat."

Little Ozzie thought, his small face puckered with effort.

(That was good. He'd have to think when he took the helm at Barnes Industries, Inc.) "The hot one. I want to save the cold one. What's in the hot one?"

"Mermaids."

The bathroom door opened with another burst of light. "All through, Ozzie. You still want that shower? Hey, you asleep?"

Barnes sat up, rubbing his eyes. "Almost."

"I'm going to sleep over here. That all right with everybody? Jim, you said there was a spare blanket?"

"In the bottom drawer there," Stubb told her.

Barnes got to his feet. "Boy, my suit's going to look like hell tomorrow."

Stubb said, "I'll show you a place that'll press it while you wait for fifty cents."

"Do you wish a pillow?" the witch asked Candy. "They will not think there is more than one if both pillows are mussed—many sleep with two. I require only one."

"That's great. Just toss it."

A dim blob of white seemed to float across the room. Candy caught it as Barnes shut the bathroom door.

The bathroom was so brilliantly lit that it hurt his eyes, although the mirrors were blind with condensation. Using a wet washcloth for a glove, he unscrewed all but one of the bulbs. His trousers he hung on a towel bar; the steam would take out what remained of their creases, but it would take out the wrinkles too. He hung up his shirt and tie and threw undershirt, shorts, and socks into the tub, got in with them and washed them out with hand soap and trod them underfoot in the accumulating water until no more bubbles came, then hung them on the bars inside the shower doors.

With what remained of the little bar of yellow, scented soap, he scrubbed his whole body. He was a hairy man, and the hair was black and curly. Each time he looked at it, he felt glad he had no daughter; she would have gotten that from him, and she would (rightly, he felt) blame him for it. Little Ozzie's hair, though, was brown instead of black. Not very curly either, unless he got it wet plunging with the penguins and porpoises. But Little Ozzie was really his son. He remembered how he had looked as a boy, and there was something of that in Little Ozzie's face. Not that it wasn't likely Lois had played around. God knows she'd had a right to.

When the soap was gone, he made the water colder and colder until he was shivering as he watched the suds stream away. He stretched his arms as wide as he could in the shower, slapped himself, then did a little dance under the stinging spray. By the time he had turned off the water and stepped from the tub, most of the steam was gone from the mirrors. He had left his eye on the shelf over the bowl, and there was something of Popeye in his reflection, he thought. "I yam what I yam." As he dried himself, he paused to caress the stubble of his chin.

The eye would make his socket sore if he wore it all night, but he felt he could not leave it in the bathroom. He hung up his wet towel and wrapped himself in a dry one, the next-to-last dry one, he noticed, before he opened the door.

Candy was standing there wrapped in her blanket. "Have a nice shower, Ozzie? You finished now?"

"Yes, certainly." He slipped past her.

"I've just got to go. I won't be a minute. Jesus, it looks like a laundry in here."

As he had hoped, the room felt warm after his cold shower. He folded his suitcoat for a pillow, covered himself from the waist down with his topcoat, and moved the thick, dry bathtowel up to his chest. He felt very snug.

Chapter 20

BELLE AND WHISTLE

The telephone rang, and he glanced through the glass panel that separated him from the girl. She was out. Probably gone to the can, gone for coffee.

The telephone rang.

He reached for his extension, sleekly black. Through the glass he could see the gold letters on the other side of the pebbled door that opened into the hallway: Ess, Eee, El, Ay, Ess. Ess, Eee, En . . .

The telephone rang.

Barnes sat up in the gray dimness. His arms were cold and stiff, and he rubbed them. As if he were still dreaming (and for a moment, he believed he was) the bathroom door swung open, releasing a flood of light. A switch clicked and the light went out. The telephone rang again.

"Hello," Candy said. There was a pause. "Yes, it's me. . . . I'm staying with her. . . . Okay. It was real nice hearing from you, you know? We thought something might have happened to you." She hung up.

From the other end of the room, Stubb's voice asked, "What was that?"

"Never mind."

"You didn't tell somebody from the hotel you were staying with Madame S."

"Huh uh. It wasn't from the hotel."

"Who was it?" Stubb's voice was sharper now.

"I said never mind. It was for me, all right? I answered it. I got the message. It was my business."

The witch asked, "How would someone know that you were to be reached in my room?"

"I don't know. I didn't ask him, and he didn't tell me."

"It was a guy then."

"Jim, shut the hell up." Trailing a corner of blanket, the fat girl stepped over Barnes. There was a grunt and a thump as she lowered herself. "Dammit, I'm not made for sleeping on floors. I don't think I ever even *passed out* on a floor, for Christ's sake. I usually find a couch or something." A scuffing noise was followed by the flapping of the blanket.

No one else spoke. Barnes stared at the dim ceiling for a time, then allowed his eyes to close. The fat girl was near enough for him to hear faintly the sighing of her breath. He could even imagine the sensation of her body heat on the bare skin of his left arm. He was chilled, and she seemed to radiate warmth like a stove.

He tried to call back the great house in the mountains, but it was lost somehow, speeding away from the speeding car, always vanishing around the next turn in the road until they no longer saw it at all, were no longer sure it had even passed that way. Then something happened, somehow the car would no longer run, and Little Ozzie was wandering the windy mountain roads on foot, alone in the dark and looking for him.

Something touched his hand. Automatically, he drew it away; the touch came again, and after a moment he realized it was another hand, very soft, small and warm.

"Ozzie." It was the faintest of whispers.

"Yes," he said, glad to be taken away from the night-shrouded mountain roads where his son could not find him, where he could not even find himself.

"You awake?"

Outside, the doorman's whistle blew.

"Yes," he said again.

"Jim's asleep. I can hear him and I think she's asleep too."

Barnes did not reply. He had opened his eyes, but they had closed themselves again. He lay in the dark, listening to her as he might have listened to some night-calling bird, inno-cent of the need for any reply.

"I feel like a hog, keeping this whole blanket to myself. Are you cold, Ozzie?"

"Little."

"There's plenty for both of us. It's for a double bed."

There was a flapping as of wide wings, and the blanket settled over him. Her breasts nuzzled at his shoulders, and the soft, warm bulge of her belly lay against his side. Two arms that were like two pillows embraced him. He rolled over and kissed her.

Her lips were moist, soft and warm as every part of her seemed to be soft and warm. She did not bite, though he for some reason had feared she would; her tongue touched his, then drew away just before they parted. She nibbled gently at his lower lip, so that he had the illusion (taken perhaps, as such things often are, from some forgotten book he had been read as a child—or perhaps only borrowed from the blond girl who had once in better days brought him a drink in the Kansas City Playboy Club) that Candy was a very large white rabbit who had somehow been transformed into a woman. So that if someone had flicked on the lights, he would not have been surprised to find she had pink eyes and a wiggling pink nose; not a carrot-chewing, wisecracking Bugs Bunny, but something like one of Peter Rabbit's sisters, caged and fed on Caesar salads and grown huge. "Nothing tricky," she whispered. "Not to-night."

"All right," he said.

"Not that I mind usually, but it's late and I'm tired. Besides, it's like . . . you know."

"All right," he said again. He did not know. He kissed her again.

She laughed softly. "You've got a nice mustache. It looks like it's going to be bristly, but it's sort of silky. Anybody ever tell you?"

"No," he said. He tried to kiss her as he had before, but she had turned her head to one side, and it was her ear he kissed. He kissed his way down to her neck, thick, soft and warm, like all the rest of her.

"Stop," she said. "You'll make me laugh and that'll wake them up for sure."

He did not stop.

She pushed him gently away and reaching down took hold of him. "Do you like that?"

"Yes," he said. "I like that very much." He wanted to kiss her breasts, but he could not reach them. He stroked them instead.

"I have big ones, but nobody ever notices," she said.

"I noticed."

"Forty-six D's. How about this? Do you like this too?"

"Yes," he said. "I like that a lot."

"Only when I take off weight—when I used to—that's where it would come off first. It never would come off my hips. Nothing but surgery or a hydrogen bomb will ever take one ounce off my hips."

"I like your hips too."

"Not me. The movies won't let me in any more." She kissed his chest and shoulders.

He visualized a rude ticket-taker who barred her from some palace of dreams with a flaming sword.

"Those damned narrow seats. Don't pinch hard."

He kissed her again, pushing close, and she tucked the blanket around them.

"I used to love to go. You remind me of that one with the mustache—I can't think of his name."

"Peter Sellers. Richard Pryor."

"No." She giggled. "I can't think of it. He's handsomer, but you're handsome too."

"That's right."

"Can you reach? I'm sorry, but you can't lie on top. I don't like that any more."

"All right." He moved until their faces were no longer together, their bodies forming an X. Afterwards, he got up first and went into the bathroom to wash. Candy went in when he left, and he lay on the floor listening to her, hearing the toilet flush, then flush again.

He hoped she would lie down with him instead of asking

for the blanket back, and she did. "Everything okay?" she said. "Copacetic?"

He had been wondering if he had caught a disease, syph or maybe herpes. She's probably thinking maybe she's pregnant, he thought. No, she isn't. He said, "Not while you were gone. I missed you."

"Uh huh. You were cold."

"Right." He chuckled.

"Me too. My feet are cold from that damn cold floor in there. Can I put them against your legs?"

"Okay."

She lay with her back to him, the soles of her feet against his calves. He made sure they were covered by his topcoat, tucking it in, then pulled up the blanket. Old Mr. Free was standing there in the dark, ready to light the hot water heater for Candy's bath. Barnes thought: That's who called. She must have told him to come up.

"I'll be gone before sundown, so what do I care?" Free said. "You like women, don't you, Mr. Barnes?"

"Yes," Barnes admitted, "yes, I do."

"You're a bigger man on the inside than on the outside, Mr. Barnes."

"Thank you," Barnes said, "but I'd rather be bigger on the outside too."

"Don't be any bigger fool than you can help, Mr. Barnes. You said you wasn't widely respected. I said I respect you, and I do. Only you've got hold of a few things you don't understand hardly at all. Right now you're trying to figure out how you can ask me about that treasure—some way that will get me to tell you what I don't know myself about something you're not even close to understanding." Old Mr. Free pointed to the wall. There was a sign on it, a white sign of painted boards with black lettering that said something.

Barnes went to it and pushed it aside and looked through the hole in the wall behind it. It was Madame Serpentina's room, but Candy Garth sat there naked on Madame Serpentina's bed smoking one of Madame Serpentina's cigarettes.

After a moment Barnes saw that the rumpled sheets of the bed were not rumpled sheets at all, but heaps of rings and diamond bracelets. The key to the room lay on the dresser near the hole, beside Madame Serpentina's hairbrush, and he knew that if only he could seize it he could open the door and go in—although it would not be necessary for him to walk down the hall and turn the key in the lock, because the wall itself would melt away, the whole house be transformed. He thrust his arm through the hole, feeling a deep pleasure.

Outside, the doorman's whistle blew thinly and shrilly. He opened his eyes, uncertain for a moment where he was. Gray light shone through the drapes. The whistle blew again. Going to catch an early flight, Barnes thought. He remembered the year he had covered the whole East Coast for Continental Compactors, Inc. The whole damned East Coast. Boston to Miami by plane a couple of times. Philly to New York on the train, riding the ferry from Long Island to Connecticut.

Candy had rolled away, taking the blanket with her—that was surely for the best. One arm was thrust out from under his topcoat, and his feet were cold. The towel lay in a crumpled heap to one side. He stood up, wrapping the towel around him. Candy looked like a bear lying there in her brown blanket, her back to him. The bed that could not be mussed was still unmussed, pristine. The witch slept like an actress in a movie, her profile, almost but not quite too strong to be lovely, outlined against the white sheet, her enormous eyes closed in sleep. Stubb lay on his back, his mouth open, his face strange without its glasses.

Barnes went into the bathroom and switched on the lights. His cheeks were blue with stubble; he rubbed it with both hands, wishing that he, or someone, had a razor; there was none in the litter of cosmetics the two women had spread over the basin table. He examined himself again, combing back his hair as well as he could with his fingers. "Oh, I'm strong at the finish/'cause I likes me spinach. . . ." His eye was in the pocket of his topcoat. He wondered if Candy had realized it was missing. She's probably wondering if I noticed how fat she is, he thought, if she's still awake.

He laughed softly to himself.

His underwear was dry; he put it on. His shirt was still a little damp at the collar, but he put that on too. All the crease was out of his trousers, but otherwise they didn't look too bad. Perhaps when evening came he would still be here, and perhaps Stubb and Candy would be gone. He would press them under the mattress then.

He made sure his empty wallet was still in the pocket, put on his trousers, switched off the light, and left. The other three were asleep. He put on his tie, his somewhat rumpled suitcoat, and his eye. For a moment he was afraid Stubb was going to wake up when he stepped out into the hall, but he never stirred.

Three doors down, that was what the bellboy had said. The latch was taped back. The room might be rented by now, but if it were, it would be locked. If anyone came to the door, he could pretend he had come to the wrong one. Or try to sell them something—they would get rid of him fast enough. He pushed gently against the door, and it swung back.

Chapter 21

STAKEOUT

The room was quiet and dark. Barnes stepped inside and closed the door silently behind him, then stood listening. Over the sighing of the vent in the wall came the heavy breathing of sleep.

Most of the bed was concealed by the jutting enclosure of

closet and bathroom, but as his eyes grew accustomed to the dimness he saw a foot—black shoe, white sock, dark trousers cuff above—that extended beyond it. He walked forward softly.

Sergeant Proudy lay on the bed fully dressed, his head still swathed in bandages. A notebook and a pencil, a small camera, and a revolver were neatly arranged on the bedside table by the telephone. For a moment, Barnes wondered if he should not empty the revolver—it seemed to be the sort of thing they did on TV—then decided not to. It was probably against the law, and he did not know how to open the mechanism anyway.

A black attache case stood open on the desk, and an electric razor nestled there among a clutter of other objects. Barnes reached for it, drew back his hand, then imagined himself making calls with a day's growth of beard. The temptation was too great; he carried the razor into the bathroom and locked the door.

Proudy's knuckles slammed against it as he was finishing up his right cheek. "Just a minute," Barnes called. "I'm almost through." A fusillade of violent rapping startled him. "Please, Sergeant, it's early. You'll wake up the guests, and they'll complain. I'll be out in a minute."

"You better be. Who are you? What the hell is that noise?"

"Just a minute."

"I'll shoot through the door!"

There had been no hint of humor in the policeman's voice. Barnes said, "It's only your electric razor. I thought I'd shave while you were sleeping. I'll be out in a minute."

"You got a gun?"

"I'm not armed," Barnes said. "You can't even trim your corns with an electric razor."

"You'd better not be. I'm going to frisk you when you come out. You can forget about wrapping it in plastic and dropping it in the toilet tank, too. I'm on to that."

Barnes looked. "This toilet doesn't have one."

"Don't get smart with me."

There was a silicone-impregnated strip of paper for shining shoes. Barnes put one foot on the basin, then the other.

"Come out!"

Something in the policeman's tone gave Barnes the impression that the revolver he had seen was pointed at the bathroom door. Under his breath he said, "Everything is bathroom doors lately," and opened the door, still muttering. It was a shock to see he had been correct.

"What'd you say?"

" 'Well, blow me down.' It's just an expression."

"I'll blow you away if you stay cute. You know who I am?"

"Of course," Barnes said. "I let you in yesterday."

"That's right. That's exactly right. You know who I am and where I am, and why I'm here. Ain't that right?"

Barnes shook his head. "How about putting away the gun, Sergeant? I'm not going to do anything."

"I'll say you're not. Turn around and put your hands against that wall. Lean on 'em. I'm going to shake you down, and if you so much as wiggle your ass I'll blow you in two."

Barnes did as he was told and felt the rapid patting of the policeman's hands—inside thighs, outside thighs, under arms. His order book was deftly extracted from the breast pocket of his suit coat. He heard the pages riffled, then the slap as the book was tossed on the bed.

"Okay, turn around."

He turned as instructed. "I just wanted to talk to you for a minute. Put away your gun and let's sit down."

"You said you had an electric razor. Where is it?"

"I left it in the bathroom."

"Switch those lights on again and point to it. All right, go over to it slow." Sergeant Proudy followed him into the bathroom, the muzzle of his revolver jammed against Barnes's spine. "Unplug it and drop it in the crapper." Barnes started to protest, and the revolver made an ominous click. "You do what I tell you. Do it *now*."

The razor sank with a soft splash, trailing a column of tiny bubbles. Barnes left the wire hanging out of the bowl. "Is that all right? If it is, how about putting your gun away? You've seen I haven't got one. I'd like to sit down and talk."

The revolver no longer jabbed his spine, and he heard the shuffle of the policeman's feet as he backed out of the bathroom. "You'd like to jump me. That's what you'd like to do."

"I could have jumped you while you were asleep," Barnes protested.

"Yeah, but you didn't. Lost your nerve. *You* sit down; sit on the bed."

Barnes seated himself gingerly, wondering what the maid would say, how she would report it to the management when she found the bed of an unoccupied room so rumpled and creased.

"I'm putting my gun back in this shoulder rig," Proudy announced. "You see it? I can get it a hell of a lot quicker than you can get your hanky, and I'm hoping, yeah, *hoping* you'll try something. Because you're going to be dead before you ever get your ass off that mattress."

"I won't try anything," Barnes said.

"God damn you, you'd better not."

"I just came here to talk to you. You're watching Madame Serpentina and Stubb and—ah—the rest of us? Isn't that true?"

"You've got this all wrong, bud. I don't answer questions. I ask them."

"All I want," Barnes said carefully, "is a little advice. You see, Sergeant, I've been offered a business proposition— by Stubb and Madame Serpentina specifically—and it occurred to me that if they were suspected of something, maybe I ought to find out about it before I give them my decision."

"What you're telling me is you're not working with them already."

"I'm not. We're friends, that's all."

Sergeant Proudy had begun to pace the room. Barnes watched him, trying to recall him as he had been the day before, when he knocked at the door. A harsh band of daylight had penetrated the drapes; when Proudy entered it, he seemed haggard, as though he were a creature of the night who lost all life and color there, as sea creatures do, taken from the water.

"I know about you," Proudy said after he had paced the room a dozen times. "You don't think I do, but I do. You don't think anyone knows, do you. Well, I do. I'm the only son of a bitch that does, but I know more about you than you do about yourselves."

"Then maybe you'll give me your advice."

"Me give you advice? Oh, no, not me." Proudy turned a humorless smile toward him. "What could I say? Quit? Your boss won't allow you to quit. I know that, and you know it too. Confess and bargain with the Prosecutor's Office for police protection? They wouldn't believe you any more than they would me. Kill yourself? That wouldn't work either, now would it?"

"I guess not," Barnes said.

"So you see, there's nothing I can tell you to do." Proudy drew his revolver again, spun the cylinder so that it made a sharp clicking, then thrust it back into his holster. "We'll fight it out, you people and me. I got a hand tied behind me: I got to work inside the law, or pretty much. You can do as you damn please. There's four of you with God knows how many millions or billions behind you, and only one of me." He thumped his chest. "That's okay too."

Barnes said, "I believe you should sit down, Sergeant. You look tired." A thought struck him. "Maybe we could go down to the coffee shop and have breakfast. Talk this over."

"To hell with you!" Proudy stopped suddenly, grinning. "Say, that's pretty good, ain't that right? 'To hell with you.'"

"I'll say. It certainly is." Fumbling at his shirt pocket, Barnes found a crushed pack of Winstons. It held only a few crumbs of tobacco. He wadded it into a ball and tossed it at the wastebasket.

"You out? Here, have one of mine. That's the way they do, ain't that right? You want a blindfold too?"

"Thanks," Barnes said. "I've been trying to quit, but thanks."

"Least I can do."

Barnes reached into his coat pocket and saw Proudy freeze. For an instant he froze himself. When Proudy spoke, he sounded as if he were choking. "What is that? Beretta twenty-two?"

"Get them up and keep them up," Barnes said, astonishing himself. "And shut up."

Clumsily, nearly dropping it, he grasped the butt of Proudy's revolver with his left hand and jerked it out of the shoulder holster. "Get in the bathroom. You can shut the door and lock it, then we'll both feel safer."

The door closed and the lock clicked. Barnes let out a great *whoosh* of breath and pulled the trigger of the little silver pistol. A small blue flame appeared at the end of its barrel. He lit the cigarette Proudy had given him and sucked in smoke.

"I got a gun too now," Proudy called through the door. "I had a backup, a derringer strapped to my ankle. You didn't think of that, did you, you smart bastard?"

"You'll be a sitting duck coming out of there," Barnes told him. He dropped the cigarette lighter back into his pocket and transferred Proudy's snubnose to his right hand. Would it shoot if he just pulled the trigger? He could not be sure.

"I'm not coming out. Just don't you come in."

Barnes said, "I'll come in when I'm good an' ready, ya swab."

There was a muted clumping sound, and he imagined Proudy climbing into the tub, hiding himself behind the shower doors. He wondered if Proudy really had another gun.

A trick sliding chart under the telephone gave emergency numbers as well as those for the hotel gift shop, valet service, and so on: Doctor, Hospital, Police, Fire. After a moment's thought, Barnes pushed the number for Hospital.

"Holly Angels," the operator said enigmatically.

"Listen . . ." Barnes discovered he did not know where to begin. "A friend of mine got hit on the head. He's acting funny now. You know what I mean?"

"*Ya want Belmont,*" the Holly Angels operator told him. "*Belmont's psycho. I kin connect ya.*" There was a click and a buzz.

"*Belmont Hospital.*"

As quickly as he could, Barnes said, "Listen there's a maniac in Room Seven Seventy-One of the Consort he's got a gun and if you don't do something he's goingtokill-somebody."

He slammed down the phone and gasped for breath. Would they come? When you called people, they didn't, not always. Sometimes not even the Fire Department came, he had heard. One of his customers had told him once that sometimes she could not even get salesmen to come, and he knew that not all the salesmen he had called to Free's had come. He toyed with the idea of telling Proudy again that he would shoot him if he came out, but that might only make Proudy come out sooner.

The notebook by the telephone showed half a page of scribbled comments: ". . . after going in. Kidnap? Dead? How disp bdy? Cart? Later maybe. Still there, 2:50. Listened at door. Sleeping and talking. Rtnd stkt cald # grl. Ans dvc. Sd where you? Call when come in."

Barnes closed the notebook, picked up his order book, and dropped both into his pocket. As he left the room, he toyed with the idea of taking the tape from the door, but that would not, of course, keep Proudy in, only delay the men from the hospital, if men from the hospital ever came. For an instant he visualized thorny-winged green beings in robes of red, one carrying a net, the other a straitjacket. No, Belmont. Madmen, then. Belmont was psycho. Better get away before they came.

A siren howled outside, and he realized with a start that he was still holding Proudy's revolver. He looked up and down the corridor to make sure no one had seen him and thrust it into the waistband of his trousers. As he was buttoning his coat, a bellman pushing a serving cart emerged from the nearest elevator.

"*How disp bdy? Cart?*" That was what Proudy had been

worried about, the waiter last night. Stubb had told the waiter to go the other way to reach the elevators, and he had done it. Proudy thought he was dead in seven seventy-seven. *"Grl"* must mean Sandy Duck, who had talked to him on her way out. She hadn't come home then, or had come home late, or just had not taken her phone off the answering machine while she slept.

The cart held an assortment of covered dishes, two carafes of coffee, silver, and a stack of cups and saucers. Barnes watched the bellman push it into the witch's room and waited until he left, then went in himself. "Ahoy!" he said.

Chapter 22

PARTNERSHIP

"Where the hell have *you* been?" Stubb came half out of his chair.

"Down the hall talking to Sergeant Proudy," Barnes told him. "You're a detective, you must know something about guns."

Candy's now-scarlet mouth formed a little *O* at the mention of guns; the witch, who had smiled slightly when Barnes entered, continued to smile.

"Yeah," Stubb said. "Yeah, I know something. I'm no crack shot, my eyes aren't that good. But I know one end from the other."

"That's great." Barnes pulled Proudy's revolver from his waistband and laid it on the table. "You take this. I don't want it, and I'm liable to shoot myself with it."

Stubb stared at the gun for a moment, then picked it up with a napkin. The cylinder popped open, and when Stubb pushed the cylinder pin six bright brass cartridges rattled onto the table. He flipped his wrist, but the cylinder would not snap back into place, and he had to push it back with his left hand. After wiping and wrapping the entire gun, he lifted the mattress of the unused bed and pushed the gun far under it. He carried the cartridges into the bathroom and flushed the toilet.

"They go down?" Barnes called. He did not think they would.

"Yeah, probably no farther than the trap, though."

Candy said, "It'll plug up now." She sounded bitter.

Stubb stepped back into the room. "I doubt it. A sewer line like that's pretty big."

"He knows everything, Jim does. I haven't found one single, solitary, God-damned thing he doesn't know more about than any other dude on earth."

"All right, it'll plug up. Madame S. can ask for another room."

The witch said, "We have been negotiating, Ozzie. We wish to forge an alliance." She sounded amused.

Stubb asked, "How'd you get it away from him, anyhow? Take it while he was asleep?"

Candy passed Barnes a cup of coffee. "Don't tell the bastard, Ozzie. If we're partners, we're partners. If we're not, we're not."

"I thought we were going to be partners," Barnes said.

"Partners means share and share alike. Jim wants to give us a lousy ten percent. That for both of us, Jim? Five percent each?"

Stubb said, "Our last offer was fifteen. Fifteen for each of you."

"Bullshit!" Candy heaved to her feet. "I'm splitting. Thanks for the coffee, lady. Sorry I've messed up the eggs, but somebody can still eat them—I'm not poison. Thank you so very much for letting me sleep on your floor. It was comfy."

Stubb said, "For God's sake, sit down. Nobody wants your eggs. You might as well finish them."

"No, what nobody wants is me." Candy looked for her

white raincoat and found it in a corner. She picked it up,
keeping her legs straight and grunting at the compression of
her belly.

"I want you." Barnes stood up too. "If you go, I go."

Candy straightened, her face pink. "Thanks, Ozzie.
You're a decent guy. I go. Come on."

"Damn it," Stubb said, "we want you too. Twenty-five
percent."

Candy stared at him. "Ozzie and me each get twenty-five."

The witch said, "You have not consulted me, Mr. Stubb."

"I don't have to. You agreed we'd give them fifteen. That
was thirty for them and thirty-five each for us. I'm giving
them another ten each out of my share. You have thirty-five;
they have twenty-five apiece; I have fifteen."

"No way," Candy said.

There was a knock at the door.

For a moment they were silent, looking at one another.
Stubb asked, "Proudy?"

Barnes lifted his shoulders. "Maybe." The witch called,
"Who is there?"

"*Maid*."

Barnes opened the door. A middle-aged woman waited
there with a dust cloth in her hand; behind her was a laundry
cart full of crumpled sheets. "You still eatin'?" she asked. "I
can come back."

Stubb rose. "We're about through, except for Ozzie. We
didn't know you'd be back, Ozzie, so we didn't order for
you."

Candy told him, "I haven't finished my eggs."

"It'll only take you a minute. I suggest we adjourn to the
coffee shop. Ozzie can get a bite there, and this lady'll have a
chance to clean."

The maid said, "It won't take long. Just make the bed and
vacuum and straighten around a little."

The witch told her, "I'm afraid you will find the bath
rather untidy. I indulged myself in an orgy of towels."

In the corridor, Barnes said, "It might be better to go the
other way." Stubb nodded, and they trooped behind him.

"What does he want?" Stubb asked when they had reached the elevators.

"I don't know."

"He thinks we're up to something, huh?"

Barnes tried to remember everything that had been said in the vacant room. The coffee and cigarette had whetted his appetite, so that as he stepped through the doors his mind vacillated between Proudy and waffles. "He thinks we're part of some vast, evil conspiracy, I believe," he said at last. "Just one cell, but an important one."

Candy said, "You're putting us on."

"No." As they dropped past Six, Five, and Four, he showed them how he had taken Proudy's gun. "That wouldn't have worked with you," he told Stubb. "And I don't think it would have with Proudy, yesterday. Actually, it wasn't a question of its working; I just got it out to light my cigarette. It's a sample novelty. I can take orders for them."

"Yeah. Let me see it." As the elevator inched to a stop, Stubb pulled the trigger and inspected the blue flame. "Doesn't look much like a real gun. Especially at the end of the barrel."

Candy called, "Come on!" She was already at the door of the Quaint. "They're just opening up, but they'll serve us."

"How wonderful," the witch replied. She was looking around; and though her dark, handsome face was as expressionless as ever, she might have been sightseeing in the tunnel of some monstrous beetle.

The Quaint was furnished in a style called (in the catalogue of the firm that had supplied its decor) Middle Colonial Double Dutch. Its tables were of thick and irregular planks reproduced in Formica. Its false windows, lit from behind by electric bulbs, were furnished with inutile shutters pierced with hearts and tulips. Its walls boasted hex signs and polystyrene reproductions of long clay pipes.

"We want a booth," Candy insisted. "A big one—we're expecting two more people." When the hostess, who wore a Dutch bonnet, a Dutch frock, and vinyl wooden shoes, had led them to one, Candy said, "You get in first, Ozzie. I'd rather not have to slide over."

Stubb said, "Still mad?"

"No, not a bit. But you two are on one side and we're on the other."

Barnes asked, "Who else are we expecting?"

The fat girl giggled. "Only me. I always say that."

A waitress appeared. The witch ordered orange juice, Stubb coffee, and Candy corned beef hash with a fried egg. Barnes asked for a cream waffle with sausage. "It's very nice of you," he told the witch, "to pay for my breakfast. If it weren't for you, I wouldn't have gotten one."

She shrugged. "This vile hotel pays. I shall charge everything to my room."

"But if we find Mr. Free's treasure . . ."

"Yes, *if*. None of you, not even Mr. Stubb, will devote himself as I. I will seek ceaselessly, for the rest of my life if necessary. Nevertheless, I know how unlikely it is that I shall succeed."

"I'm more of an optimist," Stubb told her.

"I know you are. So are most, and that is why they prefer roseate dreams to the great, hidden truths."

"We'll see who hangs in longest." Stubb looked across the table at Barnes and Candy. "Have we got this partnership settled?"

The witch said, "Nothing is settled, Mr. Stubb."

"What the hell does that mean? Those were my shares. Don't I have a right to give them to these two if I want?"

"No. The thing has become preposterous. I do not understand why you wish to have these people involved with us, and I do not believe they will be of the least use. But if we are to have them, let us by all means arrange it as the fat woman originally suggested: on equal shares."

Candy said, "No offense taken, but I've got a name. I'd appreciate it if you called me by it."

"As you wish."

"Equal shares it is." Stubb grinned. "That's decent of you, Madame S."

"I have two provisos, however. No other partners are to be taken in. Nor are our shares to be redivided among ourselves. Each will claim one quarter."

"All right with me," Stubb told her.

"Very well; now we must see that there is something to claim. Miss Garth, I know that Mr. Stubb wishes to question you about all that passed between Mr. Free and yourselves. Before he begins, however, I have one or two questions I will ask.

"Last night the telephone rang, and you answered. You spoke in such as way as to suggest that it was Mr. Free who called. Specifically, you said: 'Hello. Yes, it is me. I am staying with her. Okay. It was real nice hearing from you again, you know? We thought something might have happened to you.' I assume that the 'her' with whom you said you were staying was myself. Who was the caller?"

"You've got a really wonderful memory," Candy said.

"I could imitate your voice as well, should the occasion arise. But that is neither here nor there. You have refused to answer my questions regarding the caller on the grounds that we had not agreed on a partnership, and thus you felt entitled to keep for yourself whatever information you possessed— this despite the fact that the instrument was in my room, and thus the call was presumably for me. Now we have come to an agreement; specifically, to precisely the agreement you demanded. Your grounds avail you no longer, and should you find new ones, I shall consider our agreement voided at once—not by my action but by your own. Who was the caller?"

"If your memory's that good, you ought to remember I said it was for me."

"I do. I did not believe you then, nor do I believe you now. Who was the caller?"

Candy grinned. "A guy who works here in the hotel. His name's Joe. Last night a bellhop tried to take us to see him, then Ozzie hooked onto that girl from the magazine, and Jim called again, and we never did see Joe. That's why I said we were afraid something had happened—Ozzie and me had

waited around, and he never showed. On the phone he asked
for you, then he recognized my voice and said was I the one
that had been singing in the club. That's why I said yes, it
was me."

The witch pursed her lips. "Go on."

"So he wanted to know what I was doing in your room, and
I said I was staying with you." Candy looked apologetically at
Stubb. "It just slipped out, Jim. I don't think he'll rat on us,
because he sounded so damn glad he didn't have to talk to
her. He asked me to tell her—that's why I said it was for me."

"Tell me what?"

"That there was some trouble about the money he owes
you, but he was trying to raise it, and he'd pay you tomorrow
night—that would be tonight now—for sure."

"And you said you would?"

"Yeah. That was when I said okay. And don't tell me I
didn't do it, because I just did."

"Very well. A second question, and I will be finished. A
blanket is hardly sufficient to cover you, and last night I
observed you to rise and take a fur from your little bag. When
you were asleep, I rose also and examined it. It is very soft
and rich, and much, much larger than the pelt of a single
mink."

Barnes interrupted. "I saw it on her bed at Free's!"

"This I have confirmation, though I did not require it. I
was about to say that though it is so large, it is the skin of a
single animal; the tail has been cut away, but one sees where
the legs were. Mr. Free gave that to you, I should guess, and
thus we know why you returned to his house when the police
released you. Am I correct?"

Candy nodded. "It filled up my AWOL bag, almost, but I
didn't want to leave it."

"Nor would I. Did Mr. Free tell you what it was?"

Candy shook her head. "He just went downstairs and
came back with it. He said here keep this, I want you to have
it, and I said it was pretty, and he said valuable too, you hang
onto it. That's everything, honest."

"I believe I know what it is," the witch said. "It is the pelt of a beaver. Yet I cannot guess what it means, or where he got such a thing. Can anyone?"

No one spoke; as the waitress brought their orders, Stubb rapped his glass with a spoon. "Maybe we're going to find out. I want to hear about Free from both of you. Not just the skin, everything you saw or heard. After that, I'll have assignments for everybody."

Chapter 23

VENDO

Outside, the morning sun shone as though winter had never come. The snow, already churned to gray sludge along the middle of the sidewalk, had frozen hard in the night, but at the edges of this beaten track a white margin pure as the plastic flakes lingering in the corners of the department-store windows remained to reflect the sunshine and blue the shadow of each passerby.

Hurrying along, stumbling and slipping sometimes in the frozen gullies, tripping and sliding on the icy ridges, Barnes yearned for good boots and thick stockings, for a sweater too, and gloves. He was cold—nearly frozen, he told himself— despite his threadbare topcoat and his hat. Hocking the coat was out of the question until better weather arrived. After a big breakfast and innumerable cups of coffee, he was not hungry, but the need for money was like a hunger in him; he longed for it as a prisoner in some Siberian camp might long for bread.

As he walked, he watched the sidewalk and the gutter. In his mind's eye, he could see plainly a bill lying in the snow where it had been dropped by someone paying off a cab, a coin trodden underfoot like a pebble. He watched the people who hurried past as well; it seemed possible—indeed, it seemed likely—that one of them would require some sudden service. He saw himself snatching a child from beneath the wheels of a truck for a fortune, collaring a runaway dog for a dollar.

His fingers toyed with the three locker keys in his pocket, but he did not go directly to the bus station. The branch post office that had served Free's house while that house yet stood was only a block out of the way; he waited patiently in line there to reach a window. "You were supposed to hold my mail," he told the bearded young clerk. "The house was torn down." He gave the address.

The clerk vanished somewhere in the back of the post office. Barnes could feel the accusing eyes of the people behind him on the nape of his neck. *I only came to buy stamps*, the eyes of a thin woman there whined, *it would only take a second*. The eyes of a portly man in a five-hundred dollar suit said: *My affairs are urgent. Very urgent.* Barnes rubbed the back of his neck and pretended not to hear the eyes.

"Nothing," the bearded clerk said, returning. "When was your last delivery?"

"Day before yesterday."

"Well, there was nothing yesterday, then. You got a new address?"

"Not yet," Barnes said. "Just hold anything that comes for me."

There were stamp machines in the lobby of the post office. He felt in the coin return of each, hoping for an overlooked dime or quarter.

That gave him an idea. Outside, he stopped at each curbside phone booth he passed. Sometimes, because he thought people were looking at him, he pretended to make calls, dropping imaginary money into the slot and groping in the cold metal receptacle as though the call had not gone through, as though he had failed to reach his party, as indeed he had.

*   *   *

The Greyhound station was a gem set in a coronet of cheap restaurants. It blazed with light and seemed designed for thousands of surging people, vivacious and gaily dressed, not for the thin, exhausted woman who slept with her exhausted infant on her lap (both worn out with weeping) or the red-headed sailor who had contrived with drunken ingenuity to sprawl across parts of several benches, or for Osgood M. Barnes with his creaseless trousers and thin-soled, frozen shoes.

There were two sample cases, and he had put them in two lockers because one would not hold them both. The lockers would be good now until evening, though he might, perhaps, carry everything to the Consort and smuggle them up to seven seventy-seven. For a moment he considered it, but he did not feel certain there would be anyone there to let him in. Candy would certainly be gone. It seemed likely that Stubb would be as well. Madame Serpentina might be there, but she might not. He tried to recall which case he had put in which locker, then realized he was no longer sure even of which of the three held his personal effects. In the end he chose a key at random, and when he swung back the locker door, he saw with pleasure the rectangular black bulk of a sample case. Thanks to his breakfast, it seemed a trifle lighter than it had the night before.

He had never called upon the restaurants around the bus station. The chain fast-food outlets would be out of the question, but some of the diners might sell a few novelties, cards behind the counter, possibly a display on the cigar case. The only question was where to start. He glanced about at the exits, and in the process noticed a wizened man rolling up the grills that had protected his magazine stand. In half a minute Barnes was there, his sample case open beside the cash register

"Now here's a nice item—dog collars that glow in the dark. Say you've got a black dog, like one of those toy poodles, for instance. When he goes out at night, you can't see the little devil. Put one of these on him and you can spot him right away. Twenty-two fifty for the card; when you sell the last collar—at the price printed right on the card—you've made forty-five bucks."

"No," the wizened man said.

"Okay, here's another one. This can't miss; they sell like hotcakes every place we get them in. I've had customers call me begging me to get them more. It's a rose, see? Just an ordinary plastic rose like you might wear in your buttonhole if you were dressed up. Just twist the stem, the petals open, and there's a lovely, naked centerfold inside. Of course, if the customer wants to, he can take that out and put in any picture he wants. He can put in his girl's picture and give it to her. Card of six costs you five ninety-nine, and you sell them for a buck ninety-eight each—a real high-profit item."

"No."

"Okay, look at this. In your location it can't miss. You get lots of mothers through here with their kids, right? Sometimes they got two or three kids, right? They're going to be on the bus three or four hours, and the mother's going to go crazy. The mother can buy *Redbook* from you, but what are the kids going to do—read *Newsweek*? On this card here you get no less than twenty-five puzzles, for kids, for grown-ups, for anybody. You get the Pigs in Clover Puzzle, the five linked rings we call the Olympic Puzzle, you get the take-apart Three-D Jigsaw Puzzle."

The wizened man leaned forward. "I used to have that one with the twisted nails when I was a kid."

"So why not order a card? You can keep the nails for old times' sake, and you'll still stand to make over six bucks clear when you sell the last puzzle."

Breath of mingled bourbon and pizza touched Barnes's face. "Say, can I look at them?"

Barnes glanced around; it was the sailor. "Certainly, sir. There's hours of amusement in every one."

The puzzles were hung on tabs punched from the cardboard. After blinking and poking several with a long finger, the sailor selected a pencil with a cord through a hole near the eraser. "How does this work?"

The buttons of the sailor's pea jacket were all unfastened.

Barnes pulled at the uppermost buttonhole and thrust the pencil through it, then pulled the cord tight.

The sailor pushed the pencil back through the buttonhole, but the cord was too short for him to take it out entirely. "Hey," he said, "that's great. How much?"

"Like it says on the card, just seventy-nine cents."

The sailor produced a wallet.

"This is my sample card, and I don't usually sell from it, but in your case I'll make an exception. I can get another card from the factory. Want me to take that off for you?"

"Hell no." The sailor covered the puzzle with one hand. "I'm gonna do it myself." He pulled out a crumpled dollar. "Got change?"

Barnes plucked it from his hand. "No, but I'm sure this gentleman does." He handed the dollar to the wizened man. "Do you have change, sir? Seventy-nine cents for me, twenty-one for this serviceman here."

"I'm Phil Reeder," the sailor said, extending his hand.

"Ozzie Barnes," Barnes said, shaking it.

"I'm from the *John Bozeman*," the sailor told him. "She's a destroyer. Docked at Norfolk now. I got two weeks shore leave."

"Congratulations," Barnes said. The wizened man handed him change; Barnes gave the sailor two dimes and a penny and dropped the rest into his pocket. Something that had been coiled tightly inside him seemed to relax slightly.

"Say, what's that one?"

"This?" It was hard to tell just where Reeder was looking.

"No. Over there."

"Oh, that? We call it the Houdini Puzzle." Barnes pulled it free of its cardboard tab. "See, the little man is Houdini, and he's locked in a cell. The trick is to get him out." He took one of the toy figure's hands and pulled; the toy figure wedged between the bars. "Wait a minute. It can be done." He loosened the figure and twisted it; a tiny bar caught it between the legs.

"Ouch!" Reeder said. He laughed.

"I'll say. Well, it can be done. I guess I'm out of practice."

"I want that one too." Reeder got out his wallet again.

The wizened man glanced at the card. "Eighty-nine cents."

"Hey, the last one was only seventy-nine."

"They got all different prices," the wizened man said. "That last one was only a pencil with a string through it." He looked at Barnes for confirmation.

"You haven't bought it yet," Barnes reminded him.

Reeder thought Barnes was talking to him. "I know. You got change for a five?"

"Sure," the wizened man said. He rang up eighty-nine on the register and gave Reeder four dollars and a nickel. "Six cents tax," he explained.

Barnes was making mental calculations. "The board's usually eleven forty-five," he said.

"So take off seventy-nine and eighty-nine for the ones that's sold. Should be about nine fifty." The wizened man turned aside to wait on a woman buying *Cosmopolitan*.

"You've already got the eighty-nine. Take off the seventy-nine and it comes to eleven thirty."

"The hell it does."

"With tax."

"What the hell do you mean, tax? This ain't no retail sale, I'm buying them to sell again."

Barnes said mildly, "You're not giving me an order, you're buying my sample."

"I still don't pay no tax. You don't collect sales tax."

Without looking up from the Houdini Puzzle, Reeder said, "You got tax from me."

"Okay," Barnes told the wizened man. "I'll knock off the tax for a quick sale. Ten sixty-five, cash."

"Deal." The wizened man rang No Sale on his register and gave Barnes the money.

Barnes stood the card of puzzles on some magazines. "Now here's another beauty for a man in your business. It's a hundred funny bookmarks, all different."

"Nothing else," the wizened man said. "I only got so much room for this kinda stuff."

"I haven't even showed you my best—"

"No more."

"Okay. When you see how the puzzles go, you'll want something else. I'll see you again in a couple of weeks."

"Not if I see you first," the wizened man said; but it was routine bellicosity, without malice.

Reeder asked, "You know where we can get a drink around here, mate? I want to buy you a drink."

"Not this early." Barnes glanced at his wrist before he recalled that his watch was gone. "If you want to buy me something, how about a sandwich? There's a place that looks good right outside the station."

As they stepped outside, a bus turned a corner two blocks up, maneuvering as ponderously as a warship.

Chapter 24

CANDY & SWEET

Candy did not leave the hotel at once. It was cold outside and warm inside, and she was conscious that her white raincoat was unlined, and that her feet, in the black rubber boots the police had given her, were without stockings. She had been arrested many times and did not greatly object to jail; she toyed with the notion of soliciting here, in a part of the city where soliciting was permitted only after midnight and with the greatest discretion. Without money to pay her fine, she might easily be held until the worst of winter was past. In the end she decided against it out of loyalty to Stubb; but when she had decided, she found herself thinking seriously of Free's treasure and "High Country."

A lobby shop selling costly women's wear had already

opened its doors. Candy browsed for three-quarters of an hour, though the woman who ran the shop was nervous about her; because she had no rings, Candy decided. She explained, when she was able to begin a conversation, that her engagement-and-wedding set was too tight since she had put on so much weight, and she had left them upstairs in her room.

The woman was nervous anyway. Candy tried on several dresses and a pants suit she liked very much. She would have suggested that she wear the pants suit while she went up for her credit cards, but she did not think it would work.

The lobby was crowded when she stepped into it again, and there was a long line of businessmen at the cashier's counter. A few were traveling together and talked about restaurants and flights; most did not talk at all. Candy found a comfortable chair and sat down to watch.

A hotel dick crossed the lobby. He was dressed like a businessman, but she knew who he was by his expression and the way he walked. He did not seem to notice her. Hookers, she thought, aren't supposed to be up this early, and besides, there's no business now. She was not sure if she had met this particular dick or not. She was usually pretty tippy when she met hotel dicks.

A bellman came out of one of the elevators towing a baggage cart loaded with suitcases, some dark brown, some baby blue. A businessman and his fat wife followed the cart. The businessman got into the line at the cashier's counter, and his wife wandered off toward the hotel shops. The bellman pushed his cart through the entrance doors. When they opened, they showed cabs pulling away for the airport.

Candy went out, standing aside to let the bellman's cart back through the door. It was cold and sunny. Eight or ten businessmen stood near the curb, their collars turned up against the wind. A doorman, resplendent in scarlet and gold braid, shrilled his whistle. Cabs arrived by twos and threes, always empty. The part of the sidewalk farthest from the curb, beside the Consort's stone flower box and plastic plants, was lined with luggage—tan, brown, blue, red, yellow, and black.

Candy turned her coat collar up in imitation of the men. "Whoever said fat people don't get cold?"

Several of the businessmen grinned at her.

Almost in the street, a businessman in a homburg was helping the doorman wave forward a cab. The next in line looked about fifty, sleekly shaven and prosperous. The three men behind him were obviously together.

Candy smiled at him. "I've got this early, early flight. Would you mind splitting a cab?"

"I'd be happy to."

"Oh, that's wonderful! Thank you so much!"

"My pleasure."

"Look, here it comes."

The bellman had not grouped the bags by color; the second largest of the blue ones had a brown one on either side of it. Candy picked it up and gave it to the cabbie to put in the trunk.

"I'm going to Salt Lake City to visit my sister," she told the businessman when they were both in the cab.

"Do you live here? I thought you were staying at the hotel."

"I was. I stopped here to see a friend, but she didn't have any place to put me up. She rooms with another girl. Now I'm going to Salt Lake and spend a week with Clara and her husband. Were you here for the hardware convention?" Candy had a vague idea there was always a hardware convention in progress somewhere.

The businessman laughed. "Hard candy, you mean. Yes, I'm in hard candy and soft candy too. Mickey's Jawbreakers; we're a division of the Continental Wax Corporation."

"I must have misread the sign."

The cab spun up the entrance ramp to the tollway, throwing them together. He said, "Wow! Sorry."

"Don't worry about it. You know, I'm kind of into hard candy myself. I guess it shows."

"You have the nicest smile, Miss. Did anybody ever tell

you?" With some difficulty he thrust a hand under his overcoat and into his suitcoat pocket.

"Do you really mean it? No, nobody ever did."

"Of course I mean it—it's true. Here. Here's what we make."

"Oh, aren't they pretty!"

"Want one? Go ahead—they're samples I brought to the show with me."

"Hey, isn't this nice! I slept late, and I thought I wouldn't get breakfast."

"That's what we call a Pink Princess—one of our biggest sellers now. It looks like a jewel, see? But it tastes better." His hand touched hers.

Candy's plump fingers fluttered around the cellophane. "It smells better too."

"Christmas is the best time for hard candy. We developed that one to go after the Valentine trade."

"I always think of chocolates at Valentine's. Big heart-shaped boxes with two layers."

"I bet you get plenty of them, a pretty girl like you."

She shook her head. "I hardly ever do unless I buy them myself."

"Valentine's Day will be coming up pretty quick now."

"I suppose."

"Tell you what. Give me your address, and I'll see you get our Valentine's Day assortment."

Candy looked stricken. "I can't."

"I understand." He folded his hands in his lap.

"I don't mean that. I'm moving, and I don't know yet where to. Most of my stuff's in storage."

He brightened. "I suppose you'll have to find a new apartment after this trip? Do you live by yourself?"

"I did, yeah. . . . I've been thinking of moving here, to tell the truth. You come here often?"

"Pretty often. On business."

"Maybe, you know, you could bring it. Meet me somewhere. It wouldn't have to be Valentine's Day."

"I'd like that. I'd like for you to try all our candies, Miss . . ."

"Garth. Catharine Garth."

"Do they call you Cathy?"

She smiled shyly. "Sometimes."

"Here's my card. I'm John B. Sweet."

Candy giggled. "Is your name really Mr. Sweet? And you make candy? Gosh, you're an executive vice president."

"You can call me John."

"I'm going to call you John B. I know too many Johns already." Holding the card, Candy glanced around. "My God! My purse! Where's my purse?"

"You lost it?"

Her eyes were round as saucers. "I must have left it back at the hotel. All my money—my ticket—"

"Where were you?"

"In the coffee shop. I know I had it there—you know, I paid the waitress. I must have left it on my seat in the booth."

He took her hand. "Don't worry, Cathy, she'll find it and turn it in."

The driver, a melancholy Pakistani, glanced over his shoulder at them. "Wha' airline?"

"I beg your pardon?"

"Wha' airline, sirs? Where you want stop?"

"Oh. United."

"John B., what will I do?"

"Well, to start with, you ought to call the hotel and see if anybody's found it. Then you should check with your airline—which one was it?"

"En double-you. Is that Northwestern?"

"Right. Check with them. Tell them you'll have to make a later flight."

"I don't even have money to pay for this cab," Candy moaned.

"Don't worry—I'll take care of it. I'll lend you twenty too, so you can get back to the Consort."

The cab rushed past a sign: RENTAL CAR RETURN.

As she had feared, the blue suitcase was locked. It was a combination lock with four wheels, the kind the user can set for himself in any of a thousand different ways. "Something easy to remember," Candy whispered to herself. The only other woman in the ladies' room glanced at her, then back at her mirror.

She tried the quadruple numbers first—0000, 1111, 2222, 3333. . . . None of them worked. Then 1234, 0123, and on a wild impulse, 8910. None of them worked either. Neither did the year. There was a cutlery shop in the airport, she knew, where you could buy Swiss Army knives. She could get one and a couple of little plastic overnight bags to carry what she wanted to keep. Let's see, World War II? She spun the little dials to 1940, 1941, then rapidly through the war years to 1946, all without effect. Anniversary? When would that woman have gotten married? Nineteen sixty, 1961, 1962. The catch slid smoothly back.

There were two pairs of shoes inside, and both fit her beautifully. She selected the lizard-skin ones because they had closed toes, and hid her rubber boots in a corner beside the vinyl-covered couch. In a moment more, she had put on panty hose and a clean wool dress. There was even a purse in the bag and some makeup in the purse, with fifty-seven cents in change and an opened package of gum. Candy put two sticks of gum in her mouth and went out into the airport lobby again, still carrying the blue bag. A line of cabs waited where she and John B. Sweet, Executive Vice President of Mickey's Jawbreakers, had arrived a few minutes before. A driver stowed her blue suitcase in the trunk while she settled herself in the back seat.

"Where to, lady?"

"The Greyhound station. The big one downtown."

"You gotta ride those things? I hear it can be pretty tough."

"No," Candy said, "I just want to check my bag there. I've got errands to do around town today, and that's the only place where I can leave it."

"Suit yourself, lady," the cabbie said. "Have a good flight in?"

"Yeah," Candy told him. "Great."

Chapter 25

THE NEIGHBORHOOD

When Candy had gone out of the Quaint, the witch said, "And now what of us, Mr. Stubb? Have you an investigation for yourself too? And one for me?"

Stubb nodded. "Soon as I finish my coffee."

"Then I must tell you I cannot oblige you. I have matters of my own to which I must attend."

"All right, but you'll have to loan me the key to your room."

"I cannot do that either."

Stubb raised his voice. "Waitress! Hey! What time you got?"

The waitress glanced at him, then at her wrist. "Eight thirty-seven, sir. We're on Eastern Standard Time here."

"Thanks, doll."

The witch said, "And what was that about?"

"A maid came to the door of our room, remember? It couldn't have been eight o'clock yet, and there she was. You really think the maids in this place come around and pound on doors at eight o'clock?"

The witch stared at him. At last she said, "It did not seem to me that she intended harm. I sense these things."

"So do I, but I don't make a big deal of it. She looked happy."

"I sensed it before the door was opened. But yes, I concur. So?"

"Let me guess, all right? The maids here probably come to work around six thirty and start off by cleaning up the meeting rooms—any place that's been used the night before but isn't being used then. After that, they probably get a list of rooms where people have already checked out. There's always a few guys with real early flights. Then maybe they do the corridors."

"What is it you are circling toward, Mr. Stubb?"

"Suppose somebody stopped one on her way to work. Suppose this person said, 'Look, honey, here's fifty bucks and a ashtray.' Or maybe it was one of the Gideon Bibles. Whatever. 'You put this in room seven seventy-seven when you fix it up, and if you'll meet me down in the lobby afterward and let me know you did it, I'll slip you another fifty.'"

"I see. She would wish to get the money at once. Perhaps she would be afraid he would leave if she took too long. You are correct, there is an assignment for us both. We must go to my room and search."

Before he knocked at Mrs. Baker's door, Stubb stood on the sidewalk for a moment to study the wreck of Free's house. As far as he could tell, it was just as he and the others had left it the night before; in fact, he could see their tracks in the snow going up and down the short walk, their footprints on the steps.

In the brilliant winter sunshine, its ruin was more apparent. Most of the front wall had been dashed to rubble. Most of what remained looked as though it might fall at any second. Stubb found himself wondering why the people who did not have houses, himself included, did not riot when houses like this, solid brick houses that might stand for five hundred years if only the governments and the banks would let them alone, were destroyed.

He looked around for the destroyers. The long-necked yellow machine waited quietly at the curb, its deadly black ball lying before its treads like a discarded toy before the paws of some great, sleepy beast. Both the machine and the ball were dusted with sparkling snow. There were no workers in sight. The houses to the left of Free's had CONDEMNED signs in red on their windows, and some of the windows had been smashed.

He walked on, then up the step and onto the porch of Mrs. Baker's house. Wires emerged from long-splintered wood where the doorbell should have been. He knocked hard, a habit acquired from bill collecting.

There was no sound inside.

After waiting a moment, he knocked again; this time he heard footsteps, slow and hesitant. A new Yale lock had been set into the door, but the old-fashioned keyhole remained. Stooping, he put his mouth to it and called, "It's just me, Mrs. Baker. Jim Stubb, remember? From the hotel last night? I have to talk to you."

The door opened. Mrs. Baker wore a gray housecoat and slippers. Her sparse hair was in curlers.

"I'm sorry if I got you out of bed," Stubb said.

"Time for me to get up anyway. 'Early to bed and early to rise, and get the jump on the other guys,' that's what the late Mr. Baker used to say. It's from Shakespeare."

"I've always felt the same way myself," Stubb told the old woman.

"Anyway, come in. Would you like some cooco? Or maybe tea? 'Cooco's a cad and a cow.' Better than milk, it means. Isn't that what they say?"

"'Tea is like the East he grows in,'" Stubb quoted from memory. "'A great yellow mandarin, with urbanity of manner and unconsciousness of sin.'"

"You're right, that's like the people here for sure. Even if I don't think folks in California's any better. Where'd you learn all that? Would you rather have tea than cooco?"

"Cocoa will be fine," Stubb told her as he stepped inside. "I went to a parochial school when I was a kid, and there were poems we had to learn. That wasn't one of them, but it was in the same book, and it was the only one I really liked."

"No amounting for tastes," Mrs. Baker's gray back announced vaguely.

The house was cleaner than Free's had been, but mustier too, as though its windows never opened and somewhere (upstairs, perhaps, in an unused bedroom) there was a vast accumulation of rags, dusty rags filling the room and spilling, so Stubb imagined them, from an open door into the hall.

They went through the parlor where Proudy had played with Puff, now silent and dark. The dining room was crowded with dark, heavy, oak furniture, the kitchen brighter than the other rooms but empty-seeming: a sink with a few dishes, a white-enameled refrigerator, a white-enameled gas stove, a table, and two chairs. Mrs. Baker filled a teakettle and put it over stiff blue flames.

"I don't generally eat much breakfast," she said. "Just cold cereal and milk. What the French call the breakfast of mushrooms, I'm told, though I'm sure I don't know what that means."

"I had breakfast quite a while back," Stubb said, seating himself at the table. "That cocoa will be all I need. Mrs. Baker, I came to ask you about the two women you told us about last night."

The kitten came out of the dining room, walked halfway across the kitchen floor before deciding Stubb was perilous, and scampered under the stove.

"You said these women didn't give you their names, remember? That you didn't even know if they were married or not, because they wore gloves. You thought they might be from the Federal Government, but you weren't sure."

"And you said not to tell them a thing till I talked to you," Mrs. Baker continued for him. "Mom's the word, that's what my own mother used to say."

"That's right. And I wanted to talk to you some more, but not then, because the Duck girl was there."

Mrs. Baker produced two china cups of the decorated sort sold in five-and-ten-cent stores when there were five-and-ten-cent stores. "We can talk while we have our cooco, Mr. Barnes. I'll eat my cornflakes too, if you don't observe." She spooned cocoa powder into the cups. "The valiant flee to eat their breakfasts on the lip of the line, as the Bible teaches us. That means that if you're brave you ought to run fast to get your breakfast, if there's just a little while to eat it in."

"I'm Stubb, Mrs. Baker. Mrs. Baker, do you ever watch crime shows on TV?"

"Once and awhile," the old woman said, puzzled. "Not very much. As soon as you turn them on they're all over but the shooting, as the saying goes. But the shooting is what troubles me." She set a cup in front of Stubb.

"The reason I asked is that a lot of people seem to have gotten their ideas of detective work from them, and you'll notice, if you watch them at all, that even when the detectives on those shows find someone very important, they just ask two or three questions and go away. Real detective work isn't like that, Mrs. Baker—people who know something important are too hard to find. I'd like to ask you a lot of questions about those women who talked to you. It isn't going to be very exciting, but I'd like to do it anyway because if I do I may find out something important to old Mr. Free as well as to me. Do you understand?"

The old woman nodded. "Every stone takes its turn."

"Yes. That's very well put, Mrs. Baker. Now, when these two women came to see you, did they telephone first, or let you know in any way that they were coming?"

"No. Just come knocking at the door like Bare-Knuckle Bill."

"About what time?"

"You remember when they tore down Mr. Free's front? A little after that. After work but not quiet dinner time, not but that all my times aren't quiet now that I don't work no longer and Mr. Baker's gone."

"You didn't look at a clock?"

The old woman shook her head.

"Between five and six—would that be about right, Mrs. Baker?"

"If I'd have known it was so important, I'd have looked. A dilly of a five o'clock scholar, that's what I am."

"Not later than six?"

She put her bowl of cornflakes on the table, flanked it with a formerly silver-plated spoon, then paused in the act of sitting down. "Could have been as late as six thirty."

Stubb rubbed his chin.

The old woman lowered herself into her chair. "No, I recompense. At five o'clock I always have the news. That nice man with the white hair."

"Bryan O'Flynn? WROM?"

"That's him. And the big story was about the president going somewhere. I used to vote, but it doesn't do any good. It's coffee that makes politicians wise—that's what the Pope said—only they don't drink enough." She took a sip of cocoa. "Hot. Cave cane 'em, Mr. Barnes."

"I've been stirring it," Stubb told her.

"Anyway, there was a lot about him. And then the strike. I think whenever they strike they should cut their pay. That would put the kibitz to strikes pretty soon. Then the weather—more snow is what they said. Then the basketball. Did you ever play, Mr. Barnes?"

"No," Stubb said. "I didn't."

"Me either. Just a lot of jumping around, if you ask me. Then about poor Mr. Free. I told you about that last night up at your hotel."

Stubb nodded.

"And that was the end of the news—practically the end, anyway. Now curfew nods to tell of parting day; that's what my father always used to say about that time of night, when the churchbells rang. We went to bed with the chickens a whole lot earlier then."

"And then the two women came?"

"Well, not right away."

"How long after?"

"I left the TV on just like I usually do, but I don't remember now just what the show was. And I went to fix my dinner. I had real Irish stew, the frozen kind. I lit the gas and put it in the oven and set the table and so on—poured my milk—and just when I was finishing they come a-tap, tap, tapping like the poor raving."

"Finishing setting the table or finishing eating, Mrs. Baker?"

"Finishing eating, but Lord, that didn't take more than a couple of minutes. Then I got up and went to the door and they came in and I turned the TV off and gave them some tea."

"How long would you say the frozen stew took to cook?"

"Wait just a shack." The old woman got up and hobbled across her kitchen to the outside door. "This is the one those nice policemen broke," she said. "I have to get it fixed."

She stepped out onto the snowy porch, and returned a moment later holding a shiny little carton. "I always keep my garbage back there until collation day. They used to come oop the alley, but now they won't, and I don't see why. Anyhow here's the stew box, Mr. Barnes. I was wrong about the Irish—Hungarian galosh, they call it. I haven't got my glasses, so you'll have to read the back yourself. I only wear them when I want to see something. How long does it say?"

Preheat oven to 350 F, Stubb read. *Ready in 20 min.* "Twenty minutes," he told the old woman.

"Then it must have been about six when they came." She filled her mouth with cornflakes and milk.

"Yeah. And that's about half an hour after Free's face was on the news. But they wouldn't have come here—next door—first. First they would have gone to Free's and poked around a little to see if he was still there, or had maybe left a note for the milkman or something. Say ten minutes for that. They got here in about twenty minutes from wherever they were. Did they have a car?"

Mrs. Baker nodded and swallowed.

"Did they *say* they had one, or did you actually *see* they did?"

"There was a car in front of the house when I got the door, and when they left I heard a startup. I saw the lights in my curtain too, now that I come to think. What lights through yonder window breaks, as they say, though naturally they didn't really break it."

"When you came to the Consort, how'd you get there, Mrs. Baker?"

"Cab." Her mouth was full of cornflakes. "Drink your cooco. It'll be as cold as a cumberbund."

Stubb took a sip. "You phoned for one and it came? Or did you go to a busy street and flag one down?"

"Phoned."

"When it came for you, did the driver stop in front of your house, where the two women's car had been?"

"I believe so, but I can't imagine where it makes no never blind."

"It means it's probably no use for me to look for tracks from the women's car in the snow. What sort of car was it?"

"Like General Matters, you mean? I didn't see."

"Standard? Subcompact?"

"Kind of bewitched and between."

"That's a compact. Old or new?"

"New, I think. It looked kind of shinish. But listen here, Mr. Barnes." The old woman scooped up more cereal. "Suppose I knew just exactly how it was—I don't, but preposing I did—what good would it do for poor Mr. Free?"

"I don't know," Stubb admitted. "Maybe none. But maybe I'd come across that car someplace else and be able to link the two up."

"If they come again, I'll look better."

"Thanks. Write down the license number if you can. Getting back to this time, you said it looked shiny. What color was it?"

"Black, I think, or midlight blue."

"Could it have been gray?"

She shrugged. "You know what they say—at night all cars is gray. Is that important too?"

"It's the usual color for cars in the General Services Motor Pool, that's all. Two doors or four?"

"Four, I believe. Two on the side I saw."

"You didn't see the women get out of the car? Or get back into it?"

She shook her head.

"When you saw the car, could you tell if there was anybody else still inside?"

"Not for curtain sure, but I don't think so."

"Was it the women who told you where we had gone?"

She shook her head again. "You wasn't even there already, when they come."

"Then how did you know? It couldn't have been more than a couple of hours between the time Madame Serpentina checked in and the time you knocked on the door."

Mrs. Baker sat silent, refusing to meet his eyes.

"If I guess, will you tell me if I'm right? You were sitting in your parlor watching TV, and you happened to overhear—"

"Well, you're a cushion! That's what my mother used to say. You make the hard things easy."

"You did overhear us, then."

"Not really overhere, Mr. Barnes." She swallowed, although all her cornflakes were gone. "Mr. Barnes, I guess you're too much of a gentleman to scald a old lady."

"I never scold people. That's not my job."

"Like you said about overhereing—I would have, you know, just sat here out there and overhered if could have. But only I couldn't, so I opened the window a little teenie and scrootched down on the floor and dropped just like Eve in the Garden of Edam. I'd been watching, you know, and I saw Ms. Snake come in, and I was overworried about poor Mr. Free."

"I'm glad you did what you did, Mrs. Baker, and if you were trying to help Mr. Free, nobody can blame you for that."

"And then later I heard Ms. Girth ask about a hotel, and somebody said the Consort. But I didn't know you were there until I tapped one of those hoppers."

Stubb nodded to himself.

"Are you about finished, Mr. Barnes?"

He took a final sip of cocoa. "No, I haven't really started yet, Mrs. Baker. I want you to tell me everything about those two women. We might begin with the way they were dressed."

"Well, if that don't beat the Dutch." Mrs. Baker shook her head in wonderment. "And the Dutch meet the Devil."

Chapter 26

A BETTER NEIGHBORHOOD

The doorman's whistle sounded less often now. Most of the businessmen were at the airport, and the hurrying crowds of office workers had thinned to sauntering shoppers. The sun was higher and the blue shadows had gone, but it was still bitterly cold.

The witch wore a ranch-mink coat appropriate to the Consort. It had a hood, and the hood was up, so that her exotic face was framed in soft fur. She walked half a block past the doorman and his line of cabs, then left the sidewalk and stepped into the path of a Cadillac sedan.

The driver braked. Although the street was largely clear of snow and ice, the big car skidded, its rear wheels sluing before it came to a stop with its bumper touching the witch's mink. She opened the right front door and got in.

"Young woman," the driver said, "you were very nearly killed."

"Perhaps."

"Not perhaps." He was a man of fifty-five or sixty, with a clipped white mustache. "I almost couldn't stop. If my reaction had been a trifle slower, you'd be dead at this moment."

"How fortunate for you that I am not. It would have been most embarrassing."

He took his foot from the brake and let the car drift toward a dozen others waiting at the light. "You don't seem much shaken up."

"It is my nature," the witch said. "Within, I am seething, often. Outside, nothing."

"Your legs aren't trembling?"

"No."

"Then may I drop you off someplace?"

"Yes. The address is sixteen twenty-three Killdeer Lane. It is in Bellewood. That is a suburb to the north."

"I'm afraid that's out of the question. It's at least an hour's drive."

"In this car, at this time of day, it will take no more than forty minutes."

"I'm afraid I can't spare that. I'm going down this street to Broad, then turning left on Broad to Nineteenth. I'll be happy to drop you anywhere along the way."

"You will take me to the address I have given you," the witch told him. "Or if you are in a great hurry, you may drive to your destination and give me your keys. I will take care of my errand and return your car there—certainly, I would think, before five o'clock. I will leave your keys beneath the seat."

As the traffic began to inch forward, the driver stared at her. "You're insane."

"No. I am only a determined woman in urgent need of transportation. What are your alternatives? You are a wealthy and distinguished man, married, with several children and many business contacts. You may, if you like, drive to a police station or merely stop where you see a policeman. I will cling to you and scream. Cry. You may drive to your destination; I will do the same thing, and it will be still worse."

"You don't even know my name."

"It will not matter. I will give a name—any name—and the police and the journalists will believe that you have given me a false one. No doubt it will be a bit of gossip that will enliven many business lunches." The witch opened her purse, took out a compact, and inspected her face critically in the mirror.

"I am a beautiful woman, but I am not asking you for a hundred thousand dollars, or even for a nice little condominium on the most fashionable side of the park. Only for an hour or two of your time. You will drive me where I wish to go, and I will get out, and you will never see me again. You will get off very cheaply—if you act now."

"You are a very clever young woman," the driver said. "But it isn't going to do you any good." He accelerated the Cadillac to make the next light.

"No. I am a deep young woman, if you like, Mr. McAlister. A desperate young woman. But not clever. To tell the truth, I am too busy to be clever."

He spun the wheel to swing the big car around a corner. "A clever and unscrupulous young woman, ready to use my position against me."

"This is not Broad Street."

"No," he said, "but this will get us to the freeway. Want to give me that address again?"

"Sixteen twenty-three Killdeer Lane. Mr. McAlister, my kind of person has been telling your kind for many centuries that you are enslaved by your possessions. It is irrational of you to resent it because occasionally your master chooses to crack his whip."

There was a radiotelephone in the Cadillac's dashboard. McAlister picked it up. As they turned onto the *On* ramp, he said, "It's me, Bill. Tell them I'm having a little trouble—I'm going to be a couple of hours late. Make my apologies, will you?"

The witch used the Cadillac's lighter to light one of her Turkish cigarettes and turned her head away as though to study the grim, costly buildings they passed.

When the Cadillac was purring down a boulevard lined with winter-naked oaks, McAlister announced, "I live here myself. I'd just driven in when you stopped me." It was the first time he had spoken since they had turned onto the Interstate.

His passenger permitted herself a slight smile. "Are you not afraid I may use that information against you?"

"Certainly I am, but you could have gotten it from the telephone book. If you try another stunt like this, you'll find I'm not such easy meat."

"You regret that you did not call the police? Do so now. There must be police in Bellewood."

He shook his head. "I said I'd take you, and I will. Just don't try it again."

The witch laughed.

Killdeer Lane was a winding residential street where large, well-kept houses stood on three-acre lots. As McAlister stopped the car in the drive of sixteen twenty-three, he asked, "How are you going to get home?"

"You have guessed already that this is not my home. That is very clever of you."

"I told you I live here. We're a community of only about three thousand, and if you lived here too I'd have noticed you."

"Unless I had just moved in."

"Let's not beat around the bush. How are you going to get back to wherever you came from?"

"I cannot say."

"Somebody here will drive you?"

"Perhaps. I doubt it."

McAlister nodded. "And I don't think you've got money for a cab. They charge double outside the city, so it's about a thirty-dollar ride. Miss—Ms. whoever you are, I'll pay you fifty dollars right now, cash, if you'll tell me how you knew my name." He slipped a calf-skin wallet from his coat and took out two twenties and a ten.

She smiled at him. "Suppose I take your money and tell you it was magic?"

"I don't think you'll do that. I think you're a young woman who keeps her bargains."

"Firm but fair. Is that not what they say of you in the boardrooms?"

McAlister nodded. "Sometimes."

"I, also. All right." She plucked the bills from his fingers before she got out of the car. "What do you call that thing that holds the wheel? Not you, the other thing."

"This? The steering column."

"I know you would know the name. Your registration, Mr. McAlister. It is held to that steering column in a little window frame. When I took out my compact, I read your name in the mirror. Was that worth fifty dollars? Here—" She held it out. "Do you want your money back?"

"No," McAlister said. "It was worth the fifty." He waited for her to close the door.

"Then I will give you for nothing information that is worth much more. I am a witch, Mr. McAlister. Discovering your name was not magic, but I am. I can often read the future . . . and do certain other things. Someday soon, you may find you require such a person. I am living at the Consort under the name of Serpentina." Without waiting for him to reply, she shut the door of the Cadillac and turned away.

Sixteen twenty-three, where she had told McAlister to drop her, was not her destination. When his car was out of sight, she walked down the driveway to the street, then down the street, stepping carefully to keep her high-heeled boots off the worst patches of ice.

Even now, in the dead of winter, it was an attractive neighborhood. All the houses were large, and most were white. They were sufficiently separated that there was no clash of architectures; each seemed set among its own groves and lawns as though it were intended to be remote and its neighbors were present merely by accident. Clumps of birch thrust pale arms through the snow, hollies and blue spruce spoke of Christmas almost a month past, Christmas now almost infinitely remote at the distant end of the year.

Moving among all this in her dark furs, her fringed black dress and black boots, the witch seemed as out of place as some tropical animal, large-eyed and slender-legged, a bit of the city blown far from its gritty streets and bright windows by the winter winds. She might have been the sister of a notorious gangster (not his wife or mistress, since such men favor florid blonds). She might have been the sister of a nun. Once a green Mercedes passed her, cracking the ice, crunching snow. She waved to the man and woman inside as though she knew them, and they, thinking that perhaps, that certainly somewhere, they knew her, waved in return.

When she had walked about three-quarters of a mile, the open lawns on one side of the street gave way to a stone wall eight feet high. She followed it for another hundred yards, and at last reached an iron gate. There was a pushbutton beside it, but it was a long time, ten minutes at least, before a dark man in a buffalo jacket pulled it back.

"Hello, Pete," she said.

"Hello yourself, Marie," Pete answered as she stepped inside. "How you doing?"

"All right."

"Nice coat. You walk?" He shut the gate again and locked it with a heavy steel bar.

"Friend gave me a lift."

"Ah, you got a *gadjo* boyfriend. Don't tell the King."

"I haven't got any boyfriend, Pete. You crazy?"

"That's the idea," Pete said. "Don't tell anybody. He'll beat you black and blue."

When they reached the door of the white brick house, he opened it for her but did not go in with her. The foyer was dark and musty; the drapes were drawn, and there was a smell of cooking, of much coffee and of ham. After a moment, a handsome, sallow woman pushed aside a curtain. There was a red kerchief knotted around her head, and she wore gold earrings and three gold chains.

"I knew you'd come," she said. "I saw it."

The witch nodded.

"You don't believe me, huh? I did. I been tellin' everybody for weeks. You ask the King."

"I believe you, Rose."

"Yes, you do."

"Is he upstairs?"

"No, I'll show you. Someday you and me are goin' to be

friends, Marie. If the King asks, tell him I was real nice to you, okay? He likes you. He talks about you. This way—" She motioned the other down a dark hall. "Maybe once a week. For him, that's a lot."

The door was closed. When the woman in the red kerchief opened it, she released a new smell, of woodsmoke and cigars.

The room itself was bright and cold. There were seven wide windows—four in one wall and three in another—and their blinds were up and their curtains drawn back. One window was half open. A big fire blazed in a big, fieldstone fireplace, watched by a big old man in a dark blue suit.

"Hello," the witch said. "How are you?"

His eyes never left the fire. "Is that the way to talk to me? I am the King."

"Should I talk like the *gadje*? Should I say hello Your Majesty?"

"Our people say King. Here you are one of us."

Her voice fell. "Always, King."

Perhaps he had not heard. A poker with cruel hooks stood beside the fireplace. He picked it up and stirred the fire.

"I have something for you, King. A gift." She held out the fifty dollars McAlister had given her; then, when he still did not turn to look at her, walked across the room to him and laid the money gently in his lap.

He glanced down. "Bah! Tens, twenties. Today they get you nothing! Paper! Just paper." He wadded up the bills, rolled his big hands back and forth, flung crumpled green paper into the fire.

"Yes, King."

For the first time he turned to look at her. "You're cold in here, Marie?"

"I'm comfortable, King. I have my coat on."

"When I was a boy, we used to move around more. We had trucks. When I was very little, there were still a few wagons, even. We used to camp every night. Open air. Open fire."

"Yes, King."

"You know how we were made? Out of the dust like other men, but ours was the dust that blew down the road. The old ways are best."

"Yes, King."

"I want to tell you stories of the days when I was a boy, but I know you have heard them all before, many times. You would only laugh when you left my house. Did you see me on TV?"

The witch shook her head. "No, King. I did not know you were on."

"If you came to see me more often, you would know these things. The man before me had built a funny car. The woman after me had trained a bird. I talked, and Felix played his violin. I made them pay me, though they did not want to. I do not think the man with the car or the woman with the bird were paid."

"The wind is free—go talk to the wind."

He laughed, and his laughter was still deep, like wooden wheels rolling over cobbles somewhere near his heart. "You have not forgotten. Not you! You are the best and the wisest and the most beautiful." His laughter faded. "But not the most generous, Marie, not the most faithful. You have come to see me, but you have brought me nothing."

"You have the money I brought, King. How can you say I brought nothing?"

"It was nothing. I burned it."

She threw herself on him, sobbing. "How can you say what I gave you was nothing? I am destitute! It was everything I had."

He pushed her away. "No, not in the pockets of my vest. Not between the buttons either." He held up the three crumpled bills.

"You felt me?"

"Of course, but I knew where to wait for the little fingers. When I was younger, I could have moved the money always ahead of them, so they smelled it in each place they went, but never found it. Now there is a stiffness in my hands."

"I did not see you, when you changed the green paper for them; but because I am I, I knew, King."

"What is this 'King?'" the old man asked.

Chapter 27

LONELY HEARTS

The lines at the post office were shorter than they had been. Barnes stood in one to buy a stamped envelope, then moved aside to address it. He put three completed order blanks inside, licked the flap, and dropped the envelope into a mail slot.

By the time he had done so, the line in front of the General Delivery window had disappeared. A clean-shaven fat man had replaced the bearded young clerk, and when Barnes asked for his mail, the fat man, after vanishing for some time, returned with a violet-coloured envelope. Barnes thanked him and retreated to the lobby, which was (however barren) far warmer than the street outside.

There he examined the letter with some curiosity. It was addressed to him, at Free's, in a precise feminine hand and sealed with red wax. He could not recall having seen a letter sealed with wax before, though he had heard about them. The wax had been stamped with a heart. He slipped a finger under the flap of the envelope, and somewhat to his surprise the wax snapped. There was a letter and a snapshot of an oval-faced young woman with dark eyes and dark hair worn just off the shoulders. A strong face, as women's faces go, Barnes decided. Calm and maybe smart.

Dear Osgood Barnes:

I know you won't remember writing to me—that's because you didn't. A friend of mine put an ad in a certain paper (I think you know which one) and met a wonderful man. I came to her apartment today and she told me about it. And then she showed me all the letters she'd gotten, and since she doesn't need them anymore, I took them. Most of them look pretty bad, so yours is the only one I'm answering.

Now I ought to tell you about myself. Yes, that's my picture, taken last year. I'm twenty-nine now. I hope you'll say I don't look it. I've never been married—that's because I took care of Mama until she passed away last year, and so I tried not to get involved with men. I'm in Civil Service here, the Bureau of Indian Affairs of the Dept. of the Interior. I used to be a secretary, but now my title is Asst. Supervisor, so I'm sort of a junior executive. I'm a Grade 3, if you know what that means.

That explained the letter-perfect typing, Barnes thought.

My phone number at work is 636-7100. At home 896-7357. Call me if you're really interested and we'll meet somewhere for a drink.

Okay?

Barnes put the picture back into the envelope and put that in the breast pocket of his suit coat. An old woman was standing near the door looking at the gaudy posters advertising the Postal Service's latest stamps: a dejected revolutionary soldier, General Wood, and Aaron Burr. Barnes edged past her.

"I don't think they ought to have real people's pictures on them," she said. "Do you? It makes the rest of us feel like we're not much."

"Well, we aren't," Barnes said. As the big glass door shut behind him and the cold struck his cheeks, he added to himself, "Who cares about us?" Wind rattled the violet paper.

There was a telephone booth on the corner; he remembered going into it when he had left the post office earlier. He went again now, fishing for dimes in his pocket, but there were already coins in the return, and he used those instead.

"Bureau of Indian Affairs. Good Morning."

It was a switchboard operator, of course. Barnes hesitated, then tried to sound like an old friend calling. "Let me talk to Robin."

The telephone buzzed and clicked.

"Hello, this is Robin Valor."

"Robin, this is Osgood—Ozzie—Barnes. You said it would be all right to call you at work. How about lunch?"

She gasped. *"Mr. Barnes! I didn't think you'd call."*

"Make it Ozzie, will you? A minute ago I called you Robin. I don't want to have to go to Ms. Valor. It seems like a step backwards."

"You really called! I can't believe it."

"After seeing that letter and that picture? Listen, Robin, any man on earth would have."

"Tell me—No, I won't ask. You said in your letter. If you'd lie in the letter, you'd lie right now."

"Anything I put in my letter is true."

"You're not married?"

"I'm divorced. That was the truth when I wrote the letter, and it's the truth now, okay? I've been divorced for two—hell, now it's almost three years."

"All right."

She said nothing for a moment, but he sensed it was not the time to talk.

"Mr. Barnes—Ozzie—I'd love to have lunch with you, but I have some things I really absolutely have to do, and I only get forty-five minutes for lunch anyway."

He laughed. "Would you believe I've already had lunch? A crazy business contact—he was going out of the city and wanted to get a bite before he left. I was planning just to drink coffee and look at you."

"Is that true? You've already eaten lunch?"

"I swear."

"You're a salesman, aren't you? That's what you said when you wrote my friend."

"That's right."

"You still live at that address? I suppose you must—you got my letter."

"As a matter of fact, I've moved. I'm at the Consort temporarily. I had the post office hold my mail. Are you free tonight?"

"Yes . . . Mr. Barnes—Ozzie—I don't want you to think I'm pushing you. But I live way out in the suburbs. Do you have a car?"

"I'll get there, don't worry. All you have to do is give me the address."

"You don't. I was afraid of that."

"Not right now. I'm having it worked on. Transmission. I can rent one."

"No. There's no reason for you to drive way out there. I get off at five, but I'll need a little time to pretty up. I'll pick you up in front of your hotel at eight. We'll have dinner someplace, then I'll drop you off and drive myself home. You don't mind?"

"Mind? It sounds fantastic!"

"That's wonderful, Ozzie. I'm really looking forward to meeting you. Now, how will I know you? You're medium height and have a mustache—isn't that right?"

"Right. Tan topcoat, check suit."

"I'll be driving a gray Buick, Ozzie, and you've seen my picture. I think I'll wear my red knit dress. See you at eight."

She hung up, and after a moment so did he, rubbing his jaw. He picked up the handset again and dropped two dimes in the slot, then pushed buttons for the Consort. The telephone in Room 777 rang eight times, but no one answered it.

The wreck of Free's house seemed unchanged. As on the previous night, a part of the facade still stood, though so much of it had been smashed that the whole structure looked like a huge dollhouse, both floors and the interiors of several rooms visible through the gaping hole. A little fresh snow had obscured the tracks the four of them had left. Barnes stared at it for a moment, then went into the ruined house, leaving his sample case in what had been the hall. For almost an hour he walked through the rooms and up and down the stair, often running his hands over the cold walls.

When at last he picked up his sample case and left, it was to walk diagonally across the street, where an old house of grimy stone, narrower and more decrepit even than Free's, seemed to stand with shoulders hunched. A tarnished plate on the door read *Dr. Makee*. Barnes knocked.

There was no sound from inside and he looked for the bell, but the button was buried under layers of paint. From nowhere, it seemed, two small black boys had appeared to clamber over the long-necked yellow machine. Barnes knocked again.

This time there was the sound of feet, and the doorknob moved. After a moment, the door itself opened a bit and a round, red face topped by a Panama hat showed at the crevice. "You a patient?" The speaker had a bad head cold.

Barnes nodded.

There was a pause. "Me too. Want to come in?"

Barnes nodded again.

"You got a appointment?"

Barnes was maneuvering the toe of his shoe into the door. "No," he said. "But I have to see the doctor. It's important."

The red-faced man nodded. "Well, if you don't have a appointment, I guess you can come in." He opened the door.

Barnes stepped inside and found himself in a dreary little waiting room. Nine worn chairs of heavy wood dotted with senile magazines stood against its walls. The walls themselves were covered with dark paper and darker pictures: a little girl who stood by anxiously while an elderly man listened for the heartbeat of her doll, dogs shooting pool.

The red-faced man sneezed and looked doubtfully at Barnes's sample case. "You're a patient?"

Barnes nodded.

"You're not a salesman?"

"I *am* a salesman," Barnes said. "But I'm not here to sell the doctor anything. I was calling on customers, and I stopped off to see him."

The red-faced man hesitated for a moment, then sat down in one of the chairs. In addition to his Panama, he was wearing an aloha shirt, Bermuda shorts, and sandals.

"How about you?" Barnes asked pointedly.

"A mental patient—that's what you mean, isn't it? No, I'm not crazy. I've got a cold."

Barnes was diplomatic. "I just thought maybe you lived here. I mean, you wouldn't go out dressed like that."

"Like hell," the red-faced man said. "You want to know how far away I'm parked? A block and a half." He pushed two fingers into his shirt pocket and produced a card case from which he extracted a business card. "Sim Sheppard's the name. I represent Sunshine Estates down in Florida. You got your retirement home picked out yet?"

"I certainly do," Barnes told him. "The little lady and I are going to Arizona—we already own a house there. She's got asthma bad. I took her to Florida once, and she damn near died. They make you dress like that?"

For a moment Sim Sheppard seemed to ponder the question. "I wouldn't say they make me—I could always quit or something, and really there's no rule about it. It's just that everybody does it, and you sell so much more that way. They see you coming up the walk like this and freezing to death, and they say to themselves, hey, he could be there now and he'd be perfectly comfortable dressed like that. Hey, *I* could be there and go around like that all the time." Sheppard paused to wipe his nose on his bare forearm. "Or maybe they haven't filled in a coupon or anything and you're just coming in cold. Practically anybody will let you in the house when you're standing out on the front step in shorts and beach shoes in the snow."

"I guess I shouldn't put you down," Barnes told him. "You probably make twice what I do. You don't wear long-johns with the legs and sleeves cut off or anything?"

"Absolutely not." Sheppard unbuttoned his shirt and

parted the front to show an orange T-shirt reading SAND IN MY SHOES COME TO SUNSHINE. "This isn't some kind of trick, especially warm T-shirt either. That's what people think sometimes. No little wires, no batteries." He wiped his nose again and snuffled. "Just plain cotton, the kind you'd be wearing now yourself if you had accepted one of our invitations to visit free of all charge except for your plane fare. Two free nights at Sunshine Manor—swimming, fishing, tennis, and badminton, all meals included."

"If my wife ever gets over her asthma, I'll take you up on that," Barnes said.

"Hats are my biggest problem. You want to wear one because they do cut the wind a little and help keep your head warm, but they can't take the snow. Up until yesterday I had a coconut straw I liked a hell of a lot, but when I put it on this morning, half the brim came off in my hand. I had to dig this Panama out of the closet. You have to buy hats and everything in advance, you know. You can't get this kind of a thing in the winter, at least not before Valentine's." Sheppard coughed.

"You have many guys working out of your agency?"

"Only three now. We started with seven before the weather turned cold. Winter is the best time to sell because that's when everybody wishes he was the hell out of here. That's what the manager tells us, and it's God's own truth. 'When the weather gets cold, the bold gets going and the gold gets flowing.' But as soon as it drops below freezing we'll lose somebody sure as hell, and when it gets below zero we always lose one or two more." He pulled a dirty handkerchief from the hip pocket of his shorts and blew his nose.

"You don't happen to know a lady called Mrs. Baker?" Barnes asked.

"Yeah, I think so. Old lady that owns a cat, lives across the street. I was in her place yesterday. Why do you want to know?"

"Just wondered." Barnes glanced again at the card he had been given. "Salary plus commission?"

Sheppard shook his head. "Straight commission."

"Oh." Barnes stuck the card into a pocket.

"You?"

"Stock Novelties Incorporated," Barnes said. "Straight commission."

"Times are tough, good buddy."

Barnes nodded, and for a while they sat without speaking, each locked in his own private hell. The mutter of the doctor's voice came faintly from the examination room beyond, rising and falling as though he lectured to a class of one.

Barnes found a tattered *National Geographic*. He did not feel like reading (he never did any more), but he opened it and flipped through the pictures. They showed an Africa without the clutter of cities and the oppression of murder. Wide, unpeopled plains swept down to sullen brown lakes; there were elephants and rhino.

A shriveled, white-haired woman came out of the examination room, and Sheppard leaned over to whisper, "I ought to tell her about our Eternity Cottages—a durable home for all of life, an eternal resting place when life is gone. The beds convert, so your kids can move back in with you if they want to, when their time comes."

The old doctor looked out, glancing from Barnes to Sheppard. He wore a white surgical coat and had a dough-nut shaped reflector strapped to his head. Sheppard rose and went in. After a time, Barnes heard him cough.

Chapter 28

ARF! SAID THE GREYHOUND

The bus that had rounded the corner as Barnes and the sailor left the station stood silent and empty now beyond the wide glass doors. Inside, the passengers who had straggled from it were nearly gone, most of them having carried their luggage to taxis, to the cars of relatives, to city busses, or down the icy city streets. A boy of about seven, wearing black shoes, navy-blue trousers, a white shirt, and a navy blazer with a crest, stood forlornly beside his little suitcase. An old man in a dirty gray sweater slept on the bench where Reeder had sprawled.

Candy had paid her driver grandly with bills; now she discovered that she had no quarters with which to rent a locker. She crossed the station to the magazine stand and asked the concessionaire for change.

"Sure," he said. Then, as he was scooping coins from the drawer of his register, "I never seen you around here so early."

Candy thought for a moment. "Yeah, I guess I have been here a few times, late. I was looking for somebody."

"You usually found him," the concessionaire said. He was a bald, wizened little man with a crooked nose, and on impulse Candy kissed his bald head as he gave her the change. The kiss left a distinct scarlet print on his scalp. "Hey!" he said. "What the hell?"

"I found him this morning too," Candy told him. She leaned against the stand and tried to throw her hips to one side like the model of the cover of *Cosmopolitan*. "You're him, Sugar. You're going to take me out and buy me lobster and champagne, and afterwards we'll go up to your place and listen to your record collection. All night."

"Like hell," the concessionaire said. "Anyway, doll, it's too early for dinner. Only a little after ten."

"Have it your way. A champagne lunch. Lunch from now till midnight."

"You don't look like you need it."

"Sure, but you do." Candy picked up an Almond Joy. "These free? For me, I mean?"

"Like hell. Fifty cents."

As she returned two of his quarters, there was a tug at her skirt. "Ma'am, have you seen my dad?"

Candy glanced down at the boy. "No, 'fraid not. If I were

you, kid—" She hesitated, staring. "Hey, maybe I have at that. What's your name?"

"Osgood M. Barnes."

"Oh, Lord," Candy said. And then again, "Oh, Lord." The concessionaire turned away, his back ostentatiously signaling that he had nothing to do with lost children in the bus station. Candy shrugged, took two more Almond Joys, and dropped them into her purse.

"Have you seen my dad?" the boy asked again.

"Uh huh. What's your mother call you?"

"Ozzie or Little Ozzie."

"Right. Well, you know, Little Ozzie, I call your dad Ozzie, so I'm going to call you Little Ozzie. That way I can keep the two of you straight. You want the other half of my candy?"

Little Ozzie nodded.

"Let's go over and sit down on those benches for a minute. Did you get any breakfast today?"

The boy nodded. "Real early. It wasn't even daylight outside."

"What was it? Breakfast, I mean."

"Cornflakes."

"Uh huh. And then your mother took you down and put you on the bus, right? And she told you your dad would be meeting you here?"

The boy nodded.

"I know your dad, Little Ozzie."

"You do?" His mouth was full of sugared coconut.

"I sure do. I'm Candy Garth, and I'm one of your dad's best friends."

"Did he tell you to come here and get me?"

"Huh uh. I just happened to come here because I wanted to check this big old suitcase in one of their lockers. In a minute we'll do that, and we can put yours in with it so you won't have to carry it around until you get settled someplace. Did your dad know you were coming?"

"I think so."

"Well, I kind of wonder about that because he never

mentioned it to me at all, and I think he would have. We were talking just this morning about what we were going to do today. Did your mamma write him a letter?"

"She said she'd phone him after I was on the bus," the boy said. "She didn't want to wake him up, and it was real early."

"Uh huh. Only she thought he still lived at Mr. Free's, I bet. The phone got taken out of there. It sounds like she had something pretty important to do, if she put you on the bus alone without making sure first there'd be somebody here to meet you."

"She was going someplace with Uncle Mike."

"Uh huh. Did she say when they'd be back?"

"Pretty soon."

"Uh huh." Candy sat silently, looking at the boy out of blank, china-blue eyes, a fat, pink girl in a white plastic raincoat and a good wool dress that seemed a bit too old for her.

The boy stared back at her from dark eyes like his father's. There was much of his father, too, in his high, square forehead and expression of innocent cunning.

"I guess I promised you some candy, didn't I?"

Ignoring the earlier half bar, Candy fumbled in her purse and brought out one of the stolen Almond Joys. "Here. Have some candy from Candy. That way you won't forget who I am. Candy Garth."

The boy said thank you.

"I'm going to have kind of a busy day today, Little Ozzie. I want to say I can't drag you around while I'm doing all this stuff, but honest to God, I can't think of anything else to do with you—anybody to park you with. I'm supposed to meet your dad tonight, and—"

"Are you?"

"Yeah, we're all going to meet back at the Consort—that's the hotel. After that, I don't know what the hell we're supposed to do. And before then, I want to find a place to stay. We'll see. Anyway, what I was going to say was that I might even run into him sooner. You never know. Meanwhile you'll just have to tag along with me. Right now, I'm supposed to be going over to the hospital to talk to this certain person I helped doctor once. He's kind of sick. You want to come along?"

"Okay."

"Fine. Now you come and help Cousin Candy put the bags in the locker. You might even help me get in to see him—I'll explain on the way over."

Belmont Hospital was a pile of gray stone, a monument (as Ben Free's house had been in a much smaller way) to the constructive urges of the last century. Its eight stories were overshadowed by the steel and glass towers of this one, but it spoke with every thick stone windowsill: *"I will remain when they are gone. When the spades of the scholars clear my walls of the soil this city will at last become, I will yet stand whole. I will last forever."*

Belmont was psycho, of course, but it was possible it was also correct, as so many of the mad are at last discovered to be. The long-necked yellow machine might have battered those granite blocks for weeks and only disfigured them; and who would dare to use dynamite when the steel and glass towers were so near? As it was, they dropped their eight-foot panes in every wind.

Candy and the boy went up Belmont's wide steps as though they had legitimate business there, the boy skipping ahead, perhaps because his energies had been refueled by chocolate, almonds, and coconut, perhaps only because they had been restored by a trifle of soiled affection, a hug on the bus. Candy labored after him, her cheeks puffed like Boreas's and as red as two apples.

"I'm his sister," she told the nurse inside. And then, recalling that she did not in the least look like Sergeant Proudy, "Not really his *sister*, but that's what we always said. We were both adopted."

"I don't know whether that makes you a relative or not," the nurse said doubtfully. She was a pallid, sharp-chinned woman with untidy black hair.

"Legally it does," Candy announced firmly. "Legally, I'm his sister. We have the same mother and father, Mr. and Mrs. John Proudy." She was already sorry she had qualified her initial assertion.

"I meant emotionally. After all, that's what we should really consider, isn't it? If we're going to let visitors in and get the patients upset and disturb the whole routine of the hospital, it has to be because we feel it will do the patients some good. What does them good, we think, is seeing someone to whom they are emotionally attached." She swiveled to face a computer terminal, and her fingers danced across the keys. "He must be quite a bit older than you. He's forty-two."

"I'm twenty-one," Candy said automatically.

"That's over twenty years."

"He was always such a kind big brother," Candy fantasized desperately. "He used to take me fishing. On hot days we went to the ball game."

"Baseball?" The nurse looked interested. "Do you like it?"

"I never really cared that much about the game, but I liked the hot dogs and soda. There used to be a vendor there who'd put sauerkraut on your wienie if you asked for it."

"Sauerkraut commonly symbolizes pubic hair," the nurse remarked pensively. "And the phallic symbolism is almost too obvious."

"Shut up!" Candy snapped. "I wasn't talking dirty. I got a kid here." She picked up Little Ozzie and seated him on the reception desk. "This is Sergeant Proudy's little son, my nephew Oswald."

"It's vital that children learn to recognize their own psycho-sexual urges."

"Listen," Candy leaned across the desk, her face redder than it had been on the steps. "I've had it up to here with you. Are you going to let me in to see my brother?"

The nurse shook her head. "Your inappropriate rage probably indicates orgasmic repression. You should see a therapist. How long has it been since you've had a satisfactory sexual relationship? One with a male who did not recall your father?"

"You dumb bitch, you think you ought to talk like that with a little kid around? You two-bit hunk of tail!" Candy reached across the desk and grabbed the nurse by her starched lapels. Like many fat people, Candy was stronger than she looked, and she shook the nurse until her arms were pinioned behind her.

"Thank you, Parker," the nurse said.

"Right-o," drawled a voice behind Candy. Then, "Ow! He kick me! That li'l boy kick me!"

He kicked him again, and again and again, the square-toed black shoes flying, tears streaming down small cheeks. Candy squirmed in the orderly's grip, mouthing words no child should hear.

Chapter 29

CITIZENS OF THE STREET

"In a wall," Stubb muttered to himself. Swiftly yet methodically, he inspected every wall, striking matches to peer at those the sunlight failed to reach, finding and lighting Free's candle, grinning bitterly at the footprints Barnes and the witch had left in the snow, smashing plaster occasionally with a hammer he discovered in a broom closet. He found no ticket, no treasure, no wall safe or hiding place.

Wearily, he walked to the house on the other side of Mrs. Baker's and knocked. A thin young woman in a soiled housedress came to the door, carrying a baby that squalled fretfully, like a toilet with a leaky valve.

"I'm sorry," Stubb said. "I hope I didn't wake him up."

"She hasn't been to sleep yet. Don't worry about it."

"Oh, it's a girl." Stubb tickled the baby's chin. "Isn't she cute!"

"Her name's Melissa."

"How about that! Listen, Melissa, I'm a detective, and I need to ask your mommy a few questions about a certain car. Can I come in?"

The young woman's jaw dropped. "Wait a minute. Are you really a cop?"

Stubb took a badge case from his pocket, flipped it open, and closed it again. "You and your family aren't in any trouble," he said. "I just want to ask you about some people who came to the house next door last night."

"Okay." The young woman stepped back. "Haven't I seen you around the neighborhood?"

"Sure," Stubb told her. "I was in and out of the place two doors down a couple dozen times before they demolished it."

The young woman nodded wisely. Her house was less clean than Mrs. Baker's and Free's had been, and it smelled of excrement.

Stubb sat on a green plastic chair at the dinette table. "I want you to think about the house next door. That way. Got it? An old lady lives there."

"I think so. I see her shopping sometimes. I don't know what her name is. Is she all right?"

"Sure, she's fine—I just talked to her. Last night there was a four-door sedan, dark color, parked in front of her house. It must have been there from about six to at least eight. Think back. Did you see it?"

The young woman shook her head.

"Were you outside anytime yesterday evening?"

The young woman nodded. "That's the trouble. We went over to my mom's and left Melissa, then we went to a movie. Ed got off at five, and we left just after that."

"You don't work?"

"Not since Melissa came. We decided I'd take at least a year off."

"What time did you get back from the show?"

"Ten, maybe. See, we had to go over to Mom's, and then

we ate with her, and then we went back to the show, and then we sat around for a while and told her about the picture. It was *Something Strange*. That was the name of the movie."

"It's good you get out once in a while. I know how it is, staying inside all the time looking after a little baby. You like the show?"

The young woman smiled. "I guess so. It scared me silly. I hung onto Ed all night."

"You want to watch out, or you'll never get back to work. It's one of those haunted house pictures, isn't it?"

She nodded enthusiastically. "There's this old house up on a rock in New England. Barbara Delacourt answers an ad for a house-sitter. See, she's supposed to take care of it while they're in Europe. What she don't know is the house eats people, and every so often they do this to feed it. Once she started to go into a closet, and the clothes hanging up and the shoe boxes on the floor all turn into teeth. I crawled right under the seat."

"You didn't have to worry—the star never gets it until the end of the picture. But speaking of haunted houses, you haven't seen anything funny going on in the place two doors down, have you?"

"Not except that they're tearing it down. They're going to tear this one down too, and the place next door. They said they'd tell us when. Ed and me only rent, but we're looking for something else, maybe an apartment if they'll take Melissa."

"They're going at it pretty slow, if they've started on Free's but haven't even told you when yours is coming down."

"Is Free their name? The place across from the Frees's is condemned too."

"The doctor's?"

"No, that's across from here. Across from the Frees's. Only with the strike, it might be a long time."

"I didn't know there was one."

"It's the construction guys. They walked off yesterday afternoon. That's why nobody's working today. Some guy got hurt as soon as they started. Some cop. I mean a police officer."

"Yeah, I know."

"There was a big number about it. The TV came. Then two construction guys got hurt too, and the rest of them walked out. Unsafe working conditions, I guess."

"I see." Stubb rose smiling. "Listen, I can see you're busy with the baby, and I don't want to take up any more of your time. You've been a big help. If the forces of law and order got more cooperation from good citizens like you, well, the neighborhoods wouldn't be as bad as they are."

The young woman looked modest. "Officer, you were just somebody nice to talk to. A break in the day."

"Thanks. Listen—that car I told you about? I don't know if it'll be back, but I will. If you see it, take a good look and write down the license number, will you? Try and see who's in it."

The man who answered the next door was large and black and yawning. He wore an undershirt and white boxer shorts. When Stubb showed his badge, he grabbed his wrist. "Hey, man, let me look at that. That say Private Investigator—you ain't no real policeman."

"Did I say I was a policeman?"

"Course you did." The black plucked the badge case from Stubb's hand. "Get your foot out my door."

"No, I didn't. I said I was a detective. I am. I'm a private detective, just like it says on the tin. I'd like to talk to you for a minute."

"You got this out the mail-order catalog."

"Sure. Where else would I get a badge like that? There's a company out in California."

"You just get out my door." The black drew back the door to slam it, and Stubb stepped inside. The black said, "Man, just what *do* you think you're doin'?"

"You said to get out of the door, so I did. I have to talk to you, and I figured you were probably freezing, standing there in your undies."

"You woke me up, man. I was sleepin'. I work third shift this week."

"Yeah? What do you do?"

"What you care? Little man, you know I could chew your ass up and spit you out."

"Sure, but you won't." Stubb looked about the room, then sat on a straight-backed chair near the lone, comfortable-looking easy chair.

"You tell me why I won't. Man, it's cold in here."

"Because you know I'm a private op, and I might be carrying a gun."

"Are you doin' that?"

Stubb got out a battered pack of cigarettes and offered one. "If I said, you couldn't be sure you could believe me."

"Guess you're right." The black accepted a cigarette and bent over Stubb's match. "Here." He tossed the badge case into the small man's lap. "Keep it. I'm goin' to get a blanket."

He reemerged from the rear of the house in a minute or so, a plain, dark green blanket wrapped about his shoulders. "How about this? Look at superman. I got me a nice, warm robe a while back, but I spilled somethin' on it. My woman's been soakin' it. Now, what you here for, wakin' me up an' botherin' me?"

Stubb told him about the car.

"Didn't see it. I don't never pay much mind to what neighbors is doin' anyway. If you do an' they're doin' bad, they'll get you for it. If they're not doin' bad, what's the good of it?"

"Will you keep your eyes open for me anyhow? I'll check with you on the weekend when you don't have to sleep."

"Man, weekends I sleep till noon."

"I'll check in the afternoon, then." Stubb stood up.

"You don't even know my name. I'm Buster Johnson."

"Jim Stubb. Somebody told me about you once—I think it was the lady down at the all-night grocery. She said you were a tough dude."

"She told you right. I does my share."

"You look it."

"See that scar?" Johnson touched his face with one finger. "That's a busted beer bottle. You put that scar on you, man, and the little children would run off out the street. On a black man they don't show so much."

Stubb nodded. "It's a shame."

"Oh, I don't know. Depends on whether you want to scare the men or cuddle up the women. I believe I'd just as soon cuddle up."

"There were two women in that car I told you about. If you've got an eye for the ladies, you might use it to keep a lookout for them."

"I might at that. Specially if there was somethin' in it for Buster."

"I haven't got money to toss around on this one," Stubb said. "But there might be some later. If you see something let me know, and we'll see what we can do."

As he went down the icy steps to the sidewalk, Johnson called behind him, "Man, you really got heat?"

A clown opened the next door. His nose was a red rubber ball; the rest of his long, smoothly ovoid face was of a white so pure as to be nearly luminous. Scarlet tears shaped like inverted hearts fell from his eyes. His collar was a wide ruff that would have honored an Elizabethan gentleman, and the buttons of his white blouse were pompoms.

"Yes?" he said.

"I'm a detective. I'd like to talk to you."

The clown nodded. It was hard for Stubb to tell what expression, if any, he wore under his sad greasepaint. "The neighbors have been complaining, I suppose," the clown said.

"What do you think they have to complain about?" Stubb asked, stepping inside.

The room was not a living room, a sitting room, a parlor, or even a bedroom. It seemed half warehouse and half shop; there were stacks of queer clothing, masks hanging from the ceiling, and painted tubs, cabinets, and chests.

With startling agility, the clown sprang to the top of a coffin too theatrically coffin-like to be real. "I'm sorry there's no place for you to sit," he said. "Perhaps you can find somewhere."

"I'll stand," Stubb told him. "I've been sitting down a lot lately."

"What do they say?"

"Your neighbors? I think you know."

"Of course. Get that clown out of here! Dissolve him like a dream! He's a menace to society." The clown pulled out a red handkerchief and pretended to blow his rubber nose. A paper butterfly propelled by a rubber band fluttered from the handkerchief and circled the room, blundering into woolen sausages and gargantuan shoes painted to look like feet.

"What's your name?" Stubb asked.

"Nimo. Nimo the Clown."

"Swell, Nimo. What do people call you when you're not wearing that makeup?"

"You understand, don't you? At least a little bit. They call me Richard A. Chester—that's my name when I'm asleep."

"Sure, I understand, Nimo. What does Richard A. Chester do for a living? If you don't mind telling me."

"Nothing," the clown said. He used his thumbs and forefingers to make a circle. "Nothing at all."

"He just sort of hangs around?"

"That's right!" The clown smiled broadly and clapped his hands, delighted. "And he shops for me, and sometimes he eats for me. And he sleeps for me."

"I don't suppose he was hanging around out on the street last night, was he? Say, sometime between six and nine?"

"I doubt it—it was too cold. But you'd have to ask him."

"Ask Dick?"

"Ask Richard. He doesn't like being called Dick."

"I'm for him. I never liked it much either. I guess if I was to come back later today I might be able to talk to him?"

"You might."

"Maybe I will, but while I got you here, Nimo, there's something I want to ask you. You know the house four doors down, the one they're wrecking?"

The clown nodded.

"Is there anything you can tell me about it?"

The clown nodded again. "They don't have any children."

Chapter 30

AND NOW THE NEWS

The newsstand was so narrow it scarcely seemed a store at all. It squeezed between a snack bar and a dry cleaner's as though someone ignorant of the ways of commerce had set out, given a trifle of waste space and a little money, to imitate an actual store. One felt that only very thin magazines, magazines filled entirely with pictures of thin, naked brunettes in the arms of hairy men, could be sold there, that only the thin papers (dated two months back) of little, one-horse towns and the thin, foreign-language weeklies of obscure Eastern European nationalities could ever be hung from the clips of its festoons of picture wire, hung beside the lavender and rose tip sheets for the horse races, the fly-spotted Gypsy Dream Keys for the numbers game. It smelled of coal smoke, printers ink, and mold.

Majewski sidled in, shoulders turned so he would not scrape the magazines from the walls, not overturn the thick stacks of the *New York Daily News* and the *Chicago Sun-Times*. "He in there?" he asked the old man who sat in the back of the store.

"Is who in there?"

"You know damn well who I mean. Barney. I want to see him."

The old man shook his head. "He's got somebody with him."

The newsstand grew darker as it crept away from the street, illuminated at first with bare bulbs hanging from bare wires and then with nothing, so that the rearmost wall, where the old man sat tilted in his chair, seemed black as ink. A voice came from the blackness now, hearty but muffled. "Let him in. It's okay."

Resignedly, the old man moved his chair to one side. Majewski turned the knob and stepped through.

The room was no wider than the newsstand, but brightly lit. It held an old wooden desk with an old wooden swivel chair behind it, a single, hard-looking, straight-backed chair, a small safe, and two men.

The larger of these leaned against the wall. He had a round, ruddy, freckled face, and he wore a police uniform. The smaller sat behind the desk. His face was dark, and he had a darker mustache mixed of black and gray.

"Nothing to worry about," the policeman said. "We've done our business, and I was just going. What's your name, son?" He was no older than Majewski.

Majewski looked at the man behind the desk, who nodded. "Joe Majewski," Majewski said.

"And you're already a bellhop at the Consort." The policeman looked at the red uniform cap Majewski wore with his overcoat and nodded approvingly. "You live around here, Joe?"

Majewski shook his head. The dark man behind the desk said, "I knew where he lives."

"I bet you do. What do you need the money for, Joe? Pay off your bookie?"

"Make the payment on my TV. If I don't give them something pretty soon, they'll take back my set."

"How about that. Well, at least it keeps you off the streets, huh?" The policeman straightened up and reached for the doorknob. "See you around, Barney."

"So long, Evans."

"What was that about?" Majewski asked as the door closed.

"What do you think it was about? I got to operate, don't I? What the hell do you think I do with the interest you pay, send my dog to college? I got to pay off the precinct, I got to pay off the juice squad, I got to pay off my alderman. That was precinct. Don't ask how much."

"How much?"

"Don't ask. One hell of a lot. If I didn't have the magazines out front, I couldn't make it. And that son of a bitch will cop *Penthouse* as sure as hell. How much do you want?"

"Seventy."

"That all?"

Majewski nodded. "I get paid tomorrow, Barney, but I got to have it before I go to work today. You know I'm good for it."

"Okay. Five for four until the end of next week. That'll be eighty-eight. If you can't make it, five for four at the end of the next week. That'll be a hundred and ten. Don't let it go no farther than that."

Majewski nodded again.

The dark man took a thick billfold from his coat and gave him a fifty and a twenty, neither new. "I trust you, Joe," he said. "Don't let me down. I got so many collections going now it's killing me."

"See you next Saturday."

"That's the spirit."

Majewski turned the knob and backed through the door, closing it after him. The old man still sat with his chair tilted, a limp, sweat-stained gray hat—an old man's hat—pulled over his eyes. A short, brisk girl was peering and poking among the magazines. She glanced at Majewski, then looked again in what actors call a double take. "I know you!" she exclaimed.

"Well, lady, you're one up on me," he told her.

"Last night when I came into the Consort, you asked me if I was Miss Garth, or if I knew who she was. And I remembered the name because later I met Candy Garth, and she seemed to know Madame Serpentina. Why were you looking for her? For Miss Garth, I mean."

"I don't remember," Majewski said. He made no effort to push past her.

The girl stared at him for a moment, then fumbled in her purse and produced a dollar.

Majewski allowed himself a slight grin. "Yeah," he said. "It's coming back to me."

"Was it Madame Serpentina who told you to look for Miss Garth?"

"Huh uh. A guy."

"A small man with glasses?"

Majewski shook his head. "I didn't see him. He phoned down to the lobby. I was hoping for a tip out of it, because I knew it was her room and the lady's a good tipper, but I haven't seen her since. To tell the truth, I've been kind of ducking her because I owe her, but now I'm set to pay her, and I'll remind her about finding the girl in the white coat for the guy up in her room."

"You said Madame Serpentina was a good tipper. Will you tell me about that?"

"Boy, you want a whole lot for your buck, don't you? Ten each for the three guys that carried up her bags."

"Was the man with the thick glasses with her then?" the girl asked.

"No." Majewski tried to edge by her. "There wasn't nobody with her. I never seen this guy. Listen, lady, I've given you one hell of a lot more than a buck's worth. I got to go."

"Here." She fumbled in her purse again. "Here's another dollar, all right? She was alone when she checked in? Did she come in a cab, or do you know?"

"Huh uh." Majewski paused and snapped his fingers. "Come to think of it, I did see the little guy with the glasses, maybe. See, when we're not too busy we're supposed to help the guests bring their stuff in from outside. Then we set it in the lobby while they register."

The girl nodded.

"Anyway, I think I saw somebody like that—little guy, thick glasses, hat pulled down—talking to her. Then later I saw him in the lobby at registration. I don't know if that was him on the phone."

"Did you see him at the hotel after that?"

Majewski shook his head. "Of course, I ain't been at work much. I work afternoons and evenings—I'm due in a couple hours."

"How about the woman in the white raincoat? Or the man with the black mustache? I was talking to him in the lobby later. You must have seen us."

"I never noticed him," Majewski said. "I ain't seen the fat lady again either."

"Here's my card." The short girl pressed it into his hand. "Talk to the people you work with. If you find out where the man with the glasses and the woman in the white raincoat live, call me and let me know. Especially the man with the glasses. Or if you see him and can tell me where he is. I'll pay ten dollars." She hesitated. "Each. Ten dollars for each one."

Majewski glanced at the card. "Okay, Miss Duck. But listen, I ought to level with you. You remember when you asked me about the little guy with the glasses a minute ago? And all of a sudden I remembered seein' him on the sidewalk?"

Sandy Duck nodded.

"Well, the reason I remembered was I just saw him walk past outside." He pointed beyond her toward the glass door at the front of the newsstand.

She rushed out, then stopped abruptly, looking up and down the street. More philosophically, Majewski followed her.

Chapter 31

COUGH!

"Take off your shirt," Dr. Makee rumbled. He himself still wore his tattersall, with herringbone trousers and a bolo tie. His gray herringbone jacket hung from the back of a chair in one corner of his examination room.

"I'm not really sick," Barnes explained. "I just want to talk."

"Take it off," the old doctor said firmly. "I don't care what the hell you came here for, I'm going to listen to your heart or I won't talk to you."

"I can't pay you."

"Take it off!" He strode up to Barnes and began to unfasten the buttons himself.

"All right," Barnes said. "All right." He pulled loose his tie and hung it on a halltree beside a dusty skeleton, then slipped out of his suitcoat and undid the rest of his shirt buttons.

"That's better." The old doctor sipped coffee from a mug on his desk and wiped his white mustache with the back of his hand. "I know you can't pay. If you could pay, you'd go to a real doctor in the medical center, not to a crazy old retired quack like me. Nobody comes here that can pay, even if some of them do. I know you're not sick, too. Or anyway, you don't think you are. I could see that the minute you walked in. A sick man walks one way, a well one another way; but a man who's sick and doesn't know it might walk like John Wayne. Hell, John Wayne walked like John Wayne when he was full of cancer. When a man your age comes in here, I always listen to his heart. Suppose you said you weren't sick, and I accepted it, and you walked out of here and fell down dead on my sidewalk. I'd never forgive myself."

He stood and adjusted his stethoscope, then thrust its dangling end against Barnes's belly. "Cough!"

Barnes coughed.

"That's not for your heart, that's your lungs." The old doctor put his instrument in half a dozen other places, occasionally rapping Barnes's ribs with his knuckles. "How long since you've had a good physical?"

"Five years, maybe. Six."

"I thought so. Now I want you to skip in place. Watch how I do it." He hopped from one leg to the other; Barnes tried to imitate him. "Good enough. You want to see how a sick man walks?" The old doctor hunched one shoulder and lurched about, dragging a leg. "This is sick!" He chuckled fiendishly and clawed with his spotted old man's hand at Barnes's bare shoulder. "Yes, Master! Igor will obey!"

Barnes recoiled, and the doctor straightened up and shoved his stethoscope against his chest again. "Nothing like a little anxiety to bring up the pulse rate."

"I just wanted to ask you about Mr. Free," Barnes said.

"Ben Free?" Dr. Makee took the earpieces from his ears, walked around his desk, and sat down. "Your heart seems to be pretty good. What did you say your name was?"

"Osgood M. Barnes."

"Well, I don't think you have a problem there, Mr. Barnes. Just the same, I'm going to check your blood pressure. Put on your shirt again, and come over here and sit down. Father deceased?"

Taking his shirt from the halltree, Barnes nodded.

"What did he die from?"

"Accidental causes."

The old doctor sipped his coffee. "You'd just as soon not talk about it, I take it. Fine with me. Sit down here and let me do the blood pressure. You can put on your tie but not your coat. You wanted to ask me something about Ben Free?"

Barnes nodded again.

"Thought you lived with him. I've seen you over there, so you ought to know more than I do. Put your arm here, level, on my desk. You got your breath? Heart pretty well slowed down?"

"Yes, fine," Barnes said. "I did live with him. You're right about that, Dr. Makee."

"You were over there when I stitched up the fella that got hit with the ax."

"Yes, I was. But Mr. Free was gone by then—we didn't know where he was. We still don't. We're hoping you can tell us."

The old doctor wrapped a rubber cuff around Barnes's arm. "I won't, because I don't know. That satisfy you? Don't know where he went when they started to wreck his house. Don't know where I'll go myself when they start on this one."

"It's not a question of my being satisfied, Doctor. We're worried about him. He's lost his home. We'd like to help him if we can."

"Out of the goodness of your hearts? I don't believe you, Mr. Barnes. People don't do those things. They think they do, but they don't. Something happens, and they think if it weren't for such-and-such I'd do so-and-so. But such-and-such is always there, except when so-and-so might put money in their pockets."

"Are you saying there aren't any humanitarians? I'd have said you were one, Doctor. You said you were retired, too. Why do you take care of your patients?"

"Thunderation, somebody's got to. Besides," the old doctor chuckled, "because I do, I can get away with just about anything I want around this neighborhood. You notice how I made you take off your shirt soon as you came in here?"

"Of course."

"Well, I do that with all of them. Make 'em strip so I can check their heart and lungs. For decency's sake, if a lady or one of these young gals has on a brassiere, I don't make her take it off. But lots of these young gals don't wear them now—you know that?"

"Yes," Barnes said. "I've noticed that myself."

"And when they do, why frequently they have these real lacy, frilly things. I like them damn near as well. You're too young to recall what it was like in my day, Mr. Barnes. But back when I was a boy, if I saw down the front of a good-looking gal, I'd really seen something. Why, I thought about something like that for a month afterward. Why when we got the Monkey Ward catalog, my ma used to tear out the pages with the ladies' unmentionables to keep my brothers and me from lookin' at 'em."

Barnes grinned. "You're not really that old, Doctor. You know, you remind me a lot of Mr. Free."

"Well, I ought to." The old doctor began to pump the blood-pressure cuff. "He was my son, you know." Barnes stared at him, and he chuckled again. "Not my actual son—Tommy died a long while ago, and I think Ben was really a few years older than I am. But we used to pretend that way, and we had a lot of fun. I was the dad because of my mustache. Ben shaved his face all over back then. He's got more hair on his face than I do now."

Barnes nodded.

"That's right, you saw him many a time." The old doctor pressed his stethoscope to the inside of Barnes's elbow and cocked his head. The air escaping from the cuff made a faint hiss, the sigh of a sleepy serpent. "Started when we were coming home on the bus one time. I'd wrenched my knee a little, and Ben gave me a hand up the steps—your blood pressure's okay, Mr. Barnes. Good, in fact, for a man like you, because you're lean. Get plenty of exercise and stay away from rich food, anything sweet or greasy. Never salt a thing."

"I won't," Barnes said. "Thanks for the tip. I hope your knee's better now."

"Knee? Oh, sure, the story. Well, sir, Ben helped me up, and then there wasn't two seats together, so I took the one up front and Ben sat about three rows back, next to a lady about my age.

"And when we were both settled down, she said something like, 'Will your friend be all right?' and Ben said something like, 'Doc'll be okay.' Only the lady was a mite deef, and she thought he said Dad'll be okay. So she said, 'Oh, is he your father? Such a distinguished looking man!' Well, Ben's always a great kidder—you could say just about anything to him and he'd go along with it. So he told her he was sixty-nine and I was ninety-one, and how we'd lived together all our lives, and so on so forth. From then on it's been a joke we pick up every once in a while."

"You haven't really known Mr. Free all your life?" Barnes asked.

"No, of course not. Only since he moved in across the street."

"How long has that been, Dr. Makee?"

"Just a few years."

"Dr. Makee, I know you think I'm prying into something that's really none of my business, but Mr. Free's—your friend Ben's—missing, and all of us who lived there with him are concerned about him. We're afraid something may have happened to him, and until we find out nothing has, we're going to keep looking."

The old doctor nodded, his face expressionless. "Have you called the police?"

"No," Barnes said. "Not yet."

"That's what most people would do, Mr. Barnes."

"We're not . . ." Barnes hesitated.

"Not what?"

"Not the sort of people the police pay much attention to, Doctor. A man in your position—you're a physician, you own this house, you have a certain status in the community."

"Can't say I've ever noticed it."

"I think—Dr. Makee, I used to be a regional sales manager for the Continental Crusher Division of Yevco Incorporated. I had a house and a wife and kid. Two cars, a gold American Express Card, all that stuff."

The old doctor nodded. "What happened?"

"A lot of things. The point I want to make is that when I lost all that, I lost it so slowly I hardly noticed it happening. The wife and the kid and the house and one car first. That was all in one lump."

"I see."

"Then my job. After that I went through five jobs in a little over a year. Each of them looked nearly as good as the last one—do you know what I mean? I know you're thinking it was my own fault, but not all of it was. Like, once I was sales manager for a small company. They got bought up by a big one, and I was out. They said I could stay around as a sales trainee if I wanted, and I told them to stuff it. Today I'd jump at that."

The old doctor nodded again.

"I'm getting way off my point. What I wanted to say was that one day I was making a call at a liquor store. The man who owned it was out front by the register, and he didn't want any. You know how they do, 'I ain't got time, come back next month,' all that bullshit."

"I can imagine."

"While I was standing there trying to tell him about the products I represented, a cop came in. The owner looked at him and said, 'Throw this guy out.' I suppose the cop got a fifth of cheap Scotch from him at Christmas; they usually do. Anyway, he grabbed me."

Dr. Makee chuckled. "The bum's rush, that's what we used to call it."

"They still call it that. It's funny, until you realize you're the bum. Anyway, the cop did it. He tossed me out so I couldn't get my feet under me, and I landed on my hands and knees on the sidewalk. When he threw my sample case after me, it hit so the latch came open. All my samples were scattered on that sidewalk. Some of them got stepped on, and some of them got lost; I suppose people picked them up and carried them home."

"I can understand how that must have hurt you, Mr. Barnes," Dr. Makee said softly.

"In a way, he'd done me a favor, because that was when I

knew where I was. That's about where all of us who lived with Mr. Free are. You wanted to know why we didn't call the police."

"You'll have to excuse an old man, Mr. Barnes. We get set in our ways, and I suppose I was thinking more about how the police used to be than how they are now. Ben would have called them himself, that's what I was thinking; but he was old like me. Ben and I, we sort of lived in the past, I suppose. It was hard for us to keep in mind how much the world's changed. You're too young to understand it, maybe. Crystals in the brain's what some of them think it is. Did you know that, Mr. Barnes? Hirano bodies. The brain's turning to glass, or something like it. Well, folks said the both of us were cracked a long time ago."

Barnes laughed dutifully.

"For you young people, it's all the same. But people my age, or Ben's age, we have to wonder what kind of glass it is. For some a shot glass, I suppose. One of those funny mirrors for Ben, I think, and if Trudie were still with me, hers might be a pretty cut-glass vase. I don't know."

"Speaking of brains, Doctor, you said once that a concussion was a brain bruise. Do you remember that?"

The old doctor shrugged. "I've said that maybe a thousand times, Mr. Barnes."

"This was just yesterday, when you bandaged Sergeant Proudy at Mr. Free's."

"Oh, him." He nodded.

"Right. I want to ask you more about Mr. Free, if you don't mind. But first a couple of questions about Sergeant Proudy. How did you know to come?"

"When he got hit with that fire ax? Because I saw it. I was watching all the hoorah out my front window. I suppose by that time the whole neighborhood was. When he got hit, it looked like a fine chance to just busybody over and see what the commotion was about, so I did."

"Mr. Free didn't call you, then."

"Nobody called me. I just came."

"Doctor, I'm not very good at asking questions, but Stubb

told me specifically to ask this one. When was the last time you saw Mr. Free?"

"I'm not much on answering 'em neither. I don't know."

"You mean you don't think it's any of my business."

"Nope. I mean I don't know."

"You were his friend."

The old doctor seemed to hesitate, his eyes roving from the yellowed, wired-together skeleton by the halltree to the window and back. At last he said, "I'd like to think so," and let the words hang, as though there were no more to say. Barnes was conscious of the warmth of the room and the smell of carbolic acid clinging to everything.

"I'd like to think so, Mr. Barnes. I know for certain, that if you'd have asked, Ben would have said he was mine. I'm getting old."

"Not mentally, Doctor."

"Old every way. I've got an old mind in an old body. I've got an old soul. That Chinese wise man . . ."

"Confucius?"

"Yes. We used to make up jokes about him. Confucius say this and Confucius say that. What Confucius really said was that in the pursuit of knowledge he forgot he was getting old. My practice does that for me, Mr. Barnes, that and keeping up with the new developments. But it doesn't stop me from getting old, only from thinking about it."

Barnes waited.

"You ask me when I saw Ben last, and I feel like I just did. But I can't pin it down. Maybe yesterday. Maybe today. Maybe it was last week, and maybe it was last year."

"I think I understand."

"It may come to me. Then again, it may not. I could tell you a hundred things we did, a thousand things we talked about, because we talked about everything. But I couldn't tell you just when it was, except sometimes that it was summer or winter or whatever because I remember what kind of clothes I wore, or maybe that Ben got himself a soft ice cream. Then too, it isn't always easy to know when you saw Ben, if you didn't see him right to his face. One way he looks like everybody else, but another way he looks like everybody. Sometimes he's just as straight as a poker. Sometimes he's stooped over like his back's giving him a lot of trouble. He—"

"Is it?" Barnes asked.

"Hurting him? I think so, but he never came to me for doctoring. I used to try to get him to, but when I started I made the mistake of telling him I wouldn't charge him. After that he wouldn't come.

"Now, Mr. Barnes, I like to take an interest in all my patients, just like in my friends. You said something about that policeman I stitched up yesterday. Why don't you quit prying into Ben Free's affairs and tell me about him?"

Barnes nodded, uncertain at first about putting his thoughts into words. "You said yesterday he might have a slight concussion, isn't that correct?"

"I believe we've mentioned it today too."

"Right. Is it possible for a slight concussion to make somebody a little confused and very suspicious of—of another group of people?"

"Paranoia? No."

"It isn't possible?"

"Slight concussions can cause some confusion, Mr. Barnes. If you've ever seen a boxer or a football player walking around and maybe even doing what he's supposed to, fight or run with the ball, but acting kind of dazed and maybe staggering a little, you've seen the results of a slight concussion. But a concussion like that doesn't cause paranoia or any other mental disorder, in my experience. Sometimes almost any kind of trauma will produce overt paranoia in a person who's had it for years and been covering it up, though. How does . . . I can't recall his name."

"Sergeant Proudy."

"How does Sergeant Proudy act?"

Barnes told him.

Chapter 32

I'D RATHER BE IN PHILADELPHIA

Little Ozzie cried until he could cry no more. He could not have said just why he cried, but he cried because he knew, in some deep part of him where the knowledge would remain till he was dead, that the world was a more horrible place than he could ever imagine. He might think of monsters or mad dogs, but the world would beat him. It would turn the people he loved and trusted to monsters; it would reveal those meant to help him as mad dogs. He wept for himself, and he wept because he knew there would never really be anyone else to weep for him.

It ended slowly. Perhaps half an hour passed between the first slacking of his tears and his last choking sob. That gave him time to look about without having to commit himself to consideration of what he saw. It was nothing anyway: a narrow room; a narrow window, high and old-fashioned looking, with bars on this side of the glass. The scuffed sofa where he lay smelled faintly of tears and dust, and creaked a little when he got off.

The door opened and a black woman in a white dress like the school nurse's took him by the arm and said come along, boy. They went into a wide hallway with tiles on the floor, a place he faintly recalled. The plaster was dark brown until it got higher than his head. Up there it was vanilla. Chocolate for kids, he thought, vanilla for grown-ups. Serves them right.

They went through a door, and the nurse pushed him through another one.

A man in a white coat was sitting at a desk. He had a fluffy beard that was not quite red and not quite yellow, sort of like ketchup and mustard mixed up. "Hi," he said.

Little Ozzie nodded, not speaking.

"Want to tell me your name? I'm Doctor Bob."

"Osgood M. Barnes."

"Is that what they call you at school?"

Little Ozzie nodded again.

"I bet they don't. I bet they call you . . . Skippy."

Little Ozzie shook his head.

"Skeeter?"

"No."

"Duke?"

"No."

"All right, Osgood. Now Doctor Bob wants to ask you a few simple little questions before we send you home to your mommy and daddy. You'd like to go back to your mommy and daddy again, wouldn't you?"

Little Ozzie shrugged. "I guess so."

"Where do you live?"

"I don't know."

"Come on, Osgood. Doctor Bob can't send you home if you won't tell him where your home is."

"I don't see how it's any use to have a doctor send somebody home if he doesn't know where you live unless you tell him."

"You're feeling defiant, aren't you, Osgood?"

"No!"

"Can you explain to Doctor Bob why it is that you don't want to tell him where you live?"

"I do want to tell you—I just don't live anyplace right now."

"Maybe we ought to talk about something else for a while, Osgood. Want to tell me where your mommy is?"

"I don't know."

"Uh huh." Doctor Bob turned away for a moment and stared out the window, playing with his beard. "There's a Coke machine and a candy machine I know about. Would you like a Coke and a candy bar?"

"No," Little Ozzie said honestly, "I'd like a sandwich and a glass of milk."

"What kind of sandwich, Osgood?"

"Jelly and cream cheese."

"How about peanut butter?"

"I don't like peanut butter much."

"Dr. Bob doesn't think they have any cream cheese down in the commissary, Osgood. I'll tell you what I'll do—if you'll tell Dr. Bob where your daddy works, Dr. Bob will have somebody bring you a glass of milk and a peanut butter and jelly sandwich."

"At the Consort Hotel."

Dr. Bob smiled. "Now we're getting someplace, Osgood. Do you know what he does there?"

"He's a salesman."

"I see." Dr. Bob stroked his chin.

"Can I have my sandwich now?"

"Why not." Dr. Bob pressed a button on the intercom on his desk. "Shirley, run down to the commissary and get us a cream cheese and jelly and a glass of milk. Peanut butter, if they don't have cream cheese. Then call the Consort, downtown. Ask if they have an employee or a guest called Barnes." He covered the mouthpiece with his hand. "What's Daddy's first name, Osgood?"

"Ozzie."

"First name probably Osgood, but don't count on it, Shirley. Any Barnes."

The intercom squeaked at him.

"Grape, strawberry, whatever they have," he said. "White bread." With a snort of disgust he released the button and turned back to Little Ozzie. "Now I want you to tell me about the fat lady who brought you here. You know who I mean?"

Little Ozzie shook his head.

"Sure you do. She has curly blond hair and blue eyes. She came into the building with you, and then she assaulted the therapist at the front desk?"

"She's not fat," Little Ozzie said. "Fat means ugly."

Dr. Bob stared at him for a moment, then nodded to himself and made a note. "Interesting. But you know who I mean. What's her name?"

"Candy."

"Do you mean that's her name, or just that she gave you some candy?"

"Uh huh."

"Did she give you candy?"

"Uh huh."

"Do you know her name?"

Seeing that "Candy" was not a satisfactory response, Little Ozzie shrugged.

"Is she your sister or a cousin—something like that?"

Little Ozzie hesitated. "I don't think so."

"Have you ever been to Philadelphia, Osgood?"

"Yes."

"You have? Fine. When was that?"

"Last year."

"Why did you go?"

"Everybody did."

"Your mommy and daddy?"

"No, they couldn't come."

"The lady who brought you here?"

"No," Little Ozzie said again. "From school. Everybody from school. We saw where they signed the Decoration of Independence."

"I see, it was a class trip."

"Uh huh."

Dr. Bob picked up his pencil and balanced it between the tips of his fingers. "The reason I asked you about Philadelphia, Osgood, is that the label in the dress the lady who brought you here wore indicates she bought it there. Do you know anything about that?"

"No," Little Ozzie said for the third time. "Can I talk to her?"

The growl of angry voices came from the hallway. Dr. Bob said, "Don't pay any attention to that, Osgood. Sometimes we have a little trouble with the sick people here. It will be all right; we'll soon have them calmed down again."

The angry voices grew louder. A woman who sounded like the one who had come for him screamed, "We'll call the police!" and he heard glass breaking. The door flew open, and a man with a brown face and stringy black hair looked at Dr. Bob. "Nah," the man said. "This ain't him." Before he shut the door again, Little Ozzie noticed he wore earrings. Little Ozzie had never seen a man with earrings before.

"What the hell!" Dr. Bob stood up. Little Ozzie got up too, beginning to feel better. Dr. Bob went out the door with Little Ozzie at his heels.

The crash had come from a glass of milk. Milk had made a star in the middle of the brown tile, full of glassy twinkles. By one point of the star there was a sandwich somebody had stepped on. Dr. Bob jumped over the star and ran out into the corridor.

People in white pajamas were milling around, mixed up with nurses and doctors and white-coat men. In the middle was the man who had looked in Dr. Bob's office. With him was a littler, younger man in a soft felt hat and a woman with her hair in a red handkerchief. They were talking more than anybody else. They waved their arms a lot and the people in white pajamas saw them and waved too.

Ozzie ducked between legs, getting closer and closer to the man with the earrings until he got caught by the woman, who held him at the end of her arms, then squatted down in front of him.

"What are you doin' here, little boy?"

Ozzie decided she smelled like cooking hamburgers outside. It was a nice smell, but he was getting pretty tired of people who asked questions. "What are *you* doing?"

"I'm lookin' for a old man named Ben Free. You know him?"

Ozzie shook his head.

"He's a real old man. His eyes look bad, and he's got a white beard. Have you seen a old man like that?"

Ozzie shook his head again.

"If you see him, you tell him Rose's lookin' for him. Tell

him Rose is the Queen, and a good friend of Mar—of Serpentina's. He knows Serpentina."

"All right," Ozzie said. He found the conversation thrilling, though he could not have said why.

"Go look now," the woman told him as a burly attendant seized her from behind. Little Ozzie darted away.

Chapter 33

WASHINGTON CALLING

"Okay, Cliff. I've got a little something going to keep me occupied, but if you should need somebody to fill in, I could probably make the time." Stubb hung up the phone.

"You look tired," Murray said sympathetically.

"I ought to. I've been walking my dogs off all morning."

"In this cold?"

Stubb shrugged and pushed back his hat. "That part wasn't bad. A lot of the time I was in somebody's house. Hell, I was sitting down then, so what am I bitching about?"

"You get paid yet?"

"Not yet. Couple of days. Thanks for the coffee."

"Hey, I didn't mean that. You're good here. Hell, Jim, you ran up a big tab and paid it all off. When was it? Day before yesterday?"

"I guess," Stubb said. "Jesus, I am tired. I guess it's the cold. Gimme a B.T.L., Murray."

"Fries on the side?"

Stubb shook his head. "I had a big breakfast."

The door flew open, admitting a few snowflakes and a blast of frigid air. "Mr. Stubb! Mr. Stubb!" and then, "Oh, God!"

The steamy air of the sandwich shop had fogged Sandy's glasses. She jerked them off and rubbed them on her sleeve.

"Winter's hell, isn't it?" Stubb said. "Same thing happened to me. Same thing happens every time I go inside anyplace. Over here."

"Mr. Stubb, I have to talk to you. It's important—terribly important. It really is."

"Sure. Important to you or to me?"

"To both of us. Something's happened."

"In that case, we'd better get a booth in back. Bring my sandwich back there, will you, Murray?"

Murray nodded and asked Sandy, "How about you? Wanna have anything?"

"Just coffee. Gosh is it time for lunch already? A hamburger and some tea."

"Regular or bellybuster?"

"Regular. Will you have lunch with me, Mr. Stubb? It shouldn't offend your sense of chivalry. I'll put it on my expense account. Usually I have a lot of trouble with that, but I don't think I will now."

Stubb was carrying his cup toward the rear of the sandwich shop. Over his shoulder he said, "I don't have one. Sure, I'll eat on your dough."

"Really, this is very good of you, Mr. Stubb. Do you know you're a very hard man to trace? You're not in the telephone book, and the front desk at the Consort didn't seem to know a thing about you. I went to the *Journal* and looked through their morgue—I know a man there—and you had a couple of clips, but none of them indicated where you could be reached. And you're a detective! You're not investigating Madame Serpentina, are you? If you are, what you said about false psychics last night has a very unpleasant double meaning."

"Don't worry about a thing," Stubb said. He had taken out his pencil and battered little notebook, and had begun to write as she spoke. "I'm working *for* Madame Serpentina. She's my client."

"Why that's wonderful!" Sandy paused, her plump

fingers fumbling in her purse for her own notebook. "But why would a psychic need a detective?"

"For the same reason detectives need psychics. You said last night that the cops go to psychics for help in finding bodies, missing weapons, and that kind of stuff, remember?"

Sandy nodded.

"And it's absolutely true. They do. But did you ever hear of a psychic telling the cops that the body was in the basement at four twelve West Forty-Eighth? No, what the psychic sees, maybe, is an old trunk and a broken clock."

Sandy nodded again.

"Swell. So suppose this time it's the psychic that wants to find somebody. She sees the trunk and the clock, right? Or whatever."

"I see."

"As Madame S. would say, I doubt it. But that's what's going on. I'm looking for a certain party, on behalf of Madame S. Those other people you met, Candy and Ozzie Barnes, are working for me."

"Are they detectives too?"

Stubb grinned. "Sure. But they don't know it."

"What are you writing?"

"This." Stubb ripped a page from his notebook and handed it to Sandy. "Maybe you've forgotten, but last night you promised Madame S. a full-page ad in both magazines—"

"One!"

"Both. You know damn well you're going to spread that material out over at least a couple of issues, which in your case means the two magazines. Anyway, you promised the ads, and I told you I'd take you up on them. That's the ad copy. Run it as soon as you can."

Sandy looked at the paper. "'It will be to the advantage of anyone knowing the whereabouts of Benjamin Free, formerly of the High Place, to communicate with us. Box XXX in care of this magazine.' That's it?"

"You assign Madame S. a box number so you can keep the

replies together, if there are any. Every so often I'll send somebody to pick them up." Stubb took a sip of coffee. "Murray! This is getting cold. How about warming it up?"

"Who is Benjamin Free?"

"The man Madame S. is trying to find."

"I don't claim to be Sherlock Holmes, Mr. Stubb, but even I deduced that. What is the High Place?"

Stubb shrugged. "You'll have to ask Madame S."

"This man Free lived there?"

"He said he did, yeah."

Murray brought Sandy Duck's tea and poured steaming coffee into Stubb's cup.

"Hell of a day, isn't?" Stubb said. "Freeze the tits off a boar hog."

"Are we going to discuss the weather, Mr. Stubb? I'd much rather talk about Benjamin Free."

"If we're going to fight, we might as well use first names. Mine's Jim."

"I'm Sandy—short for Alexandra. As you've probably noticed, I'm short for Alexandra myself. Alexandra should be nearly six feet and use a lorgnette. But I know a little karate."

"No, I don't want to fight, Sandy. I was just trying to fill in with that crack about the weather. Murray was still close enough to hear. I can tell you everything I know about Ben Free in two minutes, and why shouldn't I? You could find it out yourself in ten. What I'd rather do is get some information from you. Last night you said I'd come to your rescue a couple of times—something like that—and you said you'd give Madame S. the ad. If I really helped you, how about helping me? Tell me what's going on. Why were you looking for me?"

"How do you know I was? Maybe I just dropped in here for a cup of tea."

"You saw me at the counter and called my name before your glasses had a chance to fog. The windows are pretty foggy too, but I think you saw me through them before you came inside. Because after you came in, you weren't hungry.

And you switched your order from coffee to tea. You weren't thinking about food while you were out there on the street; you were thinking about me."

"You know, you're really a pretty good detective."

"Yeah, but nobody in the world knows it but you and me."

"Madame Serpentina must, since she hired you. Anyway, you're right. I was looking for you. A few minutes ago I ran into one of the bellmen from the hotel, and he told me he'd just seen you walking past. I decided nobody would want to walk very far in this cold, so I started looking in the shops for you."

"Why?"

Sandy lowered her voice. "Something big, really *big*, happened at the office this morning."

Stubb nodded, sipping his coffee.

"Mr. Illingworth—he owns and edits both magazines— old Mr. Illingworth got a call from the Government. From someone very highly placed in the Federal Government." Her voice was tense with excitement. "They had heard about my story. They wanted to see an advance copy."

Stubb leaned back, his eyes nearly closed behind the thick lenses of his glasses.

"Mr. Illingworth was—was just beside himself, if you know what I mean. I mean, government repression, after all these years! He has this friend on *The New York Times* he hasn't seen since I don't know when. They just exchange cards at Christmas, but Mr. Illingworth called him up. They must have chatted for half an hour. Mr. Illingworth looked ten years younger."

"Swell. Are you going to let these Government people look at your story?"

"Of course. We're going to cooperate—at least for a while—and keep records of everything. Then maybe we'll publish an exposé of the whole business. With luck, we'll make the big papers and some of the journalism reviews—the *Times* promised Mr. Illingworth they'd hold off until we gave the word. We've already started a thing for the next issue of

Hidden Science. He and I finished it just a minute ago. We say the magazine is in desperate trouble—not financial—and we ask all our precognitive readers to look into the matter for us, and to advise us how to act as well as tell us how it will come out."

"Shrewd."

"One of the things we really want to know, of course, is how they found out. The Government, I mean. If there's some sort of agreement among the various psychics about that, well, we'll be watching for it carefully."

"I'm psychic too," Stubb said. He raised his right wrist and pressed it to his forehead. "I can tell you right now."

"You can?"

"Sure. When the wreckers were tearing down Ben's house, he got himself on TV. I'll tell you about that some other time. The tape ran on the five o'clock news. Somebody saw it and came looking for him. You remember Mrs. Baker, the crazy old lady that came up to Madame S.'s room about the same time you did? She was there because they had contacted her, and she knew our names—she had them wrong, thought I was Ozzie Barnes and so forth, but the names themselves were all right. They picked one of us up. It's just a guess, but mine would be that they got Candy at the precinct before she was sprung. But it doesn't matter, because all four of us went to Madame S.'s room in the Consort. Hell, it couldn't have been hard, because that crazy cop . . ."

"Mr. Stubb? Jim?"

"I just had an idea, that's all. It's something that happens to me about once a month. Listen, Sandy, do you want to buy into this?"

"Yes, certainly, if I can. That's what I wanted to talk to you about. I don't know why this very important government agency is interested in Madame Serpentina, but if they are, it's a big story. I may be able to sell it to the *Times* or one of the national news magazines. If it's really good, I might even be able to use it to get a job on one of those magazines. I wanted to ask you to help me go after it."

"Sure. Was I just supposed to do that from the greatness of my heart?"

"I was hoping for your help, yes. I suppose I could say that I hoped we'd find some area of mutual interest."

"Fine. Money." Stubb grinned at her.

"I haven't got much."

"Compared to me, you're probably rich. Listen, I know you think a lot of Madame S., but she hasn't been a damn bit generous about bread for expenses. So here's what we'll do. You've already offered to pay for my lunch."

Sandy nodded.

"That's fine, that's a start. I want you to give me a hundred bucks now, with the understanding that it's not mine. It's a loan that I'll pay back when—and if—I collect from Madame S., and I can use it as expense money while I'm working on her case."

"I don't have a hundred dollars in my purse, or anything like it."

"You can write a check. They'll cash it for us at the currency exchange down the street, which is good because we're going to need a hunk of it for a cab right away."

"And what do I get, besides a ride in a taxi?"

"Information. I tell you what I know about Free, and I let you tag along, shoot pictures if you want to, until the hundred runs out. When it does, we talk. You can buy in again for another hundred or so, or we can break up the act. What do you say?"

She sat staring at him and gnawing her lipstick. Half a minute passed, and Murray brought their sandwiches and a greasy bill on greenish paper. At last she said, "It's not the magazines' money, you know. It will be mine. My own."

"You're talking about selling the story and maybe even getting a new job. The magazines pay you to do that?" Stubb picked up a quadrant of his club sandwich and smeared salad dressing down the side. "You got that little camera with you?"

"Yes, I always carry it. You didn't say you'd call Mr. Illingworth if I didn't give you the money."

"That's because I won't. I'm no blackmailer. I'm offering to let you buy into the story. If you want to, fine. If you don't, that's fine too. But if you don't, don't come around with your hand out."

"You'll tell me what that idea you just had was?"

"Sure. That's the first thing I'll tell you. Then you come along and watch me try to make it pay off. If I find out anything, you'll hear what it is. Only you'll have to keep the lid on it until I say you can write about it—which shouldn't be long."

"All right, a hundred dollars. You're hoping for a clue to the whereabouts of this Mr. Free?"

"Indirectly, yes. More specifically, I'm hoping for a clue to those government people who called about him. So now, cooperation cuts both ways. What did they tell your boss?"

"I don't know a lot of it. He wouldn't tell me."

"That's what I figured. Did he say what agency?"

Sandy shook her head.

"Department of Justice? FBI? CIA? Treasury? Internal Revenue?"

"He didn't say."

"Just that it was a government agency?"

"Something like that."

"Man or woman?"

"I don't know."

"But it could have been a woman?"

"I told you, I don't know." She gave a little shake of exasperation. "If he didn't say, how could I? I wasn't listening in."

"Not even to his end of the conversation?"

"No. He was in his office with the door shut."

"And you didn't ask him questions when he told you your piece was going to get checked over?"

"Of course I did. It's just that he didn't answer them. He was full of the idea of letting them have their head, then springing the whole thing on the readers and making a big splash. He didn't want to talk about the call. Mr. Stubb—"

"Jim."

"Jim, I can see you mean well, but you don't know Mr. Illingworth. He's an old man—over seventy—and cranky. He was running the magazines before I was born, and he knows perfectly well that he'll still be running them when I leave for a better job. He keeps the business under his hat."

"They must have told him where to send your article on Madame S. Wouldn't he have made notes? A name and address? Maybe a phone number?"

"I suppose so."

"In a pocket notebook, or in something he'd leave there on the desk?"

Sandy pursed her lips. "Probably on his blotter. Really important things—printer's deadlines and meetings with the distributor, things like that—he usually writes on his blotter. It's a habit he has."

"Any reason we couldn't go in and have a look at it?"

"After he's gone home, you mean? I don't see why not. I've got a key. But, Jim—"

"Yeah?"

"It wouldn't be fair for you to concentrate on that part of the story. I could do that myself. The reason I came to see you, and the reason I'm giving you a hundred dollars of my own money, is that I need you to help with the part that concerns Madame Serpentina. She's the one they're interested in, after all. Not Mr. Illingworth. Not me."

"Not her either," Stubb said. "I just told you, and if you're going to write about this, you'd better learn to listen. It's Ben Free. And don't worry about me concentrating on one part of the case or another—I concentrate on all the parts. Now finish your hamburger and we'll cash your check and take a ride over to Belmont Hospital."

"Belmont?"

"Sure. That was my idea of the month. I told you already—these government people must have been watching Madame S.'s room at the Consort. They saw you come in, or maybe go out, and that's how they got onto you. Swell. But somebody else was watching too. Hell, you got stopped by him while you were leaving, remember?"

"The policeman with the bandaged head!"

"That's right. Sergeant Proudy. He was watching us, and there's a damn good chance he saw whoever else was. This morning, when I was giving out assignments to the gang, I told Candy to go over and have a word with him, but that was just because she'd helped the old doc patch him up and he seemed to like her better than the rest of us. I wanted her to find out what he knew or thought he knew that made him think he ought to stake us out. She's probably been and gone by now—I hope she softened him up for us."

Chapter 34

CALLING ON BELMONT

"Hello," Captain Davidson said. "Can I help you?"

The dark woman glanced at him. "No." She wore snow-flecked mink, spike-heeled boots, and a hat with a veil, old-fashioned but elegant. She was not tall, but she looked tall, only in part because of the heels.

"You're a Gypsy," Captain Davidson said.

She appeared not to have heard him.

"It's the first time I've ever seen a Gypsy throw away the chance to take advantage of somebody who offered to help."

"This is a wonderful world; a world far larger than you suppose."

The captain glanced up at the dark facade of the stone building. "One of your tribe's in Belmont?"

"Several, I understand. Have you influence at this place?"

"I hope so. One of my men's in there."

"We have common cause, then."

"Somewhat."

"I am Madame Serpentina," the witch said. She held out a black-gloved hand.

"You mean that's what I can call you."

"Of course. You are a very intelligent policeman, and so you know that. And what may I call you?"

He told her. "I've got the Thirteenth Precinct now, but I used to be on Bunco. I knew a Gypsy once who took two old ladies for forty thousand dollars."

"How terrible that there should be such evil among our people. How thankful you must be that there is none among your own. Captain Davidson. Shall we go inside?"

As they started up the steps, a cab swung out of the traffic and braked at the curb. A plump young woman hopped out as agilely as a plump brown bird, took a step or two toward them, called shrilly, "Madame Serpentina!" and whipped out a little camera with a gesture so much like the drawing of a gun that Captain Davidson's hand started for his own. There was a brief flash, brilliant and yet lost in the vastness of street and sky, forlorn amid the sunshine and sparkling snow.

"It is you," the witch said.

"And me." Stubb walked around the rear bumper of the cab as it pulled away.

Davidson growled, "I know you, P.I. What the hell's your name?"

"Jim Stubb." Stubb thrust out his hand.

It was ignored. "I'm Davidson. Captain, Thirteenth Precinct. You wouldn't be trying to recover the loot from some kind of a scam, would you?"

"You mean this lady here?" Stubb glanced toward the witch. "I work for her."

"I see. I didn't think you were licensed, Stubb."

"I'm not—not yet. But the law doesn't say a man has to have a license to get a job, only to advertise services. I'm just a working stiff, and right now I'm working for this lady."

Davidson turned to Sandy Duck. "You too? You just took our picture."

"I took hers," Sandy said. She handed him a card.

"And what are you two doing here?"

"I don't believe we have to answer that."

"You do unless you want me to run you in. I could bust Stubb for operating without a license, and forget about that smart bullshit he loves spreading. I could take both of you on suspicion of fraud."

Sandy's mouth opened, and her eyes grew wide. "Oooh! Would you? Mr. Illingworth would be so happy! I get to make one call, don't I? I could call the office. He'd get me a lawyer and everything, it would be wonderful!"

"You think so, do you?"

She had turned away and was chattering to Stubb. "You see, I belong to this little club—we call it Input for Smaller Magazines. And there's one person in ISM who was arrested in a protest, fingerprinted and everything, and she's bragged about it until the rest of us are absolutely sick."

The witch said, "I have listened to enough of this trifling. Captain, I advise you to arrest this foolish woman—it will make you both very happy. Mr. Stubb, if you still consider yourself in my employ, come inside with me and help me if you can."

She went up the icy stone steps without waiting to see whether Stubb or anyone else would follow her. All of them did, Sandy hurrying after the detective, and Davidson bringing up the rear.

Inside, the captain showed his badge to the nurse with the disordered hair.

"Oh, we're so glad you've come, officer. It's been such a long time. They're upstairs in two seventeen."

"You called the police?"

"These horrible people broke in here—three of them, officer, a woman and two men. They asked for someone, and when I told them he wasn't here, they demanded to search the whole hospital. I tried to stop them, but they *ran* upstairs and started a riot."

"I see," Davidson said. "What do they look like?"

"Why, you can go upstairs and see for yourself, officer."

"Right now, I'd like to have you tell me."

The nurse considered. "They're foreigners of some kind, I'm sure. One of the men has a big mustache—of course some American men used to have them too—and rings in his ears. Latent masochism, or maybe overt. The woman has a long skirt, and her hair's tied up in a red scarf. They're very dark. Do you think they could be from India?"

Davidson nodded. "About five hundred years ago. And you're holding them until the precinct sends somebody over. Around what time did you call?"

"Goodness, it seems so long—so much has happened." The nurse looked from Davidson to Sandy and Stubb, then back again. "Actually, it's been less than an hour, I suppose."

"You called Precinct?"

"I don't know what that means. Dr. Roberts told me to call the police, and I did."

"What was the number?"

"The telephone number? I don't remember. The one in the front of the directory."

"That's headquarters, downtown. The wagon's not here yet, but the Gypsies know some of their people are in trouble. They've even had time to send somebody. You ought to be hearing from their lawyer soon—they'll sue." Davidson glanced at Stubb, then looked around for the witch. "Where'd she go?"

Stubb grinned. "I'll be damned if I know. One minute she's here and the next she isn't. Probably up to two seventeen. Isn't that where the lady said they were?"

The nurse banged a glass paperweight on her desk. "You mean she's gone up without permission? We can't have this!" She snatched up a telephone fitted with a voice suppressor.

"You going up to see them too?" Stubb asked Davidson. "I'm here to see about my sergeant," Davidson said. "Unless they're guilty of something—which you can bet your ass they are—and unless we can prove it—which you can bet your ass we can't—I don't give a damn about them."

The nurse slammed the telephone back into its cradle.

"We'll get her. I've warned Marcia, up on the second floor."

Davidson said, "Good. Now I'd like to ask about Sergeant Charles Proudy. The way I heard it, you picked him up at the Consort this morning."

"You wish to visit him?"

"No, I'm here to talk to his doctor. Who is it?"

The nurse swiveled to a terminal, pushing buttons as if to blow up a continent. "Here he is. Delusions of grandeur and persecution. Violent. Dr. Roberts."

"Is Roberts here now?"

She nodded. "I'll find out if he'll see you."

"I'm going up to see him. And don't tell me you'll sic your goons on me—that will be interference with an officer in the performance of his duty, and they'll be in the slammer before you can say white coat. Also I'll knock their God-damned teeth out."

"I'm sure Dr. Roberts will see you, officer. Just let me phone—"

Stubb took Sandy's elbow. "Come on!"

"What is it? Why are we whispering?"

In an alcove behind them, an elevator waited with open doors. Stubb pushed Sandy into it as the glass paperweight struck the wall. "Wonder how many chips she's got in that thing." The doors jolted shut.

"Where are we *going*?"

"I told you—to talk to Proudy. What do you think the chances were of us getting in to see him with that cop around?"

"You don't even know where he is!"

"Sure I do—seven seventeen. It ought to make him feel right at home, because he was in seven seventy-one at the Consort. When that crazy broad at the desk got his record, I read the number. It's no trick to read a three-digit number upside down. Speaking of tricks, though, did you see where Madame S. went when she left?"

As the elevator bumped to a stop, Sandy shook her head.

"Me neither. And she didn't take this elevator, because it

was there after she was gone, and nobody brought it back down. Hell, we'll probably never know. Come on."

They stepped into a wide hallway, sunny at the far end where a window faced the west, with a plaster ceiling and plaster wall painted yellow from four feet above the floor; in spots the dark linoleum had worn through to the boards. There were benches along the walls, and on them sat men in unstarched gray-white cotton pajamas and slippers. A few looked up, but it was without interest or intelligence.

"You think this Sergeant Proudy will be here?"

"Not out in the hall," Stubb said. "From what I heard downstairs, he's been cutting up too rough." One of the silent men stood, pulled down the trousers of his pajamas, and began to masturbate.

"Jim, I'm scared."

"Don't be. It's been a hell of a time since that poor guy's seen a woman who didn't look like the boss. Now he wants one last little hunk of fun out of life, and he's so doped he won't remember you five minutes after you're gone."

"Suppose they gang up on us?"

"Suppose they don't?"

The door to one of the rooms along the hall opened, and a husky young man in starched white stepped out. "I'm sorry, folks," he said. "But this floor's off limits to visitors."

Stubb flashed his badge. "I'm here to see Sergeant Proudy—Thirteenth Precinct."

The young man hesitated. "He really is a policeman, then?"

"Sure, he's a cop. Before he got sick like this, a pretty good cop. Where is he?"

The young man looked at Sandy. "Are you from the police too?"

Stubb said, "No, she's his sister-in-law. The girl down at the desk said since I was going to see him, she could come up with me."

"We've had a lot of trouble here today. . . . You *are* a policeman?"

"The hell with this," Stubb said. "Get out of my way."

From behind him, Davidson called, "Don't do it, son. Make him show you the buzzer."

Sandy whirled, and Stubb turned wearily to look at him.

"Hello, Stubb. Hello, Miss Duck. Can I ask just what you're doing here?"

The attendant said, "They came up to see the policeman in seven one seven."

"Do tell. So did I. Actually," Davidson smiled at them, only a trifle grimly, "I wanted to see his doctor first. But when they phoned his office, he wasn't there, so I figured I'd come up and see Chick. Did you say this guy told you he was a police officer, son?"

"I didn't," Stubb declared. "I just showed him a badge. This girl's my witness."

The attendant said, "He said he was from the Thirteenth Precinct. Are you a real cop?"

Stubb chuckled. "Show him your buzzer, Captain."

"I will," Davidson said. He took a badge case from the pocket of his coat and held it out. "Take a good look this time, son."

"And I didn't say I was Thirteenth Precinct, I said Proudy was. I said, 'I'm here to see about Sergeant Proudy, Thirteenth Precinct.'"

Sandy interjected, "That's the truth, Captain."

"What does the badge say—Junior G-Man?"

"Actually, it's 'International Private Investigator,'" Stubb told him. "Want to see it?"

"I'll wait. In fact, I won't have to see it at all, if you'll tell me what the Gypsy girl's interest in Proudy is."

Stubb shrugged. "As far as I know, she hasn't any."

Sandy pulled at his sleeve. "You mean Madame Serpentina's a real Gypsy?"

"That's right, lady," Davidson said. "And out on the street, this guy said he was working for her, and she confirmed it when she told him to come in and help her. Now I find him up here asking about Chick." He glanced at the attendant. "Right, son?"

The attendant nodded.

With a squeeze of Stubb's arm that said please don't tell, Sandy lifted herself on her toes and raised her voice to match. "Captain, I'm sure Mr. Stubb meant no harm at all! Why Mr. Stubb is one of the nicest, finest—"

Through the closed door of a room nearby, a voice called, "Mr. Stubb, is that you? Please, please help! It's Nimo!"

Chapter 35

INITIAL INTERVIEW

Dr. Bob pushed open the door of Candy's room, glanced at her, then looked up and down the hall before stepping in and closing the door.

"How are we today?"

"Strung out. What was that they shot me up on? It felt like I was packed in cottonwool, and now the cottonwool's going away."

"Would you like a drink of water?"

"Hell, yes. I'd like a drink of anything."

He took the cap from a white plastic container, ran in water from the little bowl in the corner, and closed the container with a top from which a flexible plastic tube protruded.

"You'll have to get used to drinking lying down. It isn't easy at first. If you'll turn your head to the side, you'll find that helps."

Candy put the tube in her mouth and sucked water until the container made a noise like an empty soda glass.

"Good. I hope you feel better now."

"My head hurts. What are you writing things down for?"

"My report. I have to put down what you say, especially how you feel. This is your initial interview."

"My head hurts because of that dope you shot in me. It didn't hurt when I came in here."

Dr. Bob nodded. "Have you ever used narcotics?"

"Sure."

He glanced up. "Did you use them today—the day you came here?"

"Huh uh."

"Yesterday?"

"No. It's been a while. I don't think I've even had a toke in a couple weeks."

"Marijuana. What else?"

"Oh, you know. Uppers to try to get skinny. Smack a few times. Coke."

"You used heroin?"

"Yeah, I had this friend that used to give me some. I just snorted it. I figured I'd let myself get a little habit and drop some weight, then I'd go to a clinic and kick it. Only I never really got to like it that much. A doc I knew told me I lacked the addictive personality. What I want to know is if I do, how come I eat so much and get crocked every time somebody opens a bottle? Is that different?"

"Usually. What's the name of your doctor?"

"I can't tell you that." Candy sounded offended. "You know, professional ethics."

"I don't think you understand. When you see your physician, professional ethics prevent him from revealing what passed between you. You, on the other hand, are completely free to tell a third party—certainly another physician— whatever you like."

"I don't think *you* understand. *He* saw *me*."

"You're a therapist?"

"Uh huh. A sexual therapist. I mean, usually I call myself a hooker, because it saves the argument. But what I am really is a sexual therapist."

"You're saying you're a prostitute."

"Huh uh, a sexual therapist. You're a doctor, right? So guess my weight. If you want, you can even feel me up, like they do at the carnivals."

Dr. Bob stared at her, rubbing his chin, then made a note on his pad.

"I'll give you a clue. I'm five eight, no shoes."

"Two hundred pounds, I suppose."

"Two forty. Now you're a really nice looking young guy, even if you are a little wide around the hips. Suppose I came up to you on the street. It's pretty close to midnight, and we've both had a few, maybe. I say, 'Listen, I'm in a hell of a bind. Take me to your place, and I'll show you a wonderful time. Anything you want. I gotta have fifty bucks.' Would you take me?"

"I suppose so."

"Doc, I suppose not. A guy like you can go into any singles bar in town and walk out an hour later with somebody half my weight that he won't have to pay for. The ones that say yes . . ."

"Yes?"

"Well, they've got some kind of trouble. Sometimes, to tell the truth, their trouble is they just can't say no to it. Sometimes they feel guilty—they're cheating on their wives or girlfriends or even for Christ's sake on their mothers. Then they don't want a girl that looks nice. They want to be grossed out. I can spot them by the way they look at me when I undress. Hey, why am I telling you all this?"

"I suppose because I'm a doctor," Dr. Bob said. "And somewhere inside you're hoping I can help you."

"I think it was the dope they gave me."

"No." He made another note on his pad.

"Get these straps off me, will you?"

"I'm afraid I can't do that. Violent patients must be restrained for the first twenty-four hours. It's a hospital rule."

"I'm not a patient."

"You are."

"Can you just *do* that? Take somebody and sock her away?"

"If you mean confine someone permanently, no. There has to be a sanity hearing, and this isn't even a permanent facility; we don't keep anyone, under any circumstances, for more than six weeks. But we can admit anyone whose behavior is dangerous to society or to himself, on a temporary basis."

"That's what you did with the cop, huh?"

"Cop?"

"Sergeant Proudy. He was in the Consort, and somebody—I forget now who it was—called about him. Jim, I guess."

"You know him then. The policeman."

"I didn't really know him. I helped bandage him."

"I saw the dressings. I gave him his entrance interview, just as I'm giving you yours. That was a very professional job."

"Thanks."

"You did it?"

"I did part of it, yeah. I helped."

"I would have said the stitches in his scalp had been made by a surgeon."

"You took the bandages off, huh? Yeah, a doctor sewed him up."

"You were working for the doctor?"

"I guess you could say that."

"Are you a nurse?"

"No."

"Not necessarily a registered nurse. A practical nurse, perhaps."

Candy snorted with laughter. "An impractical nurse. That's me."

"I wonder if you could tell me who the doctor was. Possibly I know him."

"I've forgotten his name. He told me—or somebody did—but I forget. That's a problem I have, a real bad problem."

"I see."

"Another problem is remembering. You'd think the two of them would get together and cancel out, wouldn't you? But they don't. I'm always remembering things I want to forget—you know, like what happened last night—and forgetting stuff I need to remember, like somebody owes me twenty."

"Perhaps we should begin at the beginning, then. I suppose that's what we ought to have done all along. What is your name?"

"Candy Garth. Listen, I didn't really do anything so bad, did I? Just shook that girl up a little. When are you going to take these straps off me and let me go?"

"Candy is your legal name?"

"Catherine. Catherine M. Garth, all right? The *M* is for Margaret."

"Do you know what day of the week this is?"

"You mean like is it Monday or Tuesday? I guess not. Usually I keep track, but sometimes I forget. See, I don't have a regular job, and I don't go to church, so it's all about the same to me. The stores are open all the time anyway, and so are the bars."

"Guess, please."

"You mean just take a stab at it?"

"That's right."

"Wednesday. How's that?"

"And what is the day of the month, please?"

"Well, this is January. I had one hell of a hangover after New Year's, but that was back a couple of weeks ago anyway. I'd say about the fifteenth."

"This is Friday the twenty-first, Candy. Where do you live?"

"You mean right now?"

"Yes."

"I just don't have what you call a fixed address right now. I've been staying with friends."

"I want to be quite open with you, Candy. When you were admitted here, we went through your purse. We weren't snooping, we—"

"Oh, God! The kid!"

"Yes?"

"I had a kid with me, Little Ozzie. Is he okay? My God, I

forgot all about him." Candy tried to sit up, the straps indenting her soft flesh, her round face red with the strain.

"Don't worry about the little fellow. I saw him myself a few minutes ago, and he was just fine."

"You've got him in here?"

"We're trying to locate his father."

Candy mumbled something, and Dr. Bob leaned forward. "What did you say?"

"Shut up. I've gotta think. Jim sent him to see that doc, but I can't remember his name."

"I'm sure it will come to you as we talk."

"I don't know where Jim will be either. What's the time?"

Dr. Bob glanced as his watch. "A quarter to three."

"Will you still be here at six?"

"I can be, if there's a reason for it."

"At six, phone the Consort. Ask for Madame Serpentina's room. Ozzie ought to be there then. We were going to meet there."

"Madame Serpentina is rather an odd name."

"Really. She's a pretty weird woman too, so I guess it fits her."

"Is she an American?"

"Why not? Every geek who can get one foot on the beach is American now. She can speak English, if that's what you mean. Half of them can't. I don't think she was born here."

"You don't like her, do you?"

"What the hell business of yours is that?" Candy hesitated. "I guess I do, a little. Sometimes. When are you going to take off these straps?"

"Tomorrow. I think I mentioned that."

"I got to go to the john."

"When I leave, I'll send in a nurse and an attendant. Until then, I'm afraid you'll have to wait. Have I mentioned that we went through your purse? We did. You were carrying no identification whatsoever."

"There were some of my calling cards in there."

"You are John B. Sweet, Executive Vice President of Mickey's Jawbreakers Incorporated?"

"Oh, him. Jesus, I'd forgotten about him. Don't call him. No, I meant the candy bars. People call me Candy, see? So I always say those are my cards. I leave the wrappers behind, anyhow."

"But you had no real identification."

"I used to have one of those little cards that come with the wallet, but I lost it."

"Can you drive a car, Candy?"

"Uh huh."

"You didn't have a driver's license in your purse."

"I got ripped off once. He took everything—my money, my license, all that crap. I never got another one. What for? I don't have a car."

"I had a friend in college who went to Italy. He stayed in a very nice hotel in Sorrento, and the bellboy there told him he could get him a girl. Do you know what I mean, Candy? For so many hundred lira or thousand lira or whatever it was."

"I know what you mean, all right. I guess better than you do."

"So my friend said okay, and the bellboy came back with a very beautiful Italian girl. . . ,"

"And when he woke up next morning his wallet was gone."

"Yes, it was. His passport too. How did you know?"

"How would anybody know? The woman needed some extra money, or she didn't like the way it had gone the night before or something. What are you after, advice for next time? You shouldn't have gone to sleep while she was still in the room. You shouldn't have done it at all."

"It wasn't me."

"Really. I never knocked on anybody's hotel room door late at night either. One of my friends told me about it. Anyway, ever since it happened, you think the john's the only one that ever gets ripped off. Bullshit. There isn't a damn thing a woman carries with her that I haven't got stolen from me one time or another—my purse, my shoes, my clothes, you name it. I've been slapped around plenty. I've had enough guns and knives pointed at me to start a war."

The door opened; a woman's voice said, "A Dr. Makee to see you, Dr. Roberts."

Chapter 36

SIMPLE ASSAULT

The room in which Barnes and Dr. Makee waited was much like the one in which Dr. Bob had talked to Candy, though it was not the same room. An examination table with restraining straps had been pushed to one side. There were several very light folding chairs. Barnes sat primly, knees together, hands clasped in lap, his sample case half hidden behind the chair. Dr. Makee almost sprawled, his old brown tweed overcoat cast off and gaping behind him, his old gray herringbone jacket open to show his tattersall shirt and black string tie.

A nurse with a clipboard looked in. "Dr. Make-ee?"

"Makee. Say it like ma's key, then leave off the *S*."

The nurse nodded and wrote something on her clipboard. "You're the patient's personal physician?"

"I was the last to treat him, I believe, before he got sent here. I'm not sure he has a personal physician."

"And when was that?"

"Yesterday. I told all this to Dr. Roberts."

"I know, but I have to have it for his record. Did he show signs of anxiety or confusion when you examined him?"

Dr. Makee shrugged. "He was anxious about his condition. He'd had a head injury, and he was afraid it might be serious. I didn't think it was, and I told him so. That seemed to reassure him. I wouldn't have said he was confused."

When the nurse was gone, Barnes said, "Well, Doc?"

"Well what? I haven't seen him yet."

The door opened again, and a tall, red-faced man with a long nose peered through. "Shipmate!" he hissed.

Barnes glanced up.

"Remember me? Seaman Reeder?"

Barnes nodded. "What the hell are you doing here?"

The sailor stepped inside and shut the door. He wore the soiled white pajamas of a patient. "I got picked up. I was in a bar—cuttin' up pretty silly, I guess."

"And they brought you here?"

"I been in the brig a lot—it wouldn't have been much fun to go again. So I just kept on cuttin' up—sillier, even—and they brought me here. The food's better, a little."

Dr. Makee said, "Stretch out both hands, young man."

Reeder did.

"Pronounced tremor. How long had you been drinking?"

"I don't know. Before Christmas."

"About a month, then. I've seen them a lot worse, but you're bad enough. Dee tees?"

"I don't think so. Anyway, how can you be sure?"

Barnes asked, "When were you supposed to be back to your ship?"

"January fifth. It was a Christmas leave."

Dr. Makee said, "I'm surprised you weren't picked up by the Shore Patrol. In my day, you would have been."

"I just kept missing the bus," Reeder told him. "Honest. There's only one to Norfolk from here, and it leaves at eleven twenty in the morning. Sometimes I wouldn't make it. Sometimes I'd get there early, but I'd get tired of waiting and go off for a drink someplace." He turned to Barnes. "You got to get me out of here, Mate. That's why I came. I saw you when they brought you up. You know the last thing my mom said when she died?"

Barnes shook his head.

"She said, 'God, you gotta take care of Baby Phil, because he won't never take care of himself.' I wasn't there, but Bubba was, and he told me. God has to get me out, and you're His chosen instrument."

"Instrument, hell. I never even met Him!"

Dr. Makee chuckled and nudged Barnes with an elbow. "Don't be too sure."

"Besides, why do you have to get out? They'll just send you back to the Navy, and that's where you ought to go anyway."

"Shit, man, not like this! You know what they're doin' here? Buildin' up a file on me that says I'm crazy as a bedbug. I want to get back to my ship."

Dr. Makee said, "I would think it's already sailed, if you're as late as you say."

"They'll hold me till she comes back, or maybe fly me—"

The door swung wide, and a burly young man with crew-cut hair led in Proudy, his arms pinioned by a canvas straitjacket. Before he could stop himself, Barnes said, "I didn't think you really used those things."

The attendant told him, "They're a lot more humane than they look. He's comfortable, but he can't hurt himself or anybody else." He glanced at Reeder. "You want this one out of here?"

"Let him stay, if it's not against the rules."

"Okay with me. Doctor?"

Dr. Makee nodded.

"At least you'll have somebody to talk to. The sailor will talk your arm off. The cop won't say a word."

"I just want to reexamine that head wound." Dr. Makee stood up. "I see somebody has changed the dressings."

"Yeah, we did that." The attendant closed the door behind him.

"Come over here, Officer," Dr. Makee said. "Sit down."

Proudy did not move. His face seemed paler than Barnes remembered it, the big nose nearly white at the tip. He watched them without expression.

"Some of 'em don't talk," Reeder said. "Besides, they been givin' him dope for sure. They give everybody dope, even me."

Dr. Makee nodded, "Well, if he won't come to me, I'll have to come to him. It's lucky he's not a tall man."

"You're goin' to get me out, aren't you, Mate?" Reeder asked Barnes.

"I don't see how," Barnes told him. "I will if I can."

"Listen, you can do it." Reeder lowered his voice. "Mate, we don't want the old doc mixed up in this, do we? You step outside with me for a minute. I know a place where we can talk. Hey, you know that puzzle I bought off you? The little guy in the cage. I think I just figured out how to get him out. I'll tell you about that too."

Reeder opened the door, and Barnes followed him. The same despondent men sat on the benches. The bright squares of light cast by the windows on the worn linoleum were longer now; the short winter day was drawing toward its close.

"There's a room back here they don't use any more," Reeder said. "The light don't work. This is one old, old building."

"I'd think they'd keep it locked."

"They do, but you can spring it if you push against the door frame. That's how you get the little guy out, right? Spring the bars just ever so little, just like you're goin' to do for me. Here we are."

To Barnes the door looked like all the rest, except that it had a fairly new lock of shining brass.

"We won't have to do it this time," Reeder said. "I left it off the latch when I was here before." He pushed against the door, but it did not give.

"Somebody found it," Barnes told him. He felt relieved.

"Yeah, probably one of the nurses saw the crack and pulled on the knob." Reeder braced his back against one side of the warped frame and put a foot against the other, grunted, and pushed the door with his hand. It swung inward.

"Dark in there," Barnes said.

"Yeah. There's a window, but they got a steel hatch over it. Nothin' to worry about in there, just old beds and stuff. Come in now before somebody sees us."

Barnes stepped inside, and Reeder shut the door.

"Look, Mate, I'm sorry, but I forget your name."

"Osgood M. Barnes."

"Look, Barnes, like I said, I've already overstayed my leave. Even if I was to go back to Norfolk now, they'd toss me in the brig. So all I got to do, really, is turn myself in here. I can go to any Navy installation—a recruitin' station, or whatever—and tell them a story, okay? Soon as I get out on the street, that's what I'll do. They got my money when they took me here, but I'm not even askin' you for bus fare. If I had it, I'd probably go someplace and have a beer, and then it would be gone anyhow."

"Okay, I won't give you bus fare. I haven't got it anyway. But how can I get you out?"

"Change clothes with me!" It was a hoarse whisper.

"Are you crazy?"

"Hell, no. The crazy ones don't want out—not really. That's why they call it an asylum. I got a fancy hotel room I was going to skip out on, and there's some dirty uniforms in there. I'll tell 'em I lost my key, they'll give me another one, and I'll go up and change and call the Navy. You wait to give me time to get away, then you tell them who you are, and they'll let you out."

"Reeder, you must be four inches taller than I am."

"It ain't that much. I—"

The creaking of a supply cart in the hall silenced Reeder for a moment. Instinctively, Barnes held his breath too and tried to step away from the door, bumping into a bed piled with rolled mattresses.

"Shut up!" Reeder hissed.

Barnes nodded, aware even as he did that the nod probably could not be seen. The furnace vent to the storeroom had been shut off, and he was beginning to feel cold.

"It'd work," Reeder said. "I swear it would. We could do it. That suit's a little big on you anyhow—"

"I've lost some weight."

"I'd hang the pants low, get it? Like jeans. And I'd kind of scrunch down when I walked. Listen, Matey, let's try it. Let's switch. If it looks too bad, I won't go. I'll leave you all your money and stuff."

"Reeder, I need the suit. I've got a date tonight."

"So wear somethin' else. Nobody wears a suit on a date anyhow. Wear a sportcoat and slacks. I'll leave you your topcoat."

"Jesus, that's decent of you."

"Listen, Matey, you're the one that's bein' decent, lettin' me do it. Don't think I don't appreciate it. You're givin' me back my life, whole years of my life."

Barnes felt sweat in his palms despite the cold. "Reeder, won't you sit down so we can talk about this sensibly?"

"No, I won't sit down, Matey. Take off your jacket and those pants. I guess I'll need the shirt too, and I might as well have the tie. Let me try your shoes too. I don't think they'll fit, but I ought to try 'em."

Barnes's eyes had adjusted well enough for him to see Reeder untie the cord of his hopital pajamas and step out of the trousers. "This is crazy," he said. "Reeder, the Navy's going to examine you and send you back to your ship. That's all."

There was no reply. Reeder pulled his pajama shirt over his head and dropped it on the floor.

"Reeder, that's all there'll be to it. I swear to you."

"I can't do it, Matey. I've seen them—just sittin' around, starin' at the floor. That's not goin' to be me. Strip!"

Barnes reached for the doorknob, but Reeder put his back to the door. "You're not goin' out for a while, Matey. Not till I've had time to get away from here."

Barnes sighed and backed away. "Reeder, damn it, all I have to do is yell."

"And you're not yellin'. I appreciate that, Matey. You're all right. I knew it when I saw you in the depot."

"All you have to do is yell too. That's what I've been trying to tell you. You're a Navy man, and you were in uniform when they picked you up. By this time they will already have notified the Navy. In a day or so someone will come to get you. Yell. Tell them you're sane, it's all a mistake. They'll examine you, lock you for a week or so for being AWOL, and that'll be the end of it."

"I like you, Matey. I like you as much as I've liked

anybody I've met in a long time. Now take off those pants."

"Reeder—"

"Take 'em off!"

"Reeder, what were you doing in that bar?"

"You heard me, Matey!"

"You said you were acting silly. I guess deductions are really my friend Stubb's department. But even Dr. Watson catches on in the end—you know what I mean?"

Reeder said nothing. He was breathing quickly and deeply, each breath sounding like the labored working of a bellows.

"What was it, Phil? I'm your buddy, your shipmate. Remember?"

"Just this," Reeder said.

"Just what?"

"This," Reeder said. "I took my clothes off like this."

Barnes stared at him, and as he stared, Reeder hit him, his right fist coming up from beneath Barnes's chin to snap his head back. Barnes's shoulders hit the mattresses as he fell, and his glass eye rolled across the dark floor like a lopsided marble.

Chapter 37

TWO NOIDS

"Wait a minute," Stubb said. "Did you hear that?"

Sandy asked, "Hear what?"

Davidson said, "I didn't hear anything, but I sure as hell *saw* something. I saw a little kid run across the hall down there."

The attendant looked at him and shook his head.

"Don't argue with a cop, son. I saw a little boy, maybe six or seven years old. What's your name?"

"Ron."

"Ron what?"

"Ron Brown, sir."

"Well, Ron, you've got a kid running around your ward." Davidson turned to Stubb and Sandy. "You two march yourselves downstairs and out of this place. You're lucky I'm not running you in.

"Then you, Ronny, you're going to go find that kid I saw and bring him to me. And if you don't, I'm coming back with a search warrant and a few good men. Understand?"

"I want to see the guy that called my name," Stubb told him.

"The damned in hell want snow-cones. You get out of here, and get out fast. Take her with you."

Sandy looked at Stubb. "I don't think we've got much choice."

He shrugged and followed her back to the elevator. A few of the quiet men on the benches lifted their eyes to look at them, but none stood or spoke.

Sandy whispered, "I always thought crazy people laughed and jumped around a lot."

Stubb shrugged again. The elevator doors parted, and they stepped inside.

"Who was it who called you?"

"I'm not sure," Stubb said. "I'm not even sure I heard my name."

The doors shuddered closed.

"Are we really going to leave?"

"Of course not," Stubb told her.

She smiled at him. "You're kind of neat, Jim—you know that?"

"I'm just doing the job. You remember the doctor's name? The one treating Proudy?"

"Did somebody tell us? No, I don't think so."

"The woman down at the desk told Davidson. Dr. Roberts. So while Davidson's talking to Proudy, maybe we can find Dr. Roberts and get him to let us see him later. Davidson won't spring Proudy out of here after he's heard him."

"I'm Bud Bensen," the tall, thin doctor told them. "I'm pleased to meet you, Ms. Duck, Mr. Stubb. What can I do for you?"

"Dr. Roberts isn't here?" Stubb asked.

"I'm afraid not. He should be, but he seems to have wandered off somewhere. Bob's a brilliant young man," Bensen's boney face broke into the briefest of smiles, "but somewhat emotional. Nervous, you know. We had some unauthorized people going though the wards this afternoon, and I'm afraid Bob was upset."

"The Gypsies," Sandy put in.

"Yes, that, as I understand it, was what they called themselves. I didn't talk to them personally, but I've been told their king—that was the word they used, king—had ordered them to search the city for somebody, and indicated this might be a likely place to find him."

Stubb asked, "I don't suppose you recall the name of the guy they were looking for?"

Dr. Bensen shook his head. "I don't believe it was ever mentioned. Is it important?"

"It might be. Anyway, it seems to me like this Gypsy king might have something on the ball. You wouldn't have a Ben Free in here, would you?"

"I'm afraid I don't know. Check with Admissions."

"The Gypsies will have done that already. They didn't believe Admissions, I guess."

"Cross-cultural distrust." Dr. Bensen nodded. "But it wasn't the Gypsies you wanted to talk to me about, was it?"

"No. We're here about a policeman called Sergeant Proudy." Stubb paused. "Maybe I should explain that I'm a detective. Sandy here's a reporter."

Dr. Bensen nodded again. "Sergeant Proudy's not one of my patients, I'm afraid."

"He's Dr. Roberts's, as we understand it. But we can't

find Dr. Roberts, and we have to talk to Proudy. Here's the situation, Doctor. Proudy thinks we're after him—"

Dr. Bensen motioned Stubb to silence and pressed buttons, bringing a new page up on the terminal on his desk. "Yes, I see Dr. Roberts has diagnosed paranoia."

"So he was watching us last night. Trying to keep an eye on what he thought we were about to do. You follow me?"

"Certainly. That type of behavior is common in these cases. Since the subject is a police officer, I would be surprised if it did not occur."

"But the thing was, somebody else was watching us too. Right, Sandy?"

The short girl nodded. "We're pretty sure of it."

Dr. Bensen smiled at her. "Who was it?"

"Watching us, you mean?" She looked helplessly at Stubb.

"We don't know, Doctor. That's what we're trying to find out. You see, we think that since Proudy was watching us, he may have seen the others who were watching too."

"I see. Why do you think these 'others' feel the need to keep you under observation?"

"We don't know," Stubb said.

Sandy leaned forward. "We think we've stumbled into something big. If we knew who was keeping an eye on us—who besides Sergeant Proudy, I mean—we might know what it is. At least, we'd have a better idea."

"And what were you doing in the hotel room last night while these people were watching you?"

"Nothing. Just talking." Sandy looked to Stubb again.

"Did it ever occur to you that someone might be listening? That they might even be using some form of electronic device?"

"Not at the time." Stubb shook his head glumly. "But then, we didn't have any reason to think somebody might be on to us. You're right though, Doc. There could have been. Or something could have been planted there this morning. I didn't think of this until later, but the maid came around awfully early."

"You have no idea why these people are after you?"

"No," Stubb said.

Sandy said, "No."

"Did you ever talk to Sergeant Proudy before he was brought here?"

"Yeah, a little."

"Did he tell you why he was watching you?"

"Not then. I don't think he was, then. Later he told a friend of mine some crazy stuff, something about our wanting to rule the world."

"And do you?"

"Want to rule the world?" Stubb looked astounded. "Hell, no."

"Why not? Surely it would be a most gratifying experience. Think of the good you could do! Besides, you could have whatever you wanted: palaces all over the world, royal guards to enforce your will, hundreds of women. Are you sure you wouldn't want all that?"

"Okay, it's a deal. But I'll tell you what—I'll trade you my shot at the job for a conversation with Proudy."

"I see," Dr Bensen said. He made a note on his pad. "Mr. Stubb, is your disinclination to rule the world based upon the feeling that you are inadequate to the task? It's a very big job, after all."

"I guess you could say that."

"Possibly you feel you're too short. Napoleon was a very short man too, shorter even than you are, I believe, and yet he came as near to ruling the world as anyone has in the past thousand years."

"Doctor, I don't like short jokes."

"I wasn't making a joke."

Sandy said, "Well, you were very rude."

"Would both of you stand, please?"

Stubb snarled, "You go to hell."

"I just wanted to show you that even though Ms. Duck wears rather moderate heels for so small a woman—no more than two inches, I would say—she is taller in them than you are."

"You're bald, Dr. Bensen. You're bald and you have bad breath. Your breath stinks, and your eyes are too close together."

"Only too true, I'm afraid," the doctor said. He made another note.

Sandy looked from one man to the other. "I didn't come here to listen to you two trade insults—I came to talk to Sergeant Proudy. If I'm going to get to see him, I'd like to be told that. If I'm not, I'm leaving. Or do you want to start insulting me?"

"Right, Alexandra," Stubb muttered. "You're short too."

Dr. Bensen said, "You're correct, of course. Yes, you're going to see your policeman." He touched a button on his intercom. "Send up Charles Proudy, please."

"Thank you," Sandy said.

"I only wanted to see how much paranoia your friend Mr. Stubb displayed. Clearly there is some—he believes that he, and you yourself, are being observed by some mysterious 'others.' He has even managed to convince you of it, at least partially. Fortunately, the paranoid fantasies aren't as well developed as I feared, although I would advise him to seek therapy."

"Aren't you forgetting something, Doc?" Stubb grinned at him. "Proudy really was watching us. You said that yourself."

Dr. Bensen nodded. "One of the most interesting points about mental disorders is that they are communicable, although they do not originate in a virus or bacterium. This man Proudy, who is pronouncedly paranoid, judging from Dr. Roberts's report, was watching you. You spoke to him, and the disorder was transmitted. Now you believe yourself shadowed by a sinister group, and you have at least partially convinced this young woman that your fears are grounded."

Sandy made a small, polite, throat-clearing sound. "I wasn't going to say this, but one of the main reasons we're here is that these people made a telephone call to my boss. They are real, Doctor."

"Do they think you want to rule the world?"

Stubb said, "We don't know what they think. That's one of the things we're trying to find out."

"That is what Proudy thinks, according to Dr. Roberts. He was found in the Consort West, living in a room he hadn't rented. As he explained things to Dr. Roberts, he was observing a group of four persons who planned a world government that would supersede all national governments. He had his badge and some other police identification, together with handcuffs and a blackjack, but his service revolver was missing. He said these people had taken it from him."

Dr. Benson looked at Stubb, who shrugged. "Doc, I wouldn't say his testimony is worth a hell of a lot."

"But you are eager to talk with him. Ms. Duck, has it ever occurred to you that the telephone call your employer got might have been made by Mr. Stubb here?"

As though by magic, Dr. Benson's own telephone rang. After listening for a moment he said, "Well, look again. . . . Of course not. Not until they have him. Neither of them can get out." He hung up.

"Trouble?" Stubb asked.

The doctor nodded. "We've had more disturbances today than we usually see in a week. Just before lunch, a woman and a boy assaulted a receptionist—or at least the woman did. She was clearly disturbed, so we held her for observation until we could notify her family. Dr. Roberts was questioning the boy, as I understand it, when those Gypsies got in. The boy disappeared in the confusion. Now they tell me there's a police captain down on seven looking for the boy, and the woman who brought him has been released from her restraints."

"He let her go, in other words?" Sandy asked.

"It certainly looks that way. He was last seen on seven, and that's a men's floor; but six is a women's floor, and there are stairs and several elevators. He'd have had to sneak past the desks on both floors, but we're so understaffed that the nurses who ought to be on duty there are often gone."

"We've never had any trouble getting by them," Stubb

remarked. When Dr. Bensen looked at him sharply, he added, "Coming up here, I mean. We weren't ever stopped."

Sandy asked, "Are the Gypsies gone?"

"Some are still here, I think." Dr. Benson glanced at his watch. "I can't imagine what's holding them up with Proudy."

"You were just fooling with us, weren't you?" Sandy glanced at Stubb, then back to the doctor. "All that stuff about our catching paranoia from him. You were just passing the time."

He smiled. "Partly, I suppose. Let me put it this way. Virtually all normal people exhibit some pathological tendencies. If you can learn—"

There was a knock at the door.

"That should be Proudy now," Dr. Bensen said.

Chapter 38

THREE CONSPIRATORS

The witch's glare would have bored holes in steel. She strained at her straitjacket like an athlete and bared her gleaming teeth like a beast.

"You want me to give her another injection?" the nurse asked. "That first one don't seem to have touched her."

Dr. Roberts shook his head. "No need to risk it."

"Think you can get her to talk when she's like that?"

"I will speak," the witch told them. "I will tell you both what will happen to you. Your children will be taliped, their eyes dropping from their heads. They will hate you, and in the end they will kill you, cruelly and filthily, in an unclean place." She began to speak words neither physician nor nurse understood. "*Marear enkranken tober malade ammalarsi . . .*"

"We'll be all right," Dr. Roberts said. "You can go now, Nurse."

"Uh huh." The nurse was still watching the witch. "Doctor, you think she's white?"

Dr. Roberts shrugged. "Race is largely a matter of self-classification."

The nurse grinned. "Yeah, you think so, don't you."

"If she told you she was white and spoke like a white, you'd probably accept her as white. If she told you she was black and spoke like a black, you'd accept her as black."

"Look here." The nurse put her forearm beside the witch's face. "She's nearly dark as I am."

"I would die before I would jump into the melting pot with either one of you!" the witch snarled.

"No foolin', Dr. Bob. Have a look here."

For an instant, some minute fraction of a second, Dr. Roberts saw—or believed he saw—a metamorphosis wild as any psychotic delusion. The witch struck like a snake, and for that instant seemed a snake. There was a gleam of scales, a blow sinuous and powerful as a cut from a bullwhip.

The nurse screamed and fell to her knees, the witch's teeth still buried in the flesh of her arm. Blood ran from the witch's lips, staining her canvas straitjacket and the nurse's white uniform.

Dr. Roberts shouted, "Orderly! Orderly!" and got both hands around the witch's neck. Unthinkably, a bronze shoulder was writhing from the opening in the straitjacket, followed by a bronze arm.

A fat blond nurse and a lanky red-headed orderly arrived at virtually the same moment, so that they stuck in the doorway, the nurse with her belly jammed against the jamb, the orderly caught between her billowing hips and the other side of the frame.

"I'll take care of this," the fat nurse said. By then the witch had Dr. Roberts by the throat, a development the fat nurse seemed to view with satisfaction.

"Well, shouldn't we do something?" the orderly asked. He crouched to look at the witch, whose jaws were still locked on the black nurse's arm. "Here now," he said. "You let go of her."

The witch ignored him. Her rapt face gave the impression that her whole attention was devoted to throttling Dr. Roberts, that she continued to bite the black nurse from a sort of absence of mind.

"Get her off," the fat nurse said.

"Maybe if you stuck your fingers in her eyes," the lanky orderly suggested. He glanced around at the fat nurse as if to see what she thought of the idea. "Hey, why are you unbuckling that?"

The fat nurse was bent red-faced over the witch. "She's half out of it already. We can't get her back in without getting her all the way out, can we?" The final buckle loosed, she slipped the witch's other arm from the straitjacket and looked at the canvas. "Have to be washed," she said.

Another orderly opened the door and looked in. "Everything all right here?" The fat nurse was between him and Dr. Roberts.

"We're taking care of it," the lanky orderly said. "Hey, shut the hatch, will you, Mate?"

"Okay." The door closed softly. Dr. Roberts crumpled unconscious to the floor; the witch released him and transferred her grip to the black nurse.

"Don't kill her," the fat nurse said. Other than spitting out the black nurse's bloody arm, the witch seemed to pay no attention.

"Jesus!" the lanky orderly muttered. "I always thought they wore stuff—you know, underwear or something—under those things." He was staring at the witch.

The fat nurse eyed him. "You sure you work here?"

"I'll level with you. This is my first day on the job."

"Really. Where'd you get your training?"

"In the Navy. I just got out. I was a Navy corpsman, see, but we only had guys in our hospital. Well, a few girls— women, I mean—but the nurses always took care of them."

"I see," the fat nurse said. "Where was this hospital, anyway?"

"Norfolk. The base hospital there."

"You're a phony." She fixed him with a plump index finger. "You stay right where you are, or I'm gonna holler my head off. I want to talk to you."

The witch dropped the black girl. "What is the difficulty now? Nurse, I regret losing my temper with these two. It will not happen again."

"You can forget it, Madame Serpentina. He's not for real. He told me he'd been a Navy medic, but they didn't have many girls in the Norfolk Base Hospital. I spent three days with somebody from there once, and he said there were more women than men; they take dependents, so they get a ton of obstetric cases."

The lanky man looked sheepish. "I switched clothes with a pal and put this coat over them. They didn't fit too good."

The witch laughed. "But you thought our Candy a true nurse! I am sorry, but it is so funny!"

"She's a fake too? Hell, she's bustin' out of that uniform."

"Yes!" The witch pointed. "Hold in your stomach or you will lose a button."

"Okay, I'm hilarious. But we have to do something fast, or they'll be on to us. Are those two dead?"

The witch shook her head.

"Then look in these cabinets. There ought to be tape around here someplace. You can wear the nurse's clothes."

"Fah! They are bloodstained."

"We'll have to risk it." Candy slammed a cabinet shut and opened another. "My God, look at the dope!"

"Here," the lanky man said. He nudged her and handed her a roll of adhesive tape.

"Great, but you can do it as well as I can—probably better, because you're stronger. Take care of the doc. Tape up his mouth first, then do his hands behind his back and tape his ankles together. I'll help Madame Serpentina strip the girl, then we'll take care of her."

The lanky man glanced at the unconscious nurse. "We

better bandage that arm while we do it. She looks like she might bleed to death.''

Madame Serpentina clicked her tongue. "So both of you are ministering angels now." She was pulling off the nurse's white shoes.

"What's your name anyway?" Candy asked the lanky man.

"Phil Reeder. I really am a sailor—seaman first—but on a destroyer. No women there. You haven't seen anything around here to cut this with, have you? I lost my jackknife when they picked me up."

Madame Serpentina said, "In that drawer," and pointed.

Candy asked, "How do you know?"

"I know. Look."

Candy did, and handed Reeder a pair of surgical scissors. "That's Madame Serpentina. You probably already heard me call her that."

"Right." He rolled Dr. Roberts over and lovingly spread a piece of wide tape across his mouth.

"She's a witch. She's magic—she really is. It's scary and pretty hard to swallow, but it's true."

"And this," Madame Serpentina said, rising with the nurse's white pantyhose in her hand, "is my good friend Candy Garth, who has saved me. What I wish to know is why the two of you, who are attempting to fly this place, came here when you heard that foolish woman scream."

"I didn't save you," Candy said. "You saved yourself. You had an arm out, and you could have gotten the rest of yourself out of that thing."

The witch waved the objection away. "But why did you come?"

Reeder told her, "I think we scared each other into it. She was goin' down the hall out there and I was comin' up it, and we heard this yell and sort of looked at each other. I thought she was tellin' me to go on and see about it, and she must have thought the same thing about me. I know I was scared that if I ran away from the trouble instead of to it, they'd know I didn't really work here."

Candy nodded confirmation.

"I have more questions. But first you, Mr. Reeder, must turn your back so that I may put on these things. Good. Candy, will you tape that woman, please. I have already from her all that I require."

The witch hesitated, and they heard the rustle of fabric.

"Now if I have understood you, one walked in one direction and one in the other. In which direction is the exit from this mad place?"

Reeder pointed. "The way I was goin'. That's the elevators, anyway."

Candy said. "There's stairs there too—I already checked them out."

"But it was not in that direction that you walked. You were coming toward this room, and your back was to them. You were not trying to leave this hospital then."

"Okay," Candy said. "I guess I got to tell." She propped her plump hips against the side of the examination table. "There's this kid. Ozzie's kid, and—"

Reeder leaned forward. "Who?"

"Ozzie Barnes. You don't know him. I found his kid in the bus station. He was looking for Ozzie, but I don't think Ozzie ever got the word he was supposed to pick up the kid there. So I figured I'd sit with him—you know, take him around till I ran into Ozzie or we met back at the hotel." She looked at the witch. "You remember when Stubb was talking at breakfast, he told me to come here and see Proudy, if I could, and find out what he had against us? Come to think of it, what are you doing here anyway? You were supposed to get some friends of yours on our side."

The witch said. "Possibly it is unwise to speak too much of these things now. Let me say only that I did what I agreed to do, and some of the friends you spoke of came seeking a certain one we both know of. They were detained. I came to free them, and as you have seen, I was detained myself. It is unimportant. Tell me quickly about the child."

Candy nodded. "I brought him here, and then I got mad at the two-bit piece down at the desk and tried to take a hunk out of her, and they got me. I guess about like they got you. They doped me up and strapped me down, and after a while this doc here— Hey, he's awake! Hi ya, Doc! He came and talked to me. After that, he talked to Little Ozzie, only Little Ozzie split when they had some kind of ruckus and went looking for me, and when he found me, he undid my straps. This was only about three rooms down from here. Then I went wandering around in those pajamas they put on me. Really, I was looking for my own stuff, my dress and handbag. But one time when the nurse at the desk was gone, I looked under it and found this big package wrapped up in brown paper. I figured it might be something useful, so I took it back to the room where Little Ozzie was, and it turned out to be her laundry, you know? The really lucky part was that she was a pretty big gal, so I was able to get into her stuff. Then I thought, hey, if I could just find a basket or a big box or something like that, I could put Little Ozzie in it and carry him out. I figured he couldn't just walk out with me, because I knew they were looking for him. So I looked and the big nurse at the desk was gone again, or maybe still gone, and I decided to risk it. Only there wasn't anything, and I was on my way back when I heard the girl you bit yell."

"You shall never know," the witch said, "how truly thankful I am that I asked you to speak quickly. Otherwise we should still have been here on the Last Day. This child, then, is still in the room where you were strapped?"

Candy nodded.

"Then you, Mr. Reeder, must bring him to us now. If anyone should see my friend Candy with him, that person might easily remember that it was she who brought him here. But if you are seen with him, it will only be thought that he has been recaptured. I have a plan for our escape. It involves coercion and perhaps torture, but those are often characteristic of the best plans."

Chapter 39

FOUR IN THE DARK

"Doctor," said the nurse who opened the door, "I hate to interrupt you, but we have a man here, and we don't seem to have any record of him."

She opened the door farther, and Barnes walked in. "I'm not really a patient," he said ruefully. For a moment his hands wandered over the coarse cotton of his pajamas. "It's just that these are the only clothes I have. Hello, Stubb. What are you doing here?"

"The hell with me, what are *you* doing here? I sent Candy, not you."

Dr. Bensen rose to look at him. "Someone hit you on the jaw," he said.

"Yes, sir." Barnes nodded. "One of your patients, Doctor. He knocked me out and stole my clothes, my wallet, and everything. Even my glass eye."

"The routine of this hospital is incessantly interrupted."

Sandy said, "You know, you look very interesting without the eye. I didn't know it was glass."

"I bet I look terrible. Have you got a mirror?"

She took a compact from her purse, opened it, and handed it to Barnes. He studied his face intently. "Blow me down. I look awful."

"I think you're cute."

"You can get another eye," Stubb told him.

"What with? That eye cost me two hundred."

Dr. Bensen asked, "What's your name? Full name."

"Osgood Myles Barnes. Listen, Stubb, do you know the one about the guy with the wooden eye?"

"I've got a hunch I'm about to hear it."

"He was a farmboy, see? Up in New England, and some-body hit him in the face with a hay rake and put his eye out."

"Age?"

"Thirty-four. So he went to Boston to buy a glass one. They had the real good ones from Germany, but they cost a bundle, and he only had twenty bucks."

"Place of birth?"

"Pottstown, Pea Ay. So just when he was about to go back to the farm—he already had his ticket—this peddler comes up to him and he has wooden glass eyes."

"Occupation?"

"Sales. What they really were was pine knots with a blue dot or a brown dot painted in the middle. So the guy bought one for twenty bucks and put it in and went home."

"College graduate?"

"No. Two years at Pitt in business administration. But everybody on the train laughed at him and his wooden eye, and he got so embarrassed about it he wouldn't go out any more after he got back to the farm."

"When was the last time you were hospitalized?"

Sandy said, "Why are you asking him all these questions?"

"My nurse will have to fill out a card."

"Wait a minute." Stubb bent over the doctor to see what he was doing. "Ozzie's not a patient here."

Dr. Bensen removed his glasses and wiped them with a handkerchief. "Frankly, Mr. Stubb, I wouldn't jump to conclusions. My nurse said she couldn't find a record of him, but he's dressed like a patient, and there is a certain child-like ambience I find suggestive."

"You're crazy yourself," Barnes told him.

"There's no need for hostility. If an examination indicates that you're sufficiently responsible to function in society, you'll be released, and your clothing, even your artificial eye, will be returned to you."

"You mean you've got my stuff? I thought Reeder had it."

"Clothing, and corrective lenses, or other objects that might be broken to produce a sharp edge, are stored for the patient until release. Have you ever been hospitalized before?"

"Does having a baby count? I had twins three years ago."

Stubb said, "I wouldn't make that kind of joke, Ozzie. I don't think it's going to go over here."

"What kind would you make?" Barnes asked.

The telephone rang.

Stubb said, "Sandy, I want you to take Ozzie and get him out of here. Right now. I'll talk to Proudy if I can and tell you whatever I find out."

Dr. Bensen was on the telephone. "What's that?" he said. "That doesn't make any sense at all."

"Where can I take him?" The short girl looked doubtfully at Barnes.

"You've got an apartment? You live alone?"

"So far, damn it."

"Well, you just got a roommate. What's the phone number?"

"Mr. Stubb, it's freezing out there. He's got to have more than those things."

Barnes added, "I'll say I do. I got a blind date tonight."

"Then she won't be able to see how you're dressed. Split, you dumb bastard. Get out of here, or you may not ever get out."

Dr. Bensen slammed down the telephone, produced a handkerchief from somewhere in his white coat, and patted his gleaming forehead. "That damn fool Roberts is telling them to discharge the Gypsies. Excuse me. I have to see what he's up to. I'll try and find out what's keeping Proudy too." He went through the doorway, and they heard him whispering urgently to the nurse in the room beyond.

"I think you're right," Sandy said. "I think we'd better go. All of us."

"In a minute," Stubb said. He was looking out the barred window at the city under its blanket of snow. It was nearly dark.

"I need clothes," Barnes muttered. "I'd like to get my eye back too, but I don't think there's much chance of that."

Sandy asked, "What are you waiting for?" She was buttoning her coat.

"I'm waiting because he's still out there," Stubb told her. "We may be able to talk Ozzie past the nurse, but I want to give Bensen time to get away from the area."

The nurse's voice penetrated the door like the anguished squawk of a gull. She was telling someone he could not use the telephone.

"That's our break," Stubb said. "Come on."

In the outer room, a man with curly black hair and pierced ears was pushing the buttons of a complicated looking telephone while holding off the nurse with one hand.

"Don't worry, Miss!" Stubb shouted. "We'll get him out of here for you. Ozzie, grab his other arm! Sandy, you hang up the phone!"

The man was thin, but wiry and a kicker. As soon as they had him in the hallway, Stubb whispered to Barnes, "Okay, let him go."

The man rushed back toward the office, arriving at the door just in time to collide full tilt with Sandy Duck and knock her down. He leaped over her like a hunted buck, the flash of white supplied by a large handkerchief trailing from his hip pocket, and vanished again into Dr. Bensen's office. The nurse shrieked.

One of the patients on the benches that lined the hall rose and helped Sandy up. The rest watched, dull-eyed. "Thanks," she said.

Stubb asked, "You hurt?"

"Just rumpled." She tried to thrust a hand down the neck of her wool blouse. "I think my underwear is in trouble."

"Here," the patient who had helped her up said. "Let me do that for you." He seemed perfectly serious and sincere.

"Never mind." Sandy tugged at a strap. "I've got it."

"Come on," Stubb said. "Let's get out of here."

"Aren't you going to help the Gypsies?"

"Not now. The first thing is to get Barnes out. Then I'll come back and see about them. I'll try to talk to Proudy too."

The patient said, "I don't think the Gypsies need much help, Mr. Stubb. There's a doctor and a fat nurse, and a Gypsy nurse and one of the attendants, and a little boy who are going around letting them loose."

Stubb turned to stare at him. "How'd you know my name? You're . . ."

"No I'm not, Mr. Stubb. I'm Richard Albright Chester."

"Nimo the Clown! Do you know, I don't think I would have recognized you if you hadn't yelled at us while we were talking to Davidson. I wanted to see about you when I got the chance, but we had something else to do first, and then Ozzie came in."

"You're a clown?" Sandy asked. They had been hurrying down the hall; now she pushed the button for the elevator.

"Not just at present, no. But I have this strange ability to become a clown sometimes."

Barnes looked at him curiously. "When the moon is full, or something?"

"No, it just happens. Pretty often, really."

The lights went out. All up and down the corridor, the lights on the ceiling went out behind their heavy glass bowls and wire guards. The long fluorescent over the empty nurse's station by the elevator blinked out. The red elevator telltale between the elevator buttons, just above Sandy's finger, winked out; and the sighing of the warm wind in the steel grills along the baseboard stopped when the EMERGENCY EXIT light over the entrance to the stairs went dark.

Sandy froze. It seemed to her that what had happened was much more fundamental, much more *serious*, than the mere extinction of light. Somehow, with her ears, with her nose, with senses she had written about but had hardly known she possessed, she knew everything had changed, though she could not have said how. She no longer walked on hard plastic tiles, but felt beneath her feet something more resilient and almost living, like the skin of an animal. Every wall save the one she faced seemed to fly away from her, off into the darkness. When she took her finger from the elevator button, that wall vanished too. A moment later she reached for it and felt nothing.

"Power failure," someone—she thought it might be Stubb—said beside her. "It won't last long."

A completely new voice remarked, "I'm doing flips. Chocolate flips." He—if it was a man—seemed to move past her in some complex fashion, then was gone.

Another voice (or perhaps it was only Stubb's again) said, "You think it's just the hospital?"

She heard herself say, "Probably."

"Who are you?" (Possibly the second voice, or Stubb's.)

"Sandy," she told it.

"You don't sound like Sandy." A groping hand touched her face and she jerked back. Somewhere a human being was howling like a wolf.

Somewhere else—outside—a car or truck was howling too, moaning down the street and far out into the city. There was a crash, muffled but unmistakable.

"Do you think it's all over? All over town?"

"I don't know."

"It must be. I can't see any lights outside the windows."

"There aren't any here. Here in the hallway. You can't tell by that."

"Anybody wanna buy a bat?"

"There was a window in that doctor's office."

"To hell with that. Where's the stairs?"

"Please! Please! We have an emergency generating system. The lights will be back in a moment."

Sandy said, "My gosh, I hope he's right." She had lost contact with Stubb and Barnes, and with the wall as well. With each tentative step she felt sure her hands would encounter it, but there was only more space. It seemed colder already.

"If you're in your room, please stay in your room."

"Harris, is that you?"

"I'm just trying to maintain order, shit-face. *O-w-o-o-o!*"

"Stop that! Harris, go back to your room."

Someone bumped into her. It was the second time in five

minutes that she had been bumped, but she was too frightened to be angry. The bumper caught her before she fell. "Lady, where's the steps?"

"I don't know," she said. "I'm trying to find them myself."

"You nurse?"

Then the lights came back. She was in the middle of the hall, with patients milling around her. The man before her was the man with pierced ears.

The lights went out again.

Chapter 40

A CROWD INSANE

"Sit down!" Dr. Bensen ordered.

Scuffling and a thump.

"What did I trip over?" Sandy asked.

"Me," someone said. "Sit down!"

"I was trying to find a way out."

"We all were. But as long as the lights are out, there's no way out."

"Heavy," someone else said. "Who's that?"

"Not heavy, just true, all right? This is the eighth floor—"

"Sixth, I think."

"Who are you?"

"—the elevators aren't running, and the door to the steps is locked. As long as the lights are off, we can't get out."

"So you might as well sit down and stay down. That's what we're doing. At least you won't break your nose."

A yowl, a louder scuffle, and a thud.

"Not on me! Nobody said for you to sit on me!"

"I hit my elbow on this God-damned floor. None of you

gives one damn, do you? I could have broken my arm."

"Is that a man or a woman?"

"A woman. You can tell by the voice."

"A man. It's too big for a lady."

"Probably Emma Cook. She's as big as a house."

"Or Corky Davis. He's as big as two houses, but he pretends to be a woman all the time."

"Or Candy. That you, Candy?"

"Yes, it's me," Candy said.

"No, it's not. I'm over here. You want to feel me?"

"Hey! Hands to yourself."

"Move over so I can sit down."

"I think we ought to go around the circle—are we in a circle? And tell who we are."

"I am the Page of Wands."

"You sound more like a woman than a little boy."

"Let's go around. Not all of us are crazy. We ought to be able to weed out the nuts soon enough."

"Is that you, Mr. Stubb?" Sandy asked.

"I'm Candy—over here."

"No, my name is Dr. Robert R. Roberts."

"Oh, you can't help that, we're all mad here. I'm mad. You're mad."

"I'm not mad!" Sandy objected. "What makes you think I am?"

"You must be, or you wouldn't have come here. M-e-e-ow!"

"Come on, let's go around," Stubb said. "I'm Stubb."

"Wallace J. Willis."

"Joan Giraud."

"Page of Wands."

"Candy Garth."

"Klipspringer."

"Nimo."

"Maude Gonne."

"Carlton C. Katz."

"Hey, Stubb, hasn't it got back to you yet?"

"No."

"No!"

"NO!"

"Corona Borealis."

"Osgood M. Barnes," Barnes said firmly.

"Jake Barnes."

"Candy Garth."

"Hey, you're not me!"

"She's not me either."

"Candy, was that you?"

"No!"

"Yes!"

"Stubb, this isn't going to work."

"Who's that? Ozzie?"

"Yes."

"Here!" Little Ozzie called.

"Hey, a kid!"

"I'm Ozzie Barnes."

"Little Ozzie, come over here," Barnes said. "It's Daddy."

"Over here, Ozzie!"

"Right here, Ozzie!"

"Ozzie, you got him?" Candy asked.

"No!"

"No!"

"Right," Barnes told her. "Everything's okay."

"Little boy, is that your dad?"

"I think so."

"It's a wise child that knows his own father."

"Who was that?"

"Page of Wands, I think," Sandy said. "Mr. Stubb, this isn't going to work. We've got too many liars."

"That's right."

"I'll say."

"Besides, Mr. Stubb, supposing that each of us was known to all the rest, by whatever label the world has fastened to each, of what good would that be?"

"Madame Serpentina?"

"No," the witch said.

"Sure you are. I'd know your voice anyplace."

"I am the person you have been accustomed to call Madame Serpentina, though that is not my name. There are others here who call me by another—which is not mine either. In the dark? Who can say?"

"What shall we call you?"

"Why need you call me anything?"

"Well, you're here, anyway. Did you get the Gypsies loose?"

(A moment of silence.)

"She's gone."

"We are free—if to be free is to be free as you are. But a Gypsy cannot be free under a roof."

"Hey, that's profound! By God, I knew somebody'd say something profound if we kept at it long enough."

"A wife is a woman who has only been wrong about one thing in her whole life."

"That's profound too."

"Death is to life what potatoes are to breakfast."

"Going broke would be like going crazy, if you could push your purse in a sow's ear."

"Knock it off, people!" Stubb ordered.

"What for? You got a better idea?"

"Philosophy is where you go when every other mind is closed."

"You won't ever get these crazies to talk sense, Stubb. And anyway, what could you do with them if you did?"

"We already said that. That was sensible, no?"

"Christ, I wonder how long this thing's going to last. The lights must have been off for half an hour already."

"There's a clock over the nurse's desk. If somebody has a watch, he could compare it with that. If he could see it."

"What's it like outside, you think?"

"Cold."

"I mean, are they busting the windows on the TV stores? That stuff?"

"I've been listening, and I keep hearing sirens."

"Put wax in your ears."

"I already got wax in my ears."

"Doesn't help, huh?"

"Somebody help him, or we'll be driven on the rocks! Doctor! Doctor! Where the hell are the doctors?"

"Where do you think? They're right here with us."

"They are us."

"We has met the enema—"

"Somebody said he was Dr. Bob."

"That wasn't him. I know his voice."

"Didn't he get bit on the arm?"

"That was Alma-Mae Jackson."

"I didn't think she'd bite anybody."

"She might slap them around a little."

"That's different."

"Listen to the sirens. . . ."

"I want to get out."

"Are you kidding? It's a madhouse out there."

"Me too. This is Stubb—Jim Stubb, the private investigator. Who are you?"

"Gypsy Pete."

"Hey, I want to join the Gypsies."

"You don't join the Gypsies. The Gypsies are like a family. You got to be born."

"I've heard of people that joined the Gypsies. The Gypsies like them, see, and they say, come on, be a Gypsy. And they do."

"That's different. Sure, that way you can join the Gypsies."

"Hey, Pete, you like this guy?"

"Hell, no!"

"No way!"

"Get lost!"

"None of those were Pete," Stubb said. "Pete, you still here?"

"Yes!"

"No!"

"I heard once how the Gypsies steal kids."

"That's fairies!"

"We do not!"

"My God, listen to those sirens. . . ."

"Yeah."

"I thought this only happened in the summer. Because of the air conditioning."

"Is it going to last all night?"

"It could."

"Probably not."

"It could last two nights, easy. How the hell do we know what's wrong?"

"Yeah, why don't we all go back to our rooms and sleep?"

"That was a doctor! Or maybe an orderly. I got him!"

"Hey, let go!"

"So what? They're bound to be mixed in."

"He'll have keys! They gotta have keys to the stairs in case there's a fire. Help me, somebody!"

"I got him!"

"That's me—let go!"

"Where'd he go?"

Stamping and stampeding.

"Where is everybody?"

"We're all scattered out again."

"He get away?" Barnes asked.

"Yeah."

"Listen, Stubb—is that you, Stubb?"

"Yeah."

"We could bust the door," Barnes said.

"It's metal."

"I don't care, I bet we could bust them. Come on, Little Ozzie, Daddy's going to bust down a door."

"I'll help you."

"Candy? Is that you, Candy?"

"Sure it's me," Candy said. "You probably think I can't, but weight's what it takes and weight's what I've got."

"Where's the door, anyhow?"

"Next to the elevators."

"Where's Madame Serpentina? I was with her. And the tall guy—Reeder."

"Reeder! Reeder was here?"

"He gave us a hand. You know him?"

"I owe him. I'm gonna knock his block off."

"He's pretty big, Ozzie."

"He's in for a susprize. I'll deck 'at swab!"

"Big talk," Stubb said. "Want to borrow my sap?"

"Jim, won't you and Ozzie shut up for a minute. Listen. Listen outside."

"All right, I'm listening. Sirens."

"Lots of sirens. All the time. Everything the pigs and the firemen have must be out there, and every ambulance in the whole damn city."

"You want to stay here, Candy?"

"No. No, I don't. But if I wasn't starving to death, I'd say yes. Have you thought about the people out there? I mean, a blackout like this in the dead of winter? The heat will be off in all the buildings. It's been off here, but this is a big, solid old place, so it takes a while to notice it. Out there, they'll have got cold in a hurry. They must have gone outside to start fires in the street. It would be garbage and stuff at first."

"The hell with that—where's the door?"

"Here's one for you, Mr. Stubb. Why is—"

"Who's that, Jim?"

"Nimo, I think. Where are you, Nimo?"

"—the door you're looking for like Samson?"

"Okay, it's a strong door. Nobody said it was going to be easy. Keep talking so we can find you."

"Because they're both unlocked!"

Chapter 41

THE LAW OF THE SEE

Behind them, the dark bulk of Belmont was soon lost among others equally dark. Moon and stars were hidden behind clouds heavy with snow, but leaping flames gave a distant, fitful light, and from time to time some wildly careening car swept by, its brights lancing the street. The air was still, and bitterly cold.

"Looks like hell, doesn't it?" Candy said. "Just the same, I'd like to get closer to one of those fires." She had no coat over her bulging nurse's uniform.

Barnes, in slippers and thin hospital pajamas, was worse off still. He did not seem to know it, pegging along bravely with little Ozzie trotting beside him. Nimo was too active to suffer, turning flips and cartwheels on the ice.

"Sandy didn't make it, I guess," Stubb said. "We lost her."

"She was with you?" Candy asked. "She'll get out okay. She wasn't a patient, after all."

"I guess Doc Makee will too," Barnes said. "What's our course?"

"Back to the Consort."

"Well, blow me down! I just remembered, I got a date wit Olive. What time is it?"

Stubb glanced at his wrist. "Six forty-five."

"Wow!" Candy looked around at the darkened buildings. "It seems more like midnight. It really got late early tonight."

Nimo capering ahead of the rest, stopped and threw his arms wide. "Lipstick!"

"Listen," Barnes told Stubb. "I got to get slicked up. She's going to pick me up in front of the Consort at eight."

"Okay, you're not heavy. I bet Candy could do it."

Nimo dropped to his knees before her. "If I only had a lipstick, I could make stripes on these pajamas. I could give myself a red nose, too."

"Jim, get him away from me! I think he's going to sing that song from *The Wizard of Oz*."

"I like it," Little Ozzie announced. "We're o-o-off to see the Wizard, the Wonnerful WizardoFoz!"

"No, no," Nimo told him. "I-i-if I only had a lipstick, they could not think me a dipstick. I would not be thought insane! With a lipstick I could stripe me, I could even overripe me, they would not suspect my brain!"

"Blow me down," Barnes muttered. "I'm cold." He glanced down a side street where a fire winked like a star as dark figures passed before it. "Those guys might be working on a haberdashery right now."

Little Ozzie looked up at him. "You wouldn't steal the clothes, would you, Dad?"

"Of course not," Barnes told him. "But there's a thing called the right of salvage—that means that if something's found abandoned, the finder gets to keep it. For instance, if somebody's already broken into some store, and there's nobody there to take care of the things, that store is considered shop-wrecked, and until the owner or the police come, anybody can take whatever he wants. Candy, will you look after Little Ozzie for a while?"

"If you'll try to get me a coat."

"Fine," Barnes said. He turned and darted across the street. Once his hospital slippers slipped on the ice, but he did not quite fall.

"I didn't know Ozzie could run like that," the fat girl said.

Stubb shook his head. "I hope he doesn't get caught. The power could come on any minute."

The boy, who had not far to look, looked up at him. "If the store is store-wrecked, it's all right, isn't it?"

Candy said, "See, Little Ozzie, the lights are sort of like having a cop watching the place."

"Or the sun could come up!" Nimo looked at the dark sky and threw wide his arms.

"Hey, you really are crazy, aren't you?"

"It could happen," he told her seriously. "*Anything* could, and something *has* to happen. I'll bet you a massage—against a kiss—that the sun will rise within a minute."

"Are you a good masseur? I bet you are. Okay, it's a bet."

"Come here," Nimo said to Little Ozzie. "Get up on me. I'll carry you awhile." He crouched, and the boy clambered onto his back. Nimo hitched him to his shoulders and stood. "See! Ozzie is that other Ozzie's son, and he has risen!"

"Okay, I owe—" Candy broke off her sentence and pointed. "Jim! Do you see that?"

"See what?"

"That sign, down there. Jim, it's the Dilly Deli. They have the greatest corned-beef sandwiches, wine, beer, all that stuff. Aren't you hungry? My God, I'm starving."

"I'm hungry," Little Ozzie announced from Nimo's shoulders.

"Sure you are! And we're going to get you something to eat. You trust Candy. Nimo, come on!"

Half a block down, the delicatessen was silent and dark, its windows filled with bread, bottles, and hand-lettered cardboard signs.

"You'd think they'd be there, wouldn't you?" Candy said. "They used to be open till nine."

"If they were there," Stubb remarked practically, "you couldn't get in and scarf a sandwich. You haven't got any money."

"What the hell do you mean, a sandwich? A super-Dilly, with pastrami, corned beef, roast beef, liver sausage, and Russian dressing, with a bowl of matzo-ball soup and a malted. Jim, can you get us inside?"

Stubb squinted at the door. "Maybe I could, but I won't."

"For Christ's sake, Jim! You want me to bust the window with a brick?"

"No, I want you to walk about another four blocks. Then I'll get you whatever you want to eat. Come on." The small man started down the icy sidewalk. After a moment Nimo followed him, carrying the boy.

Panting, Candy waddled after them. "Jim, this better be good. My feet hurt and my legs hurt, and I'm cold. And I'm so God-damned hungry I could eat my own arm."

Nimo was scratching the crown of his head, arm held high and hand bent in an exaggerated gesture of rube puzzlement. "We're getting close to my clownhouse," he said. "I can show you an unlocked window, but there isn't much in my Peterpantry."

"Nah," Stubb said. "It isn't that. We're going to the Sandwich Shop. Candy just reminded me—it's Friday night."

There was a bonfire in the middle of the street; stores on both sides had been broken into, but the looting was nearly finished now. A few children, newly dressed in heavy clothing, pawed through what remained. A few adults stood warming their hands at the fire occasionally tossing rubbish onto it: fragments of a broken counter, papers, scraps of carpet, and the heads and limbs of mannequins. "Somebody hurt?" they asked, seeing Candy's uniform. She nodded and hurried after Stubb and Nimo.

A liquor store farther down had been abandoned even by the pillagers, a cold, reeking cavern of darkness and broken glass. She hesitated, knowing nothing remained, yet unwilling to leave its odor, the failed promise of warmth and cheer. It seemed to her that they might have left a single case, even if it were only of half-pints, half-pints of rum or some filthy cordial, for those like herself who passed in the street. She began to curse softly as she puffed along. She knew a great many evil words, and she was still cursing when they reached the entrance of the Sandwich Shop.

"Now we've gone from door to door," Nimo said, "without ever getting in. I wish the dark Delilah would clip this lock too."

"You're crazy," Candy told him as she came puffing up.

"He means Madame S.," Stubb explained as he examined the lock. "He thinks that she, or one of her people, picked the lock of the emergency exit. He's probably right."

"Jim, she was right there talking to us."

"Sure, but where were we? How close to the door? She could have been working on the lock while she talked. Or she may just have had the tools and given them to one of the others."

"I don't suppose *you've* got any tools like that?"

"Used to, but I hocked them."

"I saw a movie once where this private detective had a little piece of plastic in his wallet, and he stuck it in the door and opened it."

"Sure. I use a credit card—that's what everybody uses. But it only works on spring locks, and not on all of them. This is a night bolt. You want to wait here? I'm going down the alley."

"I don't even go in there when the lights work."

Nimo said, "I'll come!"

"Not with Little Ozzie, you won't. He stays here with me." Candy took the boy from Nimo's shoulders, hugged him for a moment, and set him down "I'm glad you've got your coat, Little Ozzie. Are you cold?"

"Pretty. When will we see my dad again?"

"When we get back to the hotel, I guess. I—"

The woman must have run up the dark street; but because they had not seen or heard her, it seemed she had not come but materialized, appearing like a ghost out of the blackness. "A nurse! Oh, thank God, a nurse! Please come, please!"

Taken aback, Candy could only ask, "Where?"

"Half a block. It's just half a block. Please! I couldn't carry her, so I was going to come here—there's a little cart thing—but she could bleed to death. . . ."

"I'm coming," Candy said. "I'm coming." She bit her lips. "Oh, Lord, my legs. If you only knew how far I've walked today."

"Please," the woman said. "She may be dying."

Candy broke into a limping trot. "What. Happened. To. Her?"

"She's my mother-in-law. They own that place down the street. Sam and me live with them. I'm not Jewish—do I look Jewish? Over there. I put her in the doorway."

In the dark, the woman crumpled in the doorway might have been a bundle of old clothes. Panting, Candy dropped to her knees beside her.

"Listen, I know about your legs. You nurses walk all day, and then with the power off and no transit—"

"Never mind. About. My legs. We need light. Any kind."

"I've got a lighter." There was a rattle as the woman who was not Jewish fumbled in her purse. "So when the power went blooey and the fires started, she went. They're not supposed to, but she went anyhow. Sam wasn't home yet. Neither was her other son. I told her I'd go—"

"What did they hit her with? A bottle?"

"I think a piece of pipe. I thought they were going to rape me, but I guess because it's so cold . . . You must be freezing."

"I am. Gimme a cigarette."

"What? What did you say?"

"I said give me a cigarette. You've got a lighter, you must have cigarettes too. I want to light it before your lighter goes out."

The non-Jewish woman fumbled in her purse again. "They took my money, my MasterCard, everything. Sam will have a fit. Is she okay?"

"Hold that lighter steady for a minute, will you? Little Ozzie, don't touch her." Candy drew deeply on the cigarette, until its end glowed almost as brightly as the shrinking blue flame. "No, she's not all right. She's got a bad concussion, maybe a fractured skull—I can't tell for sure. She ought to be X-rayed. Until we can do that, she ought to be kept warm; lying out here in the cold's the worst thing in the world for her. What is this? This cigarette?"

"A Virginia Slim. She could die?"

"I never tried them. Always hated the ads. Yeah, she could

die. The last concussion I worked on, the doctor thought the guy was going to be just fine. I helped bandage him up. Only he wasn't fine—he went kind of crazy. That was only a couple days ago. God damn it, I wish the lights would come back."

"Can't you bandage her here?"

Candy shook her head. "She's not bleeding bad, and fooling around with her like that in the dark, I might do more harm than good. Didn't you say she owned a place around here? Can't we get her inside? We might be able to find something to cover her up with."

"The Sandwich Shop, down the street. Do you think we can carry her?"

"Sure, only we gotta be careful not to bang her head. If the skull's fractured, another bump might do it."

"I'll help," Little Ozzie said.

"You're a good kid. Okay, you take one foot, and this lady can take the other one. I'll grab her under her arms."

Chapter 42

MS., IN THE PICKWICKIAN SENSE

"The lights came on" as one newspaper was later to describe it, "and everybody went home except the firemen."

Electric clocks showed five minutes till six, watches seven thirty-five. Dr. Makee, who had waited it out in the physician's lounge, went home to bed. Alexandra Duck, who had found Sergeant Proudy in the dark and spent the rest of the blackout talking with him, let herself into the offices of *Hidden Science/Natural Supernaturalism* and looked up the address of The Flying Carpet, a supper club, in the telephone directory before switching on her word processor and starting work on an article on possession. Francisco Fuentes, who had spent the blackout guiding guests up the Consort's fire stairs with a flashlight, sat on a step and wiped his forehead while he listened to the cheering; in the past hour and forty minutes, the temperature of the stairwell had dropped to thirty-eight degrees, but Francisco was sweating anyhow. On the thirteenth floor, Monstro, the computer who was the Consort's actual manager ("your innkeeper"), went off emergency power with an electronic sigh.

Mrs. Baker, who had been possessed for years by a small addiction to scented candles cast in the shapes of religious figures and animals, had gone through the blackout easily and with a good deal of pleasure, scurrying about the house (while Puff repeatedly hunted and dispatched her heels) lighting and tending various members of her collection in an ecstasy of justification. Now, quite suddenly, the lights were back, and the little silver-plated snuffer that had gathered dust for twenty years had its hour. A picture bloomed on the TV. Mrs. Baker decided to leave one candle—the bayberry Santa she had never quite been able to bring herself to light at Christmas—burning in case the lights went off again.

"If you're seeing me now," the announcer announced rapidly, "and you know you *haven't* been seeing me for an hour plus, you also know that we've been experiencing the worst mid-winter power outage to hit a major U.S. city. There's been a certain amount of rioting and looting, and several fires, including a four-alarmer at Forty-fourth and Dennis. We switch to Renee Falcone with the mini-cam."

Flames roared up the screen. Mrs. Baker, reflecting that Forty-fourth and Dennis was not terribly far, belted her robe and stepped out the front door. Sure enough, there was reddish light in the sky in that direction. "Lady bug, fly always home," Mrs. Baker muttered. "Your house's on fire, and your children in the barn."

When she stepped back inside, a sincere-looking black man was standing before a small restaurant with a broken window. He said, "Phil, as you know there are a thousand stories around the city tonight as a result of the blackout, but this is one of the most heartening I've come across. Mrs. Benjamin Potash was just taken from here in an ambulance. Mrs. Potash is a widow, and she owns this place. When the lights went out, she and her daughter left their apartment about six blocks away hoping to protect this little diner. They were attacked, and Mrs. Potash was struck on the head, but her daughter found an off-duty nurse who treated Mrs. Potash and helped carry her here. When they got here, they found two men, one of them one of Mrs. Potash's regular customers, prepared to defend it if the looters came. Well, the looters did come, and the customers tried to scare them off by telling them they had a machine gun. That didn't work, and the looters smashed this window to get in. The customers didn't really have a machine gun, but they had a garden hose, the one Mrs. Potash uses to wash down the kitchen floor. They turned the hose on the looters, and in this subzero weather, it can't have been very pleasant. Now I have with me Mr. Murray Potash, who has just arrived."

The sincere-looking black man thrust his microphone toward a plump and pimply white youth. "Mr. Potash, were you able to speak to your mother before they took her away?"

"Huh, uh." The youth shook his head. "I got here just when they were pulling out."

"Is your sister here?"

"Sister-in-law. I think she rode in the ambulance with Mom."

Mrs. Baker changed the channel.

Outside, a car door slammed. Mrs. Baker paid no heed to it, but a few seconds later there was a knock at her door. She had not bothered to put the chain back on after she had looked at the fire; she did so now, opened the door a crack, then shut it and took off the chain again. When she opened it the second time, a statuesque brunette stepped inside.

"My," Mrs. Baker said. "How nice you look! That's real leopard, isn't it?"

The brunette pirouetted. In her fur-trimmed boots she was over six feet tall. "I've got a date tonight, and this outfit's my pride and joy. Do you like it?'

"You're a regular gelded lily, I declare. But if you have yourself a social engagement, shouldn't you be at home waiting for your young man?"

"I'm picking him up, Mrs. Baker. It's only a few blocks from here, and I'm early anyway, so I thought I'd stop by and see you. Have you remembered anything more since we were here?"

"Well, that's delightful. Won't you take a cup of tea? Tea gladdeneth the heart of man is what the Bible says, but I think it works better for women. On the TV now they're always talking about women's Liptonation. Are you a Lipper, Miz, Miz . . . ?"

"Valor, Mrs. Baker. I'm Robin Valor. Please don't be embarrassed. At your age, you've met so many people. It's no wonder you can't always keep them straight."

Mrs. Baker shook her head. "Perhaps I oughtn't to say this, Miz Valor, but the truth is I couldn't keep them straight before I met them."

The brunette smiled. "It's Miss, Mrs. Baker, not Ms. I'm an old-fashioned girl just like you, and they say Ms. means a divorced woman working in an office."

"I'm an old-fashioned girl too," the old woman said, setting a little tray, with a flowery teapot and matching cups, on a small table. "That's why I say Miz. Why, we always said Miz when I was a girl. Miz Ledbetter, Miz Carpenter; why I remember Mama talking about them a million times. Excuse me for a moment while I get the water. Kettle's on."

She toddled out, and the brunette took a pair of wire-framed glasses from her purse, then rose and strode across the room to examine the television. It was still on (though Mrs. Baker had turned the volume all the way down) and showed a gaggle of solemn and rather stupid-looking men in yellow hardhats inspecting an electrical substation. But the brunette paid more attention to the knobs and the back than to the picture on the screen.

"Here we are," Mrs. Baker announced, returning with the tea kettle. "Good thing I've got a gas cook-stove. Stayed on all the time. House didn't even get cold, even if the furnace fan wouldn't blow. I've got that fireplace, but there's nothing to put in but paper these days, and I need the paper for Puff's kitty box."

"I'll bet you were brought up in a small town," the brunette said. "Am I right?"

"Oh, yes." Mrs. Baker nodded, pouring steaming water from the tarnished kettle.

"Where was that, Mrs. Baker?"

"The town? Oh, here. Right here, except this was a small town then. Mr. Baker and me, we bought this house ten years after we were married. We'd been living in rent. It seemed like such a long time then, ten years. Almost sixty years I lived right here in this house, walking from this parlor to that kitchen."

"I see."

"It's all changed, of course. This was a real nice town. The boys that played in the street, they was full of hell, they'd do anything, but they weren't mean. They didn't want to hurt anybody, not really. Just play tricks and have fun. And men used to come selling with a hearse and wagon. Not just milk. Ice and vegetables, and fish when it wasn't too hot. They don't do that any more."

"I don't suppose anyone does, anywhere."

"I saw them on the TV, in some other country. But do you know, all those American companies are coming in there too? All the ones that stopped everything here. I saw it, and the TV said the people liked it, and I suppose they were just telling the truth, they really do, or they wouldn't buy those things. I wanted to yell at them not to do it, don't you do it, only of course they couldn't hear me. I would have wrote them a letter, but they couldn't have read it. Lots of times when I watch the TV, I feel like some kind of ghost." She retreated to the kitchen with the kettle, leaving a wisp of steam hanging in the air.

The brunette looked speculatively around the room, then shrugged. This time she remained seated and did not take her glasses from her purse.

"They're all just the same as we were, except slower,"

Mrs. Baker continued, coming in again. "Sometimes I think if only the ordinary people here could sit down and talk to the ordinary people there, those people would never let things go the way they are. But look at the way we do here. We don't try to change the way things are. If one of those boys down the street steals a car, why he goes to prison for years. But if some rich man that's had everything a person could want all his life steals a million dollars, the only thing that happens is he doesn't get elected again unless he's pretty lucky. The comics in the paper have all these men that fight against crime. If they were real, they'd go and find that man and shoot him. Maybe if we were real, we'd do the same thing."

"I was just wondering," the brunette said. "You've lived here so many yars, Mrs. Baker. Was Mr. Free your neighbor when you moved in?"

"Let me think," Mrs. Baker said, sitting down. "Goodness, how time fleas, just jumps away whenever you try to catch at it." She dabbed at one eye with a corner of her robe. "You'll have to excuse me, Miz Valor. I always cry when I think too much about back then."

"I don't care if you cry."

"It was a lady," Mrs. Baker said, still blotting her eyes, "that used to give me cookies. Or anyhow one time she did. You know what they say, 'Let them beat cake.' Well, they did. Or it did. Maybe it was only once. It was a great big sugar cookie with a great big raisin in the middle. Except that wasn't here at all. That was Miz Carpenter down on Oak Street when I was a little girl."

The brunette glanced at her wrist. "I have to go soon, Mrs. Baker, but before I do, I'd like you to tell me anything you can recall about those four people who used to live with Mr. Free. Perhaps you won't find that so traumatic."

"There was nothing foreign about it, it's just that it makes me sad to think about all those old times. Pretty soon I'll be dead, and then I won't feel sad any more, so I figure I'd better get it done now. People always complain if a child laughs or an old person cries, but pretty soon they're quiet, and that's for a long time. A lot of children have started to die young again, have you noticed?"

The brunette shook her head impatiently.

"Why, pretty soon people will be saying, 'Farewell to this vile of tears,' just like they used to. I don't suppose you ever read Dickens, Miz Valor?"

"No. Is he a newspaperman? Someone Mr. Free knew?"

Mrs. Baker nodded. "Isn't it strange that you should mention that! Yes, Mr. Free knew his Dickens well, I think. We used to read him too before we got the TV, and one time I said to Mr. Free—he helped me carry some groceries home—'Why, thank you, Mr. Free. You've been a wonderful help,' and he said back, 'What we've got to do is keep up our spirits and be neighborly. We'll come all right in the end, never fear!' Which wasn't exactly *apres* poor, because what I had was potatoes and canned goods and things, and not any kind of spirits. But it was Dickens, and I knew it. I said right away, 'Why that's Dickens, Mr. Free, isn't it?' and then I explained about not having any liquor in the bags, but I invited him for a little sherry if he would like some. I always keep a bottle in the house because it benefits me so when I have the cold. And he said he had used the word—the word *spirits* was what he meant—in the Pickwickian sense."

"I had understood that Mr. Free was a rather uneducated man."

"Why, I don't think—bless me, Miz Valor, here I've been sitting and jabbering and not giving you any tea. It'll be stewed to prunes." She picked up the flowery teapot and decanted pale brown liquid into the brunette's cup.

"Would you say that Mr. Barnes, for example, was well educated? More so than Mr. Free?"

"Why he would be bound to be, wouldn't he?" Mrs. Baker asked. "They go to school so much longer than what we did. We never learned but readin', writin', and 'rithmetic. That was the way we used to say them. Nowadays you young people don't even bother with those."

"Are you teasing me, Mrs. Baker?" the brunette asked.

"Me?" Mrs. Baker shook her head. "Course not! Why I'm

innocent as a limb. I suppose Mr. Barnes is very well educated, in the modern manor."

Chapter 43

A FRIEND OF CROWLEY'S

"Marie," the King boomed, "I want you to meet a special friend of ours."

The special friend was a tall and very spare old man with a bristling white mustache; he wore a loose gray tweed suit that was either British or a remarkably good imitation of it. When the witch extended her hand, he bowed over it, brushing her knuckles with dry lips.

"I am very pleased to meet you," she said. "I cannot welcome you to this house—it is our King's, not mine—but I join him in welcoming you to the encampment of the Last Free People."

"I thank you," the elderly man said. "Indeed, I thank you very much, Mademoiselle."

"When we shorted the juice to get you and Rose and the rest of our people out of Belmont, Mr.—uh—" The King snapped his fingers.

"Illingworth, Mademoiselle," the old man said. "Cassius Illingworth, at your service."

"Mr. Illingworth was able to help us quite a bit. It turned out he knew about the tunnels downtown where the power lines run. He drew a map, and Bella and some of the other young guys went down there and fixed things."

"I am a journalist, Mademoiselle, and in a lifetime a journalist acquires many bits of queer lore. During the Second World War, those tunnels were prepared for use as air-raid shelters. How preposterous it seems now to suppose that German bombers might have reached this city in nineteen and forty-two! Yet it did not seem preposterous then; many serious-minded men believed it. And afterward, when everyone except a few laborers employed by the utility had forgotten them, they were used as a meeting place by certain—ah—seekers.''

The witch regarded him speculatively.

"He knows about that too, Marie." There was sly pleasure in the King's smile. "See, when you came here and asked me to help you find this Ben Free, Mr. Illingworth was one of the first *gadje* I came across. He says he never met this Free, but he knows people who have."

Illingworth nodded. He stood with his back to the fire, big, age-spotted hands clasped behind him. "I have the honor and pleasure of editing and publishing certain journals of the occult, Mademoiselle. I believe you have already met one of my staff, Miss Duck."

"Ah!" The witch nodded. "So you are her employer."

"I am, Mademoiselle. I have that honor."

"Mr. Illingworth used to belong to the Golden Dawn," the King said. "He's been in the business a long time."

"You knew Aleister Crowley?"

"I did, Mademoiselle. He was perfectly charming, despite all you may have read of him, and a fine mountaineer. We climbed together in the Himalayas on several occasions, and we are still not wholly separated, though our essential energies are now on different planes. I have been so fortunate as to communicate with him on several occasions."

"He was called the wickedest man in the world," the witch said.

"He was, Mademoiselle. In fact, I believe I had the honor of originating the phrase, though I did it only to please him. For all Aleister's penetration, he was like a little boy in one respect: he loved to shock. Years later—at least it seems to me like years now, though perhaps it was only a year or so—in Smyrna, I was sitting with him in a cafe when we heard the major domo tell a tourist couple, giving that little movement of the head that those diasporic Greeks (if I may coin a term) use so well, that Aleister was the most evil man God permitted to remain on earth. The tourists were very impressed indeed, and I think I never saw him so happy. Certainly I was never to see him so happy again."

"Marie hasn't had your experience," the King rumbled. "But she has the gift."

Illingworth nodded politely. "Your people are famous for it, all over the world."

"Most of us fake it—I do myself." Suddenly the King smiled. "So does Marie, sometimes. But with her, sometimes it's the real thing."

"Fascinating." For a moment, Illingworth studied the witch. "Just what is the real thing, dear? Telekinesis? Precognition?"

She shook her head, then nodded. "I do not seem to be telekinetic at all. I am strongly precognitive. A bit of telepathy, though I have met people who are much better at that than I. I am also a fairly good medium, particularly with the nonhuman spirits—elementals and so forth."

"Demons, Mademoiselle?"

The witch hesitated, then nodded guardedly. "They have other, and better, names; but occasionally, yes."

Illingworth smiled, showing a row of teeth as white and uniform as cups on a shelf. "I've been by the Free house, you know. I thought I caught a whiff of sulfur."

"You are interested in him yourself, then."

"Only on your King's behalf, my dear. We'd spoken earlier—"

The King nodded confirmation.

"—and of course he gave me the address. As it happens Mr. Free and I had—ah—certain mutual friends, so I was quite concerned when I heard he was missing and perhaps deceased. I thought his home might hold some indication of his whereabouts."

He sighed. "I found nothing. That is, nothing indicative of his present situs. A rifle that might have slain red men in its day, and a watch with a picture of a lovely lady dead, I suppose, well over a century. Beautiful old things left behind in an abandoned house, though I have taken them under my aegis now. We whose interests run beyond the marches of the visible world, beyond the fields we know, as Lord Dunsany once so finely put it while we were musing at White's, we are prone to an itching discontent of place—"

"Regular Gypsies," the King added helpfully.

"Precisely so, sir. Precisely. I would suppose I have myself, in a lifetime, I grant, more than notably long, slept in a hundred beds, hotels and such-like temporary accommodations excepted. At one time or another, I've made my abode on every continent, excepting only Australia and Antarctica; and though I've not relocated now for over thirty years and am as I suppose a bit long in the tooth for Antarctica, I might adventure Australia yet. Indeed, the warm, sunny, dry climate that characterizes so much of that 'Land of the Southern Wind' would seem more suited to my old age than our savage winters. I have sojourned upon many islands too, of which Great Britain was the largest and Capri perhaps the best. It has been spoiled now, I am given to understand, by tourists. Tiberius Caesar said much the same thing."

"You were speaking of Benjamin Free," the witch reminded him.

"So I was, my dear. I only meant to say that an examination of his mementos led me to suspect that he was not—I will not say an initiate, but not an initiate as I have been accustomed to using that term. I doubt that he was ever admitted by others to a knowledge of the occult mysteries, to the ceremonies and services of the Secret Masters; although he may well have been one of those persons—more common than we are wont to suppose, if I may say so—who have acquired occult power and even occult authority by developing their superphysical capacities."

"I'm sure you are correct," said the witch, who was happy to have this shadowy old man believe Free unimportant. "Nevertheless, I would be glad to find him, and grateful for whatever help you can give me. He was kind to me, and I would like to repay him, if he is still among the living and in difficulties; and I feel certain he had something yet to teach me."

Illingworth gave the King a broad wink. "And what payment do you offer for my services, Mademoiselle? I will not ask for that little hand in marriage; I fear there might be royal objections, although I feel sure we should be as happy—in the words of that other Benjamin, that marvelous old Franklin who used to visit the Hell Fire Club—as two bugs in a rug. No, I won't even request it for a son or grandson, for I have none, though they would be the luckiest boys in the world now if I did. But what about a kiss, my dear? Do you think you could bear to kiss this raddled old cheek, for such a prize?"

"You've found him!" the witch exclaimed.

"My dear friend," Illingworth turned to the King. "You are the luckiest man on earth, do you know that? Your subject here is a woman of such surpassing loveliness that she is beautiful even with mouth agape. You kings have all the best of it anyway, enjoying the pleasures of the *droit du seigneur*, savoring the blossoming as it were, then allowing us poor devils of husbands to sweep up the petals."

"Where is he?" The witch caught Illingworth by the sleeve.

"Well, now," he said. "Well, now, I suppose I should tell you about it. You don't object to my smoking?"

"Not at all; I would like one myself. I have no more of my own."

He opened a large, old-fashioned silver cigarette case. "They're Players, I'm afraid. One keeps up the old habits, the dear old luxuries, and they become more luxurious every year, and more dear. There's a little tobacconist's down on Fourth Street that stocks them for me. I warn you, they're strong for American tastes."

The King said, "I'm a cigar smoker, Cas. I'll try one."

Illingworth bent forward with the case. "An honor—ah— Your Majesty."

"Just King. Call me King."

"And a light. A light for you, Mademoiselle? And for myself now, if you will excuse me."

"Is he safe?"

Illingworth puffed smoke, a smoldering old dragon. "Hmm? Oh, Mr. Free. Why, yes, so far as I know. Perfectly. I don't really know the people who have him, you see—"

"Have him?"

"Perhaps I should explain. When your king communicated with me, mentioning the names, I might add, of certain esteemed mutual acquaintances, and informing me of Mr. Free's disappearance and his own concern therefor, it struck me, and indeed I might say struck me almost at once, that I had heard the name. Have I mentioned, my dear, that I have the honor to be the editor and publisher of both *Hidden Science* and *Natural Supernaturalism*?"

"I know that," the witch said impatiently, but Illingworth was looking at a corner of the ceiling, or possibly the visage of posterity, and did not appear to hear her.

"They are small publications, if you like. Indeed their page size is but five by seven and a half, seldom does an issue have a folio in excess of one hundred—often my little staff and I are delighted to see that advertising, the support, largely, of a few stalwart friends who have clung to us through the years, permits a page count in the nineties. Each title appears but half a dozen times per year; no slick paper for us, and no covers from famous photographers, no pictures of five-hundred-dollar-an-hour trollops. On a magazine rack, beside the great periodicals of the day, ours are small and shabby enough.

"But appearance is less than everything. And though in saying it I defame the God of the Age, no, Mammon Himself is not everything. These tiny and yet precious bundles of inexpensive paper—inexpensive, that is, in the eyes of men who need not pay for it—are the respected journals of those who seek to penetrate the veil of illusion and reach Ultimate Truth. And what is that but to say the sole class of mankind having any importance on the rolls of eternity? I have conducted these publications for more than thirty years, and thus I—even I, who have no more than the most rudimentary powers, the powers any man on earth might develop with very little application—even I have a certain, shall we say, cachet? A cachet, then, among many of the leading psychics of our day."

"You—" the witch began.

"Did I say *many*? I might in complete honesty have said *all*. Yes, my dear?"

"You contacted some of these people?"

"I did indeed. There are certain ones—persons whom I am accustomed to call the Secret Masters. No, not the Secret Masters of this our world, who are said to dwell among inaccessible peaks, but certain personages whom I know to be more than legends, personages who dwell (sometimes amid the most humble circumstances) within ten leagues of where we sit, those whom I name the Secret Masters of the City."

The witch said, "I would have called Ben Free such a one. Or one who is above them."

Illingworth lifted a finger to his lips. "My dear, I beg you not to speak here of Those Who Are Above. Let it suffice to say that tonight, when your King's dread minions consented to the restoration of the dynamos, I was approached by a certain individual. I was told of a location and given what I may call without too much inaccuracy a key. I called your King with my happy news and was told that you, my dear, were expected shortly. And now, if you will consent to ride in an old car with an old man . . . ?"

"You are going yourself?"

Illingworth smiled again. "My dear, it is I who bear the sesame, if I may so phrase it, that will fling wide the portals of the enchanted cavern. Besides, I wouldn't miss it for gold."

Chapter 44

SPINACH

If Stubb had been paying more attention to his surroundings and less to Candy, or if Candy had been paying attention to anything, they would, as they entered the Consort's bar, have seen Oswald Barnes standing before the hotel's main entrance.

If they had, they presumably and understandably would not have recognized him. He wore an overcoat with a rich fur collar, like a theatrical impresario; from beneath it protruded pants legs that plainly belonged to a gray pinstriped suit of bankerly cut, legs terminating, regrettably, in the sort of black patent-leather shoes worn with a dinner jacket. On his head sat a black homburg that might have graced the Ambassador to the Court of St. James. His hands were tastefully attired in gloves of the thinnest and softest pigskin, and he clasped them behind his back as he waited, humming a little tune about being strong to the finish. If he was cold, he showed no sign of it.

Five minutes after Stubb and Candy had gone into the bar, two things occurred at once. A small and slightly soiled boy came running down the sidewalk toward Barnes. And a large and gleaming gray auto pulled up to the curb in front of him. Little Ozzie called, "Daddy!" and Robin Valor inquired, "Osgood Barnes?" like unrehearsed actors stepping on each other's lines.

Barnes was a man of many flaws, but slowness of thought was never one of them, and he was abundantly blessed with that instinct America values above all the rest, the one that makes a man grab all he can. He swept Little Ozzie into his arms and stepped into the gray car with almost the same motion. "Yes," he said. "I'm Osgood Barnes. At your service—very much so. Little Ozzie, what are you doing here? Why aren't you with Candy?"

"Mama said I was supposed to live with you," Little Ozzie announced firmly. "I rode on the big bus."

Barnes shook his head ruefully. "I'm divorced," he said. "Did I tell you that over the phone?"

The gray sedan left the curb with a crunch of ice. "I think so," Robin murmured. "Anyway, I assumed it."

"Well, I am. And this is my son, Osgood Myles Barnes, Junior."

Robin glanced across at him and smiled. 'Hi, Osgood."

"Ozzie," Little Ozzie said.

Barnes added, "You can call me that too. Little Ozzie, where are the people who were supposed to take care of you tonight?"

"I don't know." The boy was enjoying the warmth of the car; he was already near sleep.

"Did you run away from them?"

"I ran away from the clown."

"Why was that?"

"Because I wanted to find you."

Barnes gave him a lopsided smile and rumpled his hair. Robin said, "We can't very well take him on our date, can we?"

When the gray sedan pulled up before the Consort again, she got out with the two Ozzies. In her four-inch heels, she was taller than both.

The doorman smiled at them. "Registering, folks?"

"No," Robin told him. "We're just going in for a moment. May we leave the car here?"

He nodded. "I'll have a boy park it for you, Ma'am."

Her hand, holding a folded bill, slipped into his. "Just leave it where it is. We'll be back in five minutes or so. If you have to move it, the keys are inside."

In the lobby, no one appeared to notice the elegant couple and the bedraggled child. A large, smooth elevator decorated like the very best type of Victorian brothel carried them to the seventh floor. Barnes knocked at the witch's door, but his knocks woke no response. "They must have gone somewhere," he said. "Probably that's why they left him with the clown."

Robin leaned over the little boy, more imposing in her scented muscularity than his mother or any teacher had ever been. Her power made him sneeze. "Where does the clown live, Ozzie?" she asked. "You came from there, so you must know."

He sneezed again, shaking his head, wiping his nose on his sleeve.

"Then he'll have to come with us," she said. "I won't mind. Will you, Osgood?"

"We can't take him into a lot of places, and if we stay long it'll get too cold in the car."

"Then we'll not stay long. First I'll drive you to a little spot I like very, very much. We'll talk on the way, and your son will fall asleep, I'm sure, on the back seat. When we stop, you can cover him with your coat. We'll go inside and I'll have a sherry or perhaps two, and we'll listen to the music. Before the car gets too cold, we'll leave again and go to my apartment. There's a spare bedroom, and you can carry him upstairs and put him on the bed. There's a very nice restaurant nearby that will send up food and wine."

Without saying a word, and much too quickly for her to protest or even step back, Barnes put his arms around her and kissed her. He had to raise himself on his toes to reach her lips, but he bent her backward until he was supporting her torso almost horizontally, crushing her big, firm breasts to his chest, his lips and tongue alive with passion at the gateway of her mouth.

At first she was too stunned to act; then for an instant Little Ozzie thought she was going to ram the long, sharp, crimson-lacquered nails of her thumbs into his father's eyes. Then she moaned, a sound surprisingly deep and anguished, and threw her arms about him, pulling him to her until it seemed they both must fall with famished lips and grinding pelvises to the floor of the corridor.

As perhaps they would, if an elevator some distance away had not opened to discharge an elderly couple and a bellman. Belatedly, they straightened up instead, Robin's lipstick smeared, much of it under Barnes's mustache, her pillbox hat with the peacock's feather lying on the carpet near the wall.

The elderly couple were much too well bred to notice anything; they walked by chatting of something neither would be able to recall five minutes afterward. Their bellman, however, smirked and offered Barnes a congratulatory wink.

When the elderly couple and their bags had disappeared into a room beyond the witch's, Robin asked breathlessly, "Shouldn't you at least tell me why you did that?"

"I don't know," Barnes said.

"Well, it was—different."

"For me too." Slowly, arm in arm, they walked back toward the elevator. "If you really want to know, it was because you said what you did. About going up to your apartment and having dinner. For my whole life I've been waiting for you to say that to me; and now that you have, I know someway that something's going to take it away so it won't ever happen, we won't ever go there and eat that dinner." He pushed the button.

"You're a little frightening, Osgood. Do you know that?"

"Ozzie. Anyway, I wanted to get a piece of paradise, sort of a sample I could carry around for the rest of my life, before that something came along and took the rest."

The elevator doors slid back.

"You are frightening, in a nice way. I feel—I don't know—as if all of a sudden I've got this pet panther. But, Ozzie, it's going to be just like I said. In fact, it's going to be wonderful—we might not order the food at all."

He grinned at her as they stepped out into the lobby. A man in a worn check suit was waiting near the registration desk. When he saw the suit, Barnes trotted over and tapped him on the shoulder. He turned around; he was long and lean, and at least half a head taller.

"Hello, Reeder," Barnes said. "Put them up. I wouldn't want to cold-cock you."

"Shipmate! Hell, I've been looking all over for you. I want to give you your stuff back." He fumbled in the pockets of the suit.

"Put 'em up," Barnes said again. Robin Valor and Little Ozzie looked from one man to the other.

"Wallet," Reeder mumbled. "Locker key."

He held them out and Barnes slapped his hand, knocking them to the floor. Then he slapped Reeder with a quick forehand-backhand, the two slaps coming so close together they sounded like one.

"Don't do that," Reeder said. He lifted his fist and Barnes hit him under the jaw, sending him reeling against the registration desk. Joe the bellman, who had been in the act of picking up a guest's luggage, dropped it and jumped between them. Barnes hit him with his left just above the belt, his fist driving into the cheap red uniform to the wrist. Joe doubled over and collapsed, his legs turned to rags.

Reeder hit Barnes on the cheek with a left and over the eye with a right, his fists flying like pistons. Barnes ducked and bored in with the hard, quick, smacking sounds a butcher makes tenderizing meat. Reeder staggered back, but the desk would not let him fall. For a moment Barnes's fists fell against him like rain. His face seemed to melt under the blows, growing soft and darkly crimson as the skin washed away. Then he slipped down, and two burly men in dark suits grabbed Barnes's arms from behind.

"Hotel security," one of them told him; Robin Valor chopped the speaker's thick neck with the edge of her hand. He turned slowly, as though half stunned, and she kicked him in the groin. Barnes whirled on the other man, landing a punch in the belly and getting a round-house right on the ear that knocked him to the carpet.

He bounced up like a superball and came at the house dick like a power saw. The dick made the mistake of reaching toward his hip pocket for a sap. Before he could get it out, his head snapped back and he fell stiffly, as a tree falls.

The other dick was still doubled over with pain. His fists still up, his good eye nearly closed, Barnes glared at the male guests and their wives, the desk clerks, and a couple of watching bellmen. Francisco, who was one of the bellmen, touched his cap in a gentle mock salute. *"Buenas noches, Señor,"* Francisco said.

"Good night to you too." Barnes let his hands drop. The knuckles of the pigskin gloves were bright with blood.

Robin took his arm. "Come on. We've got to get out of here."

He nodded reluctantly, looking at the felled house dick. "Blow me down," he said. "He had a real punch."

"The police will be here any minute."

"Aye, aye, Cap'n, sir. Where's Swee'pea?"

"I'm Olive, remember? I've got his hand. Come on now."

Outside, snow was falling once more. The soft flakes sifted into Robin's furs and settled on Barnes's black and shining hair. "I've lost me cap," he said.

Little Ozzie held up the homburg. "I got it."

The gray car waited at the curb a few steps away from the bright lights of the entrance. As Barnes settled the stolen hat on his head, they heard distant sirens. "Hurry up!" Robin snapped.

"They've been running all night because of the blackout," Barnes said. "I doubt if they'll send the Swat Team to a fistfight. Little Ozzie, when you got my hat for me—thank you very much—did you by any chance also get that wallet he tried to give me? Or the key?"

The little boy shook his head.

"Pull up in front of the door," Barnes told Robin. "I'll be right back."

Before she could stop him, he was sprinting for the entrance. He leaped a stack of luggage and burst through the inner doors while Francisco and the Agatha Christie fan were still applying water-soaked towels to Joe. The house dick Robin had kicked was nowhere to be seen, but the other dick was on his feet again, grasping Reeder by the arm. "I dropped a brown wallet and a key," Barnes told him. "I want them back. Now."

The dick only glared at him. Barnes began poking around the floor, kicking at disturbances in the thick carpet that he thought might conceal the locker key. He found the dick's sap, tossed it in the air, then dropped it into his own pocket. A white-haired woman guest discovered his wallet and handed it to him with a disconcerting look of hero-worship.

Francisco called, *"Paging Meester Jeem Stubb!"*

The sirens died away beyond the doors, and two policemen came in. Barnes walked into the street-level bar where Candy and Stubb had ordered a final drink. He was tempted to stop for a quick one, but it could only be moments before someone told the policemen what had happened and pointed to the bar.

Outside, the gray sedan still waited, its rear bumper nearly touching the front bumper of the squad car. Barnes got in and saw that Little Ozzie was already sleeping, stretched out on the back seat. "I thought they had you," Robin said. "God knows what I would have done." She put the sedan out into traffic.

Barnes shrugged. "You couldn't have done anything."

"I have friends around town. I could have phoned some of them."

"Sure." Barnes patted his pockets. "Don't give me a cigarette. I'm trying to quit."

"Good for you. But you're frisking yourself for one right now."

"That's okay, I know I don't have any."

She laughed. She had a good, throaty, big-girl laugh, Barnes thought. It made you want to make her laugh again. He said, "I might have a cigar."

This time it was more of a chuckle. "Look in my purse."

It was between them on the seat, and he looked. "What are you doing with cigars in your purse? Good ones, too." Each was cased in its own aluminum tube. Barnes opened one, sniffed the cigar, and pushed in the dashboard lighter.

"Light one for me, will you?"

"You smoke cigars?"

"Where'd you think I got these dark good looks? I'm half Spanish, *mi amigo*. All us Spanish ladies smoke cigars—it's sort of a family tradition."

Barnes drew on the cigar until it was evenly lit, then passed it to her. "You said you were at the Bureau of Indian Affairs. I thought maybe you were part Indian."

"No, it's just that I had an affair with an Indian once. Chief Smoke Eater—he was a fire chief."

This time it was Barnes who laughed. "I notice you've got a little gun in there too," he said.

Chapter 45

DETECTIVES

"Paging Miss Cathy Garth!"

"For me?" Candy looked at Stubb.

"That's what the man says."

"Should I answer it?"

He tried—quite successfully, since Candy was in no condition to be minutely observant—to appear not to care. "Up to you."

"I guess I better." She waved at the bellman as he passed. "Right here. I'm Cathy Garth."

"House phone three, Ma'am." The bellman pointed. "Thank you very much," Candy said. Stubb walked her over to it, and she asked him, "What'll I say?" whispering as though the other party could hear her already.

"'Cathy Garth,'" he told her.

"Cathy Garth," she repeated, and picked up the telephone. "Cathy Garth speaking."

Stubb listened, pretending not to listen.

"Yes? . . . Oh, hi! Hi, John. . . . I'm right down here in the lobby. . . . Could I ever! I'm starved! Anything."

The bellman who had paged Candy was coming around again. "*Jim Stubb! Paging Mr. Jim Stubb!*"

Stubb stopped him. "Me too?"

"This is a different party, sir. He gave me a letter for you."

Stubb took it. "Mysterious, isn't it?"

"I guess so, sir. We haven't had the murder yet, but when we do, we'll call in the Yard."

"But it will actually be solved by an eccentric peer who hasn't done any real work since the Second World War," Stubb finished for him.

The bellman grinned. "How about a poisoning in the Quaint?"

"Happens all the time, only they die outside." With the feeling that luck was about to change, Stubb gave the bellman a five. "The fat girl didn't tip you, did she?"

"Ladies seldom do," the bellman said. "Thank you, sir."

As he turned away, Candy seized Stubb's arm. "Jim—" She belched softly. "Jim, you've gotta help me. That was a john I met this afternoon. His name's Sweet."

Stubb nodded encouragingly.

"He was going to the airport, see? Back home after some convention. I went with him, only it turns out he didn't go. I guess they had more snow out there than we got here, and some flights got cancelled. Then the lights went out, same as here, and it got screwed up worse. So he said to hell with it like anybody would. He said there weren't any cabs by then, but he hitched a ride back with a business acquaintance— that's what he said—that lives here and had his own car."

"Is this going anywhere?" Stubb asked. "If it isn't, I'd like to sit down."

"It's there already. I mean, he's here. I'd told him I was staying here, so the guy dropped him here and he got a room and he's been looking for me ever since, hoping I didn't get my flight either. He'll be down in five minutes. Jim, how do I explain this nurse outfit?" The fat girl's voice rose to an anguished wail. "*I didn't tell him I was a nurse!*"

"You could split before he gets here. Come on, and I'll get us into Madame S.'s room."

"Jim, it's dinner and at least a hundred bucks, and I'm starving and I haven't got a dime. So what do I tell him? Do I say I'm a nurse now? You're my friend, Jim. What do I say?"

Stubb scratched his chin reflectively. It was too warm in the lobby; he felt hot and tired. Suddenly his eyes went wide, and he nudged Candy. "My God, look!"

She looked. "That's him, isn't it?"

"You're damn right it is, but where'd he get the clothes?"

"Stole 'em, I bet. But where'd he get that fox?"

They watched until Barnes, Robin, and Ozzie disappeared into an elevator. "You're right," Stubb said. "He must have got them in the blackout. Hey, that gives me an idea for your nurse's clothes."

"I stole them?"

"No. You went to a costume party. This john thought you were catching a plane, right? Why'd you go to the airport anyway?"

"Never mind, I did. What's your idea?"

"You couldn't get your plane, so you came back here— only earlier, and you called up a girlfriend and she told you about the party. You didn't have time to rent a regular costume, but the girlfriend's a nurse and she loaned you those. You were tired and the party wasn't much fun, so you had a couple of drinks and came back here. That'll also explain why you're a little juiced, which you are."

"Okay, that's great."

"Meaning, 'Now be a darling and get lost.'"

"Jim, it won't look good if he sees me talking to you."

"Don't worry, I'm not well dressed enough for a pimp," Stubb said, "or the right color either." But he was already turning away, losing himself even to himself in the crowd in the lobby. The letter felt thin and dry between his fingers; he wondered vaguely why he had not put it inside his coat. There were no statues in the Consort's lobby, no palms or ferns, and out of long habit he did not want to open the letter where someone might read it over his shoulder. Neither did he want to remain close enough to see the man who came for Candy. With a surge of others, he entered an elevator.

He got off at the seventh floor. No one answered when he tapped at the door of the witch's room. He stood for a moment and listened, fearing that Barnes had taken his tall brunette there. No sound came through the thin panels, and there was no answer when he tapped again, positioning himself before the peep-hole.

The room had not been occupied since he had searched it with the witch that morning. The big bed where she had slept was still smoothly covered by its quilted spread. The drapes he had opened then had been drawn again—that was new. A chaise had replaced the other bed.

He switched on all the lights and checked the bottom of the table, the television, and all the lamps again, then slipped out of his trenchcoat and jacket and threw them on the bed. The room seemed warm. He had tossed the envelope onto the table when he came; now he picked it up, peering at it through his thick glasses, fingering it, pushing back his hat.

I should have asked that bellboy questions, he thought. That's what comes of stopping at the Irishman's to drink with her—I'm a little bombed myself. He must have had a good laugh out of me. Man's writing, only one sheet inside.

He tore open the envelope.

> Jim— Need you on a case. This is a tough one, but the sky's the limit. $200/day & exp., could be a long one if you set yourself up right with the client. Call me PDQ. I'm in 877.
>
> Cliff

Stubb smiled to himself, picked up the telephone and dialed. A moment later he could hear it ringing in the room directly overhead.

"Room eight seventy-seven."

"It's Stubb, Cliff."

"*Jim! This is great. I was afraid I wouldn't be able to get hold of you.*"

"How did you know I was in the hotel?"

"*I didn't, not for sure, but I've been asking around for you, and I ran into Bill Kramer. You remember Bill? He's the security chief here now.*"

"Big guy, crooked nose."

"*Hell, Jim, everybody's big to you. My height, maybe two hundred pounds.*"

"So you ran into him. Your wife throw you out of the house or something?"

"*Would I stay here? Listen, Jim, you're getting pretty damned independent. The last time you called me you were begging for work.*"

"I'm not begging any more. I've got something."

"*You called me just for old times' sake?*"

"Right."

"*Jim, you're not licensed.*"

"I didn't say I had a client. Just a little job for an old friend. I told you. How about finishing the story? You ran into Bill Kramer."

"*I said, have you seen Jim, and he said, yeah in the coffee shop this morning with another guy and two gals—*"

"He said 'gals'?"

"*All right, so Bill's not a very bright guy. If he was he'd be working for me. Yep, he said gals. You and two women and another guy in the coffee shop. He said after that he checked to see if you were registered and you weren't, but he figured maybe you were shacking it with one of the women.*"

"He's running a riding academy now, huh?"

"*Jim, every place's a riding academy now. Nobody gives a shit unless you rip the sheets or wake up the couple in the next room. Where are you?*"

"In the hotel."

"*Hell, I know you're in the God-damned hotel, you just told me. What's your room number?*"

"That's confidential, Cliff. You know how it is."

"By God, you're getting cocky. This afternoon you were begging me for a job."

"Yeah, and you wouldn't give me one."

Stubb hung up. Leaving the spindly chair beside the telephone stand, he kicked off his shoes, threw himself into a larger, more comfortable chair, and put his feet on the bed. Smoothing the note, he reread it and stuffed it into his shirt pocket. A smile crossed his waxy face. He stretched, went into the bathroom and relieved himself, washed his hands, then sat down at the telephone again and dialed.

"Front desk? My name's Jim Stubb. Am I being paged?"

"Yes, sir." The clerk paused. *"We've been having a little disturbance here, but I believe you are."*

"What's the message?"

"I don't know, sir. You can find out by calling the bell captain, sir. One nine."

"I can find out from you too—" Stubb began, but the clerk had hung up. Fuming, Stubb banged down the handset, picked it up again, pressed one nine, and identified himself.

"The message is call eight, seven, seven, sir."

"I thought it was. I don't know why I'm wasting my time with this Mickey Mouse." Stubb cradled the handset a second time and grinned, then pressed the number.

"Hello? Eight seventy-seven."

"It's me again, Cliff. You've got the kid hollering for me, and I'm getting sick of tipping him."

"Jim, you didn't have to hang up on me."

"Only if I wanted to look at myself when I shave. You want to say I'm not tall enough to look in the mirror? Go ahead, say it. It isn't true, but say it."

"Jim, you're trying to put words in my mouth. I never said anything like that to you."

"Like hell."

"Okay, maybe I kidded you a couple of times. But Jim, it was only kidding. Now I need you. What the hell did I say in that note? A hundred and fifty a day? I'll make it two hundred."

"You said two C's. Make it three."

"Now you're kidding. Two fifty."

"Goodbye, Cliff."

"Jim, don't hang up. Three hundred. Okay."

"Plus expenses."

"Plus expenses, right."

"It's a deal. What's the job?"

"Come up to the room, Jim. Hell, you know I can't talk about it on the phone."

"You've got a big, big client, and they've told you, you own the mint. You've got every man you've got on it already. What is it, Cliff? CIA? Saudi Arabia?"

"You're working for me now, so knock it off. For three hundred a day you can get your ass up to this room."

"I don't start till tomorrow, right? Any rough stuff?"

"You start right now, Jim—I'm paying you three hundred for the rest of tonight. No rough stuff at all, I swear to God. A pussycat, so get your ass up here."

"Like you say, boss."

"That's the spirit."

"Stubb hung up, nodding to himself. "It sure is," he whispered.

He found his shoes, jammed his feet in them, and put on his jacket and trenchcoat. Lifting the mattress, he thrust his arm under it and pulled out Proudy's gun. In the bathroom, he stood on the toilet to retrieve the cartridges from the top of the medicine cabinet.

Chapter 46

A LITTLE TIPPY

"My coat," Candy muttered. "My God, I haven't got a coat."

A woman nearby turned toward her. "I beg your pardon?"

"I said I don't have a coat," Candy explained. "I was just talking to myself." After a moment she added, "I've been in the bar. Must have left it there."

The woman nodded. It was not clear whether she was agreeing that was the most probable explanation or acknowledging that Candy had indeed been in the bar; perhaps both.

Candy turned away, doing her best to walk straight and succeeding pretty well. There was a long rack of coats, with a shelf above for hats, in a narrow room that formed a buffer zone between the bar and the lobby. A weary redhead stood behind a small counter that closed the entrance.

Candy smiled at her with as much charm as she could manage. "Can I get my coat? My boyfriend has the checks."

The weary woman shook her head. "You'll have to get them from him."

Candy bit her lip. "Please. I want to go home."

"Like that, huh?"

Candy nodded.

"Which one is it?"

Candy peered into the narrow room, trying to imagine what sort of coat a nurse might wear. "I don't see it," she said. "It's dark blue and, you know, big."

The weary woman nodded. "I think I remember it. You've been here a while, huh?"

"I guess so. There was the blackout and everything. He's really very nice, except when he has too much to drink."

"And you don't have a hell of a lot of choice. Honey, I know how it is. Wait a minute."

There was a bowl for tips at one side of the counter. While the weary woman's back was turned, Candy took three dollars.

"Here you go. This's it, right? Pretty lining in the hood."

Candy nodded. "Thanks so much." The coat looked large and warm, a silky blend of wool with some softer fiber.

"You got bus fare?"

She was afraid the weary woman would take it from the tip bowl and shook her head. "I'm fine. I'll go home in a cab."

"Yeah, that would be better—on the bus, some creep might take advantage of you."

"I'm all right," Candy told her. "I just shouldn't have had that last one."

"You talk pretty good, but I keep thinking you're going to fall down. Maybe you ought to go out in the lobby and sit for a while."

"Okay, I'll do that." As she left the coat room, however, she was gripped by the conviction that she would forget the stolen coat when she got up, and struggled to get her arms into the sleeves before dropping into a providentially empty chair.

She thought she recalled Sweet's face, but it was nowhere in sight. After a minute or two, she decided he might be screened from her by one of the rectangular imitation-marble-sheathed pillars. She tried to stand up; but when she should have been on her feet, she discovered she was still in the chair. Something wasn't working, she decided. She would rest a bit and try again.

An elevator door opened, and the tall brunette who had been with Ozzie Barnes came out, followed by Barnes himself and Little Ozzie. Barnes went over to the registration desk and knocked down a tall man in a check suit. That's done it, Candy thought, I've got the DT's. She put her hands to her face to see if she could feel crawly things. It reminded her that her makeup must surely be gone. A crowd of people surrounded Ozzie and the tall man; faintly above the hubbub she could hear the solid crack of punches, but the liquor had erected its diaphanous, nearly impermeable curtain between her and reality: she was warm, languorous, and happy.

The crowd vanished and Ozzie with it, though she had never noticed its going. As though she had known all along they would be there, she took a compact and a lipstick from the right pocket of the blue coat. She had powdered and rouged her face and was applying the first dab of lipstick when Sweet sat down beside her.

"Well, *hello*," she said. "It's wonderful to see you!" To

herself she sounded like Mae West in an old, old, late, late, late-night TV movie, and she giggled.

He misunderstood. "I know it took me a while. I wanted to freshen up, change clothes."

"Me too, only I didn't. John, am I getting this on straight?"

He looked at her judiciously. "Fairly straight."

"I might as well tell you, because you'll guess pretty soon if you haven't already. I'm a little tippy." Fearing he did not understand her, she added, "A little in the bag."

"When you were on the phone, I thought you might be two or three ahead of me." He smiled.

"You're sweet." She kissed him, then realizing what she had said, giggled again.

"Want to give me a chance to catch up at dinner?"

"Do I ever! I don't think I've had a bite since you gave me that candy in the cab. I'm just absolutely, utterly, fabulously starved. I could eat a billy goat stuffed with soldier buttons."

"You shouldn't drink on an empty stomach."

"I'm finding that out. Don't you want to hear my adventures today?" She was still not sure she could stand up.

"Sure, and I want to tell you mine, but let's do it over dinner. I've had them bring my car around."

He stood, and she held out her hands to him. "I didn't—*urmp!*—think you had a car." A belch caught her unaware.

"I rented one. They've got an office here in the hotel." With his hands to draw her up and steady her, she came out of the chair more easily than she had expected. "You didn't tell me you were a nurse."

"I guess I didn't." She and Stubb had made up some story, she knew, but it was lost in the warm, amber fog. "You didn't tell me you were so strong, either," she said. It seemed the right thing to say.

"I used to play football, believe it or not. Iowa State. Over this way."

He had her firmly by the arm, and she was grateful for it, leaning on him with an uncontrollable heaviness. "I'll be okay when I walk a little."

"I'm sure you will. Did they call you back? To the hospital where you work?"

"That's right. It wasn't really an emergency—did I say that okay? Emergency. Well, it was, but we didn't think so at first. So I went. I went back in a cab just almost right away after I left you." She decided to lie. "I'll tell you the truth, with us just meeting and then breaking up like that, John, I didn't really feel like going on the trip. All the holiday feeling went out of it. I've been feeling down since Christmas, for God's sake. You really did like me, didn't you, even if I'm so heavy?" She had forgotten it was a lie.

"Very much."

"So anyway, I went to the hospital. And there was a lot of trouble there and I had a big talk with one of the doctors about it. And then the lights went out, and I stayed because of that, but after a while I left, and there was this man there—a visitor, you know—that I know and I've met him several times and he's really pretty nice even if sometimes he can be pretty mean. It was dark and we couldn't get a cab. I was so tired and awfully cold."

"Certainly."

"You don't have a cigarette, do you? I've been out forever."

"Right here." He lit it for her on the dashboard lighter. They were in the front seat of a big car, though she had no notion how they got there. She toked the cigarette like a joint, drawing in the smoke and holding it with a sort of rapture.

Then letting it out with a gasp, "And there were rioters all around. This man is nice, but he's pretty small and I was scared. Do you know what I kept thinking? I kept thinking about those old Westerns where the Indians try to kill all the people on the wagon train. It's no different for us, except the Indians are inside with us now, so it doesn't do any good to pull the wagons in a circle. That's funny, huh?"

"That's why we require a strong government," Sweet said. "The savages all throughout society are only waiting for the lights to go out."

Candy nodded. "Then things got complicated, and I found this woman somebody had bashed in the head. Her daughter-in-law was with her. I fixed her up as good as I could there in the dark, stopped the bleeding, tried to keep her warm and all that stuff. I'm afraid I probably got a little blood on my uniform."

"That's too bad," Sweet said.

"And then the lights came back on, and I felt like the U.S. Cavalry was there. We got an ambulance for the woman, and this man and me—we were back together by then—went to a bar and had three or four drinks to unwind. Then I went back to the hotel and had a nightcap. Anyway, I thought it was a nightcap. And then I went out in the lobby and the bellhop was calling my name. That was the best part of the whole damn night, which I guess isn't saying a whole lot, but it was." She snuggled against him. "It was just awfully God-damned nice, and it still is."

Sweet nodded. "I'm glad we shared that cab."

"I'm glad you couldn't catch your plane. Or me either. You're married, I bet?"

"My wife and I are separated."

"Uh huh."

"Well, practically separated."

Candy sighed. "That's good."

"That we're almost ready to break up?"

"That you're still married. I mean, after all these years . . ."

"Twenty-two."

"See? I'm a girl—" Her stomach jumped. "Oh, my God, I hope I'm not getting hiccups. I'm a girl who has kind of had it rough sometimes, if you know what I mean."

Sweet nodded.

"And one thing I've *hic!* noticed *hic!* Oh, my God! Is that when guys get to be over about thirty, it's *hic!* better if they're married. You see, John," she laid a hand on his arm, "guys that aren't usually aren't because they're just so God-damned selfish. *Hic!* Excuse me. Will you excuse it, please?"

"Certainly."

"It's all take and no give with them. They don't know how to treat a girl *hic!* and that's why they haven't got one. Like you're taking me out to dinner tonight. A guy who wasn't married wouldn't do that, or he'd just take me to some cheap place. This *hic!* isn't just some cheap place we're going to now, is it, John? I'm starved. I could *hic!* eat a—eat a . . ."

"It's probably the best restaurant in the world," Sweet told her.

"Won'ful." She snuggled harder, one big breast pushing at the side of his right arm, her belly almost in his lap. "Now tell *hic!* me all about it or tell me about your wife or something. I want to hold my breath."

Chapter 47

EGYPTIAN DARKNESS

They might, perhaps, have been a princess and a magician hunted by the white trolls of deadly winter; and indeed the ancient Packard, lumbering and high-wheeled, seemed rather an enchanted carriage—perhaps a funeral carriage—than a car, as it trundled between banks of snow, leaving the hunched, white, black-windowed masses of the city's buildings behind.

The largest of them seemed also the slowest in pursuit, their towering forms now hardly to be glimpsed against the night sky. Smaller structures still clawed at the Packard's sides with signs half defaced with snow. Ahead lay empty fields where only a few farmhouses kept watch over the road. Ahead too, a 747 droned out of the low clouds, its landing lights blazing like fireworks.

Illingworth appeared to watch it with satisfaction,

nodding to himself. "They are flying," he said. "I had feared they would not be. The snow and so on."

"Is that where we're going?" the witch asked. "To the airport?" She had a lap robe over her legs, and she was smoking one of his cigarettes.

He nodded.

"I had thought from what you said that these were local people."

"You must learn above all—do you wish me to call you Madame Serpentina? Your King called you Marie."

"The former."

"As you wish. I was saying, Madame Serpentina, that you must learn above all not to ask questions. One looks. One listens. One observes. Perhaps on rare occasions one asks some favor. But one does not question, ever."

"I know that. I asked you, not them."

A chain-link fence had appeared on their right, seeming to guard miles of mere empty ground.

"But it is a habit that must be broken," Illingworth told her. "Who can say what is near, or what is far? Perhaps we will fly—perhaps only you—perhaps neither of us. Watch. Observe and learn. Leave questions to the owl, that wise bird of Minerva, who asks the only important one."

"Very well, I do not ask. I merely comment. If the airport is our destination, we might have reached it more swiftly on the Interstate Highway."

"Indeed we might." Illingworth chuckled. "You are wise, at least, in the ways of the city, Mademoiselle. But is the shortest path thereby the best? Especially when it is also the plainest? I ask only as a matter of information."

The witch said nothing, grinding out her cigarette in the Packard's rusty, narrow ashtray. A gate appeared in the fence, flanked by a small metal sign:

MILITARY AREA
KEEP OUT

Illingworth heaved at the Packard's wheel. Skidding a bit, the big car turned up the gateway and creaked to a halt.

"I should do this, Mademoiselle, and not you. But perhaps you will indulge an old man?" He held out a complicated-looking key.

The witch took it and stepped onto the running board, and from there to the ground. Illingworth had switched off the Packard's headlights, but the trifles of moonlight that leaked through the clouds were reflected by the snow that lay everywhere. The phrase *darkness made visible* floated into her consciousness from some source she could not identify.

She drew her coat more tightly about her, wishing she had put on her gloves. The snow creaked beneath her high-heeled boots, but they did not sink into it—it had been packed, then, by other visitors since it had fallen earlier that day. The military of the sign? Those who were said to hold Ben Free? There seemed no way of knowing.

The gates were closed with a heavy chain. Pulling the lock toward her, she found herself outside herself, viewing everything (the old-fashioned car, the high gate with its sinister crest of barbed wire, the endless snow, the lowering structures she could now see beyond the fence, and her own dark figure) as an Edward Gorey drawing. The people in those drawings seemed always bent upon dismal errands toward bad ends. Was that her own fate? To seek Truth not in a well but down a black tunnel that wound on forever?

The key turned easily, or perhaps she had only twisted it with more force than she realized. The lock and the heavy chain were bitterly cold. She let them drop and pushed one side of the gate back; as she did so, a faint blue light kindled far behind one of the dark windows of one of the dark buildings. It should have cheered her, but it did not.

Illingworth's old Packard crept forward with snow breaking like rabbit bones under the wheels. The car had seemed cold to the witch when she had ridden in it; now in memory it was a haven of warmth and comfort, possibly even of safety. She wanted to get back in at once, but she knew the entrance to such a place could not be left open. Laboriously she closed the gate and snapped the icy lock. When she looked for the blue light again, it was gone.

Despite the size of the Packard, the high front seat was cramped. Illingworth leaned across it easily to throw wide the door for her, then held out an age-spotted, enormously long hand. "Thank you, Mademoiselle," he said.

She was seized by a desire to retain the key, but she gave it to him as though no such wish had entered her mind, carefully noting the pocket—the right outer pocket of his overcoat—into which he put it.

His sharp knee came up, then subsided as he pushed down the long clutch pedal. The hand that had taken the key settled on the cracked bone knob of the vertical gear-shift and pulled it back with a solid *chunk*! "Like a tractor," she said, surprising herself. She had spoken too softly for him to hear, or he was too intent on steering the big car into the narrow space between two of the dark buildings. He should have been a farmer, she thought. That is a farmer's face, those are farmer's hands. He would have sons by now and grandsons, red cattle upon wide green fields, plantations of yellow corn. Something went wrong, many years ago, for him.

Then she recalled that she had entertained similar thoughts about Ben Free, an old man so clearly rural confined to a rotting house in a city slum. She tried to recall just how Free had looked on that rainy evening when they had sat staring at his flickering TV, but the face that rose in her mind was not Free's but the King's. She realized for the first time that something had gone wrong many years ago for him too, and for all his dark, singing, swindling people.

The Packard ground to a stop. "Wait a moment, Mademoiselle, before you get out," Illingworth said. "I have given you very little advice on our drive, if only because I have so little to give. I know," he hesitated for a long moment. "I know hardly more of what you face tonight than you do yourself."

"You have advised me not to ask questions," she reminded him.

"I have, yes, and it was good advice; I stand by it still. Do not question—observe. Accept what you see and try to learn from it. You are aware, I hope, that there were races upon this earth before our own."

"Certainly."

"Good, though in the light of so much physical evidence— However suppressed, and in my opinion, as I have said so very many times in the pages of *Hidden Science* and *Natural Supernaturalism*, it cannot remain suppressed much longer, if only because of our Government's drive to increase coal production. You are aware, I hope, that a vast amount of evidence has been found in Devonian coal, the very best souvenir—you know French?—we have of the Carboniferous Period? Where was I?"

"You were speaking of physical evidence."

"Of course I was. Nails, knives, jewelry, all sorts of things we are prone to assume can be created only by human beings—folly, all of it. The world is so much older than we suppose, and since the Elder Days certain Powers have striven with the most admirable patience to enlighten our race, our little band—I will not say band of brothers save as Cain and Abel were brothers, but of cunning apes."

The witch nodded. She felt almost certain the old man's sudden loquacity was intended to give those within the dark buildings time to prepare, and she listened with less than half her attention.

"They have appeared to us in many forms; if there has been one constant among them, it is that we have most often thought them cruel. If Moloch demanded the immolation of children, yet Jehovah was a God of Wrath. The rites of Isis were called unspeakable, and perhaps not only because they were not to be spoken of. Yet they offer us everything— wealth, power, life prolonged. Most of all healing and serenity of mind. It may be that they are terrible only because they are good."

"I know all this, Mr. Illingworth," the witch said. "In fact, I could deliver your lecture myself; but the powers you speak of are not here. I would sense them if they were. These can be no more than the acolytes of the acolytes. If they hold

Free, they are nevertheless a great deal further from the truth, from the center of Authority, than he is."

"My dear—"

"As for all those things you say they offer us, you have not so much as touched upon the crux. Wealth and power we have already too much of—we suffocate. Longer life? We outstay the lion and the elephant. Hardly a day passes that we do not meet some man or woman who should be dead, who has outlasted his own time by decades; you are such a one yourself, Mr. Illingworth. As for healing, it is not we who require it but the world, which requires to be cured of us. Serenity would indeed be a benefit, but we do not seek it; if we did, we might find it required us to abandon wealth and power, and we love them too much. No, what we require from whatever Powers may be entitled to give it is some indication of how far we may go. Like tigers, we must kill to live, and like rats destroy; but we do not know what is permitted to us, and that ignorance paralyzes those who might otherwise refrain, while the worst of us kill every living thing and ruin all they reach." *I have been inspired,* she thought. *I myself sought power and never knew a word of that.*

"Mademoiselle," Illingworth said softly, "look about you."

Tall figures stood at the right side of the Packard, some almost at her elbow. They wore ankle-length capes, and their heads were the heads of jackals.

"Goodbye," Illingworth said. "Need I tell you, Mademoiselle, that I wish you well?"

The witch nearly surrendered to a wild urge to lock herself in. "You are not going with me? Did I not hear you say you would not miss this for gold?"

"Perhaps I shall see you later tonight."

One of the jackal-headed figures opened the Packard's door.

"I know you," the witch said. "Are you not the servants of Upuaut, the Pathfinder? Or should I call him here Khenti Amenti, the Ruler of the West?"

The jackal-headed figures said nothing, staring boldly into her face with bright eyes, then looking away. Their jaws moved, and it seemed for a moment that, even in the faint light reflected by the snow, she could see scarlet tongues caressing white teeth and hairy lips. She was no longer certain the jackal heads were masks and wondered if she had been drugged. She had eaten nothing, drunk nothing; yet perhaps some odorless gas had been released in the Packard, perhaps the cigarettes Illingworth had given her had contained some hallucinogen.

"You are of good omen, I know," she said. "You lead the procession of Osiris."

At that, the jackal-headed figures turned from her, falling into single file as they walked between the dark buildings. They were very tall, and their footprints in the snow seemed the tracks of beasts. The witch hesitated for a moment, then stepped from the running board to follow the last.

Standing motionless beside his car, Illingworth watched her go. I could never give it up, he thought vaguely. The old Packard; but soon nobody will be able to fix it for me. I could get a Ford. (He still thought of Fords as small, cheap cars, the coupes and hunchbacked sedans of his youth.) Ford be damned! I'll get a Buick.

He took out his old-fashioned silver cigarette case again and lit a Player with the lighter built into the end. Someone had given him the case, and he tried to recall whom. Dion Fortune? When its flame was snuffed, the night was too dark for him to admire the art-deco design. Very modern though, he thought. More modern than anything they make these days. But smoking in the cold was bad for your heart; he had read that someplace.

He dropped the unconsumed cigarette into the snow and entered one of the dark buildings. A young man at a desk nodded to him. He nodded in return and went past him into another office where a duffle coat hung on a hook and an older man (though Illingworth thought of him as young) sat behind a larger desk.

Illingworth tossed the key onto the desk. "Well, sir," he said, "I've done it."

Chapter 48

THE CARPET NIGHT OF OZZIE

The gray sedan swung off the Interstate, then off the side road and into a plowed parking lot, now walled with snow. As Robin had predicted, Little Ozzie was still asleep on the back seat; and as she had suggested, Barnes covered him with his fur-collared coat.

"You think he'll be all right?" Barnes pushed the lock button down; he tried to close the door quietly, and Little Ozzie hardly stirred.

"Of course. He'll be warm under there, and anyway, we won't be inside long. Besides, you can come out and look at him if you're worried. I'll give you the keys so you can run the engine a little."

A blue neon sign blinked overhead: FLYING CARPET. One thousand feet above it, a big jet was coming in with its landing lights blazing and its windows shining.

It looks like a whole city, Barnes thought. Like the flying saucer in that movie.

He handed Robin out and closed her door as softly as he had closed his own. There were cars enough in the lot to show the Flying Carpet was doing business. He and Robin walked across the ice and the hard, black asphalt together.

Inside, it seemed a bar like any other. Robin found them a table near the little stage. There was a *Reserved* sign on it, but she handed it to a waiter, who took it without protest. The stage was dark, making the whole bar very dark.

"You phoned a reservation?" Barnes asked.

Robin shook her head. "They don't take them. I come here a lot."

"The sign said reserved."

"For the owner and his friends. I'm a friend."

"I see." Barnes realized with some surprise that he was jealous.

"No, you don't. Buck knows a hundred women. I'm one of the hundred. If he comes around, I'll massage the back of his neck and rub his shoulders with the jugs, that's all."

"Bullshit!"

The waiter had reappeared; he said, "Yes, sir. Bullshot. Pink lady, Miss Valor?"

"What's the new one you told me about, Jack? A screwdriver. I'll try it. Ozzie, don't be mad. Let me tell you something funny Jack saw one time. A crowd was sitting around in a bar—not this place, another one—listening to some guy with a guitar, and after a while one woman stands up and kind of staggers over to the bartender and says, 'You got a screwdriver?'"

Three white musicians and two black ones were settling into the positions on stage: piano, drums, bass, saxophone, and vibraharp. The whites looked too young to be very good.

"So the bartender made her a screwdriver," Robin said.

It was "Sophisticated Lady," booming and whirling, filling the room with music somehow palely green, music like a perfumed green chiffon scarf, a swirling green chiffon skirt. The waiter brought their drinks; Barnes sipped and listened.

When it was over, Robin said, "Good, huh?"

"No mikes? No speakers?"

She shrugged. "This isn't Symphony Hall, and they're not recording."

Barnes nodded.

"You know what it made me feel like?" Robin asked. "Delaguerra. Did you ever read that?"

Barnes shook his head. "Who's Delaguerra?"

"A tough cop, a long time ago in a story called 'Spanish Blood.' A thirties story. Delaguerra said, 'I never shot a deer

in my life. Police work hasn't made me that tough.'" Robin
grinned at him. "I guess I thought about that because I told
you I was half Spanish, out in the car. That was why I read
the story, back when I was just a kid—because of the title."

Barnes grinned back. "I'm surprised you didn't order a
margarita."

"Spanish, not Mex. Half Spanish and half devil. You
know what they say about Spanish women? 'A lady in the
street, an angel in church, and the devil in bed.' I don't go to
church."

"I don't either, but I wish you did so I could take you."

"Our family swore never to go back until there was
another Borgia Pope. How do you feel about strippers,
Ozzie?"

"I'm not usually close enough to feel."

"I can fix that."

"What?"

"I said I can fix it. I'm a friend of Buck's, remember?
Watch my purse."

She pushed it across the tiny table, drained her screwdriver, and vanished into the darkness. The band was beginning a new number, "Now's the Time." Barnes opened her
purse and got out a fresh cigar and a folder of matches, letting
the purse remain open on the table while he lit the cigar. In
the flare of the match, he could see that the little automatic
was gone. He recalled its bright chrome, the black grips
showing a horse with an arrow in its mouth. A lighter like the
one he had bluffed Proudy with? She had made a joke of it in
the car, and it seemed too early to ask her about it.

She's gone to the john, he thought. My God, what a jerk I
am! She has to pee, and she's afraid somebody will jump her
in there. It happens all the time to women, and what the hell,
in a place like this . . .

Then he remembered he had seen her compact in the
purse. When women went to the john, in his experience, they
always took their compacts.

"Now's the Time" sang itself to sleep. The sax player
propped his instrument against the piano, got a mike from a

stand at one side of the stage, switched it on, tapped it half humorously with a fingernail, and said, "Now then, ladies an' gents, an' all you just plain folks out there too, if you will but be so very kind as to give me an' my boys a chance to grab a drink while all them chicks back there are gettin' undressed up for your pleasure, why we'll be back practically 'fore you know we're gone. Why don't you just have another drink your own self?"

There was laughter and a little applause. The sax player grinned, switched off the mike, walked over to Barnes's table and sat down. "You Mr. Barnes?"

Barnes nodded and held out his hand. "Call me Ozzie."

The sax player shook it solemnly. "You call me Binko, 'cause that's my name. Last name. Won't tell you my first one 'cause it's one of them Fauntleroy things, you know? Don't nobody use it. Just call me Binko. Ozzie, now that's a cool name. Make me think on all them flyin' monkeys an' that stuff. You see *The Wiz*?"

"On TV."

"Should have seen it on the big screen, man. I went in about seven an' come out after midnight. Seen the last show an' ate three buckets of popcorn. I figured you was Barnes, Ozzie, 'cause they say look for this handsome, real sharp dude with a mustache. What it is, they ain't no announcer for our little *do* tonight. That eye don't hardly show, so since you got experience in this line of work, would you do it?"

"Binko, do you happen to know a girl called Robin Valor?"

"Course. Everybody here know Robin. Just a minute ago she was sittin' with you, an' you're smokin' one of her cigars this second. Robin got the bitchin'est cigars I ever saw any woman to have, white or black, an' I'll tell you true, man, whenever I get the chance, why I hit her up. She don't mind. She's real nice about givin' out one."

Barnes took one of the aluminum cylinders from Robin's purse and handed it to Binko. "She put you up to this," he said.

"Her, man? No, not me. Robin's 'bout as sharp as a chick

ever gets, but I don't take no orders from her. Buck told me. Every night, Buck lay down the bread for my little combo, so he call the shots."

"I didn't see anybody talking to you."

"Hey, what's the matter, man? You think we out to get you? We just want you to fill in. They slip me a note—maybe you didn't notice I had this long rest there while ol' Sunky went to town on his vibes? I hang up my ax an' step over to one side an' kind of turn my back, an' that's when I read it. You goin' to do it? Or you just want to sit here like some royal-ass high an' mighty clown an' make faces at me while I tries to lead my combo an' announce both?"

"I'll do it," Barnes told him. "I'd just like to know what Robin's up to."

For a moment, a mask seemed to fall over the sax man's face, or perhaps one fell away. The easy, affable smile vanished, and it seemed to Barnes that it was the face of another man altogether, a man he did not wish to meet again. Then the smile returned, broader than ever, white teeth flashing in the dimness. "That's my man! You my man!" A kitchen match scratched at the bottom of the table, and Binko rotated Robin Valor's cigar in the flame, puffing with care and obvious enjoyment, then extinguishing the match with a delicately launched breath of smoke. "Now you ain't goin' to find it's much of a chore at all. When we come back, you get up there an' tell the folks a couple jokes. You know some jokes? You know how to tell them?"

"Yes, I know some jokes."

"That's fine. They shouldn't be *too* blue—you know what I mean? Or some of these motherfuckers will walk out. But they shouldn't be Sunday School jokes neither. You know what I mean about that?"

Barnes nodded.

"You *are* my man. Then you tell them how the Dixie Dukes—that's us—goin' to play 'Basin Street.' An' you get yourself off the stage an' let us do it, but you don't come back to this table here. You go off that way—" Binko pointed, "an' while you're waitin' off to one side, the next act goin' to tell you how to introduce her. Got it? Now here come my drummer and ol' Sunky already, so get yourself set."

Under a spotlight, Barnes said, "Good evening and welcome to the Flying Carpet. If you've just arrived in our fair city, we're glad to see you. If you're going, well, we're sorry to see you go, but glad you stopped here first. Do you know we've got direct service to China now? Just ask for Dragin' Home Airlines."

No one laughed. As far as he could see, no one was paying the slightest attention. He tried to flick his cigar the way Groucho used to. "Tough, huh? If you think you're tough, wait till you get the chicken over Denver.

"Did you hear about the cabin attendant and the handsome pilot? This pilot was really good looking and made terrific money, so the stew was thrilled to death when she brought him his drink up in the cockpit—"

There were a few scattered chuckles.

"Don't laugh, you're flying with him. She brought his drink and he asked her to marry him. Naturally she said yes. Then he said, 'Since we're going to be man and wife, I want you to do so-and-so right now.' Well, her mother had always told her never do so-and-so. You know what I mean? This isn't the one where you wait till the kids are in bed—this is the one where you wait till they've gone to camp. And so she was so embarrassed she ran out of the cockpit and clear back to the tail section—airplanes have great names for places— and she was back there trying to get hold of herself—the pilot had hold of himself already—and she saw Father Rooney sitting in an aisle seat reading his breviary. So she asked him about it, even though she got as red as a cherry—I love this story—when she had to tell him what the pilot wanted her to do. And he said, '*Niver!* Tell that limb of Satan you'd sooner die! Me dauther, you must leave this vile occupation and niver see the pervert agin!' Well, that was pretty serious, quitting her job, and besides the pilot was a very good-looking guy and made a lot of money, so she went up the aisle a little farther, and there sat Brother Philbert saying his rosary. The stew told him all about the pilot, but he just jumped up and went back to ask Father Rooney. So she went up the aisle a little farther, and there sat Sister Mary Elephant grading papers. So she told her about it—she was starting to enjoy telling it by now—and Sister Mary Elephant fainted.

"So she went farther up, nearly to the front of the plane, and there was Cardinal Cogan himself, with his hands folded, looking out the window and smiling a little. So she told *him*. And he said, 'Bless you, my child, not till after you're married, and may you both be happy.' So she said, 'That's wonderful, your Archship'—he was a St. Louis Cardinal—'but why is it that you can say that when Father Rooney told me to quit my job and Sister Mary Elephant fainted and Brother Philbert and so on and so forth?' And the cardinal said, 'My child, what do those three know about sophisticated sex? They're all flying tourist.'"

There was some real laughter from the tables this time and a dutiful belly laugh from the sax man behind him. The laughter faded quickly, leaving only a little mumbled conversation and the occasional clink of glass. Barnes tried to look at his audience, but he could see nothing beyond the spotlight. "And now," he said, "'Basin Street'! Done as only the Dixie Dukes can do it!"

The spot faded to darkness. At the first wail from the band, he turned to his left. When he had taken a couple of steps, he could see a naked redhead smiling at him from the wings. She had freckles.

On the rough brick wall behind her, someone had spraypainted: KILROY WAS HERE.

As Sandy Duck's little car rolled into the parking lot, its headlights picked up a small boy who stood weeping in the snow. Moved by a motherly instinct she would have hotly denied, Sandy got out, picked him up, and sought to comfort him. "Now, now," she said. "Now, now, now." It seemed foolish even to her, but she could think of nothing better.

"My—my—Daddy—"

"Yes, he's gone, isn't he? And you're lost, poor little tyke. Where did he go?"

Mutely, the boy pointed to the winking electric sign atop the low, brick building at the end of the parking lot.

"The Flying Carpet?" Sandy asked. "I'm going in there. I'll take you with me, and maybe we can find your Daddy."

As she spoke, a side door opened. For an instant, the naked figure of Ozzie Barnes appeared there like the scarlet devil who materializes in a magician's box; two naked women pulled him backward, and the door swung closed again.

"On second thought," Sandy said, "I don't think I'll go there after all. Not tonight. Maybe you'd better come with me."

Chapter 49

SERVING THE COUNTRY

The waistband of her nurse's skirt had parted an hour before. One of the lower buttons of her blouse had broken its thread and slipped unnoticed to the carpet; three more had been pulled through their holes. Her belly, drum taut and flushed with wine, protruded through the triangular space, pressing firmly against the table and spilling (as it were) three inches over the snowy tablecloth.

The table held a large platter of French pastries and bonbons, and a very large glass of champagne. Slowly, she reached for one of the bonbons and held it up as though to examine it in the candlelight. It was raspberry. "This . . . last one," she said.

"Certainly."

She put it slowly into her mouth as though performing an onerous duty, and although she was already leaning nearly as far back as the tall chair permitted, contrived to lean back farther still until her head rested against its red leather cushion. Delicately and unsteadily she raised her glass to her lips and washed down the raspberry bonbon with champagne. When she set the empty glass on the table again, a solicitous waiter refilled it.

Another, taller, waiter arrived bearing a white telephone, which he plugged into a connection in the floor. Sweet identified himself and listened for half a minute or so. "Of course I need help," he said. "I need all the help I can get."

She said nothing. Her eyes were half closed. Her cherry-colored face, propped and cradled by three chins, wore the expression of sleep, though her left hand wandered with hesitant slowness over the surface of the tray.

Sweet beckoned the tall waiter, and when the waiter stooped to disconnect the telephone, tapped him on the shoulder and extended the handset. "It's for you."

"Yes, sir," the waiter said. He gave his name; there was a long pause. "I'll have to speak with the manager, sir." He returned the handset to Sweet. "Don't hang up, sir. I'll bring the manager. Just a moment."

Sweet nodded a little grimly, and the waiter hurried away.

She fingered a pastry, a tiny mountain of colored cream and meringue. For a moment, it almost seemed she was going to put it down, then she nibbled at the edge and licked her lips.

The white handset lay on the table in front of Sweet. He picked it up and put the palm of one hand over the mouthpiece. "I really am a vice president of Mickey's Jawbreakers," he said.

If she heard him, she gave no indication of it.

"I wanted you to know. They made me do this. I was contacted at the airport; they bounced me off my plane."

The pastry was nearly eaten. She opened her mouth a trifle wider, pushed the last of it in, and took a swallow of champagne, leaving the glass lightly rimmed with pink cream filling. Dazedly, she looked around for her napkin. It had dropped to the floor beside her chair; she used the edge of the tablecloth instead.

"I'm sorry," Sweet said.

A lean, foreign-looking man in a business suit hurried over to their table two steps ahead of the taller waiter and picked up the handset.

"I am Paul de Vaux, the manager here," he said breathlessly. "Yes, yes, we have been informed. . . . I will give the instructions." He listened for a moment more, said, "Yes, yes," again and hung up, then turned to Sweet. "You will be in need of assistance, Monsieur. Walter," he indicated the taller waiter with a minute movement of his head, "will supply it. There will be no charge for these dinners."

"You had been contacted before," Sweet said. It was not a question.

"Yes, yes. Concerning the dinners. Not concerning the assistance. Now we have been told of the assistance, and we are most happy to cooperate. Walter, this gentleman has been given your destination. Is that not so, Monsieur?"

Sweet nodded.

"You must do as he directs. It is already late; there is no need for you to return here tonight. I myself will punch out for you, and I shall expect you tomorrow at the usual time."

The manager turned on his heel and strode away. The shorter waiter was already gone. For a moment the taller waiter stood looking from her to Sweet. "Would you like me to dispose of the telephone, sir?"

"You might as well. Get your coat too, it's colder than a welldigger's ass out there. Then come back."

"Yes, sir."

"And Walter, there'll be a good tip in this when we're through. Not from them," Sweet nodded toward the telephone. "From me."

"That isn't necessary, sir," the waiter said. "I'm happy to serve my country."

When he returned, he was wearing a lumberjack's red plaid jacket over his waiter's uniform. He and Sweet shifted the table to one side and managed to get her to her feet. She had kicked off one of her high-heeled shoes. They seated her again, and the waiter found it. He slipped the other from her foot as well and thrust them both into the side pockets of his jacket. "This way will be better, sir, believe me. She'll balance better and be able to give us more help."

The restaurant was nearly empty, but it seemed to Sweet that a hundred eyes watched them. He mumbled, "You've done this before, have you, Walter?"

"Every so often, sir." He glanced speculatively at their charge. "Usually the ladies just drink—you know. Two or three more than a lady should. I don't know if this is going to be easier or harder. Harder, I expect."

"I think you're right," Sweet told him.

"Then there isn't any use waiting, is there, sir? Let's get her up again."

She said, "I can . . ." Her hips slipped forward; she began to slide from her chair.

"Get her, sir!"

Both men grabbed her arms.

"Up, sir! Get her up!"

"Lay down," she said loudly. "And a mint. Want a after-dinner mint."

"You're going to be fine," Sweet told her desperately. "You're not going to be sick. Just stand up and come with us. You can lie down in my car."

She tried to embrace and comfort her straining belly, but the men's grip prevented her. They urged her forward as they might have rolled a tun of wine, a vast cask difficult to bring into motion, teetering, difficult to turn or halt. As she moved, the split skirt slid down, slowly escaping her monstrous waistline, hanging precariously for a step or two on the protuberance of her hips. Sweet tried to catch it, but when both his hands no longer supported her, she began to lose the vertical orientation they had achieved by so much labor, and he was compelled to prop her up again. The skirt escaped, sliding to her knees, then to the floor. Inevitably she tripped over it, but her own contribution to her support was so slight it scarcely mattered.

"Her coat's in the check room," he told the waiter.

"To hell with her coat," the waiter said succinctly.

"Mine too. We'll take her out to the car. Then I'll come back for our coats."

"Cold out there."

"I can take it."

"Hot," she said. "Me. Warm. Really."

"You won't be for long," the waiter told her.

Sweet asked, "It hasn't started snowing again, has it?"

The waiter shook his head, but Sweet, on the opposite side of her, could not see him.

A big man and a slender woman in a sable wrap were coming through the door as they reached the vestibule. For a moment, the newcomers stared in amazement, then the woman collapsed into helpless laughter.

"Shut up," Sweet told her. "You don't know what's happening."

"Me neither," Candy said. She belched, breathed the cool air of the vestibule, and immediately felt better. "Why are you so nice to me?"

"I like you," Sweet said.

"You too."

The waiter pushed open the door with his foot. A little new snow had fallen; the most recent automobiles had left twining, opalescent tracks in it like the trails of arctic pythons. The cold air felt wonderful. Her face was hot, her belly overwarm as well as overfull. (At last! At last! Full to bursting, dead, solid full, with every scrap of hunger crowded out.) When she stepped out into the snow, her feet felt cool rather than cold.

"You don't have to hold me," she said. "I'm okay now."

Sweet told her, "I'd rather hold you."

"You're sweet." Taking her arm from the waiter, she turned, enfolded Sweet, and kissed him.

"Thank you," he said when he could speak again. "But we have to go to the car now."

"All right." Candy slipped and nearly fell. The waiter caught her. "I'm all right," she insisted.

"Sure," the waiter said.

"Hey, you remind me of somebody. My boyfriend."

"I thought he was your boyfriend."

"No, he's my . . ." She could not think of a polite word and was not certain there was one. "My boyfriend, you know, he didn't have—" She belched again. "Any more money. That champagne. How much did I drink?"

"Couple bottles," the waiter told her. "Where's your car, sir?"

"Black Caddy," Sweet grunted. "Other side of the van." Candy was leaning most of her weight on him.

"Nice car."

"Rented."

"We'll have to put her in back."

Sweet nodded. "It's not locked."

"Okay, sir. Just hold her for a moment while I get the door open."

For a moment Sweet did so, as Candy took two tottering steps toward the black car. One bare foot slipped in the snow, and she fell.

She fell slowly and yet inevitably, as a ruinous warehouse collapses under a surfeit of rich goods, or a tall, broad maple (and indeed, her red-gold hair and round, flushed face suggested one) under the intoxicating weight of a thousand fruiting vines.

Sweet tried to support her and nearly fell with her. She sought to hold herself up, or at least to break her fall, with the arm the waiter had released. That, too, failed her, her hand skidding from under her in the snow, which had not yet been much packed. Her belly and her face buried themselves in the loose snow.

"Oh, God!" Sweet said. He jerked a handkerchief from his pocket and mopped his sweating face.

"Wait a minute, I'll help you with her, sir."

"If you hadn't let go it wouldn't have happened."

"All right," the waiter said. "All right."

A jet with blazing lights roared past, a thousand feet overhead. Futilely, Candy struggled to stand.

Chapter 50

MURDER MYSTERY

The room over the witch's was not a room at all; it was a suite. Stubb glanced appreciatively at the white-and-gold mirrors and the Louis XIV carpet before seating himself on a spindly chair of velvet and gilded wood. He liked small chairs, and this one smelled of money.

"Drink?" Cliff asked.

"I've had too much beer already," Stubb told him. "On an empty stomach, too. Think you could order your star operative a sandwich from room service? I haven't eaten since lunch."

"Whatever you want." Cliff picked up the telephone.

"Then make it a hot roast beef, medium rare. Coffee. How come I've got an in on this one?"

"You don't happen to know . . . ?" Cliff squinted at the label pasted on the cradle.

"Two eleven."

"Thanks." He dialed. "A hot roast beef sandwich *au jus*. Put plenty of meat on it. Two coffees, and they'd better be hot when they get here. Room eight seventy-seven in five minutes, understand?"

As he hung up, Stubb said, "I asked you how come I've got an in, Cliff."

"Who said you've got an in?"

"You did."

"Like hell!"

"You said three hundred a day."

"And I meant it, Jim. That's solid."

"Enough to buy me off the case I was on. This afternoon you wouldn't have me for fifty."

"For God's sake, Jim, you know the business! When you called, I didn't have this job."

Stubb stood up. "If I meet the boy in the hall, I'll tell him to take the sandwich back."

"Okay," Cliff threw up his hands. "You always were a smart monkey. It ever get through to you that you'd be better off if you weren't quite so God-damned smart?"

"And a foot taller." Stubb sat down again.

"Yeah, I know what you mean. All right. There's a murder, and you knew him. That's all, Jim. That's everything—I swear to God."

"Uh huh. No rough stuff. That's what you said. Ben Free?"

"You knew somebody snuffed him?"

"It's him, then."

"That's the name we got, yeah." Cliff took a snapshot from the breast pocket of his coat and handed it over.

The old man lay on a filthy floor that might have been concrete. The back of his shirt was soaked with his blood, and a pool had formed beneath his chest. Only the side of his face was visible, but it was Free.

"Twice in the back," Cliff said. "Big slugs. We've got a line to the ballistics lab, but they haven't made them yet. Probably forty-fives or three-fifty-sevens. He went right down. Probably never knew what hit him."

"He stayed up long enough for the guy to shoot twice."

"There's that, yeah."

"Where?"

"Hold on. Jim, I'll brief you, but I want to ask you a couple of questions first. I don't want you to go into your act again, but God damn it, you're working for me. How'd you know who it was?"

"Just a guess."

"All right, how'd you guess?"

"You said I knew him. I know a lot of characters around town, but you know most of them yourself, and you've got guys on the payroll who know them too, so it wasn't one of those. That left people I knew way back and people I know

now in my private life. Somebody who knew the guy way back isn't worth three hundred a day—the odds against his having anything worthwhile are terrific. That left my private life. Most of the people I know like that are women, but you indicated this was a man, you said *him*. And you've been here in the hotel for a while, you said, trying to get hold of me, but I haven't seen anything in the paper. So it was probably today, and I asked myself about men I know, privately, that I haven't seen in the last eight or ten hours."

Cliff snorted. "And he was the only one? Horseshit."

"No, he wasn't the only one, just the one that seemed like the best bet. I didn't think anybody with big money would be interested in any of the others, so—"

The door to a bedroom opened, and a delicate-looking blond stepped out. As well as Stubb could judge, she was five-two or five-three in her heels. She carried a purse nearly as big as a hatbox, and she had been outfitted by somebody who got a thousand dollars for a cute little blouse to wear shopping.

"I'm terribly sorry, Mr. Rebic," she said. "But I really think it's time you introduced me."

"You're the boss, Ms. Whitten. Jim, this is—"

She did not give him time to finish. "My name is Standbridge Whitten, Mr. Stubb. Since my friends obviously can't call me Standbridge, they call me Kip. I can't imagine why, but I rather like it."

She extended her hand, and Stubb rose and took it.

"I'm Mr. Rebic's client. Isn't that what you call it? Client?"

"Sure," Stubb said. "Lucky Mr. Rebic."

"Earlier, you asked to be . . . briefed? I was eavesdropping quite shamelessly; Mr. Rebic put me up to it. He refused to brief you because I had told him I wished to speak personally with each of the men who would help me find my uncle's—"

"Ben was your uncle?"

"Yes. I'll explain in a moment. You see, I feel that even if a man—or a woman—is a professional, he can feel, he is *capable* of feeling, a real loyalty. If not to his employer then to the cause of justice. To the right, if I may put it so. Don't you agree, Mr. Stubb?"

"Call me Jim, Ms. Whitten."

"Only if you'll promise to call me Kip. My father, the late General Samuel Whitten, always said the most loyal soldiers were the career soldiers, those who were practically mercenaries. His men called him 'Buck' Whitten, though not to his face to be sure. He liked to believe it was because he had never lost his rapport with the rank and file. Do you consider yourself a mercenary, Mr. Stubb?"

"I consider myself a day laborer, Kip. Did Ben have money?"

Cliff raised a hand. "Wait a minute, Jim. A briefing's okay, but you ought to answer a few questions yourself. Was it your impression he did?"

Stubb shook his head. "Not a cent."

The blond girl's fingers touched his. "Are you quite sure, Jim?"

"His house was falling apart, and he loved that house. A couple of times I tried to raid his refrigerator, but there wasn't a damn thing to eat. Every once in a while one of us would feel sorry for him and buy him something."

"You lived with my uncle?"

"For a few days," Stubb said. "Yeah."

"Did he ever speak to you of having—I don't know, it could be anything. Something valuable. Something hidden." She pressed his hand.

"He was your uncle, and you don't know what he had?"

Cliff said, "Watch your mouth, Jim."

"That's all right, Mr. Rebic—perfectly all right. He has a right to ask these questions, a right to understand. No, Mr. Stubb—Jim—I don't know. Only Daddy knew, and he's no longer with us."

"I think you'd better explain," Stubb told her.

"I'll try to. Many years ago, when they were quite young men, my uncle chose to leave our family. To go off on his own, as it were. He was under something of a cloud, if you understand me."

"They didn't like him."

"He had been wild, I suppose. He and my father were twins, Mr. Stubb. As happens so often, one twin sought attention through accomplishment, the other through rebellion. My great-grandfather was a Rockefeller partner, and our family is still very well off."

Stubb nodded. "Yeah, I kind of thought it might be."

"My uncle Benjamin—that was his real name, Benjamin Whitten—apparently announced that he meant to make his own fortune and tell the rest of them to go to Hades."

"Good for him."

"But when he had gone, they discovered that a certain extremely valuable article had disappeared. Please don't ask what it was, because I don't know. I wasn't even born when all this happened; and by the time I was old enough to care, no one was left but Daddy, and he wouldn't tell me."

"Whatever it was," Stubb said, "it's probably long gone."

The girl pursed her lips. "I don't think so. You see, before he died, Daddy was conducting certain investigations of his own. He said that if Uncle Ben sold what he had, he would know. And that he hadn't sold it yet, not in all those years."

Cliff leaned forward, rubbing his hand. "That means it just about has to be a piece of art or a rock, Jim."

"If he was sharp enough, maybe willing to go to Amsterdam and take in a partner, he could get a rock cut up without anybody knowing."

"He might, okay, but it would be tough. Anyhow, my first guess is art. If it had been a rock, it would probably have been in a safe or a safety deposit box someplace, and they wouldn't have let a wild kid get at it. Art you've got hanging on the wall, even if there's a lot of insurance. He could just take it down and stick it under his coat. A nice little Rembrandt, maybe."

Stubb cocked an eyebrow at the girl. "What about insurance, Kip? Your folks collect any back then?"

She shook her head. "We—I, now that Daddy's gone—do

own certain valuable paintings, Mr.—Jim. The same company has insured them ever since I can remember, and at Mr. Rebic's urging I called them. We've never had a large claim. Ever."

Cliff said, "It's obvious, isn't it? To collect, they'd have had to say Ben stole it, and they didn't want to. Hell, he was old General Buck's brother. They kept their traps shut, hoping he'd come home. Then the rest died, and Buck started looking for him, only he didn't find him."

"Then the General died himself," Stubb finished for him. "And Kip learned—someway—that Uncle Ben had been murdered. I'd like to hear about that, Kip."

The blond girl suddenly looked a little tired, though her back was as straight as ever. "I didn't learn that Uncle Benjamin was murdered, Mr. Stubb. I saw him on TV and went to look for him."

"Sure. You spotted him right off, even though he had left the family before you were born."

"But I *did*. Don't you understand, Mr. Stubb? He and Daddy were identical twins. Daddy passed away only last September. This man had a beard, but otherwise he looked precisely the way Daddy had."

Stubb nodded, half to himself. "Last night two women came to talk to a woman named Mrs. Baker, looking for Ben Free. Were you one of them?"

"I had a right to search for my uncle!"

"Sure. Did you? Was one of them you?"

Kip nodded.

"Who was the other one? Some girl working for Cliff?"

"No. I—I hadn't engaged him then. A friend."

"Not an investigator?"

"No."

Cliff said, "Then she hired us, and we got on it right away."

"Not quick enough to save him," Stubb said softly.

"Hell, Jim, we couldn't have. He was already dead by then. But we found him and took the picture you saw."

"Yeah. You call the cops too?"

"We had to. Anyway, Ms. Whitten didn't want to leave him lying there. He was her uncle, for Christ's sake."

"For Christ's sake, I hope he was. What time?"

There was a discreet tap at the door.

Stubb opened it, and the Agatha Christie fan pushed in a cart redolent of beef.

"Hell," Cliff said. "Your sandwich—I'd forgotten about it."

"I hadn't."

"Ms. Whitten, will you take the other coffee, please?"

"Certainly not. Anyway, I much prefer tea."

Cliff extended a ten. "Bud, you think you could get the lady a pot of hot tea, fast?"

"Quite so," the Christie fan said, taking the ten. "I should be delighted."

Stubb was already chewing a bite of beef and bread. He swallowed as the door closed. "What time, Cliff? When'd you find him?"

"This afternoon, around two."

"Where?"

"The basement of his house, by the stairs. You know where the house was—you were staying there with him until last night."

"I also went back this morning and checked over the house. He wasn't there."

"Including the basement?"

"Including the basement."

"That's worth knowing. Was this for the other client, Jim?"

"Let's say it was for me. I was worried about him. He was an old man, we had liked him, and we thought nobody knew where he was."

"You thought?"

"Somebody knew. Somebody took him back there and wasted him after I left. You want my guess about it?"

"Hell yes, if you've got one."

"Somebody was looking for whatever it was Free had. Call it the McGuffin. They got hold of him sometime yesterday, slapped him around. He said, okay, take me back to my house, I'll show you where it is. That basement was dark as hell—I had to light matches, and they probably hadn't known to bring a flashlight. Free made a break for it. When he got close to the steps there would have been a little light, and somebody panicked and shot him."

Cliff looked dubious. "An old guy like that?"

"Yeah, an old guy like him."

"Jim, I can't buy it." Cliff looked at Kip, but Kip did not return the look; she was watching Stubb, her piquant face expressionless.

Cliff said, "Sure, amateurs get panicky, but just the same."

"I didn't say it was an amateur. I don't think it was. You said maybe a forty-five, and that's not an amateur's heat. Your mistake is that you think it must have been somebody like you."

"Get on with it."

"Free must have been nearly eighty." Stubb was no longer talking to Cliff, but to Kip. "That would make your daddy close to sixty when you were born, Ms. Whitten—not really impossible, but not likely either. Anyway, he was about eighty, but big, and I'd guess that for an old man he was still pretty strong. Cliff here could have tied him up and put him on a shelf. I could have handled him myself if I had to, and I'm no giant. But I don't think you could have."

Kip's hand was inching toward her purse.

Stubb rose, knocking over his chair, and suddenly held Sergeant Proudy's gun. "Don't touch that," he said.

The hand relaxed.

"That's better. Now take it by the strap and toss it very gently right at my shoes. I've never shot a woman, and I don't want to start now."

The purse hit the floor with a thump.

"That's better. I hate to tell you this, but that was the first thing that gave you away. That big bag didn't go with the rest of your outfit, so I started wondering what you had in it. Then too, last night I talked to Mrs. Baker, after you and your girlfriend did. She'd been questioned by a couple of pros, not by two society girls."

Kip said, "Jim, I can explain this."

Stubb crouched by the purse, opened it one-handed, and whistled. "You must have raided Grandpa's bureau. A Colt New Service. Looks like it's been jerked off the deck of a battleship. Cliff, you packing?"

Cliff shook his head and held out his arms so that his jacket hung open.

"Fine. Kip, I won't ask you what happened down in that basement. Maybe he knocked you down before he tried to run. Maybe he tried to take you, and lost you in the dark. But who are you really?"

There was a tap at the door, and for an instant Stubb turned to look. The carpet flew at his face. When it hit, he did not even feel it.

Chapter 51

BLOOD MONEY

The older man behind the desk nodded. "So you have. It's the truth."

Illingworth asked, "Do you require anything further from me?"

"You mean you want to be paid."

"I would not have put it so crudely."

The older man chuckled. "You didn't."

"But since you yourself have raised the issue . . ."

"Did she say anything?"

"Very little." Illingworth took a slender tape recorder from his coat pocket and handed it over.

"Wonderful gizmos," the old man said. "Just amazing. You didn't try to pump her?"

"I was instructed not to."

"Uh huh." The older man leaned back in his chair, his fingers making a steeple over his vest. (Illingworth noted with approval that he wore a watch chain.) "I'm afraid I'll have to listen to this before you leave. But first your pay, right. If you want, we can see that the money is deposited in any account you want. Just give me the number."

"If it is all the same to you, sir," Illingworth said, "I should prefer cash."

The older man smiled faintly. "Yes, the income tax."

"Would cash be convenient?"

"Very." The older man slid open a drawer and tossed a bundle of money onto his desk. "Count it," he said. "Should be old bills, mixed numbers."

"There is no need of that. I have confidence in you, sir."

"Glad to hear it. Then I can make you a better deal, if you want. This's five thousand, right?"

"That was the agreed-upon sum, yes."

"Say the word and we'll more than double it. You own those two little magazines. Well, it turns out an eccentric millionaire set up a five-thousand-dollar grant in trust, at interest, for them quite some time back. To be paid this year, if they were still being published. A grant to encourage your kind of science. Not taxable, of course. All you'll have to do is use it for your operations and put the money you'd have used if you hadn't got it into your pocket."

"I see."

"It's all the same to us."

"I see," Illingworth said again. "The grant, I suppose." He sighed. "There should be a good deal of prestige, too, in the grant."

"You do have confidence in us. I'm glad to see that."

"Not really. It's just that throughout my life I've prided myself upon being a civilized man, and this would seem to be some sort of test of it."

The older man (who was so much younger than

Illingworth) chuckled. "You're right, anyway. If we wanted to chisel you, we could chisel you a dozen different ways, whether we gave you cash or not. We could arrange for a stickup, for example, when you got home."

"I'd prefer you not do that."

"Well, *chacon à son goût*, Mr. Illingworth. Now you wait out there while I run the gizmo. I'll phone and give somebody the word when you can go."

Illingworth went out. The younger man was no longer at his desk, and there were noises from outside. The windows were white with frost, but the lights that flashed against them, vanished, then flashed again appeared to proceed from the headlights of automobiles.

The door to the inner office opened, and the older man came out, pulling on a duffel coat. Without nodding to Illingworth or so much as looking in his direction, he hurried out into the cold. For a moment, Illingworth was tempted to reenter his office and take the bundle of money from his desk. Caution and more than thirty years of petty journalism intervened. He went to a window instead and used the heel of his hand to melt a peephole in the frost.

There were several cars and several men with flashlights too. He tried to identify the older man by his duffel coat, but almost any of the crowding figures could have been his.

A car door opened. Rather surprisingly, Illingworth thought, the overhead light came on inside the car. A small man in a trenchcoat was pushed out and fell in the snow, his hands still clasped, as it seemed, behind his back. Two men lifted him to his feet again. Perhaps he said something— Illingworth could not be certain. One of the men struck him hard enough to twist his head around, the sound of the blow coming faintly through the frozen glass. A door in the building opposite opened, and a man led the small man inside.

Illingworth heard the rattle of the door at his elbow just in time to step back. The man in the duffel coat came in, followed by a big man in a black raincoat and a petite blonde in blue mink. All three went into the inner office, and someone shut the door.

Plainly the man in the duffel coat—whoever he was—was not listening to the tape. Illingworth speculated vaguely on what might occur should he attempt to leave. He looked through his peephole again. The cars that had brought the small man were gone; it might be possible for him to return to his own car, to back it from that alley between the buildings.

It might not, as well. He might be killed, he thought, if he tried. Almost certainly the grant in trust would be lost. He found he did not believe in that grant anyway. He believed in poltergeists and shapeshifters and all manner of impossible things, but he did not believe in the grant. He would never see a penny of it. He thought of going back and asking the older man for the cash instead, but the humiliation would be too great. If only he escaped, got out without being ruined, perhaps . . .

As a young man he had been a good judge of time, so good that once when his watch, his beautiful gold watch with the fine-china dial and the double lids, had failed him, he had carried no substitute while it was being repaired. Now time seemed to slip away. Time was running faster. "Time is, time was, time's past." He recalled many afternoons when he was twenty that had been longer than the longest days were now. He mused on them for a moment, how they had tied the Airedale to Dr. Cooper's bulldog to make them fight, watching, later, from the white bench under the elm.

There was more noise outside. He rose to look, drawing his coat about him; it was cold in the outer room, so cold his peephole had frozen again.

Cars, one black, or gray, or perhaps green—in the headlights, the dancing flashlights, it was difficult to say. The prisoner was a slightly larger man this time, nude, Illingworth thought, under a blanket. His hands were tied in front of him, so he was able to hold the blanket around him, but he was blindfolded like the other. Illingworth wondered if they had blindfolded the Gypsy princess too, after they had led her away.

A big, handsome woman followed the blindfolded man carrying his clothes, or at least carrying a bundle of clothes that were presumably his. She talked for a moment with one of the men with flashlights while their prisoner did a little dance in the snow, lifting one bare foot, then the other. The man with the flashlight took the clothes from her, and she started toward Illingworth's building.

He backed away from his peephole and lit a cigarette, but she seemed to pay no attention to him when she came in, though she paused to stamp the snow from her boots. He thought her extraordinarily attractive for a woman of her size—she must have been almost six feet—despite a complexion nearly as dark as the Gypsy's. On her shining black hair she wore a little fur hat with a peacock's feather, a hat made to match her sweeping coat; even the tops of her boots were trimmed in the same spotted fur. Their heels rattled like musketry as she marched into the older man's office.

When she had gone, Illingworth went to his peephole again; almost at once he heard the click of the latch behind him. The big man in the black raincoat was coming out. Illingworth nodded to him in a way he hoped was reserved yet friendly.

The big man's hand went to his shirt pocket, but came away empty. "You wouldn't have another cigarette, would you?"

"Certainly." Illingworth held out his silver case.

"Thanks a lot. I smoked all mine on the drive out here." He took a cigarette and lit it with his own Zippo, then extended his hand. "I'm Cliff Rebic."

"Cassius Illingworth."

"Very pleased to meet you, sir. You a government man?"

"No," Illingworth told him. "I'm a publisher."

"Ah. Newspaper?"

"Magazines."

"Ah," Cliff said again. "I'm a private investigator—got my own agency." He fumbled under the black raincoat and brought out a card. "You never know when you might need a competent team of investigators, Mr. Illingworth, and if Doyle & Rebic's good enough for General Whitten's bunch," Cliff jerked his head toward the inner office, "it's good enough for anybody."

"I see. They employed you."

"Yes, sir, they did."

"They employed me as well." Illingworth paused, studying the ceiling. "You might say they enlisted the very competent reportorial staffs of my magazines."

"No kidding. How much they pay you?"

"That, I fear, must remain confidential."

"Yeah, sure. I know how it is. It's just that I thought knowing might be useful to me in my profession, you get me? Like maybe pretty soon they might want Doyle & Rebic again, and I'd like to know what the traffic will bear. Doyle's dead, by the way. I'm president."

"And similarly," Illingworth said, "I should like to know just how much they paid you. Not for publication."

"Then there's no problem, right? Tell me, and I'll tell you."

"You would rely upon my veracity."

"Sure."

"And you would not modify your answer, based upon my own?"

"Hell, no."

"Then this is what I propose." Illingworth produced a pocket notebook and a pen. "We will each write the sum, each fold his slip of paper, and exchange them."

"Got you. Here, I got my own notebook."

For a moment there was silence except for the scratchings of the pens on paper and the faint sounds of an automobile on the road beyond the gates. Cold haunted the bare room like starlight.

"Okay, you ready?"

Illingworth nodded, and Cliff handed him a folded scrap of paper. He crumpled it without reading it and let it fall to the gritty floor as he gave Cliff his own.

"What the hell is this? 'Thirty pieces of silver'?"

"You will not recognize the quotation," Illingworth told him, "but *quod scripsi, scripsi*."

He turned away, and as he did so, the sound of the automobile altered. Snow creaked and snapped under rubber wheels. John B. Sweet's rented Cadillac was entering the compound. Nearby, the engines of a propeller-driven plane sputtered to life, one after another.

Chapter 52

THE LAUGHTER OF THE GODS

"Are you all right?" the witch asked Stubb.

"I'm about blind, and my head hurts."

"Blind?"

"They took my specs." The waxen-faced little detective rubbed his eyes, then his temple. "Or maybe they just dropped off when Cliff sapped me. Wait till I get that son of a bitch alone."

"You must tell me what befell you."

"Madame S., I'm about to puke. Right now I don't have to do one other damn thing."

"It is important, or at least it may be so. Tell me!"

"Wait a minute." Shakily, Stubb got to his feet, one hand at his throat. "Well, I've had it."

"Had what, you fool?"

"The gold watch, the handshake, the testimonial dinner, the scroll signed by our chairman, the stucco bungalow in Florida, the whole damned schmeer. Point me at a toilet."

"There is none. If you are sick you must swallow it."

"I was talking about me. You know, climb in, pull the handle. Hey, what the hell!" His forearm had brushed the breast of his trenchcoat. Reaching inside, he drew out his glasses. "Son of a bitch." He wiped the thick lenses on his sleeve. "Cliff must have stuck them in there. Or the girl did. Sure, I bet it was her." He put them on with an expression of satisfaction and looked around at the bare room, the rusty tin chairs, and the witch. "Say, what happened to your eyes? Have you been crying?"

"Mr. Stubb, you are the most irritating man I have ever encountered, and I have encountered a great many such men. Forget my eyes—they are plants that must be watered if they are to grow. Will you please tell me what happened to you? I repeat that it may be of importance, and I remind you that you are in my employ."

"Madame S., except for expenses, you've never given me a nickel."

"I have very little money, but I assure you that you will be paid. Though it is doubtful now, very doubtful, that you will ever be in a position to render me the slightest service."

"We'll see about that."

"Then let me hear no more complaints. Tell me!"

"I did already. I got the gold watch—the all-day thirty-buck tour. I got shanghied. I got—"

"Yes?"

Stubb pulled one of the folding chairs across the gray, splintered floor and sat down. "I got the case I've been waiting for all my life, I guess. The big time. Rich, lovely girl not even as tall as I am." Suddenly his face twisted into a snarl as real as any savage little beast's. "Don't you sneer at me, sister. She was!"

"I was not ridiculing you," the witch told him. "Nor did I look at you in any way different from the way I now look."

"Okay." He relaxed, taking off his glasses and polishing them automatically on his sleeve. "Only maybe she wasn't really rich. Maybe somebody was slipping her the bread to put up a front. She'd gone to some good schools, though. She talked like it."

"You loved her."

"I wanted to," Stubb said. "But it was . . . Hell, you'd never understand, Madame S."

"I would try."

"It was like . . . I don't know. The Late, Late Show when you get up and yawn and empty the ashtrays because you know it will be over in a minute. Everything was perfect, just perfect, except I knew—oh, hell!"

"What is it?"

"I should have told you right off. Free's dead."

"You are certain?" The witch's eyes opened so wide that for an instant Stubb could see the fires behind them.

"Pretty sure. They said so, and they showed me a picture. He was lying on a concrete floor, and there was a lot of blood."

"But you did not see him."

"No, I didn't actually see the body. So yeah, it could have been faked. I don't think it was."

"Perhaps not. Yet those like Free so often reappear long after they have been counted among the dead. Someone struck you, I think."

"Cliff Rebic. You don't know him. I've worked for him, off and on. He sapped me too. He'd told the kid, the bellhop, to come back with tea for the girl. I forgot about that. I looked around, and Cliff sapped me."

"Unfortunate."

"You bet. When I came to, he had cuffs on me, and a blindfold, and he was sitting with me in the back of a car. I could smell his aftershave. The girl was driving. She had great perfume, and anyway, every so often they said something. He was working for her, or at least working for the people she worked for. Okay, that's how they suckered me. What's your story?"

"It is really not much different from your own. Today I defrauded a certain one, the namesake of one who possesses much authority, below. This I did knowing his name, yet thinking nothing of it. He sent—"

The door flew open; and Barnes, still naked except for a bandage over his eyes, staggered blindly through it. The man who had pushed him from behind tossed a bundle of clothing after him. He tripped over one of the tin chairs and fell.

"What the hell," Stubb said. "How'd you get so screwed up?"

"Is that you, Stubb?"

"Sure it's me. Hold still a minute." Stubb's short, dirty fingernails scrabbled at the adhesive tape, ripping it away with much of Barnes's eyebrows.

Barnes yelped.

"Best way to do it. Get it over with fast. Now wait till I get my pocket knife out and I'll cut you loose."

The witch said, "They permitted you to keep such a thing?"

"Sure. What could I do with it? It wouldn't cut those cuffs, and anyway I couldn't get at it."

"And they permitted me to reclaim my handbag. But poor Ozzie has been stripped to the skin."

"They threw his stuff in with him," Stubb pointed out.

"I guess I did it myself," Barnes said. "I mean, mostly I took off my own clothes." He was rubbing his wrists.

The witch observed, "You have a tale to tell."

"All right, but I want to get something on my tail first. Jesus, can't you at least shut your eyes?"

"As you wish. See, I hold my bag before them."

Barnes picked up a pair of check pants and swore.

"They rip you off?"

"I'll say they did. These are mine."

"Hey, you're right. Your old suit. Didn't you lose it in that hospital?"

Barnes nodded. "A sailor named Reeder took it."

"And you went out while the blackout was still on and rolled some other guy for his."

"No, I didn't. I got it from a store. Hey, look—Fruit of the Loom! They even found my old underwear."

"Nifty. I hope they washed it. Put it on." Stubb stroked his chin. "You know, Ozzie, they're not as smart as they think they are, or they would only have bandaged one eye."

Barnes was feeling the pockets of his suit. "Yeah, I lost my glass one, and it's not here, either. You could tell, huh? When I read the label?"

"I could tell whether you looked at the label or not. Now put the damn clothes on—Madame S.'s getting tired of holding up her bag. They must have gotten their hands on this Reeder. That or he was working for them all along. You haven't seen him since we skipped the hospital?"

"Hell, yes, I saw him. I tagged him a good one in the lobby of the Consort for taking my stuff."

"No problem, then. They knew we were in the Consort. A house dick spotted me eating breakfast there this morning. He told Cliff Rebic, and Cliff would have told them. They might have known it even earlier—"

"But they did!" The witch interrupted, speaking from behind her purse. "That girl—she worked for Illingworth. He brought me here."

"You mean Sandy?" Stubb asked.

"Yes. That Alexandra Duck." The witch hesitated. "Perhaps she did not know. I would have sensed it, I think, and I did not."

"Illingworth's the guy that publishes those magazines?"

"He says so, yes."

Stubb said, "I doubt if he was working for them himself before this morning. She said they called him then. But they knew to call him—hell!"

"You have thought of something?"

"Just Mrs. Baker. They put a tail on her. Maybe even one of Cliff's guys. The two girls went to grill her, and he watched to see where she'd go. Or they staked her out themselves. She went to the Consort to talk to us. You can put down your bag now—Ozzie's got his pants on."

The witch lowered it. "And now you, Ozzie. Why were you brought in naked?"

"I don't think I'm going to tell you that."

"Oh, really?" The witch's face twisted in the suggestion of a smile. "Mr. Stubb has told his story."

"I didn't hear it."

"You will, if you wish—from me, if not from Mr. Stubb himself. But from Mr. Stubb surely."

"I'm still not going to tell you what happened to me. That's my business!"

"If you will answer just one question, I will desist, at least for the time being. Was it something you are now ashamed of?"

Barnes nodded.

"So for Mr. Stubb also. He was given—might I call it the opportunity of a lifetime?"

Stubb said nothing.

"And he failed. He was brave, yes. And intelligent too, though he would call it smart. But at the crucial moment, distracted. It was not so much different for me. I too . . ."

"You looked the wrong way too?" Stubb patted his pockets. "Anybody got a cigarette?"

"No. But I failed. I was shown deities—the ultimate deities, so was I told. And they were as I had always believed they would be, Phra the Sun; Khepri, who is Life; Ked, God of Earth; Nu of the Waters, of the Waters of Chaos. But it was all wind."

"I never believed in religion myself," Barnes said. "But if they hurt you, I'm sorry."

"You sacrifice to Kuvera, the Lord of Treasure," the witch told him. "Also to Isis of Erech. And because you know nothing of them, they drive you as with scourges."

Stubb said, "It doesn't sound like you did so well yourself."

"I did not. The worst thing is not to be ignorant of the gods. The worst is to mistake those who are not gods for them. At the very moment when I thought to be elevated, I found myself mocked and reviled. If it had been only the laughter of men and women, I should not have cared. I have heard that many times, and it is but the rattle of pebbles in an empty jar. But I heard the voices of the gods—of Mana and Skarl and Kib, and Sish, the Destroyer of Hours. Or of whatever the true gods may be."

Barnes touched a finger to his lips. "Somebody's coming."

All three fell silent, listening to the footsteps. The door opened, and a middle-aged man in a duffel coat came in. He looked cold—there was snow on his shoes, and the white touch of winter on his cheeks, and a little frost had begun to form on the barrel of the Thompson submachine gun he carried.

"Good evening," he said. "I thought you might appreciate an explanation of what's happened to you and where you're going."

Chapter 53

IN VINO, INCERTUS

"It's about time," Stubb said. "Who was Free?"

Barnes snapped, "Where's my kid?"

"I said I was going to explain," the man in the duffel coat told them. "I didn't say I was going to let you people quiz me, and I won't." The index finger of his right hand found the trigger of the Thompson.

Ignoring what he had just said, the witch asked, "Are you going to kill us?"

"We're going to do what we're told to do with you," the man in the duffel coat answered a trifle wearily.

(Stubb polished his glasses and put them back on, leaning forward in his chair.)

"If our orders are to eliminate you, then you will be eliminated, yes. If we're told to do something else with you, then we'll do that." He cleared his throat and spat into a corner. "The trouble with you people is that you won't do what you're ordered to. You can never see that when you do what the leader says, everything works out, and when you don't, it all breaks down. Everything breaks down."

"You are mad!" the witch said.

"I am the leader," the man in the duffel coat told her.

"He's just a little blasted," Stubb said. "Don't you smell the booze?" To the man in the duffel coat he added, "I wouldn't mind a shot myself, sir. How about it?"

"You think you're going to throw it in my eyes and take my gun." The man in the duffel coat shook the Thompson, making the cartridges in its drum magazine rattle.

"Hell, I don't want to throw it—I want to drink it."

Barnes was shrugging into his checked jacket. "You said you were going to explain. Get on with it. I'd like to hear it."

The man in the duffel coat chuckled. "So would I. I can't wait to hear what I'm going to say. That's Groucho, I think. Groucho Marx."

"I know. I used to be a stand-up comic myself."

"So you did. All right, I'll start with you." The man in the duffel coat looked from Barnes to the witch, and from her to Stubb, the muzzle of the Thompson following his eyes. "But first, I think it would be best if all three of you were sitting down."

Barnes dropped into a chair.

"Good. Let me begin with the founding of our great nation—"

"Are you really crazy?" Stubb glared at him.

"No, I'm our leader, as I told you. Our country was founded on the principle of the destruction of the wild by the civilized. Let me—just for a moment, if Mr. Stubb will excuse it—go back thirty thousand years before Christ, when the ancestors of the Indians crossed what are now the Bering Straits to occupy what some people have called an empty land. Those Indians represented civilization. The beavers felled trees and built lodges, but the Indians killed the beavers and skinned them."

Barnes said, "Then the whites came and skinned the Indians."

"Precisely. But the frontiersmen who destroyed the Indians and their culture were destroyed themselves, with their culture, by the settlers who followed. Those settlers lost their farms to the banks, and the banks sold them to companies who have brought the advantages of corporate existence—immortality and amorality—to agriculture.

"In the cities, the same thing occurred. The early city of independent shops and restaurants is properly being displaced by one of chain outlets, so that progressively greater control is exercised. Perhaps none of you has ever understood before why they are called that—chain outlets."

None of the three spoke.

"You see the progress? The old stores had to sell things their customers wanted. As they're eliminated, the need for their kind of slavery is eliminated too, and the chains can sell whatever they want. Their customers have to buy it because there's nothing else to buy. I ask you, all of you—how often have you gone into W. T. Grant's and found there was nothing at all you wanted?"

They stared at him. Stubb said softly, "Sometimes I feel like I'm in the wrong movie. You're Wolfe Barzell, and you're about to turn us over to Mike Mazurki."

"And you are Elisha Cook, Jr. in glasses," the man in the duffel coat told him. "You don't have to look at me like that, I'm sure you must have thought of it yourself. Where was I?"

The witch said, "You were about to tell us our part in all this."

He laughed, throwing back his head and taking two unsteady steps to the rear until he leaned against the door jamb. "Your part? My dear, demonic, dumb bitch, I can't have been about to tell you that. You don't have one. Like Short there says, you're in the wrong picture. There are no parts for any of you in this one. It's the truth. You've been extras and bit players, all of you, all your lives. Now you can't even do that."

One hand left the Thompson and groped in the side pocket of his duffel coat. In a moment it reappeared holding a silver flask. Clamping the Thompson under his arm, he unscrewed the top and drank. "Who said he wanted some?"

"Me, sir," Stubb told him. "Short."

"Catch!" He tossed the open flask. It left a narrow streak of whiskey on the floor.

Stubb drank and handed the flask to Barnes, who offered it to the witch, then drank too when she refused.

"Let me put it like this," the man in the duffel coat said. "The Indians used to be Americans—that's what an American was. Then the trappers were Americans, the Americans of their day. Then the farmers, with their buggies and plow horses and white clapboard houses. Even today when you look at a picture of Uncle Sam, you're seeing what those farmers were like dressed up to go to the county fair. Only farmers aren't real Americans any more. Neither are Indians. Poor bastards of Indians aren't even foreigners, and we like foreigners more than Americans, because foreigners are the Americans of the future. The trappers are gone, and pretty soon you'll be gone too."

He felt in his pocket for the flask, then seemed to remember he had thrown it to Stubb.

"You aren't Americans either." His voice grew angry and a little deeper. "There isn't one of you, not a God-damned one, that owns a designer sheet. Or a set of matched towels. You don't wear *anybody's* jeans, and you don't jog. You're shit. You're just shit."

"I would sooner die!" The witch's vehemence startled all three men. "I would sooner die than wear your blue jeans and be seen!"

"You're not American," the man in the duffel coat repeated. "That's what I've been saying."

"And have I ever claimed to be? Or wished to be? I am a Gypsy and a princess. And a dupe, because you have made me one. But I will speak for the Indians too, because they were nomads when they were shaped by their own thoughts and not by yours, and we are nomads now, who will remain so though you slay us." She gasped for breath; it was almost a sob.

"You have overcome us, but you have not conquered us. To conquer us you must beat us fairly, and you have not beaten us fairly, and so you have struck us to the earth, but you have not won. To conquer us, you must have dignity too, and for that reason you have not conquered us. A man may flee from a wasp and be stung by the wasp, but he has not been conquered by the wasp; it remains an insect, and he is still a man. You deck yourselves like fools and chatter and hop like apes, and your princes marry whores. That is why even those you have crushed to dust will not call you master, and none will ever call you master until you meet a nation more foolish than yourselves."

Grinning at the man in the duffel coat, Stubb applauded. Barnes took it up.

For a few seconds the man in the duffel coat was silent, shifting the muzzle of the Thompson from Stubb to Barnes and back. Then he said, "All right, I was trying to explain. I thought maybe it might do some good. We've been told to send you to the top, so that's where you're going."

Stubb said, "This sounds more interesting than the philosophical stuff—I never really liked that. You're flying us to Washington?"

The man in the duffel coat shook his head. "I said to the *top*. To the people who really run things, run the whole world. They want to see all four of you, I'll be damned if I know why. You'll leave as soon as the other one gets here." He chuckled. "You don't know it, but you're lucky. In a few more years, you wouldn't just take a plane—you'd have to go above the stratosphere, into outer space. It's the truth."

"The High Country," Stubb said.

"That's right, the *High Country*. It started just after Pearl Harbor, when everybody was afraid the Nazis might come up Chesapeake Bay. The government was exposed as hell, but it would have harmed morale to move it to some place like Kansas City, although Senator Truman and some others were for it. So they decided to put the key men on a plane and shuttle them around."

Barnes asked, "You mean President Roosevelt? My dad used to talk about him."

The man in the duffel coat shook his head. "The President's not one of the key people. Never has been. Basically a front man. These were the decision makers. *High Country*'s the code name for the plane, you see. A lot of it was wood. Saved stratetic metals for bombers and fighters. Even back then they were working on it, making it bigger in flight. Harry Hopkins, I think it was, made some joke about spruce growing at ten thousand feet. You get it?"

Stubb nodded. "Sure. Am I supposed to laugh?"

"In those days, they had to land and take off again every eight hours or so. But while they were in the air, nothing could get them unless Goering figured out a way to get his high-altitude fighters over here. So one of the things they worked on was ways to keep the plane up longer. Maybe you heard of Howard Hughes's *Spruce Goose?* The big seaplane? That was an idea that didn't work out. Now they never have to land at all, and pretty soon they'll be too high for—"

A younger man opened the door and peered into the room. "We need you out here, General."

The man in the duffel coat glanced at him. "Trouble?"

"Not serious, sir." The younger man shrugged. "But maybe you can think of something."

"You people stay where you are," the man in the duffel coat told them. "I don't want to lose you, and if you leave this room, one of the sentries will probably shoot you." He shut the door behind him, and they heard the snick of the lock.

Barnes was the first to speak. "Well, what did you think of that?"

Stubb stroked the bruise on the side of his head. "What do *you* think?" he said. "I'm tired of being smart. I think I ought to listen to somebody else's ideas for a while."

Barnes hesitated. "In the first place, Mr. Free came off that plane. 'The High Country'—that's what he said, right?"

"Or he wanted us to think that's where he came from. Or *they* want us to think that's where he came from. But, yeah, maybe he did. Is there any of that Scotch left?"

"This?" Barnes held up the flask, which was decorated with interlacing triangles. "About one good shot, I think."

"You want it, Madame S.?"

The witch shook her head.

"Then I'll take it." Stubb wiped the top of the flask with the palm of his hand. "Let me ask you both a question, and I'm not doing it just to keep myself entertained—though God knows I've been on that trip often enough. This time I really want to know. Why us?"

Neither answered.

Stubb upended the flask, swallowed, and shook himself. "Smooth. But now suppose this general was giving us the straight goods. What makes us so damn important that these guys who fly around up there all the time want to see us? Or suppose he was lying—that makes it worse. Why'd he want us to think that plane was where Free came from?"

The witch said, "I have a better question. Better because you know the answer. Before you heard the young man say general, you employed an honorific. You knew him for an officer, or at least suspected. How?"

"Nothing spectacular, Madame S. He had on plain-toed brown shoes with a spit shine, and that girl I told you about said her father was a general. Maybe he's not her father, but she probably thinks of him as a father or an uncle—she said his name was Samuel, so that would be Uncle Sam—and when most people have to make up a lie in a hurry, they use whatever they've got their minds on at the time."

Barnes asked, "You didn't believe him?"

Stubb shrugged and drank the last sip from the flask, then paused staring at its decorated silver sides. "It seemed like he was the boss. Would they pick a guy to run things who'd get shaky and start fighting a bottle? Hell, maybe they would, you never know. Maybe he's bankrolling them, and they had to. But if he was really a smart guy, the kind you'd expect to find in charge, and he wanted to lay a number on us, that might be a pretty good way to do it. He knows we're going to ask why's he telling us all this? So he gives us an answer— because he's smashed."

The witch said, "That is very wise. But why does he wish us to believe these things?"

Chapter 54

NOW LOADING

"All right, Lieutenant, what is it?" the man in the duffel coat asked.

"She's here, sir. We've got the shuttle plane warming up."

"I know, I can hear it."

"Only we can't get her out of the car, sir."

"You mean she has a weapon in there? Use gas."

"She's already unconscious, sir, or nearly. We just can't get her out." As they stepped into the freezing night, the younger man pulled out a handkerchief and wiped his forehead.

The black Cadillac stood dark and silent upon the snow while two men and two women peered through its windows. The younger man indicated the men. "They brought her here, sir."

One stepped forward, hand extended. "I'm John B. Sweet, General Whitten. Vice President, Sales, Mickey's Jawbreakers Corporation."

The man in the duffel coat shook hands with him, letting the Thompson hang from his left hand, its muzzle pointing at the trampled snow. "We've spoken by telephone," the man in the duffel coat said.

"We certainly have!" Sweet agreed. "I just wanted to let you know in person that at Mickey's we're always anxious to do our part."

"We'll put in a good word from you. I suppose the other man is from that restaurant you recommended?"

The second man stepped forward too but did not offer to shake hands. "I'm Walter Pearson," he said.

"You drove?"

"Yes, sir. I served their meal too and helped Mr. Sweet take her out to the car."

The younger man interrupted to say, "How'd you get her in there? That's what I want to know."

"Like you would anyone else, sir. Mr. Sweet kind of steadied her. I opened the door and gave her a little push."

"You're entitled to some sort of reward," the man in the duffel coat said. "What would you like?"

"Just a ride home, sir."

"You're a patriot, Pearson. I wish we had more like you. Mr. Sweet here will have to take this car back. It's rented, I believe?"

Sweet nodded. "From Avis. We always use them."

"But you won't be flying home until tomorrow sometime. Take Pearson where he wants to go." The man in the duffel coat turned to the younger man. "Now, what's the problem?"

"We can't get her out, sir. That's all. The door's too small, and she must weigh over three hundred pounds."

Sweet said, "I doubt it."

"I do too," the man in the duffel coat told him. "Her dossier says two fifty."

The younger man said, "You ought to see her, sir."

"You're right, Lieutenant." The man in the duffel coat strode across the snow. "Got a flashlight?"

Robin Valor muttered, "This is more like it," and opened the Cadillac's right rear door, turning on the dome light.

Candy sprawled across the back seat. Her eyes opened briefly when the light came on, then closed again. Heart-shaped candy boxes and drifts of fluted paper cups littered the floor.

"You were feeding her in there?" the man in the duffel coat asked Sweet.

"I had some samples. Valentine's Day assortments and our four-star collection of liqueur chocolates. She saw them."

"Umm," the man in the duffel coat said.

"I didn't think she'd eat them all, just on the drive out here."

"I doubt that it made much difference." He glanced from Sweet to the waiter. "Let me get this straight. You, Sweet, drove her to the restaurant in this car? She sat in front with you?"

Sweet nodded.

"You ate. Pearson helped you get her out of the restaurant and into the back seat. Correct?"

Both Sweet and the waiter nodded this time.

"You rode in back with her, feeding her candy to keep her quiet. I don't object to that in the least, by the way. Pearson drove. Is that right too?"

The waiter nodded, and Sweet said, "Yes, sir."

The man in the duffel coat studied the black car for a moment and shook his head. "Caddies used to be great, big cars. I own one. Remember how they used to be, Sweet?"

"I certainly do, General. These are easier to park, though."

"I suppose. Tonight a certain elderly gentleman came in an old Packard. Magnificent car. Possibly you saw it?"

"Yes, sir," Sweet said. "I think I did." He pointed. "Down between those two buildings."

"You didn't by any chance note the license number too? Either of you?"

Sweet shook his head. So did the waiter.

"Good. Observation is a wonderful thing, but it's like politeness—or a thirst for good hooch, or any other appetite. You have to know when to turn it off."

He handed his Thompson to the younger man, walked around the front of the car, opened the left front door, got into the driver's seat, and closed the door. His head and shoulders jerked forward, and he got out again.

"Now try her," he said.

The younger man handed the Thompson to Sweet and opened the right rear door again.

From the other side, Robin Valor called, "I've got an idea

too. I'll get in with her, if you can handle her when she comes out."

The younger man muttered, "I'd rather be in North Africa with Patton. Be ready to help, Pearson."

Inside the Cadillac, Robin was fumbling in her purse. For a moment, the weak light caught the gleam of steel. Her right fist dropped below Candy's gargantuan thighs and jabbed. Candy jerked far more impressively than the man in the duffel coat had, and her blue eyes opened wide. Robin jabbed her again.

With a muffled roar, Candy turned on her, her thick arms enveloping the dark woman, who screamed. The younger man drew a forty-five automatic from beneath his coat and flourished it uselessly.

"Shut up!" The man in the duffel coat leaned into the Cadillac and tried to grasp the struggling women, then drew back a bleeding hand.

As though the car had spit them out, the two fell through the open door and onto the snow, Robin under Candy, whose fingers were tangled in her hair. Kip took her huge revolver from her purse and struck Candy's head with the butt twice in rapid succession, the impacts of steel on bone nearly merging, like the left-right blows of a good welterweight at the speed bag. The younger man and the waiter rolled Candy off Robin and helped Robin up.

"Christ almighty," she gasped, "I thought she was going to kill me." Flapping her arms, she tried to dust the snow from her coat.

The waiter got her purse from the back of the Cadillac and handed it to her.

"You did it!" Kip exclaimed. "What did you stick her with, Robbie? A knife?"

"Nail file." Robin was still panting, her dark cheeks flushed with blood under her makeup. "She came down on top, knocked the wind out. I didn't have any more grit than a kitten."

The man in the duffel coat was looking at Candy. "Two hundred and eighty, perhaps," he said. "Divided by four, it's still close to a hundred pounds each. You men are lucky you didn't have to carry her out of that restaurant."

Sweet had knelt beside Candy. "Is she hurt?"

"Possibly. Kip has a good forehand, and that's a big gun. If she hit her in the temple with it, she may have done some real damage."

"Behind the ear, Daddy," Kip said. She had put her revolver back into her purse.

"Lieutenant, take one leg; I'll get the other. Sweet, take one arm and try to get your hand under her shoulder. Pearson, you take the other shoulder."

All four straightened as well as they could, and Candy's head and feet rose.

"You're not getting her derriere up," Kip told them.

The younger man grunted, "We can't."

The man in the duffel coat bent for a moment as he might have to see if the muffler and tail pipe of a car were dragging. "Try to move her. It should slide over the snow."

It did.

"Where we taking her?" the waiter gasped.

"Around the far side of the building, then back to the plane."

Having tested his engines, the pilot had shut them off. The plane stood angular and silent at the beginning of a snow-dusted runway, its propellers motionless. The leggy blonde painted on its dark fuselage looked a trifle embarrassed by the folding steps pushed against its side.

The man in the duffel coat motioned for them to stop. "Sweet, Pearson, thank you again, on behalf of this country. Goodbye, and remember that loose lips sink ships."

They nodded and hurried away.

Kip and Robin stood guard over Candy while the man in the duffel coat and the younger man went inside and brought out Stubb, Barnes, and the witch.

"You're going to have to carry her onto the plane," he told them.

"We can't," Barnes protested, looking down at her.

"If you don't," the man in the duffel coat said, "we'll shoot you down where you stand." He raised the Thompson. "And if you do, I'll tell you what became of your son."

Wordlessly, Barnes stooped to take Candy's ankles.

Stubb had knelt in the snow beside her. "We don't have to carry her," he said. "She's awake."

Her eyes were still closed, but there were tears at the corners. Slowly, one small, plump hand came up to touch the side of her head.

"Where's Little Ozzie?" Barnes demanded.

Robin said, "You didn't care so much about him a couple of hours ago."

Kip added to Stubb, "And you didn't care so much about her. I saw the way you looked at me. You would have dropped her for me any time I wiggled a finger."

The man in the duffel coat murmured, "You see, you are all traitors—as are we who betray ourselves." His mouth twisted in a smile. "It's the truth. The simple truth."

"And I?" asked the witch. "Have I been false to any goal, to any promise? I never promised these three anything, nor have I betrayed any of them. You don't need to lecture us about that poor girl there. We know she would give up Mr. Stubb or any other to follow her belly. But what of me?"

The man in the duffel coat was still smiling. "You've remained faithful, you say? To what?"

"To knowledge! To the ideal of ultimate truth."

"You've followed every lying spirit, no matter how wilful or how weak. When you were at the end of your search for the ultimate truth, you were utterly deceived by that silly old man we sent to your King, a few actors in costume, and some colored lights in a hangar." He paused. "We tried to take all of you down as far as we could. You, Marie, were the only one who never reached a point beyond which we could make you go no further."

Stubb asked, "Why?" Candy was sitting up in the snow, her legs extended and spread, her paunch in her lap. He crouched monkey-like beside her with an arm about her shoulders.

"Because those were our orders from on top. To test you and send you there. All of you failed, I think. Now we've wasted too much time already. Get her on her feet."

"Wait." Barnes had taken Candy's hand. "You said that when we did, you'd tell me about my son."

The man in the duffel coat nodded. "When you get her up those steps and into the plane."

Barnes and Stubb pulled; the witch joined them, lifting with all her strength. Candy rose and tottered, and twice nearly fell, but in the end lurched up the little ramp as she had once lurched up the stairs in Free's house. A young man in a flight jacket stood at the top with a pistol in his hand.

"He got away from us," the man in the duffel coat called to Barnes.

Chapter 55

WITH THE ARMY AIR CORPSE

Stubb got Candy into a seat, where she rocked back and forth rubbing the side of her head. The seats were of metal punched with holes. There was a partition between them and the forward part of the plane. Its door stood open, but the young man had stationed himself there with his gun. Stubb decided he was the copilot; one of the seats in the cockpit was empty. A rectangular patch on the left sleeve of his flight jacket seemed to show a winged propeller, though it was too dark to be sure. It was cold, and the roaring engines outside were deafening.

Slowly and almost clumsily, the plane banked. Lights from the active, commercial parts of the airport showed through the downside windows, seeming very far away. Beyond them lay only snowy darkness. A faint blue light burned toward the rear of the plane, and there was an even fainter light from the instrument panel in the cockpit.

Candy croaked, "Has anybody got a cigarette? Please?"

Stubb shook his head.

"Ozzie, please? Cigarette?" She made smoking motions.

"I'm out," Barnes told her.

The witch opened her purse, then snapped it shut again. "I have none either. I recall now that I got my last from Mr. Illingworth. You do not know him."

Stubb said, "Publisher of *Natural Supernaturalism* and that other one. Sandy's boss."

"Look!" Candy pointed out a window. The city seemed to fill the sky, an untidy constellation. "It's beautiful! My God, isn't it beautiful?" Her voice was slurred.

"Sure," Stubb said. He pressed her hand.

"Mr. Illingworth smoked English cigarettes," the witch continued. "Players. One can buy them everywhere in this country now, but he did not know that. I have always preferred what are called Russian cigarettes, though mine were made in Turkey. But now that I have neither, I find myself wondering if my preference were not a pose, as I am certain his was. I doubt that he either was willing to admit he played the *poseur*, even to himself."

Candy asked, "Has anybody got any liquor?"

No one answered.

"Or aspirins. Alka-Seltzer. My head hurts."

"Mine too," Stubb told her. "And I can't even remember to carry Sight Savers."

Barnes, who had been slumped with his head in his hands, tapped her on the shoulder and pointed toward the young man, who was fumbling under his flight jacket.

"Oh, thank God!"

The young man held them out to her, shouting to make himself heard. "Camels okay, Ma'am?"

"I love 'em!" Candy staggered from her seat. Stubb caught her and held her up, bending to peer at the package as she extracted a cigarette.

"Li'l too much wine with dinner," Candy said. "Sorry."

The young man nodded. "I know how it is, Ma'am. Sir, if you want one too, take it."

"I will," Stubb said. "Thanks."

When they were back in their seats again, Stubb patted his pockets. Barnes said, "Here," and extended a folder of matches.

Stubb lit both cigarettes. Candy asked, "Would you like a drag, Madame Serpentina?"

"No, thank you. I shall wait." She was seated nearest the young man in the flight jacket, and she spoke loudly enough for him to hear. "Unless perhaps—"

"Sure," he said, and once more held out the pack.

Madame Serpentina took one. "You need not bother, Mr. Stubb. I still have my lighter."

Stubb was staring at the matches. "Can I hold on to these, Ozzie? Where'd you get them?"

Barnes thought for a moment. "They're Robin's, I guess. When they gave me my old clothes back, they switched the stuff in the pockets."

Stubb stared at the matches. He could think of nothing, nothing but crazy talk he would rather die than utter. The idea that they were in the wrong movie came back to him with unexpected force, but now it seemed to him that they were not actors but a part of the audience. He had flown to California and back once, and both ways had sat in the plane watching a bad film. He wondered who was flying it now. Reagan, he thought. Ronald Reagan in *Hellcats of the Navy*. But no, that had been on old Ben Free's TV, Free coming out of the kitchen and switching on the TV, the heavy, old-fashioned tommy gun in his hands.

Perhaps that was what the script had called for. It was the wrong movie, and now though he had bought his ticket only a minute ago, it was nearly at an end. The lights would go up, and he would walk out of the theater with the rest of the audience. To what streets?

Then he realized he was thinking about death, his own death, that his mind was circling his death like the roaring old airplane circling the city, climbing, climbing, never quite ready to admit where it was. Why had he always thought of death as dark? Why not a flash of light, an end to the pictures on the dirty, sagging screen of his eyes? When Cliff, that son of a bitch, had sapped him, he had seen flashes of light, had seen the stars, not the dark.

I'll get up now, he thought. Go out like I was going to buy a candy bar, hide in the john. I wonder if the fire exits are locked? Maybe those go right to the stars without your having to go through the other thing. The lobby. They're not supposed to lock the fire exits, but sometimes they do, wrap chains around the handles, padlock them.

Christ, look at me. I'm supposed to be a tough guy; and look at me, I'm scared to death, my palms are wet. Only nobody ever really thought I was a tough guy but me. Maybe Candy. Because I'm so God-damned little, but little doesn't have a thing to do with tough. I wonder what Cliff thought, that son of a bitch. Wait till I get hold of him; I'll teach him what to think.

I wonder whatever happened to the clown, and was he gay? I think so, maybe he was, he was the kind of guy who gets hurt so much by women when he's still young that something breaks inside him, and he goes gay. Comes out, that's what they call it. He comes out and gets all those broads off his back, off his back forever—no wonder he's gay. I'd be gay too. Gets AIDS and dies.

Wait till I get my hands on Kip, that rich bitch. I'll kill her. You know what did it to me? It was Candy, first of all. A tramp, sure she was, I knew the minute I saw her in old Free's front room, but she kind of liked me, she kind of went for me, I know she did.

And I kind of went for her.

And so I thought, hell, I don't have to go my whole life paying for it, and even if I pay her for it, it's better I should pay somebody who kind of likes me, kind of keep the thing in the family, as the family used to say.

Then I met Sandy, and she kind of liked me too, and she was an inch or so shorter than I am. Hell, an inch easy if we took off our shoes. And she kind of went for me. She didn't want to show it because she was on that career trip, but she did. Hell, we could have danced together, maybe if I ever get down alive we will. She was cute too.

And then I met Kip, and oh, Jesus, it was like I could see the best part of all, like right at the end where Linda Loring calls Robert Mitchum from Paris just before the credits roll. Only they didn't. Jesus, wait till I get my hands on her, I'll beat her, I'll tear her clothes off, I'll strip her naked. But, Jesus, if she ever kissed me and said, "Jim, I'm sorry, I'm so sorry," I'd pick her up and hug her and kiss her, and we'd go out and do—

Something. Something wonderful. Have a drink, or go stand on the bridge and look at the river, drive up into the hills in my convertible and look down at the city. Because if Kip ever told me she was sorry, I'd have a convertible.

"I hope she's okay," Barnes said.

"Sure she's okay," Stubb told him, pressing his hands together so Barnes would not see them shake. "Why shouldn't she be okay? We're the ones that aren't okay."

"I think maybe she's passed out again. Maybe you ought to take that cigarette away from her," Barnes said.

"Oh, you mean Candy." Stubb pulled the cigarette from her fingers. He had finished his own and ground it out on the metal floor. There were still a few puffs left of hers.

The young man in the flight jacket said, "How about lighting me, sir?" He had his pack of Camels out again. It still did not look quite right.

Stubb handed him the butt. "I got to go," he said.

"There's a thing in back," the young man told him.

He walked back toward the blue light. His ears were popping, and the slanting, shaking floor made it hard to walk. After a moment, he realized what the rubber funnel and hose were for. A sniff brought a faint odor, with the smell of oil and a thinning cold.

He stood facing the funnel, his back toward the front of the plane, and examined the match folder. It was black, printed in white: a stork in a top hat on both sides, one leg separating the words STORK CLUB. Much smaller lettering on the fold gave the address—3 East 53rd Street, N.Y.C. No zip.

He did not know Candy was behind him until she tapped him on the shoulder. "Is there any water back here, Jim?"

He dropped the match folder into his pocket. "Haven't seen any."

"The guy said there was."

"Maybe he was putting you on. He's probably dead by now anyway. What the hell would he know about water?" He could not bite back the words.

"I'm really—there it is."

It was a sheet-metal container with a spigot. A clamp beside it held an aluminum cup with a folding handle. He filled the cup for her, and she emptied it, a few drops furrowing what remained of the powder on her cheeks. "I'm thirsty as hell," she said. "I guess a lot of that stuff was salty."

He motioned toward the water can.

"Yeah, do it again. I didn't want to say this, but I'm a little sicky too. You know? I'll go back up front if you want me to." She drank again.

"It's all right," he said.

"Hold my hand, will you, Jim? You know that was the best meal I ever had in my life. I want to keep it down."

"It was the knock on the head. They sapped me too, and I damn near chucked myself."

"And my ass is sore. Why should my ass be sore?"

"Search me."

"Anyway, I want to puke, but I know if I do, in twenty minutes I'll be so hungry I'll be sucking my fingers."

"They cheated," Stubb told her.

"What does that mean, Jim?"

"All of us got what we wanted, and we couldn't handle it. Except you—you could have handled it, if only they hadn't sapped you. It's no fun, getting it on the head."

"Everybody got what they were after?"

"Yeah."

"Madame Serpentina?"

"She won't talk much, but I think a rap with God. Except

it turned out he wasn't the real McCoy, and she bought it."

"Oh, wow!"

Stubb braced himself against the motion of the plane. "You're always asking me what I mean, so what the hell's that supposed to mean?"

"Most of us wouldn't even want it. I always figured I'd have to talk to Him when I, you know, went upstairs. I haven't been looking forward to it much."

"You'll charm the pants off God."

"Jim, I don't think he wears any."

"Then you've got it knocked. Anyway, what about Mary Magdalene? He went for her big. I bet you're nicer than she was."

"Who's that?"

"A girl like you."

"You're stringing me."

"No, I'm not."

"How would you know anyway? You go to church?"

"When I was a kid, my folks made me go to parochial school. We used to talk about it—just us kids. We thought that was really a thrill, because there weren't so many X-rated movies around then."

"When was that, Jim?"

"Let's see. Twenty, twenty-five years ago, I guess."

"Not you. God and Mary Whatshername."

"Oh, them. Two thousand years."

"That long, and people are still talking."

"God gets a lot of press."

"Uh huh. What about Ozzie? Did he get what he was after too?"

"Women. Showgirls, he called them. He was in a joint, and they got him to stand up and announce, and to tell a couple of jokes. Then he went backstage and the girls crowded all around him. He made it sound like there were about a hundred, but I doubt it. They took his clothes off. I don't think he could get it up."

"You don't think?"

"He wasn't too clear about it. I think he ran away—onto the stage again."

"Sounds like fun. I wish I'd seen it."

"Me too."

"I'm not going to ask about you."

"Thanks."

Candy belched and giggled. "I guess I'm feeling a little better. Only it seems like the floor's still tilted."

"It is," Stubb told her. "We're still climbing."

Chapter 56

APRIL IS THE CRUELEST MONTH

A new universe waited above the snow clouds. The moon shone brightly there, and all the stars were out. The clouds themselves had become the surface of the earth, as to our eyes the clouds of Venus are Venus herself. They were an unending mountain range, silvery white peaks linked by enchanted vales; and the air about them feigned never to have known the smoky filth of human life.

A single pencil wrote there, as though God were still at labor upon the Book of Genesis. It traced a narrow line across heaven, and this line too seemed silver and white in the moonlight, pure, only slightly bent against the night sky, untroubled as yet by any word that should produce a world.

The pencil drew a circle, perhaps. A great circle.

They rose to it. Once or twice the witch glimpsed the line of its tracing, but neither she nor the others saw the pencil itself, though it was far larger than a Boeing 747, though a 767 might have landed upon one of its wings, a DC 10 upon the other.

The sound of their engines altered subtly, waxed, waned,

droned. Turbulence made their aircraft pitch and yaw; Candy clutched her belly with both her hands as if afraid she would be sick after all. Stubb wrestled futilely with a seat belt that could never be made to go around her. White knuckled, the witch clung to the sides of her seat. Barnes swore and muttered, stroking his chin, pulling his ear.

There was a clang, a bang as though the plane were about to break apart in mid air. The roar of the engines faded to a whisper. Outside the windows, there was only night, without moon or stars.

The young man in the flight jacket took a deep breath and said, "Well, we did it again."

The four of them looked at him. No one spoke.

"I hope it didn't scare you."

Candy said, "I've been scared so long . . ." Her voice trailed away.

Stubb told her, "You didn't act like it, sweetheart."

"How could I act? Sicky. Woozy. That's how I acted, but I've been scared ever since they put me in that loony bin. Even when I was stuck full of dope or half looped. I couldn't get high enough to get away from it."

The young man in the flight jacket cleared his throat. "Folks, I wouldn't want to hear any classified information."

The witch said, "You must be tolerant. We are all a bit on edge."

"Me too," the young man told her. "Well, it's over now." He thrust a key into a keyhole in the fuselage overhead. A section of it angled down, unfolding a thin stair of white metal. A faint light shone somewhere beyond the top of the plane.

The young man grinned. "This is a *C*-class Fort. The limejuicers didn't want it, so your guys took out the dorsal turret and put this in. We're magnetically coupled, and when you go up those steps, you'll be walking right through the middle of the field. I'm supposed to warn you that it messes up watches. If any of you've got one you care about, you'd better leave it with me. I'll return it when we come back to pick you up."

Stubb said, "I don't think—"

The witch said, "I do," and slipped off a delicate little dial ringed with brilliants. She smiled at the young man in the flight jacket. "Already it does not keep good time, so perhaps I should wear it, no? Perhaps your magnetism would mend it for me?"

He smiled back and managed to touch her hand as he took the watch. "I doubt it, Ma'am. It's probably better you leave it with me." He glanced at the watch's tiny face, then at the chronometer on his wrist. "Twenty-four hundred. It's not so far off, Ma'am."

"And when shall you arrive to take us to solid ground again, Captain?" The witch had risen from her seat.

"It's Colonel, Ma'am," the young man told her. "I'm an Army Air Force officer, a Lieutenant Colonel, not a Pan Am pilot. We'll come for you when they tell us to."

Candy asked, "Do most people stay long?"

"Not most of them, no, Ma'am. Usually it's just a few hours. But not very many go up there, and we never take some of them down."

"*Ahhh!*" The witch breathed the word with a note of moaning wind. "Perhaps they come down without your assistance?" She made a pushing gesture.

"I doubt that, Ma'am. Now if you folks will just go up. We've already lost a little more time than we should have."

Barnes and Stubb looked at each other, then at the airy metal stair. "I want to help Candy up," Stubb said.

Barnes nodded, smiled at the two women, and went up briskly.

"I go next," the witch said. "Oh, I am not brave! I only fear I will not go at all. Candy, can you climb them? With myself before and Mr. Stubb behind?"

"I'm cold sober. Of course I can."

"I wish a kiss first, Colonel," the witch said suddenly. "After all, it may be the last. And because I did not know of your rank."

For an instant she smiled, and there was something so bewitching in her smile that it seemed strange she did it so seldom. She might, the young man thought, have conquered the whole world with that smile; he tended to think in such terms.

Then she threw her arms about him and kissed him. "You do not object?" she asked, still clinging to him.

"Why, no, Ma'am."

"My breath is not sweet, perhaps. It is so late, and it has been so long since I have eaten. I cannot even recall the last time now. I am very tired, and yet I must do more tonight, and I cannot say how much more."

The young man said, "Your breath is just as sweet, as—as a breeze in April."

"Good." She kissed him again. "I see you like it as well as I, but now I must go. You have been so kind. I would not wish to entangle you in difficulties with your superiors."

She looked around. Stubb had started up the stair, reaching behind him to extend a hand to Candy. Because he was two steps higher than she, their eyes were at a level.

The young man said, "Uh, Ma'am, would you like a sandwich? I've got one up front."

"Oh! Very much!"

"Just a minute." He ducked through the doorway. The sandwich, wrapped in waxed paper, was Spam on dark rye. He handed it to the witch, who kissed him again, then started after the groaning Candy. When the witch was halfway up, she turned, took a dainty bite of bread and meat, and blew him a kiss.

He blew one in return and stood watching until the slender figure in dark fur and black lace had disappeared into the darkness of the gigantic aircraft above. Then he pushed the folding stairway up, relocked the hatch, and after a minute spent staring idly around the now-vacant plane, went into the cockpit.

A Navy officer waited there, leaning back in the pilot's seat, his hands behind his head. He asked, "All finished, Bob?"

"Yep." The young man sat down in the copilot's seat.

"Took you long enough."

"I guess."

The Navy officer threw a switch on the control panel. Instantly they were dropping, then swooping downward in a long glide.

"Where are we?"

"Eighties. Pretty far up. Four of them?"

"Right. Two men, two women."

The old Fortress swung into a wide, easy bank. "What were they like?"

The young man considered. "Spies," he said.

"Spies?"

"That's what I'd say. You know, sometimes they look like diplomats, sometimes millionaires or politicians or whatever. Right, *compadre*? Well, these were spies. Not Army Intelligence. OSS, I guess."

"How 'bout that. False whiskers?"

"I don't know. Maybe. One had a mustache."

"Come on, what were they like?"

"Okay. Seedy-looking guy with one eye. Face beat up, like he'd been in a fight. Average height or a little under, too old for the draft. Looked like he could be anything as long as it wasn't too honest, maybe a bookie, something like that."

"A pimp."

"Maybe, if he had a little more scratch. Kind of good-looking, shiny black hair, Clark Gable mustache. He was the first one up the steps, and if it scared him he didn't let it show much."

"The other guy?"

"Jockey size. Thick glasses, trenchcoat."

"What about his face?"

"I don't remember—just the glasses. That was the whole thing about him. He was one of those guys nobody notices. Know what I mean?"

"I suppose. I didn't see him."

"Neither did I. That's what I'm telling you."

"Okay, now the good part. What about the women? You said there were two."

"Yep. One you had to notice. If you flew over the county fair and got a picture of the crowd and she was in it, she'd be the first one."

"Nice looking?"

"I guess if she lost a couple of hundred pounds she might have been. Blond, must have been close to six feet."

"That where you got the lipstick, Bob?"

"Huh?" The young man wiped his mouth with the back of his hand. "You kidding me?"

"How'd I know? You got lipstick all over you. Want to borrow my handkerchief?"

"I've got one."

"You figure this fat girl went around hiding behind doors and romancing generals? Over and above the light colonels, I mean."

"It wasn't her, it was the other one. Anyway, the fat girl was a nurse, and she looked like she'd been through hell getting here. Her coat up covered most of it, but the top of her uniform was ripped up, and the skirt was gone. I forgot to say the little guy was second up the steps. Now, he would be great at hiding behind doors or anything else. You'd never spot him. He was worried about the fat nurse and kept turning around trying to give her a hand."

"Quit stalling, Bob. Get to the other one."

"You want to be filled in or don't you? Dark and pretty. Heck, not pretty, but she'd make a pretty girl look like something from the dime store. Beautiful. Like the Dragon Lady—foreign looking, with a little bit of cute accent. Around five six. Lots of neat little curves."

"Russian?"

"She looked awfully dark for a Russian. Maybe Rumanian or something."

The Navy pilot glanced at his altimeter. "Bob, what the hell do you know about Rumanians?"

"Nothing, I guess. Count Dracula—wasn't he supposed to be Rumanian?"

"Hungarian, I think. She bit your neck, huh?"

"No, she just talked kind of like that. She let me keep her

watch for her." The young man thrust his hand into the map
pocket of his sheepskin flight jacket. "It's gone!"

Chapter 57

LONELY AS A CLOUD

The room was large and well-furnished in the heavy, masculine style Barnes had always imagined prevailed at the
Harvard Club. It held leather armchairs, a massive walnut
table, and a globe; the walls were paneled in walnut and hung
with black-and-white photographs of battleships and par-
ades. There was no sound of engines beyond a slight vibra-
tion, unchanging as the stale air, that shook even the heavy
table ever so slightly. Only a few feeble yellow lights in
the trembling chandelier seemed alive, ringed by dead
companions.

He went to the globe and spun it. India was pink; so was
one side of Africa, and the bottom. Had there really been
such a green country as French West Africa? He had never
heard of it, and yet it seemed to occupy half the continent.

The crown of Stubb's balding head appeared in the hatch,
then his forehead and the glasses whose opacity reminded
Barnes of sunglasses, though they were without tint.

Then came Candy's red, straining face, bedewed with
sweat despite the cold, and the shoulders of her dark blue
coat. It occurred to Barnes that it had been unfair to take his
new clothes and give him back his old ones while letting
Candy keep what must have been a stolen coat and the stolen
nurse's uniform.

He wanted to sit in one of the big leather chairs and
welcome Stubb and Candy with a few well-chosen remarks,
but he also wanted to search for Little Ozzie, though he knew

he could not possibly be here. Torn between the two, he went to the hatch and helped Candy up the last two steps, then assisted the witch (who had just blown a kiss) in the same way.

"Thank you, Ozzie," she said. "Those were a bit difficult with heels so high."

She was holding a sandwich, and she held it as if it would turn pumpkins to coaches. At its wave the hatch closed, leaving only a smooth, inlaid floor.

"But what kind of place is this? A club for men, is it not? But where is the bar?"

Stubb had been looking around too. "On the other side of those doors, I'll bet. Whoever lives here wouldn't want to mix their own drinks, and they wouldn't want the bartender to hear what they're talking over. He brings 'em in, gives 'em out, and goes."

Candy had sunk into a chair nearly wide enough to hold her. "Nobody here," she gasped.

Barnes said, "Not when I came up either. They must be someplace else."

Candy shook her head, fanning herself feebly with one hand. "Nobody. At all. Anywhere."

The witch stared at her for a moment, then pressed her fingers to her temples.

When she let her hands fall to her sides again, Stubb asked, "Madame S.?"

"I do not know—it is difficult because you three are here too. Ghosts, yes. Perhaps someone also who is not a ghost, but much, much of the afterworld."

Barnes objected, "Somebody told those people on the ground to send us up here."

The witch nodded. "So they said, at least; but many have been telephoned by the dead. Who can say?"

"I can." Candy stopped fanning herself and waved feebly at the other chairs, the table, and the globe.

Stubb said, "This isn't all there is to it. It can't be."

"But it's where they meet them," Candy panted. "Who comes up here? Big shots. President—senators. They meet them here. So they'd think of meeting us—have somebody with a gun, like down below and in the plane. There's nobody here, so there's nobody here."

Barnes objected, "Somebody has to fly this—this whatever it is."

"They can fly themselves, if you want them to, with a computer or something."

Stubb was peering through a doorway. "Not locked," he said. "Little hall with lots of narrow doors."

Barnes followed him as he opened one. The flare of a match showed a desk and chair, a map of Europe tacked to a wall of unpainted plywood. With both of them inside, there was barely room to turn around.

Barnes said, "When I was a kid, my dad took me with him when he went to see some lawyer. He had a chair like this."

Stubb blew out the match, lit another, and picked up a letter from the desk. "Office of War Mobilization," he said. "Ever hear of it?"

Barnes shook his head.

"Me neither. The date is June seventeenth, nineteen forty-three."

"That's crazy," Barnes told him.

"I know." Stubb blew out the match. "I've been telling myself that for the past couple hours."

Candy looked in, filling the doorway and blotting out what little light spilled from the paneled room. "You guys find the bar yet?"

"Not yet," Stubb told her.

"Let me know, okay? I've still got a headache. A couple shots would do me a world of good."

From the end of the hall, the witch called, "I have found something. Two somethings. Come and see!"

The first was a stairwell, at the top of which one of the faint yellow lights still burned. The cramped steps wound on high risers through the ceiling to end before a door as narrow as the cubbyhole office's and considerably lower. The second was a window about a foot across. The witch was staring through it as they arrived. She moved aside to let Stubb look.

He remained only a moment or two, whispered, "Jesus Christ," and turned away. Then it was Barnes's turn.

Without moon or stars, light streamed up from below. They flew, as it seemed, over an endless milky sea. Above them spread a vast dark that eclipsed the sky. Cowled engines hung on pylons suspended from that darkness like crowding stalactites.

Behind him, Barnes heard Candy say, "I'm not going up that. Forget it."

He knew she was talking about the steps, but he did not turn around. He said, "This has been here almost fifty years. Flying," and did not know he had spoken aloud until Stubb answered him.

"Look at those props."

"I am," Barnes whispered. "Most of them aren't turning."

Stubb seemed not to have heard him. "They refuel it. They have to. Refuel it the same way they brought us up. Or somebody does because they're still taking orders from up here. You know about the jetstream?"

Barnes nodded, then realized Stubb was talking to Candy.

"It blows west to east and makes it quicker to go from L.A. to New York than the other way, even in a jet. I guess it blows two or three hundred miles an hour. You could glide a hell of a long way in a two-hundred-mile-an-hour wind. If you had a few engines to help out when you needed them, maybe you could glide forever."

Barnes said, "Radar—" and Candy, "Pilots—" almost together.

"This whole thing is wood. Didn't you hear what the guy down on the ground said about the *Spruce Goose*? It wouldn't give much more trace on radar than a flock of geese. About the pilots—I don't know. Yeah, it seems like they'd see it every once in a while."

The witch said, "The pilots of airplanes see many strange things. They have learned not to speak of what they see if they wish to remain pilots."

"This isn't a flying saucer," Barnes objected.

"Who spoke of them? Let us call them unidentified flying objects. Some are lenticular, yes. Some are not. We do not know what they may be; that is what *unidentified* means."

Barnes nodded and turned away, looking out the port again and half expecting that everything would be changed, as things change in a dream. Far below, tiny yet unmistakably huge, he saw their racing shadow spread-eagled on the clouds, a rippling cross of black.

"In the old sailing-ship days," the witch continued, "it was said to bring evil fortune to see the sea serpent. Captains who saw it could not obtain another command. That was when the captains were so much nearer the water and watched the water and the sky always. Now they watch their instruments and are more fortunate."

"I don't know about the rest of you," Stubb announced, "but I'm going up these steps. That door must lead out into the wing, and I want to see it."

They watched him climb the narrow stair, the toes of his shoes making a hollow, thumping sound on each. The door was so small that a man of average height would have had to duck to enter it. Stubb would not have had to, but he ducked anyway, ducked to be seen, Barnes thought. The little door swung closed behind him.

"Well?" asked the witch. "Shall we wait for him? Or explore?"

Candy said, "They must have had grub on here. There might be something left."

"On the level above, I should think. Here they received their visitors, as we have seen. Here also were their desks and papers, for they might need something while they conversed, some fact or document. But there are two levels at least. Perhaps three. Above this they would eat and sleep, I suppose."

"You mean I've got to climb those things?"

"No. You may stay here, if you like. Mr. Stubb will be so happy to find you awaiting him. Perhaps Ozzie and I will bring you the food you crave, and some whiskey too, if we remember to do it."

"I'm not staying alone in this spooky place."

"As you wish. Ozzie, please go first. These steps are so very steep, and I should not like to have you peeping up my dress."

Something in her tone told Barnes she had known of the hole he had made in the wall of Free's house—that she had known and had posed for him, dressing again or turning out her light when she did not want him to see more. He stared at her.

"If we were alone, it might be otherwise. Now go up."

He shook his head and mounted the little stair, finding it more difficult in the oxygen-poor air than he would have thought possible and hearing the witch's laughter in the click of her heels behind him.

A narrow landing held the door through which Stubb had gone and another, larger, door that had been hidden by the ceiling when they had stood on the level below.

Beyond it was a wide room with a score or more of chairs and sofas, a dry fountain, and basins and boxes filled with dead, dry earth. Overhead spread a dome of tinted panes that dyed the moonlight.

"Here they took their ease," the witch said, "surrounded by precious things. They were very clever, these men, very cunning, though not wise."

Barnes was examining one of the chairs. Its fabric had torn under the pressure of its stuffing. When he touched it, it tore again, rotten with age. "This place is in a lot worse shape than the other one," he said. "I don't see anything precious here."

"They are gone," the witch told him. "And the suns of many years have done the damage you see. But water played in that fountain once, streaming from the horn held by the undine. I shall not trouble to explain the symbolism of horns or undines to you now, but here, so far above the seas and lakes of Earth, water was a precious thing. Fools would have said, 'We must drink it, use it to make breathable the air, and so we will hide it in tanks.' These men said, 'We will put it in a fountain for our pleasure. Then it will make breathable our air, and we may drink it when we choose.' There were flowers here as well, and flowers too are precious things." She laughed. "The visitors saw the gracious room, the little offices, and thought those here lived spartan lives. They knew that when the structure is so large, mere space costs very little. It is the load, not the emptiness, that brings down the airplane. Is it not so?"

Candy came panting up behind them. "I didn't think they'd hold me," she said. "You should have heard them crack! I waited . . . minute . . . each step."

"Here is the living illustration," said the witch.

They went forward through the sere, ruined garden, with the witch leading the way, a witch of yellow, rose, and purple as she stepped from one shaft of moonlight to the next.

"It's like that *Wizard of Oz* movie," Candy puffed, holding out one hand to test the light. "Whores of a different color, remember?" If the witch heard her and understood her, she gave no sign.

Beyond the garden were half a dozen shadowy rooms filled with instruments and winking glass. A few of the yellow lights still burned in them; where their illumination was insufficient, the witch held her cigarette lighter aloft like a torch.

Beyond these laboratories was another hallway, and beyond that, Stubb's back. They saw him open a door at the end of it, and through the door glimpsed the familiar, bearded face of Ben Free as he turned in the pilot's chair to see who had entered.

Stubb's voice came to them faintly, carried on the thin whistling of the wind. "Good morning, General Whitten," Stubb said. "Or was Whitten a lie too?" The door closed.

Chapter 58

GENERAL BUCK WHITTEN

The witch burst into the cockpit like a panther. "What thing is this! You have betrayed me, betrayed us all!" She whirled on Free and dropped to her knees. "And you, Master, you live! This traitor told me you were dead." Barnes followed her in, Candy lumbering after him.

Free said, "Sit down. Some of you, anyway."

Stubb had taken the copilot's seat. There were two more at the rear of the cockpit, apparently intended for a navigator and an engineer. The witch and Candy sat there.

The witch hissed, "Inside the wing, you said, and I see you here. You would speak with the Master behind me!"

"I've never crossed a client yet," Stubb told her. "When we were looking for Mr. Free here, you never said you didn't want me to talk to him unless you were there. If you had, I wouldn't have agreed to it."

"You told me you were going in the wing!"

"Sure, and I did. It was dark as hell in there, but I got far enough to see there were steps inside those things that held the engines so the mechanics could go down and work on them in flight. By then the matches I'd gotten from Ozzie were running out, so I went back."

"And we were gone," Barnes said. He was standing behind the witch's seat.

"Right. So I figured you had probably headed toward the front of the plane, and I went that way too. I've got most of this worked out, I think."

Free said, "You recognized me when you saw me here, but you had not recognized me on the ground. I suppose that was only a few hours ago."

Stubb nodded. "Yeah, I should have, but you were younger and you had a clean shave, and it was too crazy. Of course that girl, Kip, had blown smoke in my eyes with the story about the twins. Is she really your daughter? She looks a little like you."

"Yes, my only child. Eventually she will kill me, I suppose."

Stubb stared at him.

"She reported to me; you must have realized that. Even then I had begun to suspect that Benjamin Free had been myself."

Barnes said, "Wait a minute. You were the man in the duffel coat?"

The witch murmured, "The Master will tell us everything, if he will. Perhaps first of all, his name."

"No," Free said. "Not first. First I want to hear how Stubb deduced my identity. I apologize for calling you Short, by the way. I was playing drunk."

"I knew it," Stubb told him. "That's why I didn't mind."

"And the deductions?"

"Hell, there was so much of it. For a long time I didn't believe it, but it all pointed the same way. To start with, Kip's gun." He fell silent.

"Go ahead," Free said. "It hurts less to talk of it than to think of it, and I have thought of it a great deal."

"It was a Colt New Service, one of the biggest, heaviest pistols ever made. Colt built them for the Army in the First World War, because they couldn't make enough forty-five autos. You still see a few around, and I suppose they'll last forever; you couldn't break one with a sledge. But why would a small girl like Kip carry a heavy, old-fashioned gun like that?"

"I taught her to shoot with one," Free said. "I had a Woodsman too, but a revolver is safer for a beginner."

"Then when we met you, you had a Thompson. With the round magazine, yet, like you were Al Capone. Those things are in museums. Then you let me keep your flask, figuring that if we each had a jolt it might loosen us up a little when we went upstairs. It had an art deco design and a bottom that said, 'Tiffany and Company, Fifth Avenue, New York.' Just like that. Everybody puts the state and zip on now. Sure, maybe it was an antique, but it pointed the same way as the guns.''

The witch demanded, "And in what way was that? You men, you are so maddening.''

Candy added, "I'll say!''

"Leave me out," Barnes told them.

Free asked, "Then you knew when we put you on the plane?''

Stubb shook his head. "I was thinking about it, but I couldn't accept it, it was so crazy. Then the plane looked funny to me, but what the hell do I know about airplanes?''

"And on the plane?''

"I guess the first thing was the cigarettes. The copilot got them out and gave one to everybody who wanted one, which was damned nice of him. They were Camels, my regular brand, and the package was almost exactly like I'm used to, only not quite. Then I got the matches from Ozzie. Matches are the oldest, corniest clue there is, you know what I mean? The Great Detective looks at the matches in the third reel, and they're from the Club Boom-Boom. So he goes there, and it turns out the guy is a regular. Anybody who's done any real investigating knows you can't trust them. A guy goes into a place, buys cigarettes, and picks up a folder of matches. He's been inside maybe three minutes and nobody remembers him for shit. Then he gives them to his buddy, who leaves them on some bar, and somebody else takes them. Sure, you follow them up, you follow everything up, but nine times out of ten it goes nowhere.''

"I see," Free said.

"But look at these." Stubb reached into his pocket and produced the matches. "They're from the Stork Club. It went out of business in the sixties; but the paper hasn't yellowed, and the matches work just fine.''

Free nodded. "So then you knew.''

"Just for laughs, I like to watch those old Sherlock Holmes

flicks," Stubb told him. "You know, with Basil Rathbone and what's-his-name."

Free smiled. "I used to enjoy them myself."

"And in one of them Sherlock says to eliminate the impossible, and then you've got to go with what's left. Of course, the problem is, what's impossible? People coming here from some time when the Stork Club was still open, when that flask was new, when people with serious business would still use those guns—was that impossible? Or was it impossible that everything would point that way but mean something else?"

Candy asked, "Is he saying what I think he's saying, Mr. Free?"

Free nodded again, and Barnes said, "Well, blow me down!"

"It is I who should have guessed," the witch said. "We know such things are not impossible."

"That's how we got onto it in the beginning," Free told her. "Please understand, all of you, that I'm going to have to explain from my own point of view. I couldn't do it from yours even if I wished to."

"Go ahead," Stubb said.

"Let me start with Bill Donovan. Does that name mean anything to you?"

Stubb shook his head.

"I met Bill Donovan when we were both hardly more than boys. We were in a home-town National Guard cavalry troop together. Real horse cavalry—it's the simple truth."

Free paused, stroking his beard. "Bill was a lawyer, an Irish Catholic whose mother had pushed him to go to college and make something of himself. I was a wealthy young man-about-town. That was what we called it then, the town being Buffalo, New York and wealthy being rich the way we thought of rich in Buffalo around nineteen fourteen."

Stubb darted an I-told-you-so glance at the witch.

"I'd had the advantage of a governess as a kid, a nice, perfectly batty little Frenchwoman I called Madame du Betes. She had taught me conversational French and German, and I used to show off in restaurants and so on. As it turned out, Bill never forgot that.

"The Great War came and we both went in as officers; Bill, who had that Irish charm, because we had elected him captain of our troop, and me because just about anybody with a degree from Princeton could get a commission then. After the war, Bill left the Army with a hatful of medals and went back to his law practice. I stayed in because I had nothing better to do and had sense enough to see that it was the only way I could keep on flying. In nineteen thirty-seven, I retired as a brigadier general. My father had died, and I wanted to take over the family business. We make glass, by the way; some of the finest crystal in the world."

Stubb asked, "How old were you?"

"Forty-eight. Don't ask me how old I am now, because I don't know. Somewhere between sixty and seventy, I think.

"Anyway, to fill you in on some things I only learned later, Bill had a partner who knew President Wilson and did some globe-trotting and fact-finding for him. Eventually Bill did some of that too. I think Bill himself knew Roosevelt back when; he was practising law in Buffalo, remember. He must have gone to Albany often, and Roosevelt has been mixed up in state politics all his life. Anyway, when Roosevelt decided America should have something like the British Secret Intelligence Service, guess who he picked?"

The witch nodded. Barnes was too rapt to nod. Candy stared at the rectangular panes that made the big cockpit seem almost a small greenhouse; she might have been half asleep. Stubb said, "And Donovan picked you."

Free nodded. "One among many, of course. The business had been almost shut down by the war, and I had a manager who could take care of what little there was as well I could. I was getting a lot of pressure from the Army to come back, and I knew that if I did, I'd probably end up in charge of a training field in Texas—not exactly my cup of tea. This was the summer of forty-two, by the way.

"*High Country* had already been built, and the top men in the nation were on her. Donovan felt the Office of Strategic

Services ought to have somebody up here too, and I got the job, I think mostly because I'd been one of General Mitchell's supporters. Supposedly, I was just coming to *High Country* temporarily, but my confidential orders were to stay as long as I could."

Barnes said softly, "I wouldn't have believed something this big could fly."

"Neither could I," Free told him. "And if it had been aluminum and steel, it wouldn't have. It's a matter of weight, really—the weight-to-lift ratio. The plywood has a layer of cedar on the outside for rot resistance, then alternating layers of balsa and spruce. When they found out it worked, they had Hughes Aircraft build one that was all spruce. You couldn't get balsa from South America any more, you see. But that one didn't fly. It was too heavy."

Stubb said, "You mentioned that plane when we were on the ground."

"Did I? Sorry, but you have to remember it's been a few years for me."

The witch interrupted. "You said it was the occult that led you to what you found. I have waited and waited to hear how that is so."

"Hitler believed in it," Free said. "And Hitler had been extremely successful. When he joined the National Socialists, he got membership card number seven—the Nazis literally had only a half dozen members. In a few years he was Chancellor of Germany. In a few more he was walking over the French army, supposedly the best in Europe. Nobody knew then that his luck would run out in Russia and Africa."

The witch said, "Those with whom he leagued himself destroyed him when he had accomplished their purposes. It is ever so with them—they break their tools." Almost in a whisper she added, "We went into the death camps too, though only we remember."

Free said, "They thought Hitler might be able to look into the future, and they thought there might be some way to duplicate that mechanically and reliably. They found out—well, you know what they found out.

"There was a tremendous effort being put into weapons development then, so one of the obvious things was to try to anticipate the result. That was my first real job—to go ten years ahead and grab the best I could and bring it back. I think you can guess what I got."

Barnes whispered, "Nuclear weapons."

"Not everything, but a lot. Enough to speed up development to the point that we had an atom bomb in less than three years. But when I'd been flown back here, back to *High Country*, I'd noticed a lot of the people were gone. I couldn't ask about that, you understand. The men on that level could have swatted Bill Donovan like a fly. I kept my mouth shut and my eyes open and went back to my own period."

Chapter 59

TWO DOORS

"After I'd gone down and been debriefed," Free continued, "I went back up and through the gizmo again for more. I'd been practically solo the first time—nobody with me but the plane and crew I'd need to get up to *High Country* again and get back to forty-two. You see, this was the only gizmo there was, and if it hadn't existed in fifty-two, I'd have had to find another one, or stay where I was until somebody brought me one.

"This time it was going to be different. Besides the plane crew, I had my pick of the available people. I took my daughter Kip and a friend she'd brought in, and half a dozen others. Kip had volunteered to work for Donovan when she learned I had, you see, and if I hadn't taken her, she might have been sent into Germany or occupied France.

"I also had a small version of the gizmo, a take-down job

big enough for a person. That was so that if *High Country* was gone we could ditch the plane and get back. On the other hand, if *High Country* or some successor—back then we thought there might be one—was still flying and we wanted to take something big home, we could do that in the plane. And of course the plane was a backup if the portable gizmo didn't work.

"This time my orders called for me to make a special effort to locate items that would be valuable to our own outfit. We snooped around the electrical stores and got onto tape recorders and some other things. Have I told you about the money?"

Stubb shook his head.

"Well, after the first time, I'd seen that it would be easy to supply myself with all the operating capital I needed. All I had to do was make a fair-sized deposit back in forty-two that nobody but Kip or I could touch. What's more, I could assure the cooperation of the FBI and the OSS, or any successor organizations, just by leaving messages saying that anyone who used certain code phrases was to get it."

Candy opened her eyes. "That was how you got my john bumped off his flight. I've been wondering about that."

"Right. Only we couldn't tell the FBI or the CIA—those were the new people—about the gizmo, so we couldn't tell them where we came from. But we needed them because it didn't take long to see that this time we weren't the only show in town. I'd already begun to suspect the men in *High Country* were using the gizmo themselves, and that a lot of them were going to periods they couldn't return from, periods in which *High Country* did not exist. At first I thought it was one of them."

Stubb asked, "When did you know it was you?"

For almost half a minute, Free stared out at the night. The snow clouds were breaking up, and the dark, tossing water of the Atlantic showed through the breaks. "There wasn't any exact time I can put my finger on," he said at last. "I felt the urge; we all did. We knew the Allies would win—it was in all the history books—so perhaps the call of duty wasn't as strong as it should have been. And I saw the future we'd built." He paused again.

"Do you know what I wanted? The old frontier. To see what this country was like before they chopped down all the trees and paved it over. The wanting got so strong sometimes I knew I'd do it sooner or later, and the more we got on the man who called himself Free, the clearer it was that he looked like me. My full name's Samuel Benjamin Whitten, by the way. Buck's just a nickname."

"You're Buck," Barnes said. "You owned the Flying Carpet."

Free nodded. "We needed someplace where we could meet people without leading anybody to the old military compound at the airport, which was where we kept our files and some sensitive equipment, like the portable gizmo. I bought the Flying Carpet and staffed it with people I felt I could trust to look the other way whenever something a little odd happened."

Barnes said, "May I ask a question, sir? When I was in the Flying Carpet, I met a musician called Binko. Was he one of the people you brought out of the past?"

Free shook his head.

Stubb said, "Ozzie mentioned him when he was telling Madame S. and me what happened to him. I asked him about the music. That seemed to be another clue."

"I suppose it was," Free admitted. "I knew I'd be hearing a lot of whatever band I hired, so I hired a band I liked."

Candy opened her eyes again. "You still haven't got to the payoff. Are you ever?"

The witch darted a glance at her. "What do you mean? Do not question the Master!"

"Really. Listen, he didn't bring us up here so he could tell you about Hitler or talk about matches with Jim or music with Ozzie. So why did he? And why did he have the people down below—that's him too, don't forget—do stuff to us? When we were in the little plane, Jim told me they tried to give all of us more than we could handle, and I was the only one who could handle it. Why do that and send us up here?"

Free said, "I wanted to answer your questions first, Miss Garth. I felt I owed you that. Now your questions have come around to the matter I wanted to talk with you about, and I admit I'm glad they have."

He paused. "Do you remember what I told you about going back to nineteen forty-two to be debriefed? I had gone ten years forward and gathered what information I could about nuclear fission, then returned."

All four nodded.

"The gizmo—the men who actually developed it called it a space-time singularity induction coil, so you can see why I say gizmo—couldn't be controlled with pinpoint accuracy then. I had left for fifty-two on August eighteenth, nineteen forty-two. I returned May thirtieth."

Candy sat up straight, her china-blue eyes wide open. "Holy God! There were two of you?"

Free shook his head. "No, though I didn't realize that at first. I was debriefed by the people on *High Country* before I was sent down, of course. They told me when the debriefing was over." Free paused again. "They also told—ordered me, in fact—not to tell anyone on the ground.

"I wasn't taken to Washington for further debriefing, as I had expected, but flown down to Langley Field and released. I spent a day there wondering whether I dared phone Buffalo."

Candy asked, "And did you?"

"Yes. I called our plant and asked to speak to the president of the company, after swearing to myself that if I answered, I would hang up. Kip came on the line and asked in her most business-like manner what I wanted. I said something along the lines of 'Are you in charge, Miss?' She recognized my voice and said—these were her exact words, I'll never forget them—'It's you, Daddy! We were all so worried.'"

"My God," Candy said softly.

"I questioned her and learned that I had gone into my office about an hour before the time our shuttle plane must have appeared in the sky of forty-two. No one had seen me since. I told Kip where I was and said that I had been called away on urgent Government business, that I would be back soon, but that I would be going to work in Government full time within a month or so."

"So you went to work for this Donovan when he asked you." Stubb made a circular motion with one hand. "It seems to me that when you went to fifty-two again and came back, you'd get stuck in a loop."

"That's what we thought," Free said. "So I didn't go. There was no point in it, after all; the people in *High Country* already had everything I'd learned about the bomb. When August eighteenth rolled around, the shuttle plane flew me down again for debriefing by Roosevelt, Hopkins, and Donovan. I told them I had just returned, and in a sense it was true."

"Kip never suspected?"

"She knew something had happened," Free said. "When I came back from Virginia, came back in that second June of my nineteen forty-two, she told me how good I looked. I was prominent enough in Buffalo then that they had quite a few pictures of me on file at the paper. I got them to let me examine them."

Candy asked, "And you looked the way you had a couple of years back?"

"You're a very clever woman, Miss Garth. No. That was what I expected, but it wasn't what I saw. Younger, yes, but different too. Stronger. I don't know." He hesitated. "Better. That's really all I can say. When I went into the plant, some of the problems we'd been having, things that had worried me for months, seemed simple. I saw where we might get a local substitute for the high silicon sand we'd imported from the Philippines before Pearl Harbor, for example. I think now that what happened was that my two selves had merged, and that the coming together made a single self that was stronger than either." He stamped one foot, and all of them jumped a bit. "Plywood," he said. "Each ring on a tree is a year's growth. When you make plywood, you peel those rings apart, then glue them back so the grains cross. What you get is a piece of wood that's stronger than both were in the old trunk."

Stubb said, "What if one of the layers were rotten, General? Wouldn't the plywood be rotten too?"

Free nodded.

"General, I'm going to tell you something you won't like to hear. When I was living in your house, you told me you had a ticket that would take you back to the *High Country*. But you told me too that it was too late for you to use it. You weren't senile, or at least I don't think you were, not really. But you were a very old man."

Free nodded. "You're telling me I'm going to die, Mr. Stubb. Every man does. Unlike other men, I know *how* I'll die as well. It's the simple truth."

"Wait just a minute!" Candy exclaimed. "You said Kip had reported to you. I heard you. That means there were two of you then."

Free did not reply. A long moment passed. At last Stubb said, "No, it doesn't. She reported after the Ben Free we knew was dead."

"Miss Garth, I think that when I went to your time, to this time now, Ben Free wasn't there. How long did you—did all four of you—live with him?"

"Three nights, Master," the witch said. "After the third, the house was partly torn down."

"I think he must have gone to some other time, although I have no idea what that time might be. To the Lewis and Clark expedition, I hope. Decades later, old and sick, he came back and discovered what he told Mr. Stubb: that it was too late.

"And when he came back I disappeared, as far as Kip and the rest were concerned. Kip thought Free had done it, and she must have been frantic. We had people monitoring the papers and the television news fulltime, as you can imagine. When one of them spotted Free, Kip threw caution to the winds. She assigned an agent to watch the house, and she and Robin questioned a woman in the neighborhood and got your names. She got the FBI to put a mail cover on all of you, and when they found that Mr. Barnes here was answering lonely-hearts ads, she had Robin write to him. Eventually she had all four of you under surveillance. Then Free returned to his house, and she got him."

There was another pause. "And she killed him," Stubb said softly.

Free nodded. "I won't tell you what she told me about it. She was lying, and I could always tell. Hell, I raised her, and that's the truth. I think she took him to the house because he—I—told her the portable gizmo was still there, built into a wall; and that when they were alone, I explained everything to her. After that she must have known she would never get her father back as long as I—Free—refused to go back.

"If you're wondering where the general is now, let me assure you he's gone. Not vanished because I'm here, but gone to a better time, taking his portable gizmo with him. He deduced the location of Free's 'ticket' you see, and carried the one he'd brought from nineteen forty-two through it.

"And now we've come to what Miss Garth calls the payoff. I don't know who you four are, but I know I'll let you live with me when the time comes. I know you'll fight to save my house, the house that was my base for so many years, and fight pretty well from what Kip told me. And that you'll try to find me when you think I may be in trouble, though all of you have troubles enough of your own. The message I left for the general I used to be—I wired a calendar clock to turn on the radio and one of your neat little tape recorders, by the way—said you should get your greatest desires. I did it because I've learned we all have to get them before we can have better ones."

Stubb said, "I don't think we have them yet. At least I don't."

Free nodded. "I'm about to give you one, I hope. There are two doors out of this *High Country*, you see. One is the one you came through. The other is the gizmo. I'm offering all of you a chance to go back, to fold yourselves in upon your earlier selves and live new lives, if you want them."

"Yes!" Candy shouted. The witch threw herself at Free's feet, as Stubb nodded and rose from where he sat.

Barnes said, "Swee' pea—"

Epilogue

FREE LIVE FREE

The ragged man and the ragged boy came down the alley slowly, picking their way between pools of melting slush. The air was cold, but the sun was bright. "There it is," the man said, pointing. "See, I told you they wouldn't bother to fence off the back. Think you can climb over that junk?"

The boy had already begun, scrambling over an abandoned stove and dodging through the gutted body of a wrecked car. The man was still clambering after him when he halted on the porch.

"Can we go in?" the boy asked. "There's a sign."

The man nodded, half to himself. The sign, crudely hand-lettered in black paint, read FREE LIVE FREE. It was a trifle weatherworn now.

Through a broken window he saw the looted kitchen and the ruined parlor beyond it, a doll's room laid open.

The knob turned, and taking the boy by the hand, he stepped over the sill.

Coffee was perking on the stove. A taller Stubb and a slimmer Candy stood beside it, she dressed in some shimmering material he had never seen, a gown of silver light.

In a wall, the ragged man thought. The old fox. Free told me he'd hidden it in a wall. He thrilled with fear, with discovery and joy, an unnamed emotion.

"Glinda!" Candy called. "Look who's here—it's Popeye!"

The sorceress's familiar voice floated in from the parlor. "Ah, Mr. Barnes!" she said. "The quadrumvirate is complete."

A Chronology of the Life of Samuel Benjamin Whitten,
Brigadier General, United States Army, Retired
b. 1889, d. 1983, age about 82

1803—"Ben Free" joins the Lewis & Clark Expedition during its descent of the Ohio River. Physiologically Whitten is sixty, though he appears younger.

1807–1818—"Free" makes periodic visits to the house at 808
South 38th Street, using the portable gizmo he brought
with him to leave the frontier and the gizmo built into
the rear door of 808 South 38th Street to return.

1819—"Free" leaves the frontier for good, bringing with him
certain valuable furs, his rifle, and other memorabilia.
Recovering the portable gizmo from a cave in central
Kentucky, he conceals it in the wall of 808 South 38th
Street behind plaster and wallpaper.

1889—Samuel Benjamin Whitten born, Buffalo, New York,
the only son of John B. Whitten, founder of Whitten
Crystal Works, and Mary Standbridge Whitten.

1917—Whitten, already a member of the New York National
Guard, enters the U.S. Army. Commissioned, he volun-
teers for pilot training.

March 1918—Lt. S. B. Whitten lands in France with the
United States Army Air Service.

November 11, 1918, 11:00 A.M.—Hostilities on the Western
Front cease. Capt. S. B. Whitten of the 135th Aero
Squadron is the pilot of a DH-4 day bomber.

1924—Standbridge "Kip" Whitten born, Manila, Philippine
Islands.

1937—Brig. Gen. S. B. "Buck" Whitten retires, aged forty-
eight, his career damaged by his support of Brig. Gen.

William "Billy" Mitchell's theories of high-altitude bombing.

May 30, 1942—Whitten vanishes from his office at the Whitten Crystal Corp. and returns to *High Country* from 1952, bringing information on nuclear fission.

June 2, 1942—Whitten returns to Buffalo from Langley Field, Virginia.

July 1942—Whitten joins the Office of Strategic Services (OSS) at the invitation of William J. "Wild Bill" Donovan.

August 18, 1942—Whitten flown to *High Country*. Enters space-time singularity induction coil and the year 1952. Returns to Washington, where he is debriefed by President Franklin D. Roosevelt, Harry Hopkins, and Donovan.

August 20, 1942—Whitten reenters the space-time singularity induction coil, accompanied by Robin Valor, his daughter (Kip), and others. He carries with him the disassembled gizmo.

September 17, 1942—All U.S. atomic research is placed under the direction of Brig. Gen. Leslie R. Groves and code-named "Manhattan Project."

December 2, 1942—A self-sustaining nuclear reaction is achieved at the University of Chicago.

July 16, 1945—An atomic bomb is exploded on a steel tower at Alamagordo, New Mexico.

August 6, 1945—The B-29 bomber *Enola Gay* drops a uranium fission weapon, code-named "Little Boy," destroying Hiroshima, Japan.

November 5, 1982—On the Five O'clock News, anchorman Bryan O'Flynn reports sightings of a B-17 and speculates that it may be on its way to an air show. (Newspapers later point out that air shows are not normally scheduled for the winter months.)

November 9, 1982—Buck Whitten buys the Flying Carpet.

Friday, January 14, 1983—"Free" returns to 808 South 38th Street and discovers the house has been condemned. Whitten vanishes from his living quarters at the airport.

Sunday, January 16, 1983—"Free's" ad appears. He agrees to allow the witch to live in his house.

Monday January 17, 1983—The witch, Osgood M. Barnes, Jim Stubb, and Candy Garth move into the house.

Wednesday, January 18, 1983—Stubb lights Candy's cigarette in the rain. "Free" watches television in the parlor.

Thursday, January 20, 1983—Kip takes "Free" prisoner. The house is partially wrecked.

Friday, January 21, 1983—Stubb searches the house. Kip and "Free" return to the house, and "Free" dies in its basement. Whitten (the man in the duffle coat) reappears at his headquarters.

Saturday, January 22, 1983 (before dawn)—The man in the duffle coat vanishes again. The witch, Stubb, Candy, and Barnes talk to Whitten ("Free") in the cockpit of *High Country*.

Monday, January 24, 1983—The man in the duffle coat deserts, using the gizmo in the wall of the house and taking with him the gizmo he brought from 1942.

Note: This chronology has been prepared at the request of the editor of the U.S. trade edition. It did not appear in the small-press edition and may not appear in the British edition. It attempts to cover only the parts of Whitten's life stated or implied in *Free Live Free*.

—Gene Wolfe

THE BEST IN SCIENCE FICTION

Buy them at your local bookstore or use this handy coupon:
Clip and mail this page with your order

TOR BOOKS—Reader Service Dept.
49 W. 24 Street, New York, N.Y. 10010

Please send me the book(s) I have checked above. I am enclosing
$_____ (please add $1.00 to cover postage and handling).
Send check or money order only—no cash or C.O.D.'s.

Mr./Mrs./Miss _____

Address _____

City _____ State/Zip _____

Please allow six weeks for delivery. Prices subject to change without
notice.

THE BEST IN FANTASY

Ben Bova

☐ 53200-7   AS ON A DARKLING PLAIN $2.95
    53201-5   Canada $3.50

☐ 53217-1   THE ASTRAL MIRROR $2.95
    53218-X   Canada $3.50

☐ 53212-0   ESCAPE PLUS $2.95
    53213-9   Canada $3.50

☐ 53221-X   GREMLINS GO HOME $2.75
    53222-8   (with Gordon R. Dickson)   Canada $3.25

☐ 53215-5   ORION $3.50
    53216-3   Canada $3.95

☐ 53210-4   OUT OF THE SUN $2.95
    53211-2   Canada $3.50

☐ 53223-6   PRIVATEERS $3.50
    53224-4   Canada $4.50

☐ 53208-2   TEST OF FIRE $2.95
    53209-0   Canada $3.50

Buy them at your local bookstore or use this handy coupon:
Clip and mail this page with your order

TOR BOOKS—Reader Service Dept.
49 W. 24th Street, 9th Floor, New York, NY 10010

Please send me the book(s) I have checked above. I am enclosing
$_____ (please add $1.00 to cover postage and handling).
Send check or money order only—no cash or C.O.D.'s.

Mr./Mrs./Miss _____

Address _____

City _____ State/Zip _____

Please allow six weeks for delivery. Prices subject to change without
notice.

POUL ANDERSON
Winner of 7 Hugos and 3 Nebulas